SHITAMACHI SCAM

Shitamachi Scam

By Michael Pronko

ISBN 978-1-942410-31-7

Also available in eBook 978-1-942410-30-0

First English Edition, Raked Gravel Press

For more about the Detective Hiroshi series and Pronko's other writing: www.michaelpronko.com

Follow Michael on X (Twitter): @pronkomichael

Michael's Facebook page: @pronkoauthor

ALSO AVAILABLE BY MICHAEL PRONKO

Memoirs on Tokyo Life

Beauty and Chaos: Slices and Morsels of Tokyo Life (2014)
Tokyo's Mystery Deepens: Essays on Tokyo (2014)
Motions and Moments: More Essays on Tokyo (2015)

The Detective Hiroshi Series

The Last Train (2017)
The Moving Blade (2018)
Tokyo Traffic (2020)
Tokyo Zangyo (2021)
Azabu Getaway (2022)

SHITAMACHI SCAM

by Michael Pronko

Raked Gravel Press 2023

(Sagi = fraud, swindle, graft, especially of older people)

* * *

"Between the big thieves and little thieves, it's the big thieves rule the land."

— Rory McLeod
The Singing Copper

List of Characters

Hiroshi

Hiroshi, Forensic accountant, main detective

Ayana, Hiroshi's girlfriend

Detectives

Sakaguchi, Chief of homicide, ex-sumo wrestler

Takamatsu, Old-school detective, smokes

Ishii, New female detective

Akiko, Detective staff, Hiroshi's assistant

Sugamo, Detective, ex-sumo wrestler

Osaki, Detective, ex-rugby player

Ueno, Detective injured by gunshot, stays in office

Nakada, tech guy for detectives

Silver Center

Ueno, works in silver center

Setsuko, main character in silver center

Sasaki, works in silver center

Keisuke, real estate agent in love with Setsuko

Kotaro, hikikomori and video guy

Natasha, Russian graduate student

Annisa, Indonesian graduate student

Sagi Scam Group

Takuya leader of group

Misaki Takuya's girlfriend, runs Olzakaya

Noguchi sagi group

Murayama sagi group

Yasui sagi group and best friend of Takuya

Developers

Imada main developer

Kurono building management and crony of Imada

Other Characters

Yumi hot yoga teacher and call girl

Watanabe head of the tax agency

Terajima works in the city office

Chapter 1

Takuya leaned against a brick wall on an old *shitamachi* "lower town" street in eastern Tokyo, vaping his favorite Cuban rum and cigar flavor. The thick trunks of cherry trees, their branches propped up with wooden braces, blocked a clear view of the convenience store, optical shop, and apartment building that broke up the row of wood-fronted shops.

Across the street was the bank. It would open at nine.

In front of the storefronts, the owners sprinkled water to dampen the dust. A few early shoppers, women arching over with age, dragged two-wheeled shopping carts. A team of older men in glowing green vests swept the sidewalk. They chatted amiably as they worked past the Silver Center and down to the *sento* public bath.

A bank employee in a crisp blue skirt and vest came out to set the automatic doors open partway. She went back in and returned with a small broom and dustpan, though there wasn't much to sweep. The men in vests had worked it over already. She clicked the broom onto the dustpan and bowed to the street before returning inside.

Takuya sucked his vape pen and checked his cell phone messages, rubbing the smooth wood handle and thinking he didn't want to be there. This wasn't his pickup. None of them were anymore. He just set up the pickups.

Yasui, his friend since high school, had phoned him at five in the morning to say he couldn't make it because his grandmother was rushed to the hospital. He'd motorcycled from Tokyo to Ibaraki in the middle of the night to be with her. Takuya remembered the place. It was the only hospital still operating in the rural area where he and Yasui had grown up. It was where his grandfather had died.

A short line formed in front of the bank, older people waiting in silence. Takuya checked his cell phone for the info. Yasui failed to upload a reference photo on the shared scheduling app, but at least he'd scouted the surveillance cameras. A wide-brimmed baseball cap and mask would be enough, but he kept his head tilted away out of habit.

Precisely at nine, the bank employee came out to welcome the waiting customers with a series of stiff bows. The line trooped in.

Takuya sucked the last of the flavor out of the cartridge and put it in his shirt pocket. He'd get this over quickly.

When the first stooped woman came out of the bank, Takuya started toward her. If that wasn't her, he could excuse himself and try the next. He checked the scheduling app for her name. "Ueno," the same as the station south of there.

Takuya pulled his black baseball cap down as she headed across the crosswalk toward him. The street was too small for a stoplight, just "*tomare*" "stop" painted on the blacktop.

Takuya met her halfway across. He leaned down and spoke in a loud voice. "Ueno-san, how are you doing?"

She straightened up and looked at him curiously. "You aren't Yasui."

Takuya pulled on the bill of his cap and kept speaking in the loud voice he used with the elderly. "Yasui couldn't come, so I'll be assisting you today. Let's get a cup of coffee, shall we?"

Ueno-san frowned and looked around.

He reached for her nylon shopping bag. "Can I take that?" The packets inside pushed the bag into an awkward shape. A large A4-size envelope poked over the top. That must be it.

Ueno-san pulled the bag forward with sprightly grace. "I've got it."

"I'm sorry. Of course." He was used to that sense of dignity and independence. They all believed they were still young.

Takuya held up his briefcase with a protective hand to stop a delivery truck that pulled up to the crosswalk. The truck driver waved them along and leaned back.

When they neared the curb sloping up to the sidewalk, two beefy men in cheap suits got out of a car hidden behind the trunk of a cherry tree.

Takuya looked back toward the bank. Two more cheap suits—a stocky woman and a tall man—started across. Where did they come from? He pretended not to see them and put a hand under Ueno's elbow to hurry her. "Almost there."

"I can see that," Ueno said.

"Watch your step." He pointed at the yellow, dotted tiles underfoot.

Before he could get Ueno onto the sidewalk, a bright red 50 cc scooter sped around the side of the stopped delivery truck.

Takuya grabbed Ueno's arm, but before he could move her out of the way, the rider reached out for her bag.

Takuya pulled her to the side. The scooter swerved. The front wheel hit the non-slip tile, bucked, and slung the driver across the concrete sidewalk. The unmanned scooter smacked into Ueno, ripping her out of Takuya's grasp and slamming her into the thick trunk of a cherry tree.

The truck driver got out of the cab and hurried to help.

The scooter rider, just a kid, lay still. His shirt and pants were sheared away, and his skin scraped raw.

Takuya wondered if he could bluff it out—decided he couldn't. He grabbed Ueno's bag and took off. The four undercover cops shouted orders to stop, which only propelled him faster.

He cut left, running as fast as his slip-on loafers let him. The soles were slippery. With his soft briefcase in one hand and Ueno's bag in the other, he was off-balance, heavy on one side and empty on the other.

At the next corner, he skidded into a left turn down a one-lane street that served pedestrians, bikes, cars, and delivery vans alike. Kids had chalked a game on the pavement.

Without looking back, he turned down the first opening

between the buildings to the right. The two-story wood walls on either side left him one choice—forward. He hurried past stacks of old flower pots, rusted air conditioners, and treadless tires, careful of the gravel and stepping stones underfoot.

He had no idea where the outlet would be. Or if there even was one. Only locals would know how to wind through these narrow paths. This was *shitamachi*, the old part of Tokyo where the lanes had been formed as footpaths hundreds of years before cars.

When he turned to look back, his right heel caught on the edge of a broken stepping stone and sheered off. He bent over and picked it up. He used to wear running shoes for pickups and had always told Yasui and the others to do the same, but he didn't do it himself. He dropped the U-shaped heel into Ueno's bag and hobbled over the tamped earth and gravel.

The two alleys at the T offered no outlet. To the right were the walls of old shops and homes. Their back doors were braced and bolted, windows boarded and barred.

To the left loomed the crusty wall of a cemetery. The tops of stupa-shaped prayer plaques rose over the wall. He could climb it, but it might be a long drop onto the graves on the other side.

Before the cemetery wall was an old home with wood-frame glass doors that opened onto an old *engawa* terrace, the half-outdoor living room of old houses. It was piled with water-damaged cardboard boxes, rattan chairs, and a busted chest of drawers.

He hurried to it and tried the sliding doors, but they were locked from inside by an old metal screw lock.

Under the terrace, dried paintbrushes, stained towels, and a trowel poked out of a plastic bucket. He snatched the trowel and slid it between the old wood of the doors. He pried and jimmied and pried again until the soft wood splintered. The doors shivered as he pushed them aside.

He set his briefcase and the bag up onto the wood floor, slipped off the heel-less loafer and the good one, shoved them into Ueno's bag with the money and documents, and slid the door shut.

He tiptoed along the dusty *engawa* to a Western-style door at the end. He turned the knob gently until the latch bolt pulled, and the door creaked open.

He peered through the crack into a dark room with a futon folded neatly on the tatami. Dusty boxes lined one wall, and a large *tansu* storage chest the other. He crept in and tiptoed to the door, listening for any sound.

Outside was a dark hallway with a lacquer wood staircase that led upstairs. A sliver of light fell from the door up there, but the house was quiet.

He eased the door shut and crept to the *genkan* at the front door. He bent down to set his shoes on the tile. Then he paused. He slid open the door of the shoebox.

They all looked too small except for a pair of outdoor sandals. He set them quietly on the tiles and stepped into them—close enough. On top of the shoebox was a worn grey bucket hat. He peeled off his wide-brimmed baseball cap and tucked it in the bag. The bucket hat smelled of stale sweat, but it would cover the top of his face.

A voice called out from the second floor, and the old wood of the home creaked in alarm.

Takuya flipped the front locks, eased out the door, closed it softly, and scanned the street. The subway station was to the left. A bus stop was never far. He pulled on a virus mask, reset his new hat, and walked with awkward nonchalance.

At the corner, he turned to cross the street. Glancing back, he saw an old man peering out the door of the house he'd cut through.

He walked on, scanning utility poles for surveillance cameras, until he got to a convenience store with a row of trash and recycle bins. He reached inside the bag for his busted loafers. One of the packets of well-wrapped money had split open. He pulled out the packet and fanned the bills with his thumb.

What should have been ten thousand yen notes were nothing more than blank paper with a fake colored edge.

He pulled out another pack and bent it to split the paper. It was the same. He pulled out the A4-size envelope and tore the corner off. Blank white paper. No documents.

He dug for his vape pen, desperate for a hit of Cuban rum and cigar, but it was gone. He must have dropped it while running. No going back now.

He slung his briefcase over one shoulder and the bag of worthless paper over the other and headed off, trying to piece together what went wrong—or who.

Chapter 2

Detective Hiroshi Shimizu bent over, hands on knees, trying to catch his breath. He had kept chasing the suspect only by some wishful momentum. He walked farther and stared down the next break between the buildings. As empty, narrow, and fruitless to check as the others. In this old *shitamachi* neighborhood, you either knew the dogleg back-ways and shortcuts, or you didn't.

Detectives Sugamo and Osaki had shot down the passages on the other side and hadn't re-emerged yet. His aching feet had come to rest on pastel squares, circles, and triangles chalked on the pavement by some local kids. He eyed the crowd of shop owners and locals murmuring but felt too winded to flash his badge. He took his handkerchief out and started wiping the sweat from his forehead and neck.

The smell of deep-fried something came from down the street. A tofu maker and flower shop stood sentinel at the entrance to the last alley he had checked. On the other side, where Sugamo and Osaki disappeared, a used bookstore with a one-hundred-yen cart stood next to a stationary store with back-to-school-specials. A convenience store broke up the jumble with its plasticky front, expediency its only aesthetic.

Osaki and Sugamo came out from a side alley. Even at a distance, Hiroshi could tell they'd also found zero. It was pointless to chase some guy who probably knew every back lane. But he'd be caught on some surveillance camera somewhere, and someone must have seen him. Maybe Ishii knew who he was. It was her case, after all, one of the most important for her task force on crimes against women.

Detective Ishii had convinced him his financial savvy was needed on her case. The scam rings were the most basic kind of *sagi*, but the way they moved the money around —the only evidence in some cases—was complicated. Hiroshi had followed the money trails of one *sagi* ring targeting women's pensions. Ishii had asked him to do more. It had doubled his workload, but she needed his white-collar crime methods.

More importantly, working on the money side of the cases let him avoid the grisly murder scenes Detective Takamatsu always dragged him to. He might not escape the murder scene today, though. It was waiting on the next street over.

For this sting of the scam ring, Ishii had explained the details at several meetings. Her meticulous planning made this one sound easy. It was all on track until the scooter came out of nowhere.

The older woman who'd been targeted, Ueno-san, was sharp as a tack, full of energy, and happy to help—or had been. Hiroshi hadn't stopped to check on her, but she'd been walloped by the speeding scooter. The rider had crumpled and was oozing blood. Hiroshi didn't stay to look before taking off after the scam ring pick-up guy.

Osaki and Sugamo strolled over from their failed chase, shaking their heads and wiping the sweat from their massive bodies. Hiroshi was as tall as they were, but he always felt like he looked up at them. Sugamo played rugby, and Osaki had done sumo. Their muscled shoulders towered over the gathering of locals.

Osaki held up his badge so they wouldn't be mistaken for criminals, and a buzz of concern circled through the crowd.

"We checked all the back alleys on our side," Sugamo said. "Did you cover all the ones on your side?"

Hiroshi wiped the back of his neck. "I think so, but he could have escaped down any of the openings between the houses. Or dropped over into the cemetery."

"The cemetery?" Osaki asked. "That's all we need."

Hiroshi could never understand how guys their size, double his weight, could run faster than he could and recover more quickly. He refolded his handkerchief and swabbed off more sweat. He felt like he did after a long kendo workout, teetering between energized and exhausted.

Sugamo looked up at the sky. "We were promised drones. We can't run around the city like this all the time."

"Maybe we'll catch a break with the cameras." Hiroshi squinted at the light poles, hoping there'd be some.

Sugamo squinted at the poles. "At least it won't be hours and hours of video. The guy got away so fast."

Hiroshi pulled out his cell phone. "I better call Ishii and give her the bad news."

The three detectives started walking back to where things had gone wrong across from the bank, peering down each side street again as they passed.

By the bank, crime scene tape had been strung up. A crime scene truck and an ambulance were parked diagonally beside the tarp-enclosed scene.

Osaki and Sugamo headed over to help, but Hiroshi stopped. He wanted to avoid the bloody scene, so he headed toward Chief Sakaguchi, head of homicide. Taller and broader than Osaki and Sugamo, with a bigger chest and belly, he wore a wool overcoat, which made him seem even larger.

Sakaguchi stared down at Detective Ishii, listening to whatever she was explaining. His ex-sumo wrestler bulk was solid and commanding, and after recent knee surgery, he'd started to move again with more spring. Like most ex-athletes, he moved with fluid grace, only at a bigger size.

Ishii was solid and robust on a smaller scale. Her street fighting skills had impressed—and saved—Hiroshi on the first case they worked together, but she was just as impressive in meetings. In both, she kept going forward regardless. Her serious approach got her put in charge of the first-ever women's crime task force.

Ishii turned to Sakaguchi. "If you want to put me on

suspension, I'll understand. But I—"

Sakaguchi handed her a clipboard. "Until one of the higher-ups decides to suspend you, I want you to go over every detail, every witness, every footstep again."

Ishii took the clipboard, but her body deflated. "This is all my bad planning." She stared at the ambulance truck.

Sakaguchi tapped the clipboard, towering over her. "Better to keep working until the review. You have no idea where the scooter came from?"

Ishii shook her head. "He came out of nowhere. He wasn't in the scam ring, as far as I know. But they're tricky, those scammers. They sometimes get sloppy since they think the older women are easy targets. But these guys were pros from the beginning." Ishii sighed.

The crime scene crew wheeled out a gurney with a rise inside the body bag as small as a child's. It seemed like the crime scene crew handled her with special care.

Sakaguchi, Ishii, and Hiroshi put their hands together and bowed as she was lifted into the ambulance truck. The other detectives and crime scene crew members did the same, stopping work to put their hands together in prayer for her soul.

Ishii's head stayed down the longest. She whispered something to herself, a vow, prayer, or apology.

When the body was gone, Hiroshi cleared his throat. "What about the scooter guy?"

Sakaguchi looked at Hiroshi. "Are you sure you want to hear?"

He didn't. Descriptions were almost as bad as seeing the bodies. He skipped reading those parts of reports during meetings and avoided all photos.

Sakaguchi cocked his head. "Second- and third-degree skin abrasions. Down to the bone in a couple of places. He'll need grafts."

Ishii wiped her face with her hands. "The runner doesn't match the description we had from Ueno-san. The guy she talked with was plump with long hair. Maybe the guy who snatched the bag was also in their *sagi* ring." Ishii turned to Sakaguchi. "Listen, if you're going to put me on suspension, at least give me access to what's happening."

"You're not going on suspension," Sakaguchi growled. "But you will be if you keep pestering me about it."

Ishii bowed and nodded. "I hope this isn't going to impact the women's crime task force."

"I don't have control over that." Sakaguchi pointed at the tarp. "I'm only here because she was killed. You said it wasn't an accident, the scooter."

"It seemed like a *hittakuri* snatch and run. But he must have known. Or just bad luck. It was all so quick." Ishii looked up at the branches of the cherry trees.

Hiroshi followed her gaze. A few blossoms had opened here and there.

Sakaguchi took a clipboard from one of the younger detectives and signed it as he took a phone call. "I've got a suicide at a train station on the Chuo Line." Sakaguchi nodded for Hiroshi to take care of Ishii and waved for one of the young detectives to pull his car around.

Sakaguchi's body cleared a path to the van he'd been using. The van fit his size better than the special model Toyota Lexus the last homicide chief requisitioned. But Hiroshi knew it was Sakaguchi's upbringing in the poorest neighborhood in Osaka that stopped him from using any high-end car. He let it sit gathering dust in the police lot.

Ishii wondered out loud. "Does that mean I'm not on suspension, or I will be, or what?"

Hiroshi nodded. "Let's get some work done until you find out."

Sugamo came over, holding out his cell phone. The screen showed the records of a repeat offender.

Hiroshi scrolled down. "What is this? Or *who* is this?"

Sugamo took his phone back. "The kid on the scooter. Quite a record." He tapped the phone. "Takamatsu always says there are no accidents. And accidents don't always have victims."

Hiroshi hummed to himself. "So, where's the non-victim recovering from his non-accident?"

"University of Tokyo Hospital. You want us to interview him?" Sugamo looked back at the crew working the scene.

Hiroshi shook his head. "No, you're needed here. Ishii and I will talk with him after we notify Ueno's next of kin."

"She didn't have any." Ishii stared into the distance. "Just her friends at the Silver Center and around this whole area. Komagome Station. She had no family. That's how she knew they were lying."

"Knew who was lying?" Hiroshi looked at Sugamo.

Ishii blinked and breathed out. "The *sagi* ring. They called Ueno and pretended to be distant relatives. That's what they usually say until they can determine if she actually has a son or grandson. But she knew who they were right away. Ueno was angry that the scammers had destroyed people's lives, leaving them with nothing for their last years. And when she heard about all the other crimes against women, she was determined to help." Ishii looked over at the ambulance and up at the trees.

Sugamo caught Hiroshi's eye and frowned.

Hiroshi leaned towards Ishii. "Let's go let her friends know what happened."

Ishii took a deep breath and brushed her hair back with her hands. "I messed up everything. At least I can do this notification correctly." She started toward the crowd of older adults gathered in front of the Silver Center at the end of the street.

Chapter 3

Hiroshi followed Ishii past the bank to the Silver Center. Ishii walked as if he wasn't there. The leafy cherry trees blocked the midday sun, and the spring breeze was cool in the shade. A local policeman stood on the corner waving traffic to another route.

More like a factory or an unwanted government building, the outside of the Silver Center was made of dull grey stone, but inside, a hand-painted banner offered a colorful welcome in multiple languages. Most new areas in Tokyo had a center for seniors, and this old part of Tokyo had one, too. It was bigger than most.

Hiroshi followed Ishii inside. This was where she'd been holding workshops for the women's task force, getting the community to protect themselves from crimes preying on the "greying population." Most of those crimes took place against women because women lived longer.

Ishii had also spent time in nightlife areas where young women were blackmailed into sex work through debts or suffered workplace abuse. And then there were the *chikan* train gropers, sexual harassment, and violence. Young or old, many crimes went unreported.

Ishii headed to the office, but Hiroshi lingered in the front entryway. The smell of steam from the *sento* bath wafted in from a side door.

A conference room opened to the right. Inside, men stood discussing a sign-up board for volunteers for repair work and gardening. Across from them, women sat below a board for volunteer house cleaning, cooking, and babysitting.

In the brightly lit room to the left, the walls held a calendar of activities, brain-strengthening exercises, games, outings, and computer classes. Above the calendar hung a sign warning everyone about the dangers of *sagi* scams. A notice for a self-defense class had sketches of pepper spray canisters, mini stun guns, kendo sticks, and boxing gloves.

At tables, kids sat squirming over textbooks, with dictionaries, pens, pencils, and paper at the ready. One or two older people sat at each table, helping them with their homework. "Study Time" in Japanese and English was chalked across a board in bright colors.

Beyond the homework tables, older kids and grey-haired men squared off at Japanese *shogi* chess boards and the neat grids of *go* boards. Young and old studied the patterns with equal seriousness, pondering their next moves. One table was dedicated to Western chess, with three kids asking questions to an old master.

Hiroshi turned to look for Ishii and followed the sound of her voice to the office down the hall. The door was held open by a chunk of wood on the terrazzo floor. The office walls were covered with printed posters and neat schedules pinned to bulletin boards. Plastic trays of applications and flyers sat atop old metal file cabinets and shelving.

Inside, Ishii talked to three women standing by their pushed-together desks. Several others had pushed in to listen. No one spoke other than Ishii. When she was done, they looked at the floor.

Next to Hiroshi, one woman dipped her head into her hands. She started weeping, and another woman handed her a tissue. One of the three women standing by their desks bit her fist. She turned away toward the tall windows at the back of the office. Everyone else shook their head silently.

Ishii doubled over into a ninety-degree bow of apology.

The other women moved towards her, reaching for her arms to pull her up and whispering it wasn't her fault. One of the women led Ishii to a chair. The woman had thick, grey hair pulled into a bun. She pushed Ishii to sit down and waved for a glass of water. The nameplate on the far desk, where no one sat, said, "Ueno." Knickknacks, a teacup, and a tray of envelopes and folders created a cozy U-shaped workspace.

A woman walked in with a vase of flowers. She set it in the middle of Ueno's desk. Everyone in the room put their hands together and bowed.

Ishii, who'd stood up when the flowers came in, pointed at Hiroshi. "This is Detective Shimizu, my *senpai* in the homicide bureau."

The women turned and bowed. The woman who set the flowers on Ueno's desk moved to the electric kettle on a small refrigerator and turned it on. The others started murmuring amongst themselves.

The woman who'd been talking to Ishii came over to Hiroshi. "I'm Setsuko Yamaguchi, assistant director of the Silver Center."

Hiroshi handed her his *meishi* name card with a polite bow.

The woman who'd set the kettle on walked over with ballerina-like poise, stopping beside Setsuko. "And this is the director of the center, Sasaki."

Hiroshi handed her another name card.

Sasaki pulled her eyeglasses on to read it and walked back to her desk for her *meishi*. She handed hers over. "Nice to meet you. Detective Ishii mentioned you."

"Is there anyone we can notify about Ueno-san? Ishii said she had no family." Hiroshi looked back and forth from Sasaki to Setsuko.

Setsuko shook her head. "We were her family. Her husband died years ago. She never had children. I don't think she had much money. Only her home. We'll take care of things. We have her documents."

"Was she living close by?" Hiroshi asked. "We need to take a look."

Sasaki nodded. "The only good thing she got from her husband. We can take you there." She pointed at Setsuko and motioned in a triangle. "The three of us have known each other for a long time, but Ueno was the last to join the Silver Center. She became the most enthusiastic. She did everything."

"Everything?"

"The accounts were the hardest. But she took over scheduling, handled applications, found teachers and mentors, and started our most popular service—the *osusowake* corner."

Hiroshi frowned. "*Osusowake*?" He had to think what that was since it had been so long since he'd heard the expression.

Setsuko nodded. "At first, we set up a 'food bank,' but no one would use it. But when Ueno called it *osusowake*, it was like sharing, not like charity. It was what family or neighbors always did in Japan, share a box of potatoes or a big bag of rice. Calling it the same as a traditional custom let people take something they need without shame." Setsuko chuckled. And wiped a tear. "A lot of pensioners are struggling, but shame is worse. Ueno knew that."

Sasaki lowered her voice. "Ueno turned the Silver Center into a community that cared for everyone's needs." She wiped tears from the bottom of each eye. "She talked with the gym owners at the fancy new gym by the station and negotiated a Silver Center discount. We've all been going to dance classes, water aerobics, weightlifting."

Setsuko patted Sasaki's arm. "Sasaki is quite the ballerina."

Hiroshi thought she had a lightness of step, but he couldn't imagine them doing weightlifting. Weightlifting made him think of Osaki and Sugamo.

Sasaki shook her head and said, "We'll arrange her cremation and funeral. She also set up a discount program with a local crematorium, so now she'll be able to use it herself." Sasaki wiped her eyes with a crumpled handkerchief.

Setsuko sighed. "At least we have all her papers."

Hiroshi looked confused. "I thought that guy made off with everything?"

Ishii rejoined the conversation. "They'd told her they could give her a better apartment nearby. All she had to do was bring the deed and a small deposit. Everything in the bag was paper, except for a few bills on the outside. I knew he'd watch her go into the bank to get the money. I wanted to see it all happen in front of me. That was my mistake."

"So where—"

Setsuko held up one hand and squeezed Ishii's shoulder with the other. "We have a system. We put our important documents together into a safe. And we rotate them every few months. That way, we all know where they are, but we can't get at them without someone else knowing."

Sasaki nodded. "We're safer that way. Kind of a neighborhood watch program for documents."

Setsuko chuckled. "And in case we start going senile. Someone can look after our interests."

A grey-haired man stepped into the room. He eyed Hiroshi and Ishii and bowed. "I just heard."

Setsuko looked at him. "You have a key to Ueno's house, don't you? They want to look around."

The man nodded.

"Neighborhood watch for keys too. We leave it at Keisuke's office." Setsuko pointed at the man. "That's Keisuke."

He bowed again.

Hiroshi waited for an introduction.

Setsuko said, "He's a *fudosan* real estate agent. He handles many of the older apartments around here."

Keisuke dug in his jacket for his *meishi* case. He handed one to Hiroshi and then to Ishii.

Ishii held up her hand. "We met one time before."

"Oh, that's right," Keisuke said. "For the talk on *sagi* that first time." He smiled bright white teeth against a casual tan. "I still have the notice up in my office. I'm more or less out of the business these days, with only a few clients left. This whole *chome* is old folks. No young families want to move here."

Hiroshi pointed in the direction of the tutoring room. "A lot of kids in there getting tutored."

Setsuko frowned. "They're planning to close the nearby school. Once that's gone, no one will ever move here." She pointed up to the second floor. "We rent the rooms upstairs to foreign students studying at Tokyo University. Students are always nice to have around. They also help out with the tutoring next door."

Hiroshi held up his cell phone for Ishii to see. "Takamatsu's on his way. We need to go." To Keisuke, he said, "I'll call you so we can look into Ueno's house. We might find something there."

Keisuke took his name card back and scrawled his cell phone number on the back.

Setsuko clasped Ishii's hands and held them until Ishii pulled away and followed Hiroshi out the door.

Chapter 4

Sugamo drove up with Takamatsu and parked outside the Silver Center. Hiroshi and Ishii got in the back seat. Without turning around, Takamatsu said, "Hospital called."

Hiroshi wondered why Takamatsu wasn't smoking, but if he pointed it out, Takamatsu would be sure to light up. He'd folded his leather jacket neatly over the seat. Ishii brushed her fingers on the soft calfskin. Hiroshi wondered if they shouldn't be searching Ueno's home instead, but they could do that later. They stayed silent all the way to the hospital.

When Sugamo let them out of the car, Ishii got out and turned to Takamatsu. "Thank you for not talking and not smoking during the drive. I needed a few minutes to reflect on how to nail the guy who did this."

Takamatsu slammed the door and strode ahead. "That's what we're going to do."

Hiroshi followed them up the circle drive and into the hospital. Sugamo stayed with the car.

In the elevator, Takamatsu looked down as he flexed his new shoes, a pair of soft, expensive-looking Italian loafers. Hiroshi said nothing. He didn't want to hear about calfskin, polish, leather dye, or whatever else Takamatsu would go on about.

Takamatsu remained quiet for oncc too. Maybe he also sensed Ishii's frustration.

They got off the elevator and walked down one long corridor after the next, past several busy wards. Takamatsu checked the diagram of the hospital buildings and waved them to an elevator up to an interconnecting ward.

When they got to the top floor, Hiroshi stopped at the nurses' station and showed his badge while Takamatsu and Ishii went to the room. He asked the nurse on duty for the charts, but before he could take photos, shouting erupted, and they both turned and sprinted down the hall.

Inside the room, Takamatsu and a young detective were pushing Ishii away from a young kid in loose jeans and an oversized shirt. Ishii reached around Takamatsu, taking swings at the kid, who dodged the punches with his skateboard as a shield. Ishii landed two hard cracks to the kid's ear. Blood spilled from his row of pierces. He grabbed his ear with one hand and kept the skateboard up with the other until Takamatsu could maneuver her toward the door.

Hiroshi took her from Takamatsu and tugged her out to the hall, and Hiroshi eased her into a chair. Ishii looked up once and nodded she was in control. Hiroshi wasn't sure, but he left her there with the young detective on guard duty and returned to the room. He peeked out to be sure Ishii was out of boxing mode.

In the bed, the patient had squirmed so hard that he pulled the IVs and sensors loose, sending the monitors beeping. From somewhere in the tangle, another alarm went off, and the nurse who arrived with Hiroshi turned it off. Another nurse pushed into the room and started checking the bandages and IVs.

The kid Ishii had been punching could hardly be twenty. The nurse who'd managed the alarms dabbed his bleeding ear with an alcohol swab. He winced and clutched his skateboard until the nurse popped a bandage over it. The kid in bed—the scooter rider—fidgeted.

The older nurse turned to Hiroshi. "We're not supposed to let anyone in here for fear of infection."

"What about him?" Hiroshi pointed at the skateboard kid.

"He's next of kin." She stared Hiroshi down.

Next of kin? Hiroshi let it go.

"I'll give you ten minutes. The first hours are vital to keep the underlying layers alive. He might need grafts. A specialist's coming in later." The older nurse tapped her watch and walked out, shaking her head.

The younger nurse adjusted the monitors and tapped her watch in the same way before walking out.

Takamatsu walked over to the skateboard kid, took his arm, and twisted him against the wall. He yanked up the kid's shirts, exposing a canvas of skin covered in tattoos. "Take a photo of this. ID."

Hiroshi pulled out his cell phone for a photo. The kid's back had a half-finished tattoo of the character Yubaba from Ghibli's "Spirited Away," the lines of the tyrannical bathhouse owner's face sharp and clear.

Takamatsu dropped the shirt and pulled up the kid's sleeves.

Hiroshi photographed the sleeve tattoo of the manga Detective Conan. The other arm was half covered by a female anime character Hiroshi didn't recognize.

The kid said nothing but stood there holding his board, his body pliant but buffed. Skateboarding demanded muscle tone.

Takamatsu pulled back the sheet over the scooter rider. Bandages covered his back, shoulders, butt, and thighs. Blood soaked through the dressings, pinkish in places, yellowish in others.

Hiroshi shuddered and turned away.

Takamatsu turned to the skateboarder. "This wasn't the usual *hittakuri* bag snatch, was it?"

The kid didn't answer. Hiroshi could tell he'd been through this before.

Takamatsu stared him down. "We can take you in and interrogate you all night. We'll find your name either way. Save us both some trouble."

The skateboarder nodded. "Kobayashi Sho."

Takamatsu waited a moment and asked him for the name and where he lived.

He continued. "My name is the usual *kanji* for Kobayashi, and the *kanji* for Sho is 'to fly.'"

"Go on." Takamatsu nodded.

"I don't have an address, but I'm registered at the city hall in Shibuya." He nodded at the bed. "And that's Yoshimitsu—"

"We know that already. He had his wallet on him. The idiot. Shoplifting, amphetamines, bag snatches. Is that all? Or is there something more here?"

Sho shrugged.

"Do you always use a scooter or a skateboard? Where do you usually snatch bags? You just pick a place with weak old people and wait?"

Sho pulled a stony face. "You won't believe me, but I don't do that. Yoshimitsu didn't want to, either, but—"

"But what? No one else will hire you? Can't imagine why. Should be plenty of places that would love a tattooed worker. Maybe in reception? Sales?"

Sho stared at Takamatsu and then at Hiroshi. His pupils were huge, a sign of amphetamines.

"And what's *your* list of misdemeanors? I'll find out as soon as I check the database, so you might as well tell me now."

Sho scratched himself and looked at his friend.

Takamatsu continued. "He was riding a stolen scooter. He's got amphetamines in his system. Seems like you do too. And fighting with police?" He pointed to the hallway where Ishii was, so far, staying quiet.

"I blocked her," Sho protested. "Am I supposed to let her punch me?"

Takamatsu pointed at Yoshimitsu. "And did I mention the lady he tried to rob died at the scene? The scooter smashed into her."

Sho looked at his friend and put his foot against the tail of his skateboard. "He borrowed it from a friend to go to work, a real job in a convenience store, and couldn't see her because of the truck. It was an accident."

Takamatsu shook his head. "Next, you're going to tell me your tattoos are accidents."

Hiroshi intervened. He didn't want Takamatsu to hit the kid.

"He reached for her bag. I was standing right there."

"I wasn't there. I was—"

"Spotting for him?"

Sho sighed.

Hiroshi took a step toward Sho. "Robbing old ladies is how you make your living?"

Takamatsu took a step closer. "Too bad he couldn't see the police because of the truck. You missed something, like half a dozen undercover cops. You feeling guilty? That's why you're here?"

Sho squirmed, silent.

Takamatsu cleared his throat. "I hate amateurs."

Hiroshi spread his arms. "Look, you're in serious trouble here, so the only way out is to leverage what you know. Tell us who paid you to do this."

Takamatsu said, "A little cooperation goes a long way." Was this a new Takamatsu? First, he was quiet in the car, and now he was patient during an interview.

Sho shrugged. "We answer posts for jobs."

"Posts?" Hiroshi asked. "On 4chan?"

Sho shook his head. "Telegram. 4chan is over. Telegram's safer. No names."

"Did you save a screenshot of the post about today's job?" Takamatsu waved for Sho's cell phone.

Sho pulled out his cell phone and started scrolling. He handed it to Takamatsu.

Hiroshi stepped over to read it. It was a simple offer of good pay for an easy job. "How do you get paid?"

Sho shrugged. "Different ways."

Hiroshi took a photo of the page. "So, on Telegram, you see a post, answer it, they tell you what to do, and you do it? Just like that?"

"Job post one day. Gone the next. You have to answer right away." Sho nodded. "They pay a lot sometimes. It's mostly deliveries. Or pick-up and delivery."

"Drugs usually?"

Yoshimitsu groaned from the bed.

Sho drew a breath. He was hesitant, but not intimidated. "One guy we met in person. He came to the skateboard park."

"Miyashita Park? Shibuya?"

"Yeah." The skateboard kid pushed back his blonde-dyed hair. Maybe he was in his twenties. It was hard to tell. "That first time was just a delivery. For the payoff, we met in the park along the Sumida River."

"It's a long river. Where exactly?"

"We skateboarded along the riverside until he called out to us."

"What did he look like?" Hiroshi hoped Takamatsu wouldn't slap the kid.

"About your height." He nodded at Hiroshi. "Hat, sunglasses, jacket. Everyone looks the same."

"Yakuza?"

"I thought he was a cop."

"They can be hard to tell apart." Takamatsu chuckled. He held his hand out for Sho's cell phone. Sho pulled up his number. Takamatsu put the number into his phone and called it.

Sho's phone buzzed, and he added the number and put his phone away.

Takamatsu put a hand on Sho's shoulder. "When we call you, you answer. When you hear from that guy, you call us immediately."

"What if he doesn't call?"

"When he doesn't get his money, he'll call."

Takamatsu leaned forward. "Search the listings on Telegram. Answer any that sound similar. Send those to us."

"There's a lot of them."

"Send them to me. All of them."

Sho toed his skateboard. "What do I get out of this?"

Takamatsu smiled at him. "Well, for now, we won't put you and sleeping beauty over there in jail for homicide. How about that?"

Sho plucked at his shirt and tapped the skateboard with his foot.

Takamatsu looked at him. "You two are loose ends."

Sho popped the tail of his skateboard, grabbed the nose in one hand, and held the board in front of him.

Takamatsu jabbed a finger in Sho's chest. "We detectives don't like loose ends, either. But we have a different way of tying them up. You'll like our way better than his."

Sho touched his bandaged ear. "Can I get out of here without her hitting me again?"

Takamatsu scoffed. "You're on your own there."

Chapter 5

Takuya pulled open the door and headed for a table at the back of his girlfriend Misaki's "OLzakaya." A few customers lingered from the lunch rush. Some had beers, but most drank tea. They had hours of office drudgery ahead of them. Most were pretending to their companies to be visiting clients or doing telework. Some might not even be employed at all. Misaki was friendly to them all. She handled accounts, personnel, orders, cleanup, and customers with little drama and less anxiety. She was sensible, practical, and punctual.

Misaki thought of the name, combining OL, or office lady, an out-of-date word from the Showa era, and *izakaya*, the name for an eating and drinking spot. The wait staff at Misaki's place pretended to be Office Ladies, the female employees who made copies, poured tea, and stuffed envelopes throughout Japan, Inc. The story Misaki had them tell, which few believed, was that this OLzakaya was their side job from a big company, the name of which they never disclosed.

The customers at the OLzakaya couldn't afford the elegant hostess bars of Ginza or Akasaka, where upper-tier managers went, so Misaki brought that experience to an affordable level in a cheaper part of town. Even with Takuya's help with a down payment, *shitamachi* was about the only place she could afford. The spot they found was far enough from the station, Komagome, to be affordable but close enough to draw traffic.

But Misaki also had known that the Nishi-Nippori location was packed with small companies doing piece work for the largest corporations. The bland buildings with unremarkable names were the working home to thousands and thousands of white-shirt-black-pants employees who, at the end of the day, needed a drink and a little fantasy on the way to the station.

A new "OL," a cute girl with pretty eyes over her mask, bounced over to take his order, *oyakodon* chicken-egg-and-rice bowl. Takuya appreciated the way she turned in her skin-tight top and short skirt. He could imagine the rest. She wriggled in her short skirt and midriff, but right now, he didn't need attention. He needed an alibi and something to eat. And better shoes.

Misaki came out from the counter and walked to his table. "Why are you wearing sandals?" she whispered.

Takuya frowned and used his gruff voice. "Getting my shoes fixed. These are loaners." The sandals had rubbed blisters on his feet.

"At the repair place on the corner?"

"Yes. Listen, in case anyone asks, I've been here all morning, OK?" Takuya avoided her eyes.

Misaki bowed to a plump customer, a regular, it seemed.

Takuya waited for him to leave. "After I finish the *oyakodon*, I need a nap—"

"Someone's in that room."

Takuya sighed. "Well, can't you chase them out?"

Misaki looked at him. "Did you bring me something to deposit? I'm going to the bank."

Takuya reached for his vape pen. Remembering he'd dropped it, he groaned.

"Is your vape pen also getting repaired?"

Takuya gave her a look. She could be annoying as hell when she wanted to be.

Misaki waved to a departing customer. He bowed and pointed to one of the signs hanging down from the ceiling with funny sayings. Apparently, he knew English. Something about beer and God.

"Are you going to clear them out of that room?" Takuya asked again.

"Sure. You're my best customer." Misaki walked off.

The new waitress brought his bowl.

"Can you bring me scallions and *togarashi* pepper? And a beer." The egg wasn't steamed enough. He had trained the first line-up of cooks, but he'd been too busy to oversee the new ones.

He moved his bag to the side and realized his shoes were in there. He didn't want Misaki to see them after he'd just told her they were being repaired, and he didn't want her to see the blank paper documents and money, either. He was going to burn it all in a metal bin in the kitchen.

The waitress brought the *togarashi* chili and spice mix. He sprinkled the red pepper and spices over the whole mess and dug in with a Chinese spoon. As he ate, he ran through the morning's disaster.

He couldn't remember when he first noticed them, but they were obviously cops once he did. He hadn't looked back once, but from their voices, they weren't a rival gang or from some government office. They yelled like undercover police in suits.

When did he first notice the scooter? Was that just a bag snatch gone wrong? It was too much coincidence. Did that old lady know about it? He didn't want to think Yasui knew, but maybe he did? No, that was impossible. They'd been friends since high school. Did one of the others in his group set him up? They'd all four worked together for three profitable years.

Takuya put more spice over the top and stirred the egg and chicken with the rice and sauce until it all turned brown.

The woman was dead. She had to be. Like most of their clients, she was small and frail, hardly as tall as his chest. The scooter squashed her against the cherry tree. One glance was enough to tell she'd been killed on impact. Nothing like that had ever happened before. Nothing even close.

He shoveled in another mouthful.

Maybe the police had gone in through the back door or had been waiting there long before he'd arrived. That started to sound even worse. They'd set this up long in advance.

He called Yasui again but got no answer. If he was with his

grandmother, the hospital might have blocked cell phone reception. He sent another message.

Misaki hurried from the kitchen, her cell phone to her ear, not looking at him. She poked her head out the front, looked in both directions, leaned back, and waved to Takuya. "The police," she whispered.

"Did they ask about me?"

"No, just a routine check. Maybe."

Takuya got up. His legs had stiffened from the run, and his blisters were raw and tender. Maybe he'd stepped on something. He hobbled to the back room. Misaki pushed him inside and hurried away.

He thought about heading out the back door, but he couldn't run anymore. Misaki poked her head in and dropped some tennis shoes at his feet.

"Where did you get these?" Takuya slid his feet out of the sandals and into the shoes, but they hurt too.

"You left them here when you did repairs in the kitchen." Misaki started to shut the door but then pulled it back open to let the new waitress in with his tray of unfinished food. She touched her arm. "You've been with him for the last two hours, OK?"

The waitress nodded. The backroom service was Misaki's idea. Customers could request a private room to have their meal and a drink with the fake OL of their choice. She charged them extra. What happened inside was up to them.

"What's your name?" Takuya motioned for her to sit down.

"Here? Mi-*chan*." She pointed at her name tag. "Isn't that what you call your girlfriend?"

"I call her Misaki. She doesn't like nicknames." Takuya spooned in the last bits of egg and chicken and surveyed Mi-chan's tight top. He'd always been attracted to small-breasted women but ended up with the fuller package Misaki had.

He dug down for the last bits of rice and washed it down with a sip of beer. "Mi-*chan*, do you think you could do me a favor?"

"In addition to lying to the police for you?" She smiled slyly.

Was this her gambit for a tip? Or was she used to requests?

Takuya cleared his throat. "I need a vape pen. There's a tobacco shop around the corner."

"I often go there for cigarettes for customers."

Takuya dug for his wallet and handed her a ten-thousand-yen note.

"Don't you want me to wait until the police are gone? I won't be a good alibi if I'm not here."

She was right. He was stuck without his vape pen until they left. He scraped the sauce from the bottom of the bowl and set down the spoon.

Mi-*chan* wiggled onto the banquette opposite Takuya and scrolled through her cell phone messages.

Takuya wondered how she managed to type with long, pink, glitter-studded nails. Real office work would be impossible. She noticed him noticing her nails and smiled as she scrolled. She thought they were attractive, but they made him think of Ibaraki, the countryside, where no woman would have nails like that because they used their hands to work.

He called Yasui again. He must know something or at least have a guess. But Yasui didn't answer again.

Takuya checked the schedule of pickups that day. Only one, an elderly woman giving her savings to the Consumer Popular Protection Bureau, a business front he had created out of a few *meishi* name cards, temporary phone numbers, and slick-looking pamphlets. He sent a message to Noguchi and told him to cancel it.

Noguchi wrote back right away, demanding an explanation.

Takuya told him he'd explain when they met at the coffee shop. Noguchi agreed, and Takuya sent a message to Murayama. Maybe he was the one behind this.

No, he couldn't be. He was sly, but he couldn't have kept betrayal hidden. And he didn't need to. He was already running his own scams, using his computer skills. Maybe Yasui would call back soon to shed some light on things.

Takuya looked up from his cell phone and smiled at Mi-*chan*. "Would you mind checking to see if the police are gone? And if so, go get me that vape pen?"

She hopped up and peeked around the door. "I think they're gone. What flavor do you like best?"

"Cuban rum and cigar." The words were all in English.

She repeated it to herself with a strong Japanese pronunciation and slipped out the door.

Takuya put his feet up, leaned back, and stared at the mirrored ceiling, wondering how things had gotten away from him and how he was going to get them under control. Someone was responsible, and he would find out who.

Chapter 6

"We need to hurry," Takamatsu said. "The place closes when the broth sells out."

Ishii pulled the car into the last open spot in a small parking lot.

"What kind of place closes so early?" Hiroshi got out of the back seat.

"The kind that serves the best ramen in Tokyo." Takamatsu got out and lit a cigarette.

Ishii clicked the locks and walked over to punch the numbers into the payment machine.

Takamatsu walked down a small street whose snack bars were shuttered. Hiroshi wasn't sure if the shops were shuttered permanently or until the night's drinking restarted.

Takamatsu pointed out a sign written in English and shook his head. To him, all English was evidence of over-tourism. He kept on to a brown-tiled building. Blocking the front window were kerosene cans on an air conditioning unit and blue trash cans stacked to the side. A whiteboard tied to a wooden chair showed what was not yet sold out for the day.

Takamatsu slid aside the frosted glass door and stepped under the dingy *noren* curtain.

Inside, large colanders rested on plastic crates, the top one full of washed *moyashi* white bean sprouts. A jumble of lost umbrellas hung from a rickety shelf holding well-thumbed manga and weekly magazines. The floor was a succession of failed repairs in concrete, grout, and laminate. One wall held posters for *enka*, *kabuki*, *manzai*, and the *banzuke* sumo rankings, and the other was covered in framed signature cards from celebrities who'd visited the shop. The cards had manga-like caricatures in bright colors, with open oval eyes and toothy smiles.

They sat on stools and eyed the wall menu: ten noodle variations, fried rice, regular rice, and steamed *shumai* dumplings. Takamatsu shouted his order, and the owner, a grey-haired woman in an oversized apron, wrote it down from her perch at the counter. Ishii called her order out. Hiroshi ordered wonton noodles, though he would eat again when he got home to Ayana.

Takamatsu ordered beer.

"None for me." Hiroshi folded his arms.

Hiroshi scanned the autographs of famous people on the wall. He didn't know a few of them and couldn't read all the stylized signatures.

The beer came, and Hiroshi accepted a small glass to be polite. He knew the beer would ruin his resolve to arrive home sober. They toasted with raised glasses.

Ishii drained hers and refilled Takamatsu's, then hers. "I don't know how that kid on the scooter could have known about this."

"But he did." Hiroshi dropped his elbow on the table. It wobbled.

Ishii shook her head. "He kept calling. He knew just what to say and how to say it. After listening in to the calls, even I felt like meeting him. He was slick."

Takamatsu smiled. "Those guys are the best actors around." He flipped his lighter in his hand.

Ishii drained another glass. The table wobbled again, so she folded a napkin, leaned down, and slipped it under the short leg of the table. "I want to go back and talk to that kid in the hospital as soon as he's conscious."

Hiroshi sighed. "You just beat up his friend."

"Without his friend." Ishii kept looking at the wall of autographs.

Takamatsu gave Hiroshi a look. "Ishii, take a break tonight. Losing someone like that on a case is tough. You need to sleep."

Hiroshi finished his beer. "I'll go with you tomorrow, but Takamatsu's right. Rest tonight."

Ishii poured her glass full and held up the bottle to the shop owner for another. Takamatsu poured more beer into Hiroshi's glass, ignoring his hand to stop, and waved the bottle for more. The owner brought two.

Hiroshi asked for water and ignored his beer. Letting it sit full was the best way not to get more. He was trying to keep his promise to Ayana to drink less after she stopped drinking. It would help her more if he could be with her in some small ways. He'd started reducing time spent on unimportant work, which helped, but he still wanted to be home.

The owner carried over two bowls of wonton ramen and set them down in front of Ishii and Hiroshi. The design along the rim of the bowls was worn with use. The broth was dark brown, darker than most, with a bit of oil floating on top.

"Yours is coming," she said to Takamatsu. "I can't carry three at a time anymore." She held out her forearm—bones, tendons, and wrinkles.

She brought back the third bowl and set it in front of Takamatsu. She got three small plates of pickled vegetables from the counter and set them down. "*Sabisu*," she said, using the Japanization of "service" for a free little extra. She returned to her spot between the kitchen and the counter and picked up her glasses and magazine.

Ishii passed the wooden chopsticks out and cracked hers in two. She poured more beer for herself.

Hiroshi watched her finish another glass. "Who's going to drive?"

Takamatsu waved his chopsticks. "Leave the car overnight. Osaki and Sugamo can get it in the morning."

Hiroshi plucked the neat slice of *chashu* pork floating in the broth. It was tender and flavorful. He took a mouthful of the thin, crinkled noodles with a pinch of *menma* bamboo shoot slice.

"That woman—"

"Ueno. Nobuko Ueno. Her name means trusting child." Ishii stared at the wall of famous names with her chopsticks in the air.

Takamatsu grunted. "She trusted you for the right reasons. She understood the dangers." He went back to slurping his noodles.

Ishii pushed her bowl away. She finished before either of them and worked on the beer. Her face glowed redder. "I started on girls coerced into porn. After the age of majority was lowered from twenty-one to eighteen, there was a rush."

"JD, *joshi daigakusei*. Female college students." Takamatsu, for once, didn't smile.

Ishii finished another glass. "Right, JD, but most of that ended up marketed as JK, female high school students."

Takamatsu frowned. "All you have to do is look young enough."

"Be made to look and act young enough." Ishii drank another swallow. "No one up the chain except Sakaguchi read my reports, but he couldn't OK all the busts I wanted to make. If it wasn't murder, he had to find a connection."

"He's head of homicide. It's not his fault." Takamatsu leaned back.

"No, it's not his fault. The women's task force was set up interdepartmentally, but that meant everyone could ignore it and not take responsibility. They need a women's task force in every section, the head of financial crime said. That was his way of ignoring it." She drank more beer.

Takamatsu didn't move to pour her more. "That's how they get to be head of sections. They know how to dodge responsibility."

"Sakaguchi's different," Ishii said. "He did a lot to help. So, this case puts it into his domain. Maybe it'll be different."

"So, what about this *sagi*? Is it all about ripping off old women?" Hiroshi had helped her sort out the bank transfers, ATM protections, and overseas accounts for her cases. The *sagi* groups had become increasingly sophisticated, as smooth with finances as with patter.

"Men die younger than their wives, and some of the women start to become senile, forgetting their grandson's names as often as their passcodes. We went to Silver Centers for talks and demonstrations. Most of them, at least in *shitamachi*, still live in neighborhoods, but they can be isolated too. The ones who live alone are the most vulnerable."

"And a bigger victim pool every year. Greying population." Takamatsu refilled his glass.

"More savings and more cash in easy-to-access places. Ueno-san organized an info session every couple of weeks." Ishii looked away. She took another sip of beer. "She contacted all the other Silver Centers in *shitamachi* to run more info sessions. She and Setsuko-san seemed to know everyone. They took over so I could focus more on the *sagi* gangs. We caught a few, but penalties aren't strict enough to scare them into divulging anything."

"They operate in tight cells or are hired by the job." Hiroshi cleared his throat. "Some of the bank scams and real estate scams work that way. Everyone has one single role once. Only one or two people know the entire operation."

Ishii looked around for more beer, her face bright red. "They ruin the final years of people's lives, and after a stint inside, they're out again and right back to it."

Takamatsu poured her half a glass and kept the bottle on his side of the table.

Ishii touched her face, testing how flushed it was. "Ueno volunteered, but she trusted me to set it all up."

Takamatsu grunted and lit a cigarette.

Ishii rolled her head to pop the cricks out of her neck and surveyed the wall of autographs. "I just don't get it. We have a Respect-the-Aged Day in September, discounts, designated seats, decent retirement age, mini-buses, and an attitude of deference and considerate behavior. And yet..."

Takamatsu blew out a lungful of smoke. "People don't live with their grandparents anymore. They forget."

Ishii still stared at the wall. "Japan's tradition of respecting ancestors, teachers, parents—anyone older—goes back to Confucian scholars and feudal manners...but it's all gone, isn't it? One of the women had her life savings drained. They owned a tofu shop. Keisuke found her an apartment, and the Silver Center took up a collection, but many of them didn't have much to give. Keisuke found her one morning. She'd starved to death. She died from the shame, Setsuko said."

Takamatsu folded his arms and smoked. "It was ingrained in society when I grew up. It was drilled into us to use the right language for our elders or risk being shamed, scolded, or worse." He shook his head. "That's where things start falling apart, lack of respect."

Ishii chuckled. "The scammers know all the right words, the formal terms of address, humble, polite verb forms. They're the most well-spoken people I've ever heard."

The owner of the shop came to take the bowls away. Ishii handed her the empties. The bottles and glasses seemed to fit into a worn place between her fingers.

Takamatsu put out his cigarette and fiddled with his lighter. "This case is now in homicide. Hiroshi will help track the finances. I'm going to find out why that kid was riding the scooter. And Ishii, you're going to bring whoever did this in. For murder."

Hiroshi hummed in agreement and took the last swallow of beer. He looked at the foam sliding back to the bottom.

Ishii looked up at the signed autographs and caricatured faces looking down on them.

Takamatsu got up to pay.

Chapter 7

Hiroshi took the subway from the ramen shop back to the station. The deadline was approaching for a thorny embezzlement case at a fish company. He'd put off finalizing it for Interpol while helping Ishii.

The case was a tricky one. The head of the family-owned fish company had fled abroad, leaving his three sisters, who barely knew the business, to face the charges. Plenty of crime happened outside families in Japan, but a surprising amount inside too.

He walked from the subway station to the building beside the main police headquarters, where his office took up a converted space off a landing. Construction in the annex building, long overdue, routed him through a shoulder-width passage beside metal dividers. The floor was covered in protective plastic taped in place.

The noise of a jackhammer taking out concrete echoed in the hall. The hammering shook the floor. Maybe he wouldn't get any work done.

When he got to his office, he pushed on his door, but it wouldn't open. He pushed again. Something blocked it. He pushed harder. "Akiko?"

"Oh, sorry!" Akiko called out from inside.

He heard shuffling, scraping, and exhaling before the door pulled back.

Akiko stood there wiping her hands. "*O-kaeri-nasai*. Welcome back."

On the floor, his rug and futon chair had been pulled from their usual places. He stepped over them with a frown.

Akiko leaned down to shut the door and dragged the rug and futon chair back to the door. "It blocks the noise."

"How long is this going to go on?" Hiroshi hung his coat on the rack and doused his hands in disinfectant.

"They were going to tear the entire annex down, but they didn't have any place to put everyone until it was rebuilt. The office staff in the main building told me six months."

"Six months of jackhammering?"

"We might have to move out for a month while they redo the stairwell."

"Why didn't anyone tell me?" Hiroshi headed to the espresso machine.

"They didn't tell me, either." Akiko shrugged. "No one in the main offices knew, either. Maybe they figured detectives were always in the field. What happened with the *sagi* pick-up?"

Hiroshi hung his coat up. "The woman helping Ishii got hit."

"Hit?"

"Killed."

Akiko stood up. "Ishii had been working on that one for two months."

Hiroshi waited for the double espresso to trickle deliciously from the two spouts. He didn't want more caffeine, but it would keep him focused until he got the fish fraud report done and made it home to Ayana.

Akiko sat down, staring at her screen. "Ishii's going to have a lot of reports. I'd better offer to help."

"Do that." Hiroshi sat down and sipped his espresso, looking back and forth as his two screens started up.

She sent a message and set her cell phone down. "The report for Interpol just needs the data from the National Tax Agency on bank transfers overseas. That guy cheated his own sisters."

"Watanabe should have sent it. He's the most helpful bureaucrat in Tokyo. And the youngest head of the tax agency ever."

"Is he?" Akiko smiled and headed for the door. "Let me in when I get back."

When Akiko pulled open the door, the sound of construction

blasted up the stairwell.

Hiroshi got up to redo the muffling. He shoved the rug and chair back in place, but the vibration came through the walls and floors like a small earthquake.

Hiroshi started filling in the report for Interpol, mostly blanks, attachments, and checkboxes. Ayana worried about the dangers of his job, but most of it involved filling out forms.

He worked on the forms for as long as possible, but his mind wandered.

Ishii's *sagi* case had turned into a murder case. Two people, the scammer, and the scooter rider, were going for that bag. He should have gone to Ueno's home to scour for clues instead of going for ramen and returning to his office.

Akiko returned with the packet held over her head. For the next two hours, they input the data from Watanabe, their contact in the tax office, into the Interpol report, along with all their findings.

When they were done, Hiroshi pressed send, and they both leaned back, relieved.

Akiko turned off her computer and gathered her things.

Hiroshi checked the time. "Oh, no. I was supposed to bring dinner back to Ayana."

"How's she doing?" Akiko giggled as she pulled her coat on and grabbed her bag.

Hiroshi shook his head. "All good so far. I've got to find more time off."

"Take leave."

"I should." Hiroshi stood up. "I'll walk you out. Keep you safe from the jackhammers."

"The whole building shakes."

* * *

Hiroshi took a taxi back to Kagurazaka and got out at the corner in front of Ayana's favorite deli. For some reason, she had started wanting sandwiches. This deli was one of the few places in Tokyo with smoked turkey, something else he had never known her to like. Smoked cheese too.

He ordered cartons of bean salad, potato salad, cold pasta, and a big packet of olives. She was eating as much as Sakaguchi. He didn't know where all the pricy foreign deli food was going. It was like she'd become a foreigner. He thought she'd revert to her childhood Japanese favorites, but Ayana shrugged when he brought it up. Best to just feed the woman.

He got two bottles of wine for himself, despite his promises, and packed everything into the shopping bag he carried all the time now. It was steep uphill from the deli, but walking loosened his legs from the morning's chase.

"*Tadaima,*" he called out from the *genkan* of the apartment. He heard voices—two voices—Ayana and another woman he didn't recognize. He kicked off his shoes and came into the living area, holding the bags up like prizes.

Ayana sat on a stool at the kitchen island.

The other woman had her back to him, but climbed off her stool and bowed gently. She looked familiar. She looked like Ayana.

Hiroshi bowed. He hoisted the bags onto the counter, walked around to kiss Ayana, and dropped a hand to her bulging stomach.

"Hiroshi, this is my mother." Ayana took his hand.

"Ah," Hiroshi mumbled. He had never met her mother in person. Only recently did they start talking about their families, hoping to do things differently. "Nice to meet you." He flipped on the tap and washed his hands.

"Nice to meet you too. I thought I'd come in person." She had the same voice as Ayana.

Ayana started to unpack the shopping bags, and her mother hurried over to help.

Hiroshi smiled to cover his surprise. "I hope you like foreign food. It's all Ayana eats these days."

Ayana's mother was the same height, with the same kind of face, only thinner. They did their hair the same. From behind or the side, they looked like sisters. Only her mother's grey hair separated them. Both wore blue sweaters, Ayana with light brown sweatpants and her mother with beige slacks.

"She was in pain this morning, so I caught the *shinkansen*." Her mother picked up a paper towel, grabbed disinfectant spray, and sprayed down the items as she took them from the bag.

Ayana gave Hiroshi an apologetic glance. "Mother, I wish you'd told us you were going to visit."

"I didn't know myself until I pulled out my travel bag."

Hiroshi saw the travel bag by the sofa. "Pain?"

"The cramps are gone as quickly as the nausea, but it hurts sometimes." Ayana took the wiped deli items from her mother and set them in order.

Working in tandem, they put some things in the fridge, left some out, and pulled out plates and bowls.

Ayana smiled. "I'm eating all day, breakfast here, breakfast at the archives, a snack, lunch, snack, dinner when I get home. That's probably the cause of the cramps. All this foreign food."

Hiroshi felt confused. "I thought that's what you wanted?"

Ayana examined the containers. "I called the doctor about it. I'll see him tomorrow."

"I'll go with you." Ayana's mother turned to Hiroshi. "Ayana tells me your work is very busy."

Hiroshi eyed the wine bottle. "Reports mostly. White-collar crime. Fraud, embezzlement, a *sagi* ring. You should be careful."

"I am careful. All of that is homicide?"

"Money makes people murderous."

Ayana's mother frowned. "It must be interesting. And frightening."

"Necessary." Hiroshi wondered when she would wipe the wine bottle.

Ayana's mother held up the bag of olives. "Is this what we're having for dinner? Things wrapped in plastic?"

"It's what I feel like eating." Ayana started to pull out plates and bowls.

She still had not wiped down the wine bottle, so Hiroshi reached out, but Ayana's mother took the bottle, wiped it, peeled off the foil, and dug in a drawer for a corkscrew.

Ayana took the corkscrew from the drawer by her belly and slid it across the counter. Hiroshi wanted to wrap Ayana in his arms and have a glass of wine while patting her stomach. Now, he was stuck in an awkward conversation.

Her mother opened the wine, took two glasses from the rack, set it on the counter, poured, swirled, sniffed it like a sommelier, sipped, and then poured a full glass for Hiroshi and a small one for herself.

They tipped their glasses in a silent toast.

Hiroshi took a grateful swallow as she deftly folded a napkin around the neck of the bottle.

His phone buzzed, and he took another, bigger sip of wine and walked to the entryway to take the call. It was Sakaguchi, the one person he could never refuse. Sakaguchi never asked for too much, so when he asked, Hiroshi went.

After a simple "OK" to Sakaguchi, he pocketed his phone and walked back to the counter for another mouthful of wine.

Ayana looked at him. "You have to go, don't you?"

Hiroshi held the glass up and sighed.

"Why don't you change your shirt?" Ayana gestured toward the bedroom.

"I'm fine."

"No, you need to change your shirt." Ayana waved him after her.

In the bedroom, Ayana wrapped her arms around him. "I didn't know she was coming."

"It's OK. I got to meet her at last."

"She just showed up at the archives. In the middle of a meeting. The other librarians pushed me to leave early."

"It's fine. It's your mother. She's welcome."

"I don't know how she even knew I was pregnant."

"You didn't tell her?" Hiroshi laughed.

Ayana shook her head. "I meant to, but—"

"Isn't that why she came?"

Ayana buried her face in his chest. "She called me this morning out of the blue. Maybe she sensed something. I told her about the cramps, and she was here a few hours later."

Hiroshi hugged her, feeling the press of her breasts and belly.

"She wanted to sleep in here with me. Can you sleep on the sofa?"

"I don't know when I'll get home anyway."

"She wants me to take leave and stay with her in Nagoya until the birth."

"*Satogaeri shussan*? Giving birth in your hometown? That's the most traditional thing you've ever done."

"I thought kendo was? Or maybe this is?" She kissed him hard on the mouth.

Chapter 8

The Silver Center entrance was shrouded by blue tarps slung between the building and the cherry trees. Media vans jammed the small street all the way to Komagome Station. Local police tapped the sides of the vans with their batons, ordering them to back up, but it was too narrow to reverse until the vehicle behind did. Hiroshi wondered if the tarps were the same ones they'd strung over the morning's crime scene down the street.

Hiroshi walked past the line of vans and flashed his badge to the guard in front of the Silver Center doors. He didn't want to see another corpse. He couldn't avoid witnessing the death of Ueno that morning—it happened right in front of his eyes. Even later, when she was wheeled out in the body bag, he shivered and looked away. Now, there was another one.

Before ducking under the tape, he stopped at a table to pull on white booties and nitrile gloves. Unlike the morning's bustle, the place was empty except for crime scene techs and LED lights. He had that sickly, fainting feeling like he always did.

Hiroshi looked for Sakaguchi, his usual life preserver at crime scenes, but didn't see him. In the office where he and Ishii had spoken with Setsuko, Sasaki, and the other Silver Center volunteers, the crew were examining surfaces and dusting the terrazzo floor for clues.

Hiroshi started up the wide stairs. The building seemed like it might have been a research facility, a government office, or a company's headquarters. Something functional and now abandoned. The landing on the second floor led into a high-ceilinged hallway. Bright lights shone down the hallway. The crime scene crew had laid out evidence on rolling tables.

Osaki and Sugamo waited outside a room at the end of the hallway. When they saw him, there was no turning back. Hiroshi felt his legs weaken.

Along the hallway, the doors had nameplates written in various scripts, *romaji* with *katakana*, Chinese characters, Cyrillic letters, posters for university events, and cheerful sayings.

To the right was a door to a large, high-ceilinged kitchen area where foreigners, Asian, but not Japanese, and two or three Westerners stared wide-eyed as he passed. Behind them, the wall was taken up by a sink, a multi-burner stove, and two large refrigerators. Pots hung from a rack along the wall. A young detective stood at the door.

Hiroshi paused, but Osaki waved him down the hall to the last room. Hiroshi peeked cautiously inside. The room was jammed floor to ceiling with metal shelving holding an array of computers, printers, video cameras, and boxes with wires springing over the top. The shelving was packed so tightly that the crime scene crew had to turn sideways to move around.

On one side was a neat display case for anime characters. They caught the camera flashes and seemed to sway and jump. A rollaway bed was folded up in the corner. Sakaguchi's huge bulk took up one of the aisles.

Osaki whispered to Hiroshi. "The body's gone. Don't worry."

Hiroshi ignored the sarcasm. "Was there a lot of blood?"

Sugamo leaned over from the next aisle. "The first blood-less site in a while. Probably an overdose, maybe that date rape drug, Rohypnol. They'll know after tests."

"That can kill you?"

"If there's enough of it."

"He took it himself?"

Osaki pointed down the hall to the kitchen area. "Maybe you can talk to them? They're gathered in the kitchen."

Sugamo held up an evidence bag with a thumb-size camera in it. "He also had these all over the building." The camera was about the size of his thumb.

Hiroshi looked at it. "It's pretty small. Do the students know about that?"

Sugamo shrugged. "The women's shower had five. They found some downstairs too."

"Who was he?" Hiroshi asked.

"All I could get out of them was that the deceased was a *hikikomori* recluse. He stayed mostly in his room but was still enrolled. All the students go to Tokyo University. One girl, not a student, came to visit him." Sugamo nodded toward the kitchen. "Some students speak fluent Japanese, but it's still hard to talk with them."

Hiroshi headed back down the hall, nodded to the young detective at the door to the kitchen, and stepped inside. The students were talking among themselves and scrolling through their cell phones but sat up when Hiroshi cleared his throat. They were dressed in sweatshirts and oversized T-shirts with the logos of far-flung universities.

"OK, everyone!" Hiroshi spoke in a loud voice in English. "I'll talk to everyone together at first. Then, I'll talk to everyone one by one." He said everything in English and then repeated it in Japanese. "Please give me all the information you have, no matter how small or unimportant you might think it is. Are we clear?"

Everyone nodded, some at the English, some at the Japanese.

Hiroshi decided to stay in English. They could bring in translators for other languages, but he didn't want to do that yet.

He continued. "I want to know about your dorm mate. What classes was he taking? What did he do most days? Anything you can think of." Hiroshi looked around the room, making eye contact. "State your name before you speak."

They all squirmed. A tall, blonde-haired student straightened up and leaned forward. "My name is Natasha. I'm from Russia. And I live at the end of the hall upstairs." She spoke in thickly accented, fluent English. "I rarely saw Kotaro. He was what you call a recluse, a *hikikomori*. I read about them, but he was the first I met."

All the students nodded.

She looked around, ready to speak for them. "We have a group to cook meals together, but he didn't want to participate. We worried about him eating, though, so we invited him anyway. He paid us back by fixing our computers."

Hiroshi looked out the tall windows, blackened by the darkness outside. "So, he wasn't completely a recluse?"

Natasha nodded, her face serious. "He told me he studied in the computer studies department at Tokyo University for eight years, but he argued with his advisor and took leave. I don't know what his real status was."

A young, dark-skinned woman with jet-black hair leaned forward. "I'm Annisa, from Indonesia. I wasn't sleeping well when I arrived, so I sometimes ran into him in the middle of the night. He'd come for hot water in the kitchen, then eat instant noodles in his room. I shared some of my fried rice."

Hiroshi wondered if this was going anywhere. "Did you ever see anyone come to his room?"

Annisa asked. "How did he die?"

Hiroshi nodded. Of course, they'd want to know. "We'll have a report for you in the next few days. But for now, we can't release details. And I hope all of you can refrain from posting this on social media—"

"It's too late." One of the Asian students who was half-sitting on the window ledge held up his cell phone.

"What's your name?"

"I'm Li Dae-Hyun. From Korea. I live next door to Kotaro. He helped me with my Japanese when I first came. He speaks, or spoke, some Korean." Li put his cell phone away and crossed his arms.

"Well, no more posting. If that was someone from this room, just stop, OK? Do you want the media out front every day? Following you to and from school?" Hiroshi paused and looked around at the students. Their eyes looked down.

Annisa looked over at Natasha. "He had a visitor. A woman."

"When was that?"

"Yesterday."

"You'd seen the woman before?"

Natasha straightened her shoulders. "Annisa said she saw her sneaking into the dorm. There's a back door we use at night. I also saw her once before when I came back late from the library. At first, I thought she might be a friend or relative or another student, except—"

"Except what?"

Annisa put her hand over her mask, embarrassed.

Natasha continued. "She looked, I'm sorry to say this, like a prostitute. She wore a short skirt, knee-high boots, a leather coat, and sunglasses."

Hiroshi surveyed the faces above their masks. The reality of what happened was catching up with them. Hiroshi let it sink in for another minute.

Annisa took a breath and spoke in clear, steady English. "I saw a man stop by a few weeks ago. He was tall and thin. Nice jacket, sunglasses, and a mask. I noticed him because he wasn't a student, wasn't old, wasn't...well, he didn't belong here."

"Who was he, do you think?"

"I thought maybe he was here about computers. Kotaro said he was doing some consulting work."

"Did he go into Kotaro's room?" Hiroshi tried not to sound excited.

Annisa shook her head. "I saw him as I was going downstairs. He was speaking to one of the chess teachers—"

"Did he know the teacher?"

Annisa frowned. "I don't think so."

"Would you recognize the man if you saw him again?"

Annisa shrugged. "I just saw him for a minute. I didn't pay attention."

"Do you remember which day it was?"

Natasha spoke up. "I think chess is only on Tuesdays."

"It was two or three weeks ago. I had a presentation that day. Yes, two weeks ago. Tuesday."

Hiroshi nodded. That simplified searching the surveillance footage.

Annisa looked down at the ground but spoke loudly. "Is it true he had cameras in the women's showers?"

Hiroshi looked at her. "We will review all the video footage, but if it's sensitive, it will be viewed by female officers." That wasn't exactly true, but he wanted to calm the women down. "And then we'll keep it as evidence. No one will ever see it."

"Unless it's already posted somewhere." Annisa shivered, and two of the other women, who looked Chinese, shook their heads in disgust.

Natasha asked, "Are we in danger? Is this something personal with him, or is it the dorm, or...?"

Hiroshi cocked his head, unsure what to tell them because he didn't know what had happened.

Natasha nodded. "Is this connected to what happened this morning, to Ueno's death? Are the people downstairs in danger? They've been so helpful to us, like family. We don't want them in danger, either."

Hiroshi held up his hands, acting more confident than he felt. "We'll have police posted here for your protection, but you need to take extra precautions and notify us if you notice anything."

The other students raised their hands to ask more questions.

Hiroshi put up his hands. "I'll be back tomorrow. I'll need to talk with everyone one by one. So please be available in the afternoon. You can ask questions then. Get a good night's sleep."

Natasha pointed down the hall. "It's too noisy to sleep."

All the students agreed and started chatting in English, Japanese, Chinese, and Korean.

Chapter 9

Hiroshi was woken by the sound of a jackhammer. The floor shook as if trying to bounce him out of the fold-out futon chair. Were they destroying the concrete floor below? Or the ceiling? He squinted at the overhead light. Akiko stared at him from the door. She pushed the door shut and dragged the carpet to muffle the noise.

Hiroshi grunted and flipped his legs to the floor. "What time is it?"

"It's 8:30." Akiko pumped sanitizer into her hands and rubbed them loudly. She went to the espresso machine. It rumbled to life, the only comforting sound of the morning.

Hiroshi sat up on the edge of the futon. He'd slept deeply, but not long. He grabbed his cell phone from his desk. Messages from Ayana were stacked on the screen. He flopped onto his desk chair and called her.

"Are you coming home this morning?" she asked. Ayana's voice was curt. The morning sickness had pushed her to one extreme or the other—fluffy or curt. Hiroshi braced himself for either.

He cleared his throat. "I think I can get off early tonight. We can take your mother to dinner."

"Well, that's just it."

"That's just what?"

"She wants me to go back with her to Nagoya. Today."

Hiroshi coughed. "What did you tell her?"

"She'll help with everything until the birth."

"But your doctor is here. The clinic is here. I'm here. What about work?"

"You're working so much."

"Did it get worse?"

"Yesterday was bad. Probably because my mother came. She could tell."

"I'll get time off."

"Save that for after she's born."

"She?" Hiroshi hadn't even considered the baby's gender, sex, whatever it was.

"I'll call you later."

"Nagoya's far."

Ayana hung up. Hiroshi stared at his cell phone. This pregnancy thing was shaking up everything he'd procrastinated about for years—like commitment, work-life balance, learning to say no, and deciding if the homicide department was where he belonged.

He went back to the surety of his keyboard. The computer opened to a file he thought he'd finished.

Akiko had sat down and put her earbuds in, so she wouldn't hear the jackhammer.

All night, he'd been checking the documents and deeds for the Silver Center. He wasn't sure what they would reveal, but if the *sagi* ring and the scooter rider were both targeting them, they must be important.

He'd been distracted by the tech guys about two a.m. They called to apologize for not cracking the computers from the *hikikomori* kid who died. Or was killed. The tech guy had launched into too much detail on how it was set up and how to break in. The encryption was more challenging than expected. The video was probably of girls undressing in the bath. Zero help.

After that, around three, he finally stretched out on the fold-out futon chair. At least the construction noise didn't go on all night.

Akiko took out her earbuds and went to make an espresso.

Hiroshi dug in his filing cabinet for a change of socks and shirt. "I'm going to take a shower."

He pulled the carpet out of the way, stepped out, and walked down the underground hallway. The construction had extended from the entryway through the hallways. Hiroshi hoped they weren't redoing the showers too.

In the locker room, he ran into one of the detectives from the main building. His wife had kicked him out of the house, so he more or less lived at the station, sleeping in the bunk room, showering, and getting his clothes cleaned nearby. Some nights, he slept in a capsule hotel or booth at an internet cafe. It was cheaper than a divorce and easier than an argument.

Hiroshi had lived like that before he moved in with Ayana, and now it looked like he might live like that again if she left for Nagoya.

The shower was restorative.

When Hiroshi pushed back into his office, Akiko pointed at the tech guys' report on the video cameras and kicked the rug back to block the noise.

"When did they send this?" Hiroshi flipped through the report.

Akiko shrugged. "They apologized for taking so long."

The door started shaking, and a voice shouted, "Hey, are you in there?" Takamatsu pushed the door, shoving repeatedly until Akiko rushed over to drag the rug aside. Takamatsu slipped through the opening and helped her set the carpet back in place.

"Would you like something to drink?" Akiko had to raise her voice over the noise.

Takamatsu shouted, "Espresso."

"You pronounced it correctly for once," Hiroshi said.

Akiko pressed the button to start grinding the beans.

When it quieted, Takamatsu smiled. "Of course, I pronounced it right. I'm practicing for the future when every word for food and drink is from a foreign language. When all Japanese words are replaced, I still want to be able to order."

Akiko giggled. "That's almost true now."

Takamatsu got a call and took it, tucking the phone under his ear while he pumped some hand sanitizer into his hands and made a big display of rubbing his hands clean.

Akiko handed Takamatsu his espresso cup set neatly in a saucer.

"Ishii can't come." Takamatsu looked at him. "Aren't you going to ask where she can't come to?"

"You'll tell me either way." Hiroshi flipped through the report from the tech guys. It had stills from the videos, nothing more than a series of dull rooms and unpeopled entryways. No showers and no sex scenes. Hiroshi felt confused. Were these...what? He held the stills out to Takamatsu. "Maybe we need to see where these videos were taken."

Takamatsu tapped the cup on his saucer. "That can wait. More important is I found the young lady who will know more than the cameras could ever tell us."

"What young lady?"

"The one who visited our video guy. The 'delivery health' girl."

Akiko smiled. "Delivery is right. Not sure about health."

Takamatsu straightened his jacket. "I talked to the tech guys first thing this morning. They tend to work at night. Not sure when they sleep. Before they found your empty rooms, they found the girl going into the room of the deceased."

"Why didn't they tell me?" Hiroshi headed for another espresso.

"You didn't go down to the tech room. You should always ask what they found the first thing in the morning." Takamatsu sipped his espresso and set it back on the saucer with a clink.

Hiroshi shook his head. "OK. Tech. Questions. Takamatsu's checklist."

"You have to have a system." Takamatsu nodded at Akiko, like Hiroshi was catching on at last. "Lesson over. Let's go talk with her."

Hiroshi pointed at his computer.

Takamatsu groaned. "Not this again. We need to be out there asking questions. There's a girl who visited a young man right before he was found dead. In a dorm room above the office where a woman worked who was killed while walking across the street. Wherever the video feeds came from—"

"Takamatsu, listen for once, can you?" Hiroshi stared at him.

Takamatsu held his arms wide.

"I'm not sure where these places are, but that kid had complicated sets of video files. Was he stealing information? Selling it? Blackmailing someone? Was he just a voyeur? Or something more?"

"Or something less."

"We should look at this before we talk to the delivery health girl."

Takamatsu took out his lighter, flipped it open, and clicked it a few times, looking at Hiroshi. "I think you got the order wrong."

Hiroshi continued. "Why does he have all the videos of empty spaces?"

Takamatsu frowned. "They're not empty all the time, are they?"

"We need to know that before—"

"Videos provide confirmation, not connection. If we find the human connections first, the videos will make sense."

Akiko stared back and forth between Hiroshi and Takamatsu.

Takamatsu flipped his lighter. "If this delivery health girl knows anything, she'll tell us. Those types avoid trouble. That's why they get into trouble. And what about the students? You're following up on them too, aren't you? More connections."

Hiroshi stared at his computer screen and sipped his espresso. If he met Takamatsu's eyes, he'd have to admit he might be right. Even on the most intricate embezzlements or tax scams, it was the human element that led to a solution, that left a trail. It was almost like some criminals wanted to be caught.

Takamatsu flipped his lighter again. "Either way, we won't learn anything sitting around here in the station sipping espresso and trying to be logical."

Hiroshi sighed. He'd been outmaneuvered. "I need to talk to Sakaguchi—"

"I talked to him. After the morning briefing. Which you missed. I'll tell you on the way."

Hiroshi's phone rang. He read who was calling and set it back on his desk.

The office phone rang, and Akiko answered it. She looked at Hiroshi as she talked.

He shook his head.

Akiko bowed as she spoke. "I'll let him know when he gets back. I'm not sure why he's not answering his phone. I'll tell him it's important." She hung up and turned to Hiroshi. "That's your uncle again. We've established quite a relationship since you never return his calls."

Hiroshi pulled his jacket on and looked at Takamatsu. "Who's going to interview all the students?"

"You are. But we need to catch the delivery health girl before she disappears. Or is disappeared."

Chapter 10

Hiroshi and Takamatsu took a taxi to Omotesando. Business people in tight black suits, shoppers in understated fashion, web designers with dyed hair, and IT wonks flowed along the wide sidewalks in their ingrained routes.

The six-lane road and lined-up buildings of chic Omotesando were more like the boulevards of Paris than the cozy, rambling lanes of *shitamachi* neighborhoods.

Hiroshi and Takamatsu got out at the Aoyama Dori Street crossing. "Hot Yoga" was spelled out in giant letters on the windows of the upper floor of a building across the street.

Takamatsu checked the name and address. "What the hell is hot yoga anyway?"

Hiroshi pointed at the glass-lined building. A multi-story banner displayed yoga poses, and an arrow pointed around the corner.

Takamatsu started across the intersection before the light changed.

Hiroshi followed him across the four-way crossing. "How did the tech guys find her so quickly?"

"They didn't. I did."

"You did?" Hiroshi stopped in the middle of the intersection, hurrying on as the light changed.

Takamatsu hurried Hiroshi to the entrance and onto the elevator. The elevator walls were covered in advertisements neatly framed in plexiglass for the shops, restaurants, and yoga studios that filled the building.

Takamatsu straightened his leather jacket in the elevator video screen and reset his dark orange tie. "A guy I arrested for stalking a few years back follows girls online. All kinds of girls."

"Isn't that against—"

"It's public video, mainly, but yes. Whenever I need to find a girl in the game, I go to him. Some image-matching software. Finds them right away."

The elevator let them out into a reception area with a counter, chairs, and posters of yoga poses. A pretty, petite woman in exercise tights and a tight hair bun bowed. "*Irrashaimase*! Are you here for a trial lesson?" She danced around the counter with two orange clipboards, forms, and pens.

Hiroshi pulled out his badge.

The receptionist blinked as she stared at the badge and looked up wide-eyed.

Takamatsu unbuttoned his coat. "We're looking for Yumi. She teaches here."

The receptionist twisted around the counter and checked her computer screen. "She's just finishing up a hot yoga session."

Takamatsu eyed a woman coming out of the automatic doors. The smell of incense wafted out. "We'll wait inside." He caught the door and went inside before the receptionist could answer.

"Your shoes!" she screamed.

Hiroshi and Takamatsu took off their shoes at the door and looked for someplace to put them.

The receptionist twisted around the counter with plastic bags to put their shoes in and carry with them.

The inside area was bright and big. Lunch tables and light chairs lined up under the windows with "hot yoga" spelled backward in big paper letters. To the left, a large wooden carving of the Hindu god Ganesh sat stoically in front of an ornately carved screen. Flowers floated in brass water bowls at his feet. The scent of sandalwood filled the air.

The room was alive with young women in loose workout clothes stretching, chatting, and practicing posing. Several filled their water bottles from a large dispenser. Shoes, bags, and towels were crammed into the cubicles of a rack. Gym bags rested on top.

One or two men stood alone in the room, but it was almost all women. Those just out of class threaded down the hallway, drying themselves and rehydrating.

Takamatsu leaned close to Hiroshi and whispered, "A lot of flushed skin."

Hiroshi ignored him and took off his jacket.

"Love their masks. Erotic, aren't they?" Takamatsu surveyed the room. "Their masks frame their eyes, the back of their necks, their ears. One good thing from the pandemic. I missed those details all these years."

Hiroshi leaned over and whispered, "That kind of comment doesn't fit in Ishii's task force too well."

"She's not here. Let's find Yumi." Takamatsu stopped a woman with a name tag to ask where Yumi was teaching. She directed them down the hallway.

Hot, dry air poured out of the rooms into the hallway. Hiroshi wiped his forehead with his handkerchief. Takamatsu shucked off his jacket, some European brand, and loosened his tie.

At the end of the hall, they stopped in front of a mirrored room where an attractive woman talked with two young women in body suits. Takamatsu gave a quick bow, and the two body-suit girls traipsed off.

Hiroshi felt his feet heating up. The floor of the studio room was baking his feet. He moved his weight back and forth, trying to lessen the burn.

Yumi's bright yellow workout shirt was printed with "Yummy" in black letters. The words undulated over her breasts. Was that an attempt at humor? At being cute? Yumi, or Yummy, looked only slightly sweaty. Hiroshi plucked at his shirt. It was already sticking to the sweat on his back.

When Takamatsu explained why they wanted to talk with her, she didn't seem concerned. She took another sip of water from the straw in her water bottle and pointed across the hall. "We can go to a cooler room to talk."

She led them across the hall to a room with a dozen surfboard-like structures fixed onto the floor. Surf yoga? The room was dark, with blue walls. It was cooler than the first room.

Yumi had a broad forehead, full cheeks, and round eyes. Hiroshi could tell Takamatsu was soaking up every detail, but so was he. She was pretty.

Takamatsu set his shoe bag and jacket on one of the surfboards and launched right in. "So, are you transitioning from delivery health to hot yoga or vice versa?"

Yumi frowned beneath her mask. "I wanted to be a flight attendant but wasn't tall enough. I took accounting classes at night for a few years, but it was boring. The accounting was interesting, but the people were boring."

Takamatsu laughed and pointed at Hiroshi. "He's an accountant."

"He looks nice, though." Yumi smiled.

"Do you have a manager?"

"No, no manager," Yumi spoke in a soft, deep voice. "Just apps. I have several. Why do you want to know?" She pulled out her phone.

"The guy you visited in the rooms above the Silver Center is dead."

Yumi stopped scrolling and looked at Takamatsu, frowning in disbelief. "Really? He...? What...?"

She looked at them for confirmation and sipped her water, shaking her head. She pulled out her phone and scrolled to an app that said, "Self-Help Delivery Health." "I think it was this one."

Hiroshi took a screenshot and started searching.

"You have to be invited."

"So, invite him." Takamatsu pointed at Hiroshi.

Yumi pulled Hiroshi's phone hand over to give him the QR code link.

Hiroshi clicked in, set it up, and sent it to Akiko to research.

Takamatsu hummed. "I guess it automatically erases, right?"

Yumi squirmed. "It wouldn't be much good if it saved every detail, would it?"

"How do you remember your regular customers?"

"They remember."

"And payment is through the app?"

"There's a monthly fee. But I take payment from clients on PayPay or whatever app they have. They all work."

Hiroshi put his phone away. "And what kind of health services do you deliver?"

"It's not against the law."

Takamatsu laughed. "We know what is and isn't against the law."

Yumi sucked on her straw. "Look, the human body is like a sponge. You have to squeeze out the toxins, one way or another, and be replenished."

"A sponge." Takamatsu chuckled. "So, this guy from yesterday?"

Yumi nodded. "Hand relief. More for the video."

"You'd visited him before?"

"I used to work for a manager. He sent me to him the first time. And then the guy kept in touch."

"It was a regular visit?"

Yumi nodded and took another long drink from her water bottle. "I keep a few regulars. Being a yoga instructor doesn't pay that well."

Hiroshi wondered if she ever managed to get rehydrated. He was dripping sweat, and he hadn't even moved.

Takamatsu looked at her closely. "You could be in danger. You know that, right?"

She sipped from her straw and twisted her head.

Takamatsu cleared his throat to get her attention. "If someone killed him. They might look for you."

"He was still breathing when I left him."

"We guessed that, or we'd be talking with you in the police

station right now. Time of death and all. That might not matter if whoever killed him knows you were there."

"Am I a suspect?"

Takamatsu looked at her. "We're not sure what you are yet. Did you give him something to arouse or loosen him up?"

"Something?" Yumi shook her head. "Some girls sell on the side, but I never do. I told you, squeeze and replenish. How did he die?"

"Just tell us step by step."

Yumi swirled her water bottle and drank some more. "I go there and give him relief. I get an electronic payment. And then I wait for him to message me again. Nothing more to it than that."

"Who was the other guy you worked for before?"

"He's gone."

"Gone where?"

"Boating accident. In Tokyo Bay."

"You don't sound sad," Hiroshi prompted. "When was that?"

"I wasn't sad. He was the controlling type. I was very young. I had debts." She shrugged. "It's over. I work for myself now."

Hiroshi looked at her. "Did the dorm room guy film you?"

Yumi looked away. "He paid extra for that. Did you see them?"

Takamatsu wiped his forehead, refolded his handkerchief, and wiped his head again. "We're looking through all the videos."

Yumi sucked harder on her straw. "He was a *hikikomori*, but he was smart. You could tell. He had all those computers and video things. He didn't say much, but he was funny. Or more like he saw the irony of things."

"Not much irony in being dead." Hiroshi looked at her. "Who would have wanted to kill him?"

"I don't know." Yumi looked at the mirrors along the front wall and straightened her posture. "He was always so grateful."

Takamatsu looked at Yumi in the mirrored wall. "We need your phone number and address."

Yumi tucked her water bottle under her arm and scrolled

through her phone until she found it and held it out. Hiroshi took a photo of it.

Yumi wiped her face with a towel and held it over her face.

Hiroshi wondered if she was crying, but her towel seemed one of the super-absorbent kinds.

Chapter 11

Takuya arrived at the *kissaten* coffee shop before anyone else. He nodded to the owner, who owed him money, not enough to be fawning, but enough to let Takuya hold meetings in the back room. Takuya thought about buying the place outright, but that would be a lot of forms and a lot of taxes. Being owed was easier.

He walked to the side room they used for meetings. It had a table, two glass block walls, a small, clear window, and a brick wall with vintage road signs bolted onto a frame. Overhead, motorcycle handlebars dangled from a ceiling frame, a road-style chrome chandelier. The *kissaten* was one of the few that still allowed smoking. In fact, it catered to smokers, with big ashtrays and lighters with the shop name.

Takuya's phone buzzed. A message from Yasui. Finally.

Takuya called him. "How's your grandmother?"

"Not so good. The doctors keep saying she's old. She's older than she told me. I found her birth certificate." Yasui's voice sounded hoarse.

"You got all my messages?"

"Yeah. I don't know what happened. I'm just glad you're OK." Yasui's voice sounded far away, full of sleep and stress.

"You can't think of anything?"

"The pickup was all set. Oh, the doctors are making their rounds again. I've got to go."

"Didn't you say you talked with someone recently?"

"Yeah, some guy got in touch with me. I'll send his contact info. He just wanted..." Yasui spoke to someone in the hospital. Takuya couldn't hear. "I've got to go. I'll send it."

Takuya trusted Yasui, but he wasn't sure Noguchi and Murayama did. He and Yasui had worked together since they first came to Tokyo. In the old days, they would have laughed about having to run from the cops. They'd had to run plenty of times. Yasui always cut right, and Takuya left, but they'd always outrun the guards and the police.

The front doorbell tinkled, and Noguchi came in. Noguchi had run with a biker gang after dropping out of high school. He had a scar along his forearm but almost always wore long sleeves. His earthiness gained him points with his targets, and his deep, confident voice helped, too. He spent all his money on motorcycles, from what Takuya could tell.

Noguchi sat down with his back to the glass block wall and ordered a morning set of toast, boiled egg, coffee, and salad. He lit a cigarette, and Takuya took out his new vape pen.

The little room was warming up from the sun hitting the glass tiles. They sat quietly until Murayama arrived. He sat down and opened his laptop. Takuya could never tell where he was looking, though it was usually his laptop.

Murayama was the only one to attend college, and he looked the part. He'd had a job out of college with a bank but hated it. One day, he crashed their computer system and walked out. He'd set up the shared calendars, bank accounts, and all the fake *hanko* seals and legal-looking forms they'd ever need. Maruyama never hesitated about what they were doing and never felt guilty. He was simply incapable of seeing things in those terms. That's why his plans always worked.

Noguchi and Yasui also contributed ideas but mostly brought the Japanese virtues of common sense and deliberation into the projects. Noguchi knew how things worked in real-time in the real world. Yasui needed everything explained multiple times until memorized, which helped them all.

Takuya had always made the final decisions on target, positioning, and information flow. He also made sure everyone had their share. He was the start-up energy on every project. As a group, the four were as smooth and stable as a four-cylinder motorcycle engine.

Takuya put his vape pen down. "Yasui's at home in Ibaraki, helping his grandmother at the hospital."

"Is she all right?" Murayama asked.

With that easy sympathy, Murayama was the most consistently successful of them. He could talk anyone into anything, but Takuya could never tell how deep his empathy went. Not far, he guessed. He was all computers, to which humans were a form of input.

The *kissaten* owner came for Murayama's order. He wanted lunch, the spaghetti *setto*. The owner complained about making lunch two hours before the official lunchtime, but after Takuya stared at him, he walked off to make it without another word.

Takuya held up his cell phone. "We can call Yasui if we need to." That wasn't exactly true, but would take suspicion off Yasui. Noguchi and Murayama both knew what had happened. Takuya wanted to be sure they didn't know why.

Takuya went over the failed pick-up, the cops, the accident, and his escape, leaving out no detail. Noguchi and Murayama listened carefully. Noguchi snickered at Takuya's broken heel and his running through the streets and sneaking through the old house, but neither of them laughed at Takuya almost being caught.

When he was done, Noguchi lit another cigarette, his third.

Murayama closed his laptop case. "I hate to say this, but it's better it was you than Yasui. He would have gotten arrested."

All the firewall procedures Murayama had set up, including rotating passwords, false user names, and secure two-factor verifications, were not much of a firewall if one of them talked to the cops.

Noguchi's morning set arrived, carried in by the owner. A waitress brought in the spaghetti set. The owner remembered Murayama liked extra cheese and set a small bowl beside the plate.

They waited for him to leave.

Murayama spoke first. "You're the one who said we should expect some close calls."

Takuya had said that when they first started. "Not for something that should have been set up right."

"Nothing's ever set up perfectly." Murayama sprinkled parmesan over the pasta and doused it with Tabasco. He twisted the spaghetti into a mouthful and chomped in, sucking loudly.

Noguchi tapped the shell of his boiled egg on the side of the plate and started peeling the shell off. "Maybe Yasui just missed something."

Takuya leaned back. The food made him hungry, a good sign, but he'd eat later at Misaki's.

"Did you talk to him?" Murayama levered his laptop screen back and forth.

Takuya cleared his throat. "He had no idea what went wrong."

Murayama nodded. "He's following protocol. Nothing written down that can be traced."

Noguchi plucked at the eggshell. "I can ride up there and talk with him in person. I want to break in my new bike on the highway anyway. What hospital is it?"

Takuya looked at the glass block wall. "Ibaraki Central. It's not far from the station."

Noguchi checked his cell phone to find the location, and Murayama helped find it on his laptop.

Takuya didn't want to tell everyone that the hospital was where his grandfather, the only member of his family he remembered, died from lung cancer. His mother died young, and his father left before he could remember. So his grandfather, a bad-tempered man who drank *shochu* from lunch to blackout, took him in. Takuya was sixteen when he died, leaving him with a month's unpaid rent and not much else.

Takuya never felt like hitting him back for the beatings the old man had given him when he was younger. When he was too drunk to get up, Takuya stubbed out the last cigarette, dropped a futon over him, and turned off the TV. The day he didn't get up again, he arranged his funeral, moved into the dormitory of a construction company owned by a distant cousin, and started work.

Takuya took a big hit from his vape pen. It was almost out of flavor already. "Maybe we should take a break. Let things cool down."

Murayama pointed at his laptop screen. "There's a week full of new appointments."

Takuya looked out the window, thinking of his and Yasui's first job working construction in Tokyo, how the work had been so exhausting not even a hot bath and a couple of beers helped them recover. Tokyo work paid better than in Ibaraki, though, and Tokyo was exciting on the one day off a week. That first job was taking down old houses. As long as you watched your head and didn't step on a nail, it was stress-free. Now, all he had was stress.

Murayama looked at his screen. "Canceling this week means a lot of lost accounts."

Noguchi looked at the schedule on Murayama's laptop. "I don't like things getting so close. I want to be sure of what happened and why." Noguchi lit a cigarette and sipped his coffee. "I'm the only one here who's been hauled in by the cops. I don't want that to happen again."

Takuya looked at him. "That was a long time ago. It won't happen again."

Murayama moved his computer screen back and forth. "It was Yasui's pickup yesterday, right? Why did you go?"

Takuya sighed. "I should have canceled. I'm glad he made a good map of all the surveillance cameras. That's what saved me."

Noguchi finished chewing his toast. "Why do you think she switched the day?"

"The old woman?" Takuya hadn't thought about that. "Switched the meeting place."

Murayama pulled his laptop open. "I think Noguchi should go

talk with him." Murayama checked his cell phone. "Until we figure it out, why don't we take a break?"

Maybe neither of them was involved. Takuya knew Murayama was smooth, but he couldn't be that smooth. Noguchi didn't seem to know anything either. He felt relieved and confused as he looked at the sunlight coming through the glass blocks and felt it warming the room.

Yasui sent a text message saying, "His name was Kurono," with an address in an upscale building in Roppongi. Takuya looked at it and then looked up at Noguchi and Murayama. "Yasui said he got a call, maybe several, from a guy named Kurono."

Noguchi leaned closer. "What guy?"

Takuya took a breath. "He's a guy who wanted us to help gather documents."

"What documents?" Murayama asked. "Isn't this the first we're hearing about this?"

Noguchi tapped his fork on the plate. "We promised to keep side projects in the open so we'd all know."

Takuya frowned. "It's just a guy who kept calling Yasui." Takuya checked his cell phone. "I don't think it's connected."

Murayama pushed his tomato-stained plate aside. "Maybe this is just bad luck. The cops do their job sometimes."

Takuya checked his phone again. Yasui sent the information. "Yasui wants me to meet with the guy." Maybe Yasui thinks it's connected. He wouldn't have sent it so quickly if he thought it was nothing.

Neither of them said anything.

"So, I'll meet with Kurono?" Takuya squirmed.

Murayama nodded, and Noguchi said, "Wear your running shoes."

Chapter 12

Walking across the intersection from the hot yoga studio, Hiroshi felt his back drying in the cool spring breeze.

"Shouldn't we watch her?" Hiroshi looked back at the entrance to the hot yoga studio.

"Maybe we are sponges," Takamatsu mused. "I'll think that over. That healthy stuff makes me need a cigarette." Takamatsu headed toward the outdoor smoking area, a smoker's oasis of plastic dividers and an overhead filter. It was the first time Hiroshi had seen Takamatsu carry his coat. He usually primped and pulled his clothes right before going anywhere.

Takamatsu lit up before he was even inside. He started chatting with the other smokers right away.

Hiroshi sat on the railing under a ginkgo tree and checked his messages. There was nothing from Ayana.

Akiko wrote, "The tech guys opened the video feeds."

"I'll come back."

"Go in the side door. The noise is unbelievable. I'm taking my laptop to the main building."

"As soon as Takamatsu finishes his cigarette."

Hiroshi waved through the glass divider at Takamatsu, who waved back and said something to two young guys with longish hair and loose-fitting coats. They laughed. He blew his last lungful into the overhead filter and put his cigarette in the receptacle.

Hiroshi waved down a taxi. "They've cracked the videos."

Takamatsu groaned and backed off from getting in the taxi. "I hate video footage."

"It could save us—"

"It could waste time."

"We'll put the videos on fast forward."

"I'm nauseated already."

They rode the rest of the way without the buzz of a single cell phone message. Maybe they were wasting time, Hiroshi thought, as they got stuck in traffic diverted around a construction project near Shibuya Station.

They snuck in the side door at the station, but they could hear the construction noise down the hall. A long-haired, plump-faced guy in a black concert tour T-shirt greeted them in the tech room. Hiroshi had never seen him before. He looked like a college kid. Maybe he was.

Takamatsu rolled his cycs at the tattoo on the guy's forearm and whispered, "Pretty soon, we'll be the only ones without a tattoo." He turned to the tech kid. "We talked this morning. You sent the video of the call girl. Thank you."

"Delivery health. Yes, that was me. I'm Nakada." He pushed back his hair with two hands. His workstation was a chest-high table jammed with computer equipment.

Takamatsu said, "I heard you were a genius with this computer stuff."

"Genius? No. Just a few tricks with the mouse and the keyboard." Nakada sat down.

Takamatsu hummed, pleased to banter. "Mouse is that little thing to the right?"

Nakada looked at him, realized he was joking, and nodded. "The mouse scares the elephant."

Takamatsu said, "Now I remember, the mouse is what you hold in one hand while you mouse yourself with the other."

Nakada smiled. "Well, don't do that on company time. They store everything on servers. I'm in charge of the servers. Every little detail's saved." Nakada turned back to the screen.

Takamatsu laughed, folded his leather jacket, and set it on a stool. Nakada's joking seemed to have earned him Takamatsu's trust and patience.

Nakada motioned for them to look at the monitors to the left. He had three set up, and more were arrayed around the work table. Their screen savers bounced around the black screen. He poked the keyboard and shook his mouse until the screen popped full of twenty-four video feeds. He set them all moving.

Takamatsu groaned. "Twenty times the usual nausea."

"We'll skip ahead. No need to look at the boring parts."

"Thank you." Takamatsu patted Nakada's shoulder.

Hiroshi let his eyes jump from screen to screen. "These are all from the *hikikomori* kid's computer?"

Nakada smiled. "These are the first twenty-four. There are a lot more."

Takamatsu groaned dramatically. "I'll call Sakaguchi and get someone down here to do this."

Nakada sped them up. Across the twenty feeds were black and white images of empty stairwells, basement corridors, blank walls, unmarked doors, gloomy parking lots, and one half-full bicycle parking lot. Each had a time stamp flickering in the lower right.

"Where are they?" Hiroshi asked.

"We're working on that." He pointed at the screen. "You can see names on some doors if you zoom in. But until we find the cameras, we won't know for sure." Nakada clicked ahead.

"There's no movement or people or other identifications?" Hiroshi coughed a bit and resettled himself on the stool.

"We have motion-sensing software, but there's six months of footage, all stored in the cloud in different places." Nakada upped the speed, but the scenes hardly changed.

"What about notations, file names, labels, dates, anything?" Hiroshi tried to sound hopeful.

"There's no system I can figure out. He must have remembered what was what, and where." Nakada pointed to a stack of laptop computers on his work table. "He bought new laptops every six months or so."

"He had money." Takamatsu sighed and flipped his lighter. "Was he doing this for someone else? Someone had to pay him."

"I'll look into his accounts," Hiroshi said.

Nakada looked disappointed not to have more. "Want to see the feed inside his own room?"

"As long as we're here." Takamatsu fidgeted.

"Here's one that might help." Nakada clicked around, and the twenty videos switched to a single shot of the room in the dormitory above the Silver Center. Between the shelves of computers and video equipment came Yumi, the hot yoga instructor they'd just talked with. She was wearing a tight skirt and a low-cut top. Nakada fast-forwarded to where the *hikikomori* sat down in the chair and readied himself. Nakada fast-forwarded through Yumi's brisk, efficient sponge-squeezing, her big eyes occasionally turning directly into the camera.

Takamatsu looked more closely. "She must have known the video was there."

"Maybe," Hiroshi said. "Or maybe she's just looking around."

Nakada slowed the speed when the *hikikomori* kid slumped in relief, gasping, thanking her, and apologizing.

When she stood up and touched his face, he started crying, his head hanging down. She pulled him to her chest until he calmed down. She hadn't even taken off her jacket.

Takamatsu reached for his cigarettes, realized where he was, and put them away. "That's the saddest thing I've ever seen in my life. Worse than hot yoga."

Hiroshi wondered if she saw it as delivering health. Maybe she did. Maybe it was.

Nakada clicked off the screen. "The motion software caught that motion in the room immediately, but the hallways and stairwells will take longer. Sorry."

"Send me a still of any rooms you identify." Hiroshi closed his eyes.

"Send me a still of Yumi." Takamatsu slipped on his jacket, impatient to leave.

Nakada stopped the videos with a single click. "The best thing is to look for any cameras, and I can check from here. We reset the feeds, so they should work here if you can find the place."

Takamatsu sighed. "You mean, check every basement in Tokyo?"

Nakada shrugged.

Hiroshi got a call from Akiko. She whispered, "Ishii's been called into a meeting with Sakaguchi, the head of the police agency, some ministry officials, and the union lawyer. My friends in the main office told me."

"Where?" Hiroshi waved at Takamatsu.

Akiko whispered, "The large conference room on the top floor. Hurry."

Hiroshi turned to Takamatsu. "Ishii's been called for a meeting with—"

Takamatsu grabbed Hiroshi's arm. "Let's go. I know where they are."

They ran to the main building through the underground passageway, dodging construction materials and stepping carefully over the temporary plastic covering.

They took the elevator up to the top-floor conference room, where all big meetings took place. Takamatsu ignored the "meeting underway" sign at the door and pulled open the door with two hands.

At the front of the room, facing the podium, Ishii sat at a table with her hands folded and her head bowed. Sakaguchi sat on a chair next to her. On the other side sat the union lawyer.

From the podium's long table, the police chief leaned forward to the mic. His droning voice echoed in the empty room. The others filling the chairs would be ministry officials, bureaucrats, and assistants. They shuffled papers and pretended to listen.

"*Sumimasen*," Takamatsu shouted as he strode to the front of the room.

The chief stopped, and everyone at the table looked at Takamatsu.

Takamatsu stopped for a curt bow. "I'm sorry to interrupt the proceedings, but we've had a break in the case, and without Ishii's assistance, we can't move forward. The suspects will only talk with her."

Sakaguchi gave Ishii an elbow to go. She hopped up, bowed ninety degrees, and shuffled out behind Sakaguchi, clutching her bag and briefcase, leaning over to apologize to the union lawyer.

Sakaguchi spoke in a loud, distracting voice. "As the supervising officer, I'll continue answering questions from the committee members. I have all the relevant reports in front of me. Let's continue with your questions."

Takamatsu took Ishii's arm and ushered her down the aisle. Hiroshi bowed and turned back to the exit. They heard a voice through the mic but ignored it and continued out.

Outside the meeting room, they ran to the elevator.

Hiroshi looked back nervously at the door, half expecting them to give chase.

The elevator arrived, and they got on.

As the doors closed, Ishii let out a sigh of relief. She reached down to slip off her high heels and replace them with walking shoes from her bag. "How did you know I was there?"

Hiroshi shook his cell phone. "Akiko."

"She knows everything," Ishii said, letting out another sigh.

"Why didn't you tell us?" Hiroshi asked.

Ishii pressed the elevator button again. "I figured it was normal, but when we got there, the union lawyer was waiting."

They got off on the first floor and hurried past the construction to the parking lot.

Ishii tossed her high heels in a trash bin on top of pieces of a torn-down wall the construction crew had left. "First, they tried to force Sakaguchi to treat these both as accidents."

Takamatsu stopped. He took a breath with his eyes closed. And then started walking again.

To Hiroshi, pushing to have them treated as accidents was

confirmation they weren't. He'd learned that much from Takamatsu. They started down the row of unmarked cars. "Ishii, are you OK to drive?"

Ishii put her coat over her shoulder and fumbled for the key fob. A beep and flash of headlights steered them to the next row of cars. "They also threatened to shut down the women's task force."

Takamatsu held the door of the car open for her. "As long as the task force is still running, let's keep it that way. Those were not accidents."

Chapter 13

Ishii parked in a small lot one block away from the Silver Center. Hiroshi got out to pay.

Takamatsu leaned against the side of the car and lit a cigarette. One lungful in, he got a call. He listened and hung up. "Osaki and Sugamo are coming to pick me up. They have something."

Hiroshi looked at him. "What about the crime scene?"

Takamatsu shrugged. "I'll circle back."

Something in the way Takamatsu spoke and smoked—enjoying it less than usual—made Hiroshi feel he should call Osaki and Sugamo to ask what Takamatsu was up to. They were too honest to cover up Takamatsu's schemes, but too loyal to talk unless forced.

But he let it go. He had to talk with the students and see Ueno's apartment. Takamatsu wouldn't be much use in the Silver Center other than going over the crime scene. And he could come back to the apartment later.

The Silver Center was abuzz with grey-haired women and a few men. They crowded the bulletin board and chatted amiably. Without children around, the hubbub sounded different but just as spirited.

Ishii pointed at the speaker in the main project room. "She's one of the best. I found her in the accounting section."

"I thought I was the accounting section?" Hiroshi whispered.

"I'll get her transferred over if they cancel the task force. She finished all the detective training at the top of her class, but they gave her a desk job. She's great at PR, especially with women. The scams affect women more since men die younger than women, and women have always had control of the household finances. Many of the women have *hesokuri*."

"Secret accounts? I thought that was the last generation...?"

"The last generation is right here in front of you." Ishii laughed.

"Oh, yes. Right." Hiroshi wondered if Ayana had her secret account. They never argued about money except when Hiroshi encouraged her to spend more without worrying.

A PowerPoint slide was projected on the screen with slides about precautions to take with *sagi* scams, who to call, how to respond, and what to say. Two local police officers stood at the side.

A man at the front, his winter jacket still on, raised his hand. "And what about the convenience stores? Can't they stop selling cards in suspicious situations? The cards are how they take the money."

The spokeswoman nodded. "The e-money cards scammers want are paid for in cash. So they're not easy to trace. We've canvased all the nearby convenience stores to ask for their cooperation." She turned to the local police officers, who nodded confirmation. "They will not sell e-money cards to anyone who doesn't have a good reason, and none for large amounts."

The crowd started talking among themselves.

She waited for their attention. "After surveying the neighborhood, we also found residents were okay with installing more cameras. We'll finish that project over the next month or two. However, those cameras only help after the crimes happen. We still need you to be vigilant. Anything else?"

The crowd shook their heads and started to get up. Everyone in the room seemed galvanized. They stood up from their fold-up chairs, loudly talking things over.

Hiroshi followed Ishii to the Silver Center office.

Inside, Ishii bowed to Setsuko and Keisuke, who was standing behind Setsuko's chair.

Keisuke looked at Hiroshi. "Thank you for your help. We appreciate it. I have the keys to Ueno's apartment if you want to take a look."

"I do, but first, I want to ask you something." Hiroshi thought for a minute. "You're a *fudosan*? Maybe you could help me with some photos?"

"Of course." Keisuke straightened up, ready to help.

"Since you know the buildings in the area, you might have some idea." Hiroshi pulled up the stills from the videos the tech guy had sent him.

Keisuke carefully extracted his glasses from his pocket. Setsuko stood behind Keisuke with a hand on his shoulder. Sasaki glanced at her, and Setsuko stiffened and pulled back her hand.

Keisuke found the right distance to focus on Hiroshi's phone and scrolled through the photos. He pulled off his glasses. "I'm sorry, I don't recognize any of these places. Basements. Lobbies. Could be anywhere."

Hiroshi took back his cell phone and frowned. "We need to find these places."

Keisuke twisted and looked at Setsuko. "Are you sure they're around here?"

Hiroshi was far from sure.

Keisuke stood up. "About Ueno's apartment?"

Ishii interrupted. "Setsuko told the students to gather in the kitchen. They're all waiting."

Hiroshi turned to Keisuke. "Let me talk with them first, and then I'll call you. Will you be in your office?"

"I can wait. No rush." Keisuke bowed.

Hiroshi followed Ishii up the wide stairs and down the hallway to the kitchen. With daylight streaming in the tall windows, the hall looked bigger.

In the kitchen and dining area, students sprawled on chairs, checking their phones. When they noticed Ishii and Hiroshi coming in, they sat up.

The cooking area had multiple burners, two microwave ovens, and deep sinks. Drying racks covered the sideboard with towel racks overhead. Everything was neat. A cleaning schedule and a trash and recycling calendar hung on the wall.

Ishii spoke first. "Thank you all for assembling today. We need to follow up on the helpful information you gave us last night with a few more questions." She turned to Hiroshi.

Hiroshi spoke in English. "We want to hear anything you can tell us, even something that might seem trivial. His death is being treated as suspicious."

The Russian student, her blonde hair down her back, spoke in English. "How did he die?"

"Natasha, right?" He wanted to be careful. Students could tell when someone was lying, and their trust would help.

Natasha nodded.

Hiroshi said, "He had an eating disorder."

Everyone nodded as if they knew that.

"And he was given a drug of some kind, which caused his heart to fail. It's one of the so-called date rape drugs. On a weakened system, that was enough. Has that drug been going around recently?"

Everyone looked down and shook their heads.

One of the students from the day before raised her hand. Hiroshi couldn't remember her name. Annisa maybe? She was from Indonesia. "I thought Japan's the only country in the world where students don't take drugs."

Hiroshi looked at her. "Annisa, right? Well, there are drugs, just not as much as in other countries." Hiroshi waited for more.

Annisa frowned. "Can you tell us what happened to Ueno? Is it connected to Kotaro?"

Ishii closed her eyes and took a breath. "It seems accidental in both cases. We don't think they're connected."

"But two in one day. They must be connected?" Annisa asked. "And so close to us."

Ishii frowned, "We're treating them as separate."

Natasha spoke up. "We'd like to do something."

"The best thing you can do is think of anything you noticed, any unusual person, anything," Hiroshi said.

Annisa put her arm around Natasha. "Ueno lived alone, so she was often here when we got back from classes. She stayed late to lock up. She brought us things, Japanese sweets." Annisa blinked back tears.

Natasha straightened up. "They keep the rent low so students from other countries can afford it. Any problem we have, visas, banking, forms, anything, they help us. Ueno especially." Natasha was getting teary-eyed too. "Ueno's the one who owns this building. I hope nothing will happen to the dorm here."

Ishii looked at Hiroshi. He hadn't considered who owned this building or whether it could matter. It must. He let Ishii continue with her questions while he sent a note to Akiko to check on the ownership of all the buildings in the area.

The students were circling Ishii, concerned their dormitory might be changed. If they had to rent, they'd have to choose between a long commute or an expensive place.

A loud noise came from the first floor, the sound of a bullhorn, followed by chanting.

Hiroshi left Ishii talking to the students and went to see what it was.

Annisa and Natasha came after him and stood beside him, looking down on the street below.

Natasha smiled. "I am happy to see that here. It's not so common in Russia these days."

Hiroshi recognized a few people who had just been listening to the explanation session on scams in the main room on the first floor. They held signs and started to organize themselves into a line.

Natasha said, "They're organizing a protest. Annisa and I started interviewing them about it as part of our grad school research."

Hiroshi felt confused. "What did you find?"

"They protest different things from time to time." Annisa smiled as she looked at them. "Today, it's against the neighborhood builders."

"Builders?"

"Developers." Annisa pointed at Natasha. "We're both urban studies majors, doing our graduate work on how Tokyo is being rebuilt. But we didn't count on people *not* wanting it rebuilt. We came here to learn how to redo our own cities."

Natasha tapped the window glass. "Our scholarships are through grants from development companies. Every large corporation in Japan has an architectural and development section. They support us in conjunction with the Tokyo Metropolitan Government."

Annisa cleared her throat. "Recently, the government started the so-called *Tokyo no sharemachi*, Tokyo stylish city, regulations. We were lucky that it included a scholarship program for international students. We're the first."

From below, the noise was getting louder.

Natasha pointed at the protestors. "The large building companies propose projects to make Tokyo more beautiful. It's a way to clean up old areas of the city and make them stylish."

Annisa said, "The problem is not everyone agrees what is or isn't stylish." She made air quotes over the last word. "And they don't agree on what areas need rebuilding. We tried to research Roppongi Hills, even though it's finished, but they wouldn't grant us permission."

Natasha said, "Even though some of the CEOs there graduated from the University of Tokyo, they didn't help us. We wonder why they want us here. Maybe just to tell them how great their renewal projects are."

"Or to pave the way for joint projects in Russia or Indonesia in the future." Annisa nodded. "But we're glad to be here anyway."

Outside, the line of older people dressed in bright colors holding protest signs about public space, local input, and community didn't seem like people who would be tricked by a *sagi* scam ring. They looked like people who could take down any such ring.

Chapter 14

After Hiroshi let the students go, he plopped down in a chair in the hall of the Silver Center to check his messages. They had reached critical mass. He went through a dozen updates on past cases, several short messages from Sugamo and Osaki, though not divulging what Takamatsu wanted, and another half-dozen from his uncle.

On top of that were interoffice emails from the police agency about construction, safety, security, and other irrelevant info. Takamatsu had told the tech guys to send regular updates. Apparently, they thought that meant every hour. His unending conversations with Interpol on their secure network confirmed and reconfirmed a bevy of minor points about half-finished cases, but moved them forward very little.

Ayana's messages were layered in between them all.

There was little hope of getting through even a fraction, even with his thumb heavy on the delete key, so he put his phone away. Maybe Takamatsu was right. It couldn't all be solved on a screen.

He went down to the first floor. A few women rearranged the desks and set out schoolbooks, pens, crayons, notebooks, and clunky, old tablet computers. Several men were setting up the chess and go boards. On the chalkboard to the side, colored letters read, "Study Time!" and "*Ganbaro*!" "Let's go!" between cheery flowers, smiling faces, and bright suns.

Ayana was the best thing he'd gotten from school, whether in Japan or in Boston. She was the part of his education, the lucky part that would last. He'd loved studying history in Japan and had liked learning English, too, but accounting was so practical and tedious that it was doomed to failure in his mind. It lit up nothing inside him. It was just there.

That line of thinking was a bad start to the call he decided to make first—to his uncle, the person who'd pushed him into accounting after Hiroshi's parents died.

Fortunately, his uncle was with a client, so Hiroshi left a message he'd stop by.

Hiroshi's cousin, his uncle's only child, had left messages, too. He liked his cousin. She was a dutiful daughter in the classic mold, married to a handsome salaryman, with one child and plans for more, a chic apartment, and good at things like birthdays and holidays and keeping in touch.

Hiroshi knew what his uncle would be asking him, and nothing more than stopping by to talk face-to-face would get it aired.

Hiroshi went downstairs to the office to tell Ishii he had personal business and would meet her in a few hours.

* * *

The taxi let him out in front of his uncle's accounting firm in Kanda. His uncle's stylish building stood out among the standard-issue offices along the streets. Inside, the soft automatic opening of the doors, the downlighting, alcoves, flower arrangement, and brass intercom panel were meant to impress with understatement.

Hiroshi pushed the call button, looked into the camera, and nodded politely. He couldn't remember the last time they'd talked in person. He'd seen his uncle once after the new year when he visited his cousin and her one-year-old. He and his uncle had gone out for drinks once with their mutual friend Watanabe from the tax office.

The panel buzzed him in, and the elevator descended for him. He rode up to the fourth floor.

One of his uncle's office staff was waiting and bowed when he got off. She was masked, but he had to admit, Takamatsu was right—the little he could see of her neck was enticing. Her eyes were beautifully shaped, with nice folds, though she kept them delicately averted.

He sat at an oval table too big for two people to talk comfortably. The shiny top caught the light from the windows too well. The ergonomic chair looked new, nothing like the butt-busters in the conference room at the station. There were also new paintings on the wall, abstract ones well done. He never knew his uncle to be an art enthusiast.

His uncle pushed the door open and held it open for the woman who'd led him in so she could enter with a tray filled with two coffee cups, sugar, milk, and napkins. Everything, as always with his uncle, was perfect. She set the tray down and backed out of the room with a neat bow.

His uncle set the coffee cups on the shiny table top. "I've gotten to know your office staff very well. Akiko keeps me updated."

"Akiko is an updater. And I've been busy." Hiroshi looked at the coffee. It seemed thick enough. A jolt of caffeine was just what he needed.

"How's your girlfriend? Is her pregnancy going fine? Morning sickness? We remember—"

"We?"

"My daughter, your cousin, had some rough patches, but in the end, it was fine." His uncle took a sip of the coffee. "Any official wedding plans?"

"We're working on it." Hiroshi sipped his coffee.

"Well, *dekichatta kekkon* is all the rage these days, I read. Baby first, ceremony second. It seems like people would want to get married sometime before the baby arrives, but some people like the baby there for the celebration. Or maybe your generation resents paying for a wedding ceremony?"

Hiroshi didn't want to think about how much that would cost. Ayana said she didn't care either way, and that was good enough for him. But maybe Ayana really would like a party of some kind. He didn't even want to think who to invite. He'd ask his cousin to plan it. She'd handle it much better and with enthusiasm.

His uncle leaned forward. "There's still the money from your father you haven't touched. Plus, the money from their house."

"Thanks for looking after it for me. I should be more responsible."

"You're an accountant."

Hiroshi sipped his coffee. Hiroshi had let the inheritance sit so he didn't have to think about his parents or what to do about the money. He *was* an accountant but wasn't quite sure what that meant. He didn't want to quarrel. He didn't have enough energy.

His uncle looked at him. "I've been calling you because I need to talk with you."

The only other serious talk they'd had was after Hiroshi's parents died and his uncle sent him to America to study accounting, interrupting his studies in history and his college romance with Ayana. What would it be this time? There wasn't any other way to ruin his life further than by making him employable, acceptable, and responsible.

His uncle looked at him. "I've had this pain—" His uncle reached for his lower back.

Hiroshi sat up. "What pain?"

"Maybe just a kidney stone."

"Those are painful."

"They found something else too."

"What else?"

"They're not sure. But I'm going to start slowing down. It's a sign."

"You said you'd never retire."

His uncle smiled. His smile was exactly like his father's, the older of the two. "I didn't think I'd ever have to. I'm rethinking things."

Hiroshi looked him in the eyes. "I'm sorry."

His uncle leaned back. "I can still drink coffee. And wine. I don't have any hobbies. Never believed in them. But now I want some.

Painting, maybe." He pointed at the new paintings on the wall.

Hiroshi looked at the abstract paintings he'd admired on the way in. "Are those yours?"

"You didn't know I could paint, did you?" His uncle laughed.

No, he didn't. The paintings had bold colors and swooping brushstrokes—the opposite of an Excel sheet. Hiroshi hummed warmly. "I thought...well..." He hadn't known at all. How could he have not known that about his uncle?

"Your father was the fun one, so artistic, music, plays, literature, reading, always going out, enjoying life." His uncle sighed. "He's the one who pushed me into accounting. So he could keep playing around. He didn't get to do that for long, sadly."

Was that why his uncle pushed him into accounting? Revenge? He didn't remember his father being playful ever. Hiroshi examined the paintings more closely. He'd always assumed his uncle was a numbers person from the beginning. Hiroshi stood up to study the paintings. "Can you give me one?"

His uncle chuckled. "Take whichever one you like."

"I'd like you to pick." Hiroshi sat down again.

"I'll send one to you." His uncle leaned over the table and put his hands together. "Hiroshi, I want you to take over the firm. I've been removing the difficult clients, adding a few promising ones, and simplifying the workflow."

"I don't know much about corporate accounting."

"You must have learned something from the work you're doing. And I've hired some crack accountants in the past couple of years. They know. They need someone to run the place."

Hiroshi took a sip of coffee.

His uncle unfolded his hands. "You're not interested. But I don't want to sell the firm. Even if I did, I'd give you a cut. From your father."

"My father?"

"He's the one who gave me the money to get this firm started. I tried to repay him, but he told me to let it roll over. He did that for you, I think."

Hiroshi swallowed.

"It took years to build this place. Relationships are how Tokyo works. Most of my clients would leave if I quit without hiring someone I trust. You're the only one I trust. I mean, deep down."

Hiroshi looked into his uncle's eyes. "Let me think about it."

"You can't be happy as a detective."

"I'm not. Not exactly."

"So what keeps you there?"

"Currently, a murder case. Two. An older woman and a young kid. It connects to scams preying on old people, a kind of slow murder."

"So, you can set up scam-proof savings plans for them. You'd have time to do that here."

"That wouldn't stop the scams."

"No, but you'd save a few people."

Hiroshi took another sip of coffee. "Ayana worries every time I leave home. More so now that she's pregnant. I could never tell her about the close calls I've had. I wouldn't tell you, either."

"So, why not work here? Security, safety, and, dare I say, comfort? Yes, it's a bit dull, but my staff are excellent."

Hiroshi wondered what it would be like to have dull work and days without drama or murder. His uncle had always been wrapped up in some tight emotional accounting of his own, work-focused and tightly ordered. Maybe he was changing.

Hiroshi's uncle leaned forward again. "You don't have to run this place old-school. Give people more holidays. Take more yourself. Shake things up. Globalize. More and more foreign firms are coming to Japan. You can run things your way when I hand it over to you. Use your English."

"I'll think about it."

His uncle stared hard at him until he met his gaze and nodded that he would think about it.

Hiroshi stood up from the ergonomic chair. "I've got to run."

His uncle talked about his grandchild as he walked Hiroshi to the elevator. And he recommended several current art exhibits in Tokyo too. That was a first.

Chapter 15

After the coffee shop meeting in the morning, Takuya spent the afternoon helping Misaki at the OLzakaya. One of the cooks had quit unexpectedly, and he didn't mind filling in until she could find a new one. He'd cooked for a year when he first got out of the reformatory in Ibaraki, and he promised himself never to get stuck over a grill, deep fryer, or boil basket again.

But now he was thinking that cooking was better than being chased by cops through back alleys, though it paid a lot less than the scams. He knew the *sagi* ring wasn't going to last forever. That's what the others were saying at the meeting.

He stood in the back door of the kitchen, vaping and staring at the ceiling panel above which he stored his savings. Maybe no more orders would come in. He needed to restock the shelves, check on deliveries, and make sure the cleaners were coming to pick up towels and mats.

Misaki had plenty on her hands dealing with the waitresses, who entered and exited like actresses. Two had quit the day before, and Misaki rejected the first new applicants. She had a good eye and only hired attractive girls, which made it easy to sell drinks, but also made it easy for them to leave when they got a better offer.

Maybe he should ease out of the scams and help Misaki expand. She needed to take some time off too. She was a workaholic. They had been to Guam over the New Year break, their first vacation in years. And she handled the money he brought home, never asking too much, though he guessed she knew.

The narrow escape through those backstreets—through that house—in broken shoes and borrowed slippers had started him thinking. He couldn't remember the last time he'd run so hard.

His legs still hurt. That was the closest he'd come to trouble, to the police, since he was young. It was luck, and luck always ran out.

The backdoor opened, and he received a delivery of cooking oil when his phone rang. It was Yasui.

"My grandmother's getting worse," Yasui said. His voice was tight and scratchy. "I've got a pickup at five."

Takuya said, "We canceled everything."

"Canceled?"

"We decided to take a short break."

Yasui didn't answer, but Takuya could hear him breathing.

"Yasui, where are you?"

"At the hospital. I told you."

"What did the doctors say?"

"They said it was up to me to tell her. I'm not sure what to do."

"I'm sorry about your grandmother."

Yasui said, "I think you should talk to the guy I told you about. Kurono. Did you call him? He was talking big payoffs."

Maybe yesterday was just a fluke. Perhaps they needed to move up, not give up, and Kurono would be the next step. "I'll call him."

"He likes to meet at that park along the Sumida River."

"I thought you didn't meet him? Did you?"

"Once, yes, in the park. I didn't tell you. I should have."

"Yeah, you should have."

"I'm telling you now. He says meeting in the park is safer. It runs a long way along the river. Be straight with him."

"Your grandmother always had a snack for us."

"She always liked you."

"The only person in Ibaraki who did." Takuya pulled on his vape pen.

"I've got to go. They just called my number to pay for whatever they did so far, which wasn't much."

"You got enough money?"

"I left most of my cards in Tokyo."

"I'll send money if you need it."

"Thanks, Takuya. Thanks."

Takuya hung up. He'd meet this new guy. It might be another step away from scams.

He took off the apron, changed his shoes, and walked to the front room. The happy hour crowd was already stumbling in, fat-bellied, middle-aged men looking forward to flirting with the waitresses. Misaki was busy behind the bar with drink orders. The evening cook would be there in an hour. Any food orders could wait.

On the way out, he told Misaki all was OK in the back room. She was too busy to do more than nod.

He vaped during the walk to the subway. It was a relief to have the right flavor again. He headed down the stairs to the platform. Before he got too far, Yasui called again.

Yasui said, "He wants to meet now."

"Now? I was heading—"

"That's how he works. I met him on the spur of the moment before too."

"OK, text me the place."

"I'll send it in a minute." Yasui hung up.

Takuya waited on the stairs until he got a text message from Yasui telling him where to meet the guy, Kurono. It was in an hour, along the Sumida River.

Takuya took the information and put it into the shared schedule app. He wanted Noguchi and Murayama to know so there'd be no confusion.

The subway lines in *shitamachi* were older and smaller, and the stations were much closer than in the rest of the city. You could walk from one to the next in little time. But they added up.

He got off at Asakusa and put his head down through the crowds of tourists until he got to the Sumida River, the main artery of old Edo. The best fireworks in the city were there, and though the city had expanded in all directions, the areas along the river still held that core of Edo feeling.

It had turned much darker with fewer lights from the buildings. There was a *tachinomi* standing bar he and Misaki liked nearby, so he headed there for a drink before meeting the guy.

The standing bar was on the corner, with windows on two sides. He pushed back the *noren* curtain, slid the door open, and stepped inside. The interior was almost as dark as the outside. The *master* was in his usual place, reading a magazine on the stool at the end, and two customers leaned on the counter, fingering their chopsticks and looking at nothing.

The *master* came over and set out a small dish of bean sprouts and boiled *daikon*. Takuya ordered sake. The *master* poured it into a small glass with a saucer that barely fit. Takuya downed a big swallow and poured the spillover into his glass. He ordered his favorite dishes: grilled eggplant, potato salad, and cold tofu.

He held his vape pen up to ask the *master* for permission, and the older man nodded *hai*, go ahead. The rum and cigar flavor went well with the sake.

His eggplant came, sprinkled with *ponzu* sauce and bonito flakes. Takuya broke one side in half with his chopsticks and ate it. It was grilled just right. The potato salad was salty with a fish flavor. The cold tofu was smaller than he remembered, but he doused it in soy sauce and ordered another glass of sake.

He had no idea who this guy was, but as awkward as Yasui was, he had a knack for people, finding them, getting them to trust him, and finding out what they had to offer.

Misaki texted him, and he wrote back he'd be back to help her close the shop. He took a photo of the food and sent it to her to make her jealous. She'd stolen the unique way of presenting a couple of the dishes from this shop for the OLzakaya.

After he finished the last nibble, he settled the bill in cash and thanked the *master*. The other two guys standing at the counter would probably be there all night.

He headed toward the Sumida River. He didn't have the guy's contact number, though he'd told Yasui to give him one of Takuya's current numbers. He had three on his one cell phone. Even three didn't seem enough some days. He had to delete the numbers after certain pickups so they couldn't be traced.

He got to the broad expanse of the river and took a breath. He hadn't walked along the Sumida River since the pandemic started. That last summer, Misaki had dressed up in a beautiful summer *yukata* for the Sumidagawa Fireworks. They'd reserved a restaurant with a good view. One of her customers had a connection. Afterward, when the crowds had left, they walked in the humid night air along the river. He'd kept the selfie of it on his Home Screen.

At the stairs down to the riverside terrace, he looked back to be sure he hadn't missed anyone. According to what Yasui told him, the guy was picky about being on time, so he kept walking. Maybe he was waiting further down. "He'll find you," Yasui had assured him.

The wind was a bit cold coming across the river. A few boats plied the water carrying who knew what under canvas tops. A few faster boats buzzed past, the wakes white even in the darkness. On the side canal that fed into the Sumida River, transport boats and the low, flat *yakatabune* party boats were tied to docks along the concrete embankment that stretched west into the center of Tokyo.

When he got to the next bridge, he could see the bridge for the Sobu Line. Had he come that far? He stopped and leaned against the railing, looking in all directions. Was the guy not going to show? Maybe he was walking too fast, or he'd missed him. Should he head back?

He could see Ryogoku Bridge. He wasn't sure whether to keep going or double back. He had passed a man who fit Yasui's description, but tall, thin men dressed well were common in

Tokyo. They blended in.

If the guy were cautious, he'd want to walk by first to check things out. Maybe he hadn't passed inspection, and the guy left. Screw it then.

He stopped to call Yasui to ask him what he thought, but when he switched to the other number on his eSIM card, he found a message from Yasui. "Meeting's canceled. Get out of there!"

That was ten minutes ago. Takuya didn't need to be told twice.

He heard a helicopter over the river and saw their searchlights. He looked over the wall and saw a yellow water taxi shoot by, going way over the speed limit south toward Tokyo Bay.

He made a quick turn from the waterside into the streets of Asakusabashi. He kept going until he could cut over to a street busy with customers going to small bars and eateries.

He kept going until he was deep into the evening crowd far from the river. He didn't mind walking quickly, but he wasn't going to run two days in a row.

Chapter 16

After talking with his uncle, Hiroshi walked towards Kanda, trying to call Ayana. He tried several times, but she didn't answer. He sent her messages, but she didn't answer. He couldn't imagine she was angry exactly. Maybe she was just stressed out being a daughter and a soon-to-be mother at the same time.

Takamatsu broke his reveries with a phone call, an urgent demand to return to the tech room at headquarters. Hiroshi texted Ishii and Akiko to let them know where he would be and called a taxi on his app.

He stood waiting for the taxi and felt more tired than he should be. He craved an espresso, but Akiko had abandoned his office for the main building because of the noise from construction. She was tougher than he was for annoyances of all kinds, so if she couldn't stand the noise, he wouldn't be able to either. A noisy espresso was no espresso at all.

At headquarters, he went straight to the tech room. It was crowded with monitors, computers, and other devices Hiroshi couldn't identify. Nakada, the tech guy, was flipping through video feeds on a large monitor and explaining how it worked to Takamatsu. Takamatsu had set his neatly folded leather jacket on a stool and rolled up his cuffs in crisp folds.

Hiroshi came in and asked, "Are these the feeds the *hikikomori* set up from his room?"

Takamatsu frowned at Hiroshi. "No, these are my feeds."

"*Your* feeds?" Hiroshi closed his eyes. There was no way Takamatsu could have gotten permission for this in the past couple of hours.

"Where do you think I was all afternoon while you were off interviewing people? I was doing serious work. You were chatting."

"I suppose you didn't bother to get—"

"There's no time to fuss with that. I let Sakaguchi know, in a roundabout way, so that he'll be ready if something turns up. We can figure out the logistics later."

"Logistics? You mean legalities."

"Same difference." Takamatsu pulled out his lighter and told Nakada to zoom in on one of the video screens. The resolution was excellent. "My very first supervisor told me that you have to do what they do to find what they did. The best advice I ever received."

Hiroshi stared at the screens. They were almost as empty as the ones they looked at earlier. "Did you tell the Silver Center you were putting cameras there? That's where this is, isn't it?"

"If I had asked for permission, they would have said yes. It's better they don't know."

Nakada looked back and forth, his hands resting on the mouse.

"And we found something more. Or Nakada here did." Takamatsu patted his shoulder. "A neighborhood camera by the convenience store caught someone on the same day. He's tall, thin, not from that part of town."

"How do you know where he's from?"

Takamatsu frowned. "He's not from *shitamachi*. Look how he dresses."

Hiroshi sighed.

Nakada leaned forward and started typing. "That image-matching technology works well, but you can never be sure. Let me run it a few more times and see what I can find."

Takamatsu made a grand gesture with his hands. "The limits of technology."

Hiroshi grunted. "I'm going back to my office." He walked out of the tech room and started down the hallway. Working with Takamatsu could drive you crazy. He was like Tokyo—old-school when he wanted, high-tech when it suited him, and a mishmash of tricks the rest of the time.

"Hiroshi!" Takamatsu called after him.

Hiroshi ignored him.

"Hiroshi," Takamatsu called again, louder.

Hiroshi stopped and turned back.

Takamatsu had his phone to his ear, waving at Hiroshi and pulling on his leather jacket. He hung up. "We have to go. It's the kid."

"What kid?"

"The skateboarder. From the hospital."

"I thought we let him and his tattoos go."

"We did, and we didn't." Takamatsu caught up with him and tugged him towards the parking lot exit. "Sugamo and Osaki are pulling a car around."

Hiroshi watched him go.

Takamatsu was already halfway down the hallway before he turned back. Despite wearing slippery Italian loafers and having no wind from years of smoking, Takamatsu moved surprisingly fast when he wanted. Hiroshi caught up at the outside door.

Takamatsu waved at the car. "Ishii's coming right behind Sugamo and Osaki. We'll need two cars. I'll call Sakaguchi for a helicopter."

"Helicopter?" Hiroshi stopped again. He didn't want to go up in a helicopter.

"It's by the Sumida River. They'll search above, we'll search below."

Outside the door of the station, Sugamo and Osaki pulled up. Osaki got out to let Takamatsu ride in front.

Takamatsu hurried to the other side. He told Osaki, "Go with Ishii. You come from below upriver, and we'll head downriver. Keep the car close. Nakada said there were surveillance cameras all along the riverside terrace. Nakada's tapping into them."

Osaki got out, unsure which car to get in. Ishii pulled up just as Takamatsu ducked his head inside, and Sugamo pulled off even before the door closed.

Hiroshi got in with Ishii, and Osaki got in too.

"Any idea where we're going?" Ishii asked and pulled out after them.

"Sumida River."

"Twenty-some kilometers."

Up ahead, Sugamo popped a light on top of the car, so Ishii did the same, driving quickly after them, heading east toward the river through the crowded streets, slowing only at intersections before racing forward again.

Hiroshi took the call from Takamatsu in the other car.

Takamatsu had the window open. The wind made it hard to hear his voice over the phone. "The helicopter might take too long, but the kid told me he was heading south from Azuma Bridge."

"The kid? The skateboard kid? That's your intel?"

"Any intel's good. If it works. And this one's working."

Hiroshi held the phone up and looked at Ishii and Osaki. "So, where do you want us to start from?" he asked Takamatsu.

"Ryogoku Bridge."

"They could duck into the streets anywhere along there."

"But they won't." Takamatsu hung up.

Hiroshi hung up and turned to Ishii. "He says they won't disappear."

Osaki said, "That's what he always says."

Hiroshi looked at the GPS. "He wants us to start from Ryogoku and walk upriver."

Ishii laughed. "How fast will they come from Asakusa? If the kid's on a skateboard, he can move faster than us."

"The guy we're after will be on foot." Hiroshi wasn't sure that was true, but it was all they had.

Ishii steered south and found a place to park near Asakusabashi. They hurried to the Sumida River Terrace, the walkway running along the river. Ishii had her friction lock baton on the back of her belt and moved her cuffs to an inside pocket.

"Who are we looking for?"

"Young skateboarders or a tall, thin guy."

They headed down the tile walkway that stretched along the river. The high fencing dipped down here and there for stairs to the water-level platform of the docks.

In some places, the blandly functional backsides of buildings pushed out to the terrace. In others, newly planted trees and well-trimmed bushes led up a flight of stairs to new apartment complexes.

Every bridge had spotlights, but it was dark in between. The walkway lights were solar and hadn't stored up much charge for the night. Fog rolled in from Tokyo Bay.

Hiroshi heard the crack-thump of wheels on the tile before he saw the two skateboarders flying toward him. They dropped from an upper wall, zipped down a short set of stairs, and were gone before Ishii could whip out her baton.

Osaki chased them several steps, but they were too fast. "We're not after them anyway, are we?"

Hiroshi turned to Ishii. "Was that the kid you punched out in the hospital yesterday?"

Ishii looked at them boarding away. "I was too angry when I was punching him, and he was too fast tonight."

"Let's spread out a bit and keep going. We stop whoever comes down next." Hiroshi took the side closest to the river and called Takamatsu.

Takamatsu spoke in a whisper. "Sugamo's driving along the road parallel to the river."

"We just had two skateboarders zip past us."

Takamatsu was winded. He coughed before he spoke. "We don't want the skateboarders. We want whoever they were going to meet."

Hiroshi nodded at Ishii. She kept her baton down along her thigh and started walking faster. Hiroshi tried to keep up.

The sound of skateboard wheels on tile came from the front,

but with the fog and dim lighting, Hiroshi couldn't see anything.

Osaki pulled up, and Ishii took a defensive stance.

A single skateboarder headed right at them. When he saw Ishii, he pushed hard with his back leg and leaned low.

Ishii jockeyed for position, but the kid wove back and forth, his leg darting out to push before he crouched and shot under her outstretched baton.

Hiroshi spun around. "Was that him?"

Ishii swiped the air with her baton. "Maybe."

"The guy we want must be ahead." Hiroshi started running.

Ishii burst past him. Despite her short legs, Hiroshi struggled to keep up.

Osaki passed them both and ran full bore at a tall, thin man sprinting toward them.

Ishii stopped with her baton ready, and Hiroshi blocked the other side.

The man's long coat flew out behind him as he spun down a set of stairs to the river and disappeared below the wall.

Osaki hurried to the stairs with Ishii right behind.

Hiroshi got to the break in the wall just as a bright yellow water taxi pulled away. The boat captain spun the wheel, gunned the motor, and left a wake that splashed against the concrete wall.

Inside the bridge of the taxi stood their man, his back to them, talking to the captain.

As bright yellow as it was, the water taxi was quickly lost in the river fog.

Takamatsu caught up with them, out of breath. He put his cell phone away and reached for a cigarette. He leaned over the embankment wall and blew smoke into the night air.

Hiroshi looked at the water. He listened for the skateboarders but only heard the river sloshing against the bank. The fog would have felt beautiful and dreamy if it hadn't provided cover for their escape.

Ishii and Osaki walked a few steps in both directions, staring into the riverside darkness before ambling back.

Takamatsu flicked his cigarette into the river. "The skateboard kid told me he was testing out new wheels. Wanted to market them in California."

Osaki nodded. "Those wheels worked. We couldn't get near him."

The sound of a helicopter came along the river, and a beam of light turned the terrace to daylight. They shielded their eyes.

Takamatsu waved at the helicopter and pointed down the river with exaggerated, futile gestures.

The helicopter hovered in place, roaming its light over the dark grey cottony fog surrounding them.

Chapter 17

After they'd parked a few blocks away from the river, Ishii led them down a dark street with high walls to the entrance to a small garden with a *noren* curtain over the entrance. In the small garden, tight-trimmed trees seemed to dance in place, leaves just starting for the spring. Underfoot, a thick carpet of moss surrounded the gravel and stepping stones. Takamatsu looked around, impressed. Ishii had taken them to one of the few places Takamatsu didn't know in Tokyo.

The *master* behind the wood counter called out, "*Irrashaimase*!" The front counter was worn down to raw beige. The walls were covered in beer posters, not retro kitsch, but decades-old posters falling apart with age. The *master* was wrapped in a thick apron and head scarf. He looked too old to work, but stood stolidly behind the counter, ready.

A waitress, who also looked too old to work, pulled back the *shoji* for a tatami room beside the main room. She left her sandals on the worn black tile, hopped up with a wheeze, and flopped out *zabuton* cushions from a stack in the corner. When the cushions were all set, she climbed down the two steps, hip twist by hip twist.

The detectives thanked her and kicked off their shoes to step up into the room. Osaki and Sugamo flopped down, stretching their legs and backs and adjusting the cushions for maximum comfort. Hiroshi felt his body unwind.

The waitress brought five bottles of beer and five small glasses. Ishii kneeled by the low table to set the bottles out, ordering a few dishes. The waitress suggested a couple more and walked back to the bar.

Takamatsu lit a cigarette and waved Ishii away from pouring beer. Everyone was too tired for formalities. They hoisted their glasses, mumbled, "*Kanpai*," and drained them.

The waitress brought pickled vegetables, deep-fried cone-shaped *shirasu* whitefish, and small bowls of grated *daikon oroshi.* A box at the side of the table held worn chopsticks, which Osaki passed around. Sugamo drained another glass and turned his over to signal he was done. He had to drive.

A large dish of *tamagoyaki,* fried, rolled egg, arrived, and beans boiled in sugar and soy sauce. Everyone started nibbling.

Ishii looked around the table. "I'm so sorry to have dragged you into all this. I feel sorry for Sakaguchi. What if they suspend him for pulling these cases under homicide?"

"They won't do that," Hiroshi said.

Sugamo took his small glass in two hands and looked at her. "It was just bad luck that the scooter hit her."

"I don't think so. I screwed up." Ishii poured herself more beer.

Sugamo refilled Osaki's glass. If he couldn't drink, at least he could enjoy Osaki drinking. "Sakaguchi told me that in sumo, you can never predict which way their head or hands will go. You have to respond in an instant. Everyone signed off on your plan ahead of time."

"I missed something crucial." Ishii picked up her beer.

Takamatsu blew out a big lungful of smoke.

The waitress brought in ceramic *tokkuri* decanters of warm sake. Hiroshi took them, set them on the table, and helped set out five small *choko* cups. The waitress' arms were so old and the skin so wrinkled, he worried she'd drop it, but she moved nimbly.

Takamatsu sipped his warm sake and lit another cigarette. He blew his smoke away from everyone.

They sat quietly, thinking and recovering until the waitress returned with a big round plate of *motsuyaki*, grilled skewers of intestine, liver, heart, and stomach. On a smaller plate was *kurikara yaki*, sea bream twisted around skewers.

Ishii fidgeted. "They were all friends, Ueno, Setsuko, and Sasaki. Friends from childhood. They all grew up in the area."

Hiroshi ordered chilled sake, and the waitress went off to get it from the refrigerated case behind the front counter. Warm sake always made him drunker.

Osaki and Sugamo were making inroads on the grilled innards.

Ishii was drinking more than her share. Even Takamatsu frowned as she finished another cupful.

Hiroshi readjusted his *zabuton* and leaned back against the wall. "What if the skateboarder doesn't call us next time?"

Takamatsu dropped a skewer into the holder for empties. "He will. Plus, we've got the other kid in the hospital. He's not going anywhere. He'll talk once he wakes up. The skateboarders are the only ones who've met the guy. The rest is just video clips and not even clear ones."

Ishii finished her drink and asked for the cold sake the waitress brought for Hiroshi. "Setsuko said something interesting to me about all this. She said all the forces were against the community."

"What did she mean?" Sugamo asked.

"I didn't think about it at the time, but I think she meant that keeping the community center, the *sento,* and the Silver Center was hard. The city office didn't help. Developers snatched up properties. Stores closed. Even people who grew up there gave up. She sometimes felt only Ueno and Sasaki, and maybe Keisuke seemed to care."

Takamatsu took another sip of sake. "When I first came to Tokyo, those communities functioned efficiently and helpfully. They solved half the crimes." He laughed.

Sugamo handed the *tokkuri* to Takamatsu and took a new glass for the cold sake.

"Am I the only one who enjoys warm sake?" Takamatsu asked.

Everyone nodded at him as he lit another cigarette.

"You're definitely the only one who enjoys second-hand smoke," Hiroshi said.

"And first-hand smoke." Takamatsu blew his smoke away at

the corner of the room.

Hiroshi frowned. "I think Keisuke and Setsuko have a thing going."

Ishii smiled.

"What kind of thing?" Osaki asked.

"A relationship." Hiroshi didn't know if a touch on a shoulder meant anything, but for that generation, it must. "Maybe it's not important."

Osaki groaned. "My mother-in-law wants to remarry, but my wife won't let her." He shook his head. "My wife says it's another kind of scam. What's that say about our marriage?"

Everyone chuckled.

Hiroshi took some of the sea bream. "So, the Silver Center has some hanky-panky?"

Takamatsu leaned over for one of the skewers. "Old sex is better than young sex. It falls off for a time, and then you realize, better get to it."

"Never slowed down for you?" Sugamo asked him.

"I'll tell you when I get old." Takamatsu laughed. "So, what about that boyfriend of hers?"

"I don't think they're involved like that." Ishii set her sake cup down. "Does that matter?"

"Maybe. Maybe not." Takamatsu laughed. "Probably knew each other since they were young."

The waitress brought skewers of tofu, *konnyaku*, and *mochi* slathered in miso paste and grilled to tight perfection. She next brought a plate of green-brown seaweed nestled in a viscous broth, topped with a slice of lemon.

Takamatsu looked pleased with Ishii's orders. "Well done, Ishii." He toasted her with his glass. "This is old-style Tokyo food."

"Anything else?" The waitress asked.

"It's delicious," Osaki told her.

Sugamo made a gesture of being full, and the waitress smiled for the first time since they arrived. She gathered the empty dishes and went to busy herself at the counter with what seemed like regular customers.

Hiroshi finished another skewer and dropped it in the container. "Keisuke seems like a typical neighborhood *fudosan.* He probably knows every small house in the area, helps the residents with moving, selling their old furniture, making deals for people moving in—"

"Go talk to him. Most of those guys are corrupt as hell." Takamatsu sipped the last of his warm sake. Takamatsu got a call. He picked up his phone and smiled at everyone, nodding as he listened.

"I was supposed to do that today, but you dragged me away. I wanted to look at Ueno's place too." Hiroshi glared at Takamatsu.

Takamatsu ignored him. "The tech guys got a hit on one of the video feeds. It's an old factory close to the Silver Center. Let's go." He started to put away his cigarettes, lighter, and cell phone.

Everyone looked at him.

Hiroshi said, "We need rest, Takamatsu, even if you don't."

Takamatsu's cell phone buzzed again. He took the call as everyone nibbled the last few tidbits. Takamatsu smiled again, thanked the caller, and hung up. "They found the water taxi driver," he announced.

Hiroshi held up his hand. "We'll do that in the morning. His memory won't change overnight."

Osaki and Sugamo looked relieved. Ishii looked drunk. She got to her knees—unsteadily—and put on the restaurant's slippers to shuffle to the toilet.

"Is she all right?" Osaki asked.

Hiroshi shrugged.

Takamatsu grunted. "She drinks more than Sakaguchi, and he's three times her size."

"Who's going to call Sakaguchi?" Hiroshi asked.

Takamatsu picked up his phone and then set it down. "Let's wait until tomorrow morning. Give him a break."

Osaki and Sugamo got up slowly, stretching their limbs, breathing in and out, and groaning.

Hiroshi would have been happy to sleep right there on the tatami.

Ishii returned. "Everyone ready?" Her face was red, and she sat on the edge of the step to switch from the slippers into her shoes.

"I'll pay." Takamatsu took out his wallet.

"I already paid." Ishii motioned for Hiroshi to hand her her coat.

Takamatsu smiled, impressed again. "We'll have to let you take us out more often."

Outside, Takamatsu and Osaki headed to Uguisudani Station. Sugamo and Ishii walked back to the cars. They'd leave one to pick up in the morning, and Sugamo would drive Ishii home.

Hiroshi waited for a taxi. He closed his eyes until the driver woke him to ask where in Kagurazaka. He'd drifted off.

When he got out, he hurried up the steps of the apartment building and into the elevator. He opened the door to their place and shuffled inside quietly since Ayana and her mother would be asleep.

The kitchen light was on. And so was the bedroom light. He stopped and listened, then tiptoed to the bedroom. But there was no one there.

A handwritten note rested on the pillow. He sat down and unfolded it. "My mother talked me into going back to Nagoya. I didn't want to bother you. Everything's fine. Let's talk in the morning."

Talk in the morning? Hiroshi yanked his cell phone out. They would talk right now. It was two in the morning, but—how could she—what was she—well, she had gone.

He flopped back and reread the note, looking for a trace of something, a light touch, an emotion, any emotion, but there were only words. He held it overhead to reread it and fell asleep in his clothes.

Chapter 18

Hiroshi walked across the bridge and stared down the canal that flowed into the Sumida River, not far from where they had chased the tall, thin man the night before, and failed to catch him.

The canal walls of concrete banks loomed over the waterline. Grey, worn stairs and creaking platforms led from the lower docks to wooden huts perched at street level. Movable walkways, long metal poles, and rope lines dangled over the pilings sunk into the murky water below.

The long, low *yakatabune* party boats rocked in the gentle waves, knocking against the wood of the docks. Some huts had ready-to-go tugboats or transport boats tied below, but the prep kitchens and reception areas were all shut down until the summer party boat season returned.

Hiroshi squinted against the brisk morning wind. Takamatsu had rousted him early enough to make him wonder if his *senpai* ever slept. He always had a tip. The name was "*Ami*-something," some shrimp Hiroshi had never heard of.

On the other side of the canal, Takamatsu lit a cigarette and pulled his leather jacket against the last of the winter wind. Not all the boat names matched the dock names. Halfway from the subway to the river, he realized he should have checked both.

Hiroshi looked down the length of the canal towards the Sumida River, and there it was, a small sign on the side of a boat blocked by crates of empty beer bottles and large coolers. Hiroshi waved at Takamatsu, who flicked his cigarette into the canal and hurried over.

The hut seemed unused. They walked up the stairs to the porch. A row of dried-up potted plants rested below a plank lined with *bonsai*. The *bonsai* were cared for, so someone must be around.

Hiroshi pounded with his fist on the door, listening for any sound from inside.

Takamatsu surveyed the expertly trimmed *bonsai* from the bottom step.

Hiroshi pounded again, gave up, and walked down. They'd only have to wait a day or two if they didn't find anyone home.

Around the far corner of the lane came an older man, bowlegged and rocking from side to side, carrying a plastic bag in each hand. He wore a knit cap and a leather coat worn down to fabric in spots. He started eyeing them but didn't slow down.

They waited for him, and when he was close enough, Takamatsu said, "You must be Terada."

The old man stopped and stared at them. "You must be cops." He brushed past them and ambled up the stairs.

Takamatsu smiled at Hiroshi and followed the man up the stairs.

The old man slid open the unlocked door and stepped inside. He left it open, and Takamatsu ducked under the door frame. Hiroshi stepped inside what would be a waiting room for party boat customers in the summer *hanabi* fireworks and night cruise season. Greyed wood benches of old planks on cut logs were stacked against the wall. Blankets and a futon were neatly folded on top. The place smelled of kerosene and tobacco.

Terada walked behind the bar counter to a sliver of space crowded with a one-burner gas stove, microwave, and refrigerator. Bonsai plants covered the countertop and the window ledge. Without a word, Terada put away his groceries. He set out several cans of tea next to a well-trimmed pine bonsai wrapped with copper training wires. "*Doozo*," was all he said.

Hiroshi took a can of black tea. Takamatsu took green.

Terada walked around the bar to a knee-high heater. He primed the knob and lit the flame with a long-stemmed lighter. The stove hummed to life, filling the room with the pungent smell of kerosene and enough warmth to counter the chill slipping in through the cracks in the walls.

Terada returned to the bar, examined the remaining tea cans, took one, and sat on a high stool behind the counter. His face was water- and sun-worn, a scraggly brown array of hard folds and wrinkled lines.

Takamatsu stepped forward. "Is this your place?"

Terada waved his hand in front of his face. "I'm just the guard dog. A friend lets me stay here. Someone broke in a few years ago." He sipped his tea, putting the screw top back on after each sip.

"What's that pay?" Takamatsu asked.

"Doesn't. Just rent. Always boats to drive in the summer. But the winter runs thin." He took a slug of tea and screwed the top back on.

"Pension doesn't even cover rent. It's a crime." Takamatsu pulled out his cigarettes and offered one to Terada.

Terada took one. "Even if the pensions doubled, most people couldn't live on them. Not in Tokyo."

They both lit up, the smoke adding to the stifling smell of kerosene. Hiroshi wanted to open a window.

Takamatsu sipped his tea, in no hurry for once. "And you drive a water taxi sometimes?"

"Whatever pays."

Hiroshi looked out the window over the canal. The sun added to the warmth from the kerosene heater.

"Who was the man you took from the River Terrace yesterday? Where did you drop him off?"

Terada sipped his tea, screwed the top on as he swallowed, and turned his eyes from his bonsai to Takamatsu. Hiroshi couldn't tell how old Terada was, but he looked older than Takamatsu. His tanned leather face squeezed his eyelids taut around black pupils and near-black irises.

Terada said, "Kachidoki."

"The marina?"

Terada looked at Takamatsu. "What else is there?"

"And his name?"

"He never said. I didn't ask."

Takamatsu looked around for an ashtray but didn't see one. "From Kachidoki, where was he going?"

Terada stared for a second with his hard black eyes, puffed on the cigarette, and flicked the ashes into the sink.

"Did he take another boat?" Takamatsu was more patient than Hiroshi this time around.

Terada tapped the ashes from his cigarette again. "The kind of boat the yachts use. They wait out in the bay when they come in for supplies. Or whatever."

"Was that what that guy was doing?"

"I didn't ask." Terada looked at Takamatsu. "Why would I?"

"No reason to." Takamatsu gestured with his cigarette hand. "His boat was a fast one?"

Terada nodded. "People like that don't drive slow boats."

"Where was he going after you dropped him off?"

"He could have gone anywhere with a speed boat like that."

"How much did he pay you for that little trip?"

Terada flicked the ashes into the sink. "It's the waiting that costs."

"He used you before."

Terada stood up and plucked the branch of a long-limbed bonsai, feeling the small fir tree limb with his fingers. "You're wasting your time with me."

"You're being helpful." Takamatsu smiled.

Terada set down the cigarette on the edge of the sink and reached for his small bonsai clippers. He held them, planning what to trim. "He pays for the wait time, the ride, and extra."

"It's your taxi boat?"

"I borrow it from a friend."

"You don't have a license."

"Not for the taxi, no. You need a special chauffeur's license. I have a license for all other sizes of boats."

"You drive big ones?"

"Tugboat's about the biggest. Do you need to see the license? Isn't that what cops always need to see?"

Takamatsu smiled and took a big drag on his cigarette. "How does he contact you?"

"How did you find me?"

"Bright yellow taxi. The riverside had cameras."

"Why did you ask me where I took him, then?"

"Cameras only go so far. Do you have the number he called from?"

"He faxes." Terada nodded at the shelves to the right of the sliding door.

"You still have the fax?"

Terada pulled in deep on his cigarette, gesturing for them to look in the trash can.

"You don't take reservations on your cell phone?"

"I do that too." Terada ran water to put out his cigarette.

Hiroshi walked to the fax machine and looked at it. He hadn't seen one in years, but Akiko said they still used them in the main offices at headquarters. He leaned over to the waste basket and pulled up a few crumpled papers. Two were from the day before. He held one up.

Terada nodded. "I didn't have any other faxes for months."

Takamatsu cleared his throat. "We'll take these. Did you store his number in the machine?"

Terada looked confused.

It was better to leave the machine. The tech guys might pull something from it, but the guy would call again.

Terada cocked his head to the side. "Why do you want him?"

"Can you let us know if he faxes you again?" Takamatsu looked for a place to put out his cigarette..

"He's my best customer."

"You don't want to be with him when we find him."

"What did he do?"

"What's your phone number?"

Terada dug into his pocket for his flip phone and squinted at the screen. He read out his number.

Hiroshi wondered if it was worthwhile to look at all the numbers. "You don't have a number for that guy?"

Terada put his phone away and pointed at the fax machine. "On my phone, I have the guy who owns this place and the guy with the taxi boats. I get some other work from time to time."

Hiroshi called Terada.

Takamatsu pointed at the phone. "Now, you can remember the number when we call."

"I used to put the names in, but there are not enough to bother with anymore." Terada fiddled with the phone. His fingers were thick and worn, the back of his hands brown and blotchy. "All I did was drive him. No crime in that."

Takamatsu reached across the counter between the bonsai to put out his cigarette in the sink. "No, it's not a crime, and if you call us, we'll make sure there aren't any others."

"What's a cop pension pay?" Terada asked.

"I don't know yet." Takamatsu offered Terada another cigarette, lit it for him, and then handed him the entire pack. "Look, if we can find him, we'll see what we can do."

"Cops never pay as much as they say they will."

"I didn't say I'd pay anything." Takamatsu stood up. "Let us know if he calls you again."

As they left, Terada's attention turned to his bonsai.

Chapter 19

Hiroshi and Takamatsu walked in silence from the water taxi driver's place to Asakusabashi Station. The area was famous for the doll displays made for the Hina Matsuri Girl's Day in March. Every window displayed regal-looking dolls in miniature kimono and black *hakama* with carefully coiffed fake hair.

The main dolls struck eerie poses from hand-carved chairs on the top tier of the red felt display. Below them were arrayed teensy lamps, flowers, tables, and gift boxes wrapped in gold thread. They stared out above these miniature treasures with unchanging eyes, presiding over all below.

Hiroshi came to a halt in front of the displays. It would take hours to set all the little pieces in place and years to acquire them all. They were surprisingly expensive. Hiroshi wondered if Ayana would want this for their daughter. Maybe she had one from when she was young.

He checked his cell phone, but there was nothing from her. Maybe she was sleeping in late at her mother's in Nagoya. He put his phone in his pocket and looked at the dolls. Where would they store it when it wasn't Hina Matsuri? He took a photo and sent it to Ayana.

"No photos," Takamatsu said, pointing at the sign and lighting a cigarette.

"Learned this from you, breaking little rules."

The smoke from his cigarette clashed with the precise, perfect world of red-felt tiers and gold screens, princesses sitting with their princes.

Hiroshi got a call. He looked at Takamatsu as he listened.

Takamatsu raised his eyebrows.

Hiroshi put his phone in his pocket. "The Silver Center office is busted up."

"Someone broke in during the night?"

"Apparently. Now we know for sure it's connected."

"Seems so. But how?" Takamatsu looked unsurprised. "What connects the Silver Center office and the *hikikomori* video kid? And the *sagi*? And the skateboarders meeting their man at the river?"

"I better go." Hiroshi started thinking about which would be quicker, taxi or train.

Takamatsu calmly slipped his cigarette into his portable ashtray.

Hiroshi took a big breath. "Who said they were connected at all?"

Takamatsu put his ashtray in his inner pocket. "I didn't say. I asked."

"Not everything connects."

"In Tokyo, everything connects."

"We should head back to the Silver Center."

"Let's walk to Akihabara. Time to think."

Whoever busted up the Silver Center was long gone, and the young detectives could work it over for clues first. Hopefully, they caught it on video. He followed Takamatsu west toward Akihabara Station.

Office workers streamed towards the office buildings of Kanda. Hiroshi couldn't imagine what all the countless companies did. Most were one small company in a larger nexus of companies. They did their part for the greater good, but what was the greater good? Maybe everything did connect, but to some people's advantage. It was more conspiracy than convergence.

A steady flow of women dressed for the early spring passed by. Their tight skirts and stylish jackets seemed odd against the masks most still wore. Takamatsu eyed them, gesturing to Hiroshi about the ones that caught his eye the most.

"Tokyo women aren't just put there for you to look at."

Takamatsu chuckled. "Isn't that why they're dressing up?"

"Women don't always like being stared at and discussed, however they dress."

Takamatsu laughed. "Where did you get that idea? America?"

Hiroshi grunted and walked on. If the tech guys could track the phone number from the fax machine, they'd be steps ahead. But he doubted that would help much. They'd have to see if there was anything at the Silver Center, go over the *hikikomori*'s room again, and see if the video feeds formed a pattern. None of that seemed promising, much less interesting.

When they got to Akihabara Station, they headed inside and down to the platform. Waiting for the train, Takamatsu started fidgeting with his cell phone, checking the messages. "Why don't you go help Ishii? I've got a couple of things to do."

"I thought we were going to check out the basement where that camera feed came from. The one Nakada found. And don't you want to help with Ueno's place?" Hiroshi followed the platform arrows to line up. Takamatsu stood where he wanted.

"Can't you and Ishii do that after you check the office? The basement video feeds don't seem productive."

"You're the crime scene specialist," Hiroshi said without concealing his sarcasm.

The train came, and they both got on. They had to push to the middle to find an overhead strap to hold onto.

Hiroshi was tall enough to see over most heads in the packed train. "You mean there won't be anything helpful at the crime scene?"

Takamatsu's eyes roamed the crowd before settling back on Hiroshi. "Three incidents so nearby. They're professionals. They won't have left any clues."

"OK, Ishii and I will follow up on the camera feed." Hiroshi checked his phone. "And where are you going?"

"The guy who ran off with the paper has to be somewhere." Takamatsu let go of the strap and waved as he pushed off the train with the exiting passengers. He was quickly lost in the crowd pushing for the exits.

* * *

At the Silver Center, Hiroshi flashed his badge to the local policeman who was explaining to a small huddle of older people that the Center would be temporarily closed. One woman pestered him for more explanation, but the cop put his hands on his belt and stuck out his chest. Two other women discussed finding an alternative space for the children's tutoring that afternoon.

Inside, past the crime scene tape, the double doors to the office stood open. Ishii was inside talking with the crime scene crew. She gestured with her white gloves as the crew bustled around.

The office was in complete shambles. The computers were upended on the floor. The four desks in the center of the room were stripped of folders, personal items, and phones. File cabinet drawers gaped. It looked messy, but thinking of who had done it, it seemed done almost too well. As Takamatsu said, it was too professional to leave clues.

Ishii came over, gesturing in exasperation. "No fingerprints, no hair, no pieces of clothing, nothing."

"Not street-level thieves. Let's let them finish up here, and we can check out the video feeds. The tech guys said it's from one of the buildings near Nippori Station."

Ishii pulled off her nitrile gloves and stuffed them in her pocket. "We can come back later to figure out the why of ripping this place apart. We need to let Setsuko and the others calm down before we talk to them anyway."

"It might take time. There are a lot of basements in Tokyo." Maybe the videos would be another dead end. "Maybe we should look over Ueno's place."

"I did that already before I got the call to come here," Ishii said as they headed down the hallway to a side entrance. She shoved it open and stomped out. The door nearly hit a policewoman who jumped aside with a respectful bow.

Hiroshi stopped on the sidewalk. "I was going to cover Ueno's place."

"Done."

"And?"

"Clean as a whistle. Two of the young detectives came with me. We went over it and over it, but it was not only empty of clues, it was the cleanest apartment I've ever been in." Ishii looked for a taxi but kept walking.

Hiroshi pulled up the address of the one building the tech guys had identified. He tried to figure out the easiest way to get there. Taxi, but letting Ishii walk off some frustration would be good.

He followed her a couple more blocks, and she received two calls and made one. It sounded like people on the women's task force. After the last call, she put her cell phone away and turned to Hiroshi.

"That was Sakaguchi. He managed to maintain control of these two cases for homicide, but they're putting a stop to the stings on the *sagi* gangs." Ishii shook her head.

"That was inevitable. It's how they think. Try the easiest thing, and if it doesn't work, give up."

"We almost had this one, so they should push harder, shouldn't they? Now, all that work is lost."

"It's not Sakaguchi—"

"I know it's not him. It's the same guy who approved the women's crime task force. Now he wants to take it away."

"They want instant results." Hiroshi took a breath. "Let's get a taxi."

Ishii looked around. "I've got a car, but we walked the opposite way." She looked around, confused about where they were.

"If we turn back, we'll get stuck with something at the Silver Center."

They walked to the next big street. After a few minutes, with no taxi passing by, Ishii pulled out her phone. "Half the taxi drivers in Tokyo are over seventy. They used to keep driving, but now, they stop and wait someplace, so you have to use this damn app."

"They don't want to waste gas. One's coming." He nodded down the street and held up his hand.

They got in the taxi and were at the building in a few minutes. As they rode, Ishii took deep breaths and stared out the window.

Ishii tried to pay with her taxi app, but the driver fumbled with the phone reader. Finally, he got it to work, apologizing for the technology he couldn't have imagined using even a few years ago.

They got out, and Hiroshi navigated to a boxy, tiled building near Nippori Station, a leftover from the late 1960s, perhaps, but reasonably kept up. It had a reception window to the left of the entrance and a row of locked mailboxes. Old notices, a trash calendar, and recycling rules were taped above the mailboxes.

A bottle of hand sanitizer stood on a frame inside the door. Hiroshi pressed the foot pedal and slathered his hands, wiping them as he headed to the reception office window. The curtains were pulled shut behind the glass over the small counter. He pressed the button. They waited. No one came.

Hiroshi knocked loudly on the window frame.

The curtain pulled back, and a man stared out at Hiroshi with a frown. He looked like he'd been snoozing.

Hiroshi showed him his badge.

He came out the door to the side, straightening his tie.

"Can I help you?" he asked.

Hiroshi stared him down. "We need access to your basement. Is it that door over there?"

"Is something wrong?" The guard reset his cap.

"We're checking basements in the area."

"Someone came for inspection a few weeks ago."

"Did they?" Hiroshi asked.

Ishii and Hiroshi stared at the guard until he went to get the keys.

"An inspection," Ishii said, humming.

Chapter 20

The guard brought out two rings of keys and a long metal flashlight. He headed to the locked metal door at the back of the entry area without a word.

Hiroshi and Ishii followed. Hiroshi wrote the tech guys and told Nakada to stand ready to check from the feeds they'd kept running in the tech room at the station.

The guard tried several keys before he found the right one. The heavy metal door swung on two big hinges, top and bottom. The guard kicked a wedge of cut wood in as a doorstop and flicked on his flashlight to find the inside light switch. He ambled downstairs one awkward step at a time.

Hiroshi and Ishii followed. The air was stale and cold. The stairs stretched down two floors and got cooler and more stale as they descended.

At the bottom, two doors, big and heavy, went right and left. The right-hand door seemed to lead under the main part of the building. The guard found the key, after several tries, and pulled back the door, holding it with his foot as he fumbled for the next light switch. A row of lights with metal bulb guards flickered to life along the corridor.

Hiroshi walked inside with Ishii right behind. The corridor was lined with pipes that ran the entire length. The insulation was painted, but cracked here and there and covered with a thick top layer of dust. On the left, a low-ceilinged area held thick pipes with wheel handles and chunky valves. He touched the rusty side of one, and it was cool, but he had no idea what it was for, water, probably.

The guard waited at the door. Ishii pulled out her flashlight and held it for Hiroshi, who walked down, examining the spaces between and above the thickly wrapped pipes.

Halfway down, Hiroshi stopped. He ducked under the pipes and stretched to look along the top of the pipes. He waved his hand to where Ishii should point the beam of light.

Before she could find the right angle, she screamed and dropped her flashlight.

Hiroshi turned. "What?! What?"

Ishii swiped her neck and hair. "Spiders. And spiderwebs. Agh!"

Hiroshi bent down to pick up the flashlight. He shone it along the pipes, the perfect mooring for an expanse of webs up to the ceiling and over to the lower ceiling across the wall. Spiders scurried along the wall and across the webs.

Ishii flipped out her friction lock baton, jammed it into the thick center of the webs, and twirled. She looked around for a place to wipe off the webs. She slipped on a nitrile glove, pulled out her handkerchief, and wiped off her baton. She ran the baton along the insulated pipes all the way to the end and wiped it off again. She tossed her handkerchief onto the floor and kicked it aside.

Wiping the back of her neck and hair again, she walked back. "Sorry. I hate spiders." Ishii put her baton away and took the flashlight back from Hiroshi.

He rechecked the video feed on his cell phone. "That's it." He could see it, but couldn't reach the back of the pipe.

Hiroshi called the tech guy, Nakada, and asked him to check the feeds. He took a video with his phone and sent it to Nakada, asking him to check if it was the same.

Nakada said he needed a minute to verify.

Hiroshi walked to the door at the end of the corridor. It was also made of thick metal with fist-sized hinges at the top and bottom and a lock in a protruding frame. Maybe all the video feeds were from this one basement, but that seemed unlikely. And how would anyone get the cameras in there anyway? And why? Was that why there was an inspection, as the guard said?

Nakada called back and said he was ready.

Hiroshi asked him to watch which camera shifted. Nakada said he'd already figured out which one. Hiroshi wiggled it to be sure. Nakada was sure. Hiroshi climbed on a pipe and started to pry the small camera off the wall, before he stopped and dropped back down.

Ishii, reading his thoughts, said, "Maybe we should leave it. It might feed somewhere else."

He called Nakada back. "Can you see me on this camera?"

Nakada took a minute to answer. "Yes. Marvelous resolution. The bird's eye lens seems to be able to focus on a particular point. Try walking back and forth."

He walked back and forth several times. "What did you see?"

"It has some sort of motion sensor and dual lenses, so there are no blind spots. Does it have a serial number or anything?"

Hiroshi climbed up, careful of spiders, and looked more closely. "It does."

"Can you take a photo of it and send it to me? "

Hiroshi pried the camera off the wall and held it up. There were small numbers and letters on the back, and he took a photo of those, then reached up to set it back where it had been. The back mount was still sticky enough to hold it in place.

Hiroshi called down to the guard. "Where does this door lead?" Hiroshi pointed at the end of the corridor.

He shouted back. "The building next door."

"Does it open?" Hiroshi shouted. His voice echoed in the narrow concrete box of the corridor.

The guard shouted back, "I can open our side, but it's locked from the other side."

Hiroshi looked at Ishii. "Looks like we'll have to do the same from the other building."

"They won't cooperate," the guard shouted.

"What?"

"The owners of these two buildings filed lawsuits against each other."

Hiroshi shouted, "What for?"

The guard shrugged.

Ishii looked at Hiroshi. They'd found one feed, and they could check the next building from that direction later. They could check the basements of all the buildings in the area, but Hiroshi wondered what they'd find. More feeds, but then what?

He pointed Ishii back towards the door. She didn't need encouragement. She wiped her baton on her sleeve and headed back.

Hiroshi looked around one more time.

Ishii had already headed halfway up the two-story staircase. The guard pushed the heavy metal door shut and locked it.

They all walked up the two steep flights of stairs to the top. There, the guard locked the door.

As they came back into daylight, Osaki called to tell Hiroshi that Takamatsu told him and Sugamo to follow up on Yumi, the hot yoga instructor who moonlighted as a "delivery health" call girl. Yumi had missed that morning's class. They were headed to her home. Osaki couldn't find Takamatsu and wanted to know what Hiroshi thought.

Hiroshi told them he and Ishii would join them at Yumi's home address as soon as they could.

Ishii looked at Hiroshi. "Should we try the other building?"

"Not now." Hiroshi put his phone away. "I think we need to find Yumi, the delivery health girl."

Ishii shook her head at the juxtaposition of it all.

Hiroshi had one more question for the guard. "What goes through that basement, water, gas, computer lines?"

The guy looked nervous. "I just let people in. I should have called before letting you in."

"Do you keep a list of who goes in and out?"

The guard looked embarrassed. "We used to. Years ago."

Ishii took a step forward. "Do you have a list of all the offices in this building?"

The guard reached for a pad of paper. He copied down a number and information from a piece of paper taped to the wall. "The building management company has one."

Ishii took the paper, and they walked out. Outside, she held it up for Hiroshi to read. "Kurono Building Management."

Hiroshi took a photo and sent it to Akiko and asked her to find out all she could about the company.

"Well, one camera down. How many did you say there were?" Ishii sighed.

"Too many. Let's check the directory of the building next door first as long as we're here."

They walked around the corner to the other building. It looked almost the same—tiled, retro, well-kept, fading. The lobby layout was identical.

The curtain on the window of the guard's office was pulled closed, so Hiroshi tapped on the glass.

A guard slid the curtains and window back and looked at Hiroshi's badge. He came around, ready to assist. He looked even older than the last guard, with longish grey hair poking out from under his peaked, military-style cap.

"Can you give me a list of all your tenants?" Hiroshi asked.

"Sure." The guard hurried back inside. In a moment, he returned with a list of the companies. He explained which ones were still there and which were not. Hiroshi asked him for a printout of all the names of tenants in his building.

The guard hustled back into his room and came back out, handing him a printout. "This is old but it's the most recent one we have. Is there something wrong?"

Hiroshi tucked the list away. "We're just following up on some building inspection."

"Aren't you in homicide?" the guard asked. "I saw your badge."

Hiroshi nodded. "We still need to know about the basements." "We'll be back later today or tomorrow. Are you on duty tomorrow?"

"It's my day off tomorrow." The guard bowed twice.

"Leave a note for your boss about us stopping by." Hiroshi walked out with the list in hand. He stopped on the steps and read it.

After reading the company names, which meant nothing to him, he noticed the management company's name. He held the paper out for Ishii to read.

She leaned over, read it, and leaned back with a question on her face. "Kurono Building Management? Same one as next door."

"Coincidence or connection?"

"I'd say connection."

"What kind of connection?"

Ishii looked away, thinking. "If it's the same management company, then who sued who?"

"And why." Hiroshi looked at the two lists of building tenants and tried to think how long it would take to go through them all.

The name Kurono, though, ran through the middle.

Chapter 21

After the failed meeting with Kurono, Takuya tried all night to get in touch with Yasui but failed at that, too. Yasui must be busy, he knew. So, he asked Noguchi and Murayama to come back to the coffee shop again.

Takuya arrived first and asked the coffee shop owner to pull a divider over the entry to the glass block room. Takuya sucked on his vape pen. The rum and cigar flavor calmed him, but only slightly. The sun rose over a nearby building and hit the glass block, brightening the room.

That made two in a row. First, he was chased by the cops down back alleys. Then, the next day, he had to flee the helicopter searchlights. He didn't have to run, but it was close enough. Three strikes was all anyone got.

That had to have been Yasui's contact, Kurono. Or maybe it was him escaping in the water taxi. It had to have been. But he hadn't seen him clearly, either.

He heard Noguchi's motorcycle arrive and the tinkle of the bell on the front door. The coffee shop was filled with regulars grabbing a coffee and breakfast before work.

Noguchi pushed the divider aside when he entered the back room and stopped to order a morning set from a new waitress Takuya had never seen before.

She backed out politely.

"I thought you were driving up to Ibaraki?" Takuya asked.

"I did. I went last night and talked to Yasui. All good with him. Though not with his grandmother." Noguchi plunked his bag down on the sideboard shelf of red brick and hung his helmet from one of the handlebars hanging from the ceiling. "I came back early to miss the morning traffic into Tokyo."

"You didn't sleep?"

"I drank coffee all night with Yasui in the hospital."

"He's really all right?"

Noguchi sat down and lit a cigarette. "I'm sure he didn't know anything about the mix-up. He thinks Kurono might have something to do with it. He seemed most worried about that." Noguchi leaned back and blew the smoke in the air.

Noguchi looked around for an ashtray. They were stacked on the brick shelf. "When you said we should take a break, I felt relieved. We've been running hard at this for a while."

Takuya sucked on his vape pen and set it down. "Give me one of those cigarettes. For old times' sake."

Noguchi shook one out of his pack and lit it for Takuya. Takuya used to smoke the same brand until Misaki made him switch to vaping. He missed smoking.

When Yasui and Takuya lived in their first cheap apartment with two rooms and a kitchen that barely fit a fridge and table, they chain-smoked every day. Noguchi lived across the street. They started talking about cycles one day when Noguchi was fixing his bike out front. After that, they met to smoke and drink beer in the gravel parking lot their cheap apartment buildings shared.

One day, Noguchi said he needed their help. It was good pay but heavy lifting, and home by morning. Yasui and Takuya laughed when they realized Noguchi was boosting tools, the same as they were. Noguchi was more organized and drove better.

He also had contacts who knew about easier work. All they had to do was act like delivery men. Uniforms and documents were easy to acquire. The transition from heavy, hard-to-sell tools to quicker-to-resell cases of wine and imported foods was a relief. The cases were still heavy, but nothing like hoisting hydraulic power saws and pneumatic drills. It was mostly acting.

Murayama was Noguchi's inside contact. He knew the incoming routes for goods from the import company where he worked after quitting his bank job. He was the tech guy, so he could find the info on imported goods and send it to Noguchi, who called Takuya and Yasui. Soon, they were working nights and saving money.

Murayama then explained the *sagi* scams, which relied on charm, not brawn. They'd all been good talkers and actors. Cash and documents were even lighter to carry and worth a lot more. They'd been a smooth-running quartet for three years, a new scam each year, and never had an argument.

"Smoking cigarettes again?" Maruyama asked Takuya when he came in. He set his computer bag down. Maruyama didn't smoke or drink other than a beer or two.

Takuya stubbed out his cigarette. The waitress came in with Noguchi's morning set of toast, egg, small salad, and coffee.

Maruyama ordered a cappuccino and sat down. "Is she new?"

"I sent a couple of girls over from the OLzakaya, but they didn't work out." Takuya took a sip of his coffee.

"So tell us. What happened?" Noguchi tapped his egg and started peeling off the shell.

"The guy didn't show. I walked along the terrace like Yasui said. But Yasui sent a message to get out of there."

"How did he know?"

Takuya had been wondering about that.

Murayama took his cappuccino from the waitress. "Maybe he was checking you out and left."

Takuya tapped the ashes into the ashtray. "That's what I thought at first, but then I heard a helicopter, saw searchlights, and a water taxi shot down the river. Maybe those were not connected, but I think they were somehow."

Noguchi put out his cigarette, and Murayama leaned back and tapped his laptop.

Takuya put out the cigarette. He liked the rum and cigar flavor better.

Murayama opened his laptop. "No other people? Nothing else unusual?"

Takuya took a breath and looked out the window. "Couples. Joggers. Skateboarders. I think we were set up again."

Noguchi said, "Again? We don't know what happened with the pick-up the other day. Wasn't that just bad luck they chose that as a police sting?"

Murayama nodded. "That's bad luck. But you got out of it."

Takuya frowned. "What about the scooter? That was also bad luck? Two in one day at the same place?"

Murayama sipped his cappuccino and searched on his computer. "Call Yasui. Let's get him in on this."

Takuya pulled out his cell phone and pressed the call button. Yasui answered after several rings, sounding like he had just woken up.

Murayama waved for him to put it on speaker. Takuya set it on the table and turned it toward the other two.

"Yasui? How's your grandmother?" Takuya asked.

Yasui mumbled.

"Anything we can do?" Murayama asked.

Yasui's voice sounded weak. "I was up all night. Noguchi came up. I appreciated that. Are you on speaker?"

"We're all three here." Murayama leaned forward. "How did you know about Kurono?"

Takuya leaned forward. "You told me to leave. How did you know?"

Yasui didn't answer for a minute.

They looked at each other.

Yasui came back. "I'm sorry. The nurse was asking me questions. I can't stand this hospital any longer. I haven't showered in two days."

"What about Kurono?" Maruyama asked.

Yasui's voice was soft. "He sent me a message to cancel, but I didn't get it in time. I fell asleep. When I woke up, there it was."

"Did he say why he needed to change?" Takuya thought it was strange to have that changed after the pick-up from Ueno had been changed. Was he overthinking things? Or not paying attention?

Yasui's voice came through the phone speaker. "Kurono said he needed to change the time but didn't say anything more. I'm sorry, Takuya. It's my fault. Again."

Takuya wasn't sure what to think. He looked at Noguchi and Maruyama. They seemed to believe Yasui.

Yasui said, "Anyway, Kurono sent another message. He said it was better to meet at his office."

Takuya pulled the phone closer. "OK. When?"

"Today. Tokyo Midtown. The outdoor plaza. He said there's a bread store there, coffee place, I guess."

"Sounds like the same as before. He can check me out first. Be sure I'm alone."

"He'll take you to the main office. Dress nice."

"Dress *nice*?"

"Kurono dresses like people in Roppongi."

Murayama leaned forward, and Takuya pushed the phone toward him. "Is there anything we can do for your grandmother?"

Yasui said, "Thank you for asking. Nothing right now. Just...we're going to take a break, right?"

Murayama said, "We've got things covered here. Don't worry. Just spend time with your grandmother. Talk to her."

Yasui went silent. "If she wakes up, I'll do that, Murayama. I don't even know much about her. She took care of me when I was young, took me to the doctor..."

Noguchi finished chewing his toast and leaned toward the phone. "We'll take care of things here. Let us know if we can do anything."

Takuya pulled the phone back to his side. "I'll meet Kurono and let you know. Take care of yourself."

Yasui clicked off.

Murayama opened his computer. "I've been checking into other options."

Takuya looked at him. He was all business. That had helped them up their level, but were they just going to keep moving from one thing to the next? They'd had to stop boosting imported goods after a close call at a distribution center with a suspicious guard. "Other options?"

"We can do things at more of a distance."

Noguchi looked at him. "How do we do that?"

Murayama stared at his screen. "SIM swap."

Noguchi pushed the pieces of eggshell aside and brushed his hands. "What does that mean?"

Murayama tapped his screen. "We get a cell phone number and tap the accounts."

Noguchi hummed. "Sounds too easy?"

"With online banking, there's always a second number to verify, so we send, verify, tap the account, and switch the SIM card back."

"Those little things?" Noguchi held his fingers up close together.

"You don't need a 'little thing' anymore. You just need the number and a one-time password, and you're in." Murayama looked at them over his laptop.

Noguchi went back to his breakfast.

Takuya said, "Maybe we can finish this before moving on to your next scheme."

Murayama pushed his laptop closed. "Sure. It's too soon. Sorry. You should meet Kurono. He might have an offer of something new. Something better."

Takuya said, "We're still agreed to take a break, aren't we?"

Murayama looked at him. "Meeting Kurono isn't a break, is it?"

"I won't go if you think that's better." Takuya looked at Noguchi, who was the most cautious.

"Go meet the guy." Noguchi lit another cigarette and leaned back. "Hear him out. He's either connected to this, or he's not. Either way, he might have something."

Murayama put his computer away. "I'm good with that."

Noguchi blew out his smoke towards the handlebars hanging from the ceiling. "You need backup?"

Takuya looked at the vintage road signs bolted to the wall. "I'll back out if it seems off. We don't owe him anything."

"Not yet," Murayama said.

Chapter 22

Standing outside of the Kurono-managed buildings, Hiroshi received the info from Akiko about Kurono, his associated companies, the owners of the building, and the tenants. It was more extensive than he'd imagined. Kurono managed places all over northeast Tokyo.

Hiroshi held his phone up. "Info on Kurono. Maybe I'll ask Keisuke about this first."

"I'll stop by the Silver Center first," Ishii said, calling a taxi on her app. "After that, we can check on the hot yoga girl."

The taxi came quickly, and Ishii gave the driver directions to the Silver Center.

The crime scene vans were gone, but yellow tape blocked the entrance. Two police were stationed outside, one on the corner and one by the door. They both carried long *bo* sticks. Seeing them at the ready, Hiroshi wished he hadn't fallen off in his kendo practice. Chasing the suspect, he realized how out of shape he'd gotten. Maybe getting out of the office more was better, like Takamatsu said.

Inside the office, Setsuko was directing the cleanup. Two women were straightening the room. Setsuko held up two desktop organizers, both broken. Files and papers were still scattered over the office.

Hiroshi stayed a step back, wondering about what the students said, that Ueno-san owned the center. What would happen to the land and the buildings now that she died? Was that what the perpetrators were looking for?

"You see, they want to destroy the whole community?" Setsuko sighed and shook her head. "We have afternoon classes, a seminar on taxes and pensions, and something else...I can't even remember. The schedule on the wall's torn down. It's better not to let the students see this mess. They're anxious enough as it is."

"What do you mean 'destroy the community'?" Ishii asked.

Setsuko looked at Ishii and then waved her hands. "Tofu makers, flower stores, stationers, the smell of deep-fried cutlets and green tea. Taking care of the kids in the neighborhood. A place for the lonely to socialize. A coffee shop with lunch specials."

Ishii looked around. "So, you know who did this?"

Setsuko looked at her. "No, but I know *what* did this."

"What?"

"Do you see how close we are to Komagome Station? It's always been quiet here, but the big companies and Japan Railways are developing everything along the train lines in Tokyo. I know things change, but we wanted to keep this place livable for the elderly and the young, the most vulnerable."

Ishii hummed, waiting for her to say more.

Setsuko looked out the window, holding a broken plastic file organizer. "If you get rid of the neighborhoods, what are you left with? Company headquarters, over-priced apartments, chain stores, and office complexes. All for show, all for profit—"

"Calm down, calm down." Keisuke, the local real estate agent, walked toward Setsuko with both hands out.

Setsuko folded her arms over her chest. "I want these detectives to understand. If they don't know what's going on, how will they help?"

Keisuke cocked his head at her until she looked away. He was a handsome man with long grey hair. He dressed neatly in understated brown, maroon, and beige. He looked younger than Setsuko.

Setsuko looked at him. "I'm just upset. I have to blame someone for Ueno's death. I've known her since we were young. Ueno, Sasaki, and I formed our own community in the years after the war."

Keisuke turned to the detectives. "She feels responsible for all of this."

Ishii's head drooped. Hiroshi knew she felt the same way.

Setsuko looked out the window. "Ueno always managed to bring food home, even when there wasn't much in the stores and even less we could afford. We shared a six-mat apartment with a small kitchen. We slept on the futon beside each other until Sasaki got married. Ueno and I lived together until she got married."

Sasaki came over and put her hand on Setsuko's shoulder. Sasaki turned to the detectives. "Ueno was a savior many a night. She carried a five-kilo bag of rice home one night, hidden under her coat like a baby. Another night, she smuggled in two crabs wrapped in newspaper. Real crabs! We had to boil them with the window open and the fan blowing so other people wouldn't know how lucky we were."

"How old were you then?" Ishii asked.

"Young," Sasaki answered. "All three of us lost our fathers in the war and our mothers to the firebombing. We stayed with relatives in the countryside for a while, and then moved back to Tokyo. Ueno started working at a real estate company and married the owner. He owned buildings all over this area. This was her husband's building, but he passed away long ago, and it became hers."

One question answered, Hiroshi thought. But he needed to find out who, besides Kurono, managed buildings in the area.

Sasaki pressed Setsuko's shoulder and pushed her into a chair. "Setsuko here was such a beauty. We always wondered what dashing, rich man she'd end up with. Her prince finally arrived."

"We had a few good years. But he liked any good-looking woman he met. And he drank too much." Setsuko looked out the window.

Sasaki smiled. "I'm the only one who had to work. Married a poor man, but he was wonderful."

Keisuke hummed, sighed, and turned to the door. "Reminiscing is my cue to leave."

Hiroshi took a couple of steps after him. "I was wondering if you know the management companies around here?"

"Some of them," Keisuke answered.

"Kurono Building Management?"

Keisuke frowned. "Come with me to my office. It's not far." He turned to the women. "I'm going to borrow this young detective. Will you be OK until he gets back?"

Setsuko, Sasaki, and Ishii nodded.

"They'll still be reminiscing when we get back," Keisuke whispered. He took Hiroshi's elbow and steered him down the street on the opposite side from where Ueno had been hit and killed.

The buds on the cherry tree branches were reddening, and a bit of blossom poked out here and there. Women tugged small shopping carts behind them, joggers headed to the nearby park, and a gaggle of school kids bumped against each other, chattering away. He felt like he had been plopped down into the 1950s.

Hiroshi turned to Keisuke. "Setsuko is very upset."

"If it's not one thing, it's another." Keisuke walked quickly. "But Ueno was quite a shock for us all. And then the student's death. And the ransacking of the office."

Hiroshi added an extra step now and again to keep up with him.

Keisuke stopped at a glass door covered in apartment listings and took out a thick ring of keys. He looked up a stairway, saw the lights were on, and waved Hiroshi in. He locked the ground floor door behind them and led Hiroshi up the steep stairs to the second floor. "When I started, I thought the area would develop. It didn't. I scaled back my expectations and found I liked this human-scale living. Not much money, but lots of good people."

Apartment listings lined the stairwell. Small diagrams with framed rectangles denoting room sizes, bath, kitchen facilities, closets, verandas, windows, and doors. Below the diagrams were columns detailing parking, pets, children, key money, thank-you money, and rent. From single rooms to two-floor homes, space was calculated in precise increments.

"You have a lot of listings." Hiroshi pushed one listing back in place.

"Most are out of date. But they look good. People in *shitamachi* don't move around much. When they do move, I get my cut. If I were in another part of town, turnover would be better." At the top of the stairs, Keisuke started to unlock the door but found it was already open and went inside.

Hiroshi followed him in. A twenty-something man sat at the back, his feet propped up on one of the four desks, tapping his cell phone. He looked up slowly.

"What are you doing here?" Keisuke asked him.

"Thought we were having a drink," the man said. He had short-cut hair and eyes that sank deep into his face. His colorful nylon shirt, gold chain, and black leather jacket were more *yakuza* than *fashionista*. He put his cell phone in his pocket and leaned forward.

Keisuke beelined for the desk opposite. "This is Detective Hiroshi Shimizu from the Homicide Department." Turning to Hiroshi, he said, "This is my nephew. He spent time overseas and is back in Tokyo making his fortune."

"Uncle, I've been back for ten years." He dropped his feet to the floor. "We can go for a drink another day if you're too busy with detectives or that girlfriend of yours."

Keisuke gave him a glance. "I can't go today."

"Did you think about my proposal?"

"We can talk about that when we go for a drink."

The nephew pulled out his card and handed it to Hiroshi. "Here, so you don't have to ask my uncle for it."

Hiroshi fumbled through his jacket for one of his cards and handed it to the nephew.

The nephew straightened his jacket as he stood. "The money's on your desk," he said with a loose salute. He unlocked the door and walked out.

Keisuke unlocked a drawer, put the money inside, and locked it before walking over to re-lock the door. "That's my sister's kid. She passed away a few years ago, so I look after him as best I can. I tried to get him to settle in here, but that didn't work. Thinks it's beneath him."

"He still works for you, though?" Hiroshi's cell phone buzzed. It was an urgent message from Osaki. "I've got to go." He texted Ishii to let her know she was on her own at the Silver Center and they'd catch up later.

"Just a minute as long as you're here." Keisuke pulled out a printed sheet and unrolled it over his desk.

It was a three-dimensional map of the area. Close to Komagome Station was a mountain of buildings, with the surrounding area leveling off to one- and two-story homes, shops, schools, and other buildings. Little corner parks were marked with cherry trees in light pink.

Small blue and red stickers had been added on top, turning the whole map into a colorful Go board with the stones partly filled in and partially open.

"What am I looking at?" Hiroshi asked.

Keisuke looked at Hiroshi. "The red dots are the management company you showed me. Kurono."

"How do you know this?"

"I keep track."

Hiroshi leaned forward, looking for a pattern. "And the blue dots?"

"They're old buildings the city office wants to tear down."

"Looks like the red dots are taking over."

"That's what Kurono's good at."

Chapter 23

Hiroshi hurried to the Nanboku Line subway, which would be faster than a taxi in mid-afternoon traffic. He got on the train, regretting not asking Keisuke more about the management company. He should have stayed there longer, waiting for him to explain.

It's what Takamatsu kept teasing him about, losing his Japaneseness in the years overseas. But Takamatsu was right. He would never quite fit if he couldn't stand the pauses essential to Japanese conversation. Waiting out the silences was the key to getting the correct information and understanding the subtext. The subtext was usually the main point.

He could go back after seeing whatever there was in Yumi's apartment. Or whatever wasn't there, which was Yumi, apparently. He wrote Takamatsu for more on her, but got no answer.

Hiroshi switched to the Tozai Line, which felt smaller than the newer Nanboku Line.

He got a seat, leaned back, and closed his eyes. How would the *sagi* scam work so well? Were people that naive? The scammers had to know what to say, how to gain their trust, how to push it to another level, and how to stay cold-hearted enough to bleed the old folks dry.

The videos were another thing altogether. They didn't fit anywhere. Why would that kid hole up in a dorm and put a camera in a basement or watch the feed of a camera someone else set in a basement?

The scooter accident that maybe wasn't an accident, the overdose that was surely murder, the carefully set up scams, and the guy escaping in the water taxi seemed like four unrelated cases.

At Monzen Nakacho Station, he hurried out to the street. He hadn't been to the lively area since Takamatsu dragged him to a series of sake bars before the pandemic. The area had a small, snug vibe, with countless bars and cozy restaurants. It ran on a small, human scale, as Keisuke had just said, resisting the pushy pretense of the busiest parts of the city.

The hot yoga call girl had selected one of the up-and-coming areas of Tokyo, but she must have moved in before rents shot up, or she made more money than it appeared. Probably the latter. But visiting recluses to relieve their frustration couldn't pay that much. Or maybe it could.

Following Osaki's directions, he turned down a street lined by wood-slatted shops. It was too narrow and zig-zagged for a car. Plants and signs jutted into the walkway. He found her ten-story building. It was neatly designed with clean white and grey tiles and stood on the bank of the Oyoko River. Each apartment had a balcony.

An anxious-looking superintendent bowed in the lobby when Hiroshi flashed his badge and hurried them to the waiting elevator. He used a key to work the controls and bowed as Hiroshi got off.

The apartment door was wedged open. Hiroshi pulled on nitrile gloves and went inside. Two young detectives stood in the *genkan* entryway beside a floor-to-ceiling shoe rack filled with women's shoes.

"I'm Adachi. Detective Ishii said you never remember names. We're the ones who helped search the victim's apartment this morning. She sent us here after that." The new, young detective smiled beneath her mask. He couldn't remember who she was. Maybe he'd seen her the other day talking with Ishii.

"Were you part of the women's task force?" Hiroshi asked.

"Yes."

Hiroshi nodded to the other female detective. She was short and stocky with eyes so thin that Hiroshi wondered if they were closed, though he knew they weren't. He bowed, toed off his shoes, and stepped onto the inner floor.

"Let me fill you in." Adachi pulled out a clipboard and flipped through the pages. "So, Detective Takamatsu was going to meet the suspect...name of Yumi...here at her apartment, but when he arrived, the door was open. He called Detective Osaki and Detective Sugamo at that point but didn't wait here. Instead, he ran out to investigate a noise he heard in the stairwell." Adachi pointed in the direction opposite the elevator.

"Did you check out the stairwell?" Hiroshi asked.

"Yes, Detective Kim and I searched it twice. All ten floors. Up and down. And the basement," Adachi replied without any irritation.

Hiroshi did not want to see another basement.

Adachi flipped a page on the clipboard. "Detective Osaki and Detective Sugamo arrived shortly after that, at 15:20. They weren't sure of the time, but we checked the entry cameras. No one has heard from Takamatsu since then." She flipped the pages back into place.

Hiroshi nodded. "And what did you find inside?"

"Detective Osaki and Detective Sugamo are still searching for clues, but during the first time through, we found nothing unusual except for her phones left behind. But someone in her, um, profession, probably owns several phones." Adachi pointed with her hand to the backroom.

Hiroshi stepped into the living room, where there was another rack of shoes. "Quite a collection." Hiroshi had never seen so many shoes. The colorful tennis shoes on the top tier must be collector items. Some were still in their boxes. The bottom rack, taller than the others, held calf-high boots.

Adachi nodded at the shoes and shook her head. "One hundred and sixty-two pairs. We've had time to count. Most are designer brands. It must have taken time to try them all on."

They stood there marveling at the shoes.

After a minute or two, Hiroshi excused himself and walked to the back of the apartment. It wasn't large, but it was packed full. The hallway was lined with bookcases filled with books. Hiroshi resisted, stopping to read the titles.

Osaki and Sugamo were in the back room. It was sunny with a large window overlooking the Oyoko River. The Oyoko wasn't nearly as impressive as the Sumida, but it was famous for its contoured lines of cherry trees. Hiroshi had strolled there with Ayana a couple of years ago in April when the river became covered in a carpet of petals broken only by the small boats plying the waters.

Osaki and Sugamo stood in front of a closet with neatly hung dresses, blouses, and skirts. A trifold full-length mirror stood in the corner.

Osaki nodded at a white desk with a shelf of folders. They were neatly labeled with women's names. On top was a neat row of books on yoga.

"Did you see the shoes?" Osaki asked.

Hiroshi nodded.

Sugamo waved Hiroshi to the other room. "Why not see the rest before you look through the folders? First, the shower and toilet."

Sugamo let Hiroshi poke his head in. A single full-length mirror took up one wall and reflected the make-up mirror on the other side, reflecting infinitely. A swing-out magnifying mirror with LED lights was attached to the side. Hiroshi looked at his image, repeating to the end of the mirrored space.

Hiroshi looked back and forth. "She could see herself from every angle."

Sugamo cleared his throat. "Press the button in the middle."

Hiroshi pressed the glowing button. The light switched from white to daylight and, after another press, back to a warm yellow.

Osaki nodded at the front room. "The new detectives pretty much knew the prices of the cosmetics. That little bottle of perfume on top?"

Hiroshi looked at it and shrugged.

"One hundred thousand yen. Special from Paris."

"She can tell us for sure if she turns up," Sugamo said. He nodded at the corner rack in the shower filled with shampoos, soaps, conditioners, and cleansers. "Same over there. Those aren't just body soaps."

Hiroshi inhaled the aromas from the shelves of bottles of all sizes, colors, and shapes.

Sugamo waved Hiroshi to the next room.

The last room held a single bed covered with a thick comforter in a flowery pink and white design. Pink, green, and yellow flowers decorated the walls. Two wood chests took up most of the rest of the space. One drawer was open. Inside were bras and underwear, organized with plastic dividers. Even the yoga clothes were chic and costly.

Hiroshi peered in. "I guess those are also expensive."

"Sky's the limit with underwear, Adachi and Kim told us." Sugamo cleared his throat. "We haven't been through them yet."

Sugamo directed them back to the bedroom. He held up a note: "Detective Takamatsu, I'll be in touch. Please wait."

Hiroshi turned it over and handed it back. "Why would she leave her door open?"

Osaki shook his head. "On top of the note, we found two cell phones."

"We should take them to the tech guys. Takamatsu came in first, so let him fill in the forms." Hiroshi pointed at the front room. "Or let the new detectives do it."

Hiroshi looked around. He'd learned from Takamatsu to examine everything closely, even if you didn't consciously register it. He said it stayed in your memory so that you could pull it up later. Hiroshi thought that was just Takamatsu being Takamatsu, but he looked around again to be sure.

One of the phones buzzed, startling them.

Hiroshi took a breath and picked up the phone.

The voice, Yumi's voice, said, "Detective Takamatsu?"

"Yumi? This is Hiroshi Shimizu. Where are you?"

"I'm taking a short vacation." Yumi's voice sounded strained and distant.

"Did you leave these phones for us?" Hiroshi picked them up.

"Yes. I left them and the files for you. I can't do anything more to help."

"Are you still in Tokyo?"

Hiroshi waited for her to explain.

"There's a file labeled 'Yumi.' That's not even my real name. You can find everything else in there."

"Are you all right?"

"I'll call again when I'm there."

"There? Where?"

"Safe," she said and clicked off.

Hiroshi handed the phone to Osaki. "Tech guys. Call and tell them you're coming, and it's important to do that now."

"Let me do that." Adachi, who'd been listening from the door, stepped over, put the phone in an evidence bag, and hurried off.

Hiroshi pulled down the file labeled "Yumi." Inside was a copy of her online bank statements. Hiroshi was usually pleased to have something to drag back to his office and mull over, but this wasn't much to work on.

With her disappearance added to the scooter, the overdose, the scam, and the chase to the water taxi, it was starting to seem like five unrelated cases.

Chapter 24

Hiroshi tried to call Yumi on the number she'd given him at the hot yoga studio but was interrupted by an incoming call from Takamatsu.

"Is she there?" Takamatsu asked.

"No. She's not with you?"

"I followed a woman who looked like her into the station, but whoever it was got away. There was someone else above me in the stairwell when I ran down after her."

"Who?"

"It was like I was in the middle of them."

"Now what?"

"I'll call you later." Takamatsu hung up.

Hiroshi held up his phone. Osaki and Sugamo looked as disappointed as Hiroshi felt.

Hiroshi stood around while the crew came in to look for anything that might help. After an hour of re-examining everything with the new detectives and texting Akiko back at headquarters, the only way forward seemed to be straight to Kurono Building Management.

"Are you sure leaving those two new detectives here is OK?" Hiroshi whispered in the hallway.

Sugamo pressed the button in the elevator. "Kim's a black belt in tae kwon do. And Adachi won the marksmanship award three years running."

"Is she carrying a gun?"

"No, but it's the focus that counts."

Hiroshi thought about that. Focus seemed the thing he lacked himself. Hiroshi followed them to the car.

Osaki was driving.

"Roppongi, you said?" Sugamo fiddled with the GPS navigation and looked back at Hiroshi.

"Yes, the Tokyo Midtown complex. Middle of Roppongi."

"I've never been in there before," Osaki said.

"Everything looks new. But that's about it." Hiroshi pulled out the files he took from Yumi's desk.

"I read that the price of the land for the whole center was the highest ever paid in Tokyo." Sugamo turned around to see if Hiroshi knew.

"The price of the surrounding land leaps up further when it's finished. They plan ahead, buy what they can of the surrounding land, and hide ownership under sub-companies and investment groups. Standard tax dodge." Hiroshi looked out the window. "I can't figure out how an outfit like Kurono Building Management could afford an office in Tokyo Midtown, though. That kind of company is usually not located on prime real estate."

"They must be great building managers." Sugamo turned back to the front.

"Great at something anyway." Hiroshi opened the folders Yumi had left for them. Electronic files would have been easier, but Akiko could scan them properly when he got to the office. Some folders were labeled with different women's names.

The variously named files mostly showed credit card payments and cash withdrawals. Bank transfers and cash deposits were large, though he wasn't sure what she should be paid. Prices could vary for all the services. It was all in order. She seemed to be good at accounting, maybe from her courses.

Then, there it was. One year ago, there were regular payments from "Kurono."

He tucked Yumi's folder in the lockbox on the floor, another addition to the new detective cars, and stared out the window as Osaki pulled around a slow-moving lane of traffic over the Sumida River. The river looked wider there because you could get an angle. In the northern section of the Sumida in *shitamachi*, the buildings seemed poised to fall into the river and blocked the view.

They headed into a walled-in expressway, which echoed the noise of the cars. With no shoulder on that stretch of expressway, he could practically touch the walls if he reached out the window.

"Find anything?" Sugamo asked.

"Regular payments of all kinds from—ready?—Kurono."

Osaki looked back in the rearview mirror. "It's a common enough name."

"It's becoming more common on this case," Hiroshi explained what he discovered about the Kurono Building Management company, then looked out the window at the bland walls flashing by.

They pulled out of the tunnel onto a wide street. Pedestrians flooded the first crosswalk from all four directions while vehicles backed up into the tunnel. When the light changed, the pedestrians hustled back to the safety of the sidewalk.

Signage flowed up the outside of the buildings for the upper floor retail. Each building was a mini-corporation, with ten floors of income flow, steady foot traffic, and the name "Roppongi" to show off.

Ayana rarely asked him to go to any of those complexes, though they offered all the things they loved—movies, music, art museums, fine restaurants, and small festivals all their own. Each of Roppongi's triumvirate of massive architectural projects also offered office space, commercial space, entertainment space, and public space—everything you needed under one roof—or maybe it wasn't everything.

Tokyo Midtown's giant obelisks loomed up in front of them. No matter how clever the design, it would never match the aspirations of old Edo, where the wealthy had sprawling wood homes with as large a garden as space allowed. The design of the skyscrapers, even the innovative ones, never escaped the cold regularity of rectangular windows with their limited, pre-framed views.

Of course, his own office had no windows at all. But try as they might, the skyscrapers never differed from each other and always felt like exercises in conformity. They couldn't differ that much. If they did, a serious earthquake and gravity would bring them tumbling down.

Osaki turned into a sloping drive to the underground parking lot under Tokyo Midtown. They spiraled down three or four stories until a spot opened up. Could that many people be driving to Roppongi?

After they got out, Osaki beeped the car lock, and Sugamo pointed to the elevator. In the lobby of the building complex, they fast-talked the receptionist and security guards and headed to the bank of restricted elevators. They asked a passenger to swipe his card and press their floor.

Kurono Building Management didn't rent the entire floor, but a security gate blocked the entrance to all the offices on that floor.

Osaki eyed the gate. The plastic door didn't look that strong.

"Let's go in soft." Hiroshi looked up at the security camera and waved.

In a minute, a young woman with a card and a cell phone dangling from red straps around her neck poked her head out of the Kurono office door. "I think you're on the wrong—"

The three detectives held their badges up.

The young woman looked at their badges and back at the office door, trying to decide.

Hiroshi waved her closer. "Use your card." He smiled encouragingly.

She hesitated, then stepped forward with the security card in her hand. "Do you have an—"

Sugamo stepped through the gate first. "We don't do appointments."

"But—" she said.

"We need to talk with your boss, Kurono."

"He's not—" she stammered.

Osaki breezed past her, and Hiroshi and Sugamo followed.

The office had a panoramic view of the city. There were no dividers between the desks, so you could see out from anywhere. The city sprawled below like a thick carpet of buildings, billboards, trains, and expressways.

The women working at the desks stopped what they were doing and stared at the three detectives.

The young woman from the front ran in her heels to catch up with them. "*Sumimasen*," she said over and over.

Hiroshi finally stopped and turned to her, speaking in a soft, easy voice. "We'd like to talk to the office manager."

The young woman held up her ID card from the red string around her neck. "I'm the office manager."

Hiroshi looked around. "Where's a good place to talk?"

She held her hand up to guide them toward an open area in the corner in front of more windows. The sofa was low and wide, slanted back so that you had to either pull off your shoes and pull up your feet or keep your shoes on and lean forward awkwardly. Was that the point, or was it bad design?

Hiroshi sat down. Sugamo and Osaki stood to the side.

The young office manager half-sat on the sofa across from Hiroshi and dug in her front pocket for her *meishi*. She wore a standard-issue plain white shirt and navy blue slacks. She handed her name card to Hiroshi.

"Tanaka *desu*. Nice to meet you."

Hiroshi returned one of his cards. "Where's Kurono now?"

"He's not here." Tanaka glanced at Hiroshi's name card but said nothing.

Two more employees came over with concerned faces. They all dressed the same, in white blouses and navy blue pants.

Hiroshi leaned forward. "So, Kurono manages buildings all over Tokyo?"

Tanaka nodded, unsure how to answer. "We have many buildings. And we're still expanding, but most are in the northeast of Tokyo."

"All in *shitamachi*?"

"Not all, but most."

"Why have the offices here then?"

"We're part of a conglomerate, so we had a deal from what I understand, for an office in this building. We often meet clients here." Tanaka smiled. Her smile held a question, but Hiroshi didn't answer. He knew what she wanted to know—their real purpose. The other women had given up all pretense of work and stood listening.

Hiroshi pulled up a still from the videos inside the buildings with the cameras. "We need to know about these two buildings."

Tanaka leaned over to look at the printout. She picked it up and looked at Hiroshi. "Do you have the address?"

Hiroshi found it and held it up for her.

Tanaka told one of the women to get the books on those buildings.

One of the women hustled off and returned with a bulky three-ringed binder. Tanaka set it on the table and folded it open. "What do you need to know?"

"Who rents the offices, and what are the basement rooms for?"

Tanaka shrugged. "Basements are basements. But it's all in here. I'll make copies of the occupants for you if it helps. I've never met a detective before." She was pleasant but spoke as if the rules made it clear what was to be done and how. She handed the large binder to one of the women. Another woman stepped over to assist. Tanaka told them to make copies.

Hiroshi leaned forward. "So, tell me about the basements."

Tanaka leaned back on the sofa. She pulled one of her legs up with both hands. "They're just basements, as far as I know. Was there some trouble in that basement?"

Hiroshi smiled at her to avoid the question. "And what is Kurono Building Management's parent company?"

She stared at Hiroshi for a moment, then looked away. "That's on the company website. At the top. Imada Industries."

Hiroshi nodded and smiled. "I'll get it from there then. One more thing, do you have a map of all the buildings you manage?"

Tanaka told the third woman standing nervously beside her sofa to bring the master map with all the buildings.

The woman shuffled away, and they waited quietly. Another woman brought tea, but the detectives shook their heads. She looked disappointed and tried to get them to take a cup. After a third try, she gave up and set the cups on the table.

The tea cooled as they waited.

The other woman returned with a black storage tube of the copies. Hiroshi wanted to open it and look through it but decided to wait. He had to imagine it was what he needed.

Chapter 25

Takuya took hits from his vape pen as he walked around the plaza in front of the fifty-some-story Tokyo Midtown complex in the middle of Roppongi. The vast plaza was as open as a concrete playing field. Tokyo Midtown aimed at sleek company employees, rich kids on dates, shoppers with high credit card limits, and salarymen who didn't really have to work. The offices loomed overhead.

When the office, retail, and entertainment complex was being built, Yasui and he had hired on as laborers on the project. To get hired, you had to know someone who knew someone, hopefully with your same country accent. The excavation site was vast enough for four full-scale entry gates and deep enough for three construction hoists. There were hundreds of workers.

One day, Yasui said they should load a truck with equipment and tell the guard at one gate the stuff was needed on the other side of the excavation project. They hauled toolboxes, hoists, conveyors, trenchers, and concrete mixers into the borrowed truck and took off for the expressway to Ibaraki. Takuya's cousin ran a construction company and was desperate for affordably priced equipment.

They repeated the heists whenever they could. Small construction companies outside Tokyo had a high demand, so Saturdays became regular load-and-drive days until a new security company took over the entry gates. After that shut down, they had to really work.

He missed that feeling of hard work. He looked up at the massive building overhead and wondered how much their heists had slowed things down. Probably not much. It had been a form of redistribution. Why should Tokyo get all the best construction equipment? The countryside needed buildings too.

He sucked on his vape pen and looked at the shop, "Bread and Coffee," on the far side of the plaza. The outdoor tables and chairs were folded and put away, with only a few left out for those willing to brave the chill. He wanted to check out the area before they met, but it was too late. He wanted to see the guy first, but it was also too late for that.

A trio of skateboarders shot past him, close enough to touch a sign prohibited skateboarding. He'd never had time to learn when he was young. He was always working.

He stopped in the middle of the plaza and checked his messages. There was only one from Misaki, asking him to come by later to help close up.

He messaged he had a meeting.

"Please!" she wrote in English, followed by a row of emojis. She was short-handed.

He said he'd be by after his meeting.

Being chased through the streets reminded him he wasn't getting younger. He'd talk with Misaki and see what she was thinking. Somehow, he'd have to change things. Being the best *sagi* guy in Tokyo was fine, but he couldn't do that forever.

As he eyed the coffee and bread shop, he paid attention to everyone who passed by. It was nearly sunset and brisk, with the sun dipping behind the buildings.

A tall, thin man in a black jacket walked by.

Takuya looked at him and looked away.

That was him.

The man nodded with his head to follow.

Takuya put his vape pen away and followed him across the plaza. The skateboarders shot past again, not quite as close. There were no guards to chase them away.

The tall, thin man led him inside Tokyo Midtown and keyed him through the security wicket to an elevator to the higher floors. When the elevator arrived, he put his card key into the slot and held out a hand to stop two people from getting on. They stepped back indifferently, the doors closed, and the elevator hummed upward.

"I'm Kurono," he said finally. He stood calmly with his hands folded in front of him. "Imada is waiting for you upstairs."

Takuya nodded.

On the correct floor, Kurono got off the elevator and stepped to another key card panel that opened the sliding glass doors into the office.

The office was huge, dark, and quiet, but the windows revealed the Tokyo vista of lights, buildings, shadows, and more lights stretching to the horizon. He followed Kurono to a glassed-in office at the far end of the office.

Inside, a tall man in a tight-fitting turtleneck bent over a stack of architectural blueprints covering his desk. He talked through his earbuds while flipping back and forth between the screens of his two monitors. He bounced back and forth as he spoke, like some light gym routine.

Kurono bowed out of the room, leaving Takuya staring out the window. In the distance, Mount Fuji was framed by the last light in a cloudless sky. It looked close.

Imada tapped his earpiece, took it out, and shook it in his hand as he looked at the screen again. Then he turned to Takuya and came around the desk.

"I'm Imada," he said, reaching to shake hands. "I hope we might do business together."

Takuya tried to sound cheerful and agreeable. "That's why I'm here, though Yasui didn't say what that might involve."

"I didn't get a chance to explain to your associate. Kurono told me Yasui had family issues."

"His grandmother is dying."

"Ah." Imada gestured. "Would you like something to drink?"

"Coffee."

"Cappuccino?"

"If you have it."

"We have everything." Imada pressed a button on his intercom phone and told someone to bring two cappuccinos.

Takuya sat down on the edge of the sofa chair and waited.

Imada cleared his throat. "Let me be direct. I hope that's OK. Saves time."

Takuya eased back on the chair. "I prefer that."

"I want to ask you to help us make Tokyo the city of the future."

Takuya had not been expecting anything like that.

Imada pointed at his desk. "Urban renewal. Urban re-design."

"It's already renewing, isn't it? You can't go anywhere without construction."

Imada smiled. "Not nearly at the level it could be. That's why I need you."

"How can I help?" Takuya felt surprised to hear himself say that, but wanted to hear whatever was coming.

"Tokyo is stuck between past and present. Only the present can move to the future." Imada pointed outside.

Takuya wasn't sure what that meant, but he peered out the window for the answer.

"The future, the future of Tokyo, is up," Imada said.

Kurono came in with two cups of cappuccino. He set them on the table between the sofa chairs.

"Do you smoke?" Imada asked.

"Vape."

"Perfect. Me too. Do you mind?" Imada got up and went to his desk. He pushed aside a few of the rolled-up plans and found his vape pen."What flavors do you like?"

"Cigar and rum." Takuya took his cappuccino, but it was too hot to drink. He lapped the foam and set it down.

"Ah, nice. Now, I'm into Virginia Tobacco. It's a real tobacco flavor. Delivered like this, it's better." Imada held up his vape pen.

Takuya pulled in a lungful of relief. The last outline of Mount Fuji had faded into the darkening sky. Only the city felt close.

Imada took another draw on his vape pen and smiled. "My new

venture is all about taller buildings. I want to offer people another way to live."

Takuya had no idea what he meant. "You mean, you want to put up skyscrapers in undeveloped parts of Tokyo?"

Imada smiled indulgently. "We want to develop the air. Floor by floor, value is added, and quality is improved. Too much of Tokyo life goes on at ground level. We want to add value above to create multiple ground levels, as it were."

Takuya wasn't sure he understood. A skyscraper added floors, not ground.

Imada leaned forward. "We've got fifty-four in this building so that we can afford a ground-level concourse."

"Did you help build Tokyo Midtown?"

"We did our part. We're just one small company. But our company is expanding, and the way to do that is by adding value through walkways, plazas, and public spaces. Then, we offer concerts, festivals, medical facilities, various services, retail options, and shorter commutes. Work and leisure side by side. Even retirement facilities. We want to do that all over Tokyo, starting in the northeast."

"They won't have anywhere to go but into your spaces."

Imada smiled. "We have three stages of development. First, remove. Second, replan. And third, rebuild. We need your help with the first."

Takuya sipped his cappuccino.

Imada leaned forward. "Our company is not as big as others. We don't have a dedicated team to work on securing rights, readying the ground, managing the properties."

"My skill set—."

Imada spread his arms wide. "I want you to think beyond bank transfers and chatting up old ladies. I want you to think bigger. Farther. Higher."

Takuya frowned. How could he know their business? But he did.

"You can help collect information for us. Documents and deeds. Help secure lost materials. Help clear the way when needed. It's simpler than what you're doing now. You won't think of another bank transfer scheme ever again. And you won't have to be chased."

How did Imada know that? Takuya wondered. If he knew that, he must have been there when things went wrong with the pick-up. The scooter wasn't an accident.

Imada looked at him. "We know what to target. You get it done."

Takuya finished the last of his very foamy cappuccino.

Imada took a big breath, looking intensely at Takuya. "We need your help. And there will be handsome returns."

Takuya wondered how much exactly. He waited for something more, but Imada stood up and said, "Kurono will have the details."

Murayama always said the devil was in the details. Was this what he meant? Takuya looked at Imada. "I appreciate your offer, but it's not for me."

Imada pulled a face and stepped around his desk, leaning back on it with his arms folded. "What about your group? The one that meets in the coffee shop. Why not ask them first? We could use all of you. We don't want to break up a high-functioning group."

How did he know about that? They must have done a lot of work to find out all about them. He realized they'd been stalked, and he didn't even notice. Takuya cleared his throat. "OK, I'll ask them."

Imada gestured at the door. "I promise you, you'll like our terms."

"Terms?"

"Compensation." Imada swept his hands in the direction of the elevator.

Kurono appeared from somewhere and stood beside Imada. "All good?" he asked.

"All good," Imada answered.

All what? Takuya thought. He walked ahead of them to the elevator, got on, pushed the button, and stood against the wall.

As the doors closed, Kurono and Imada stood side by side in the hall, not bowing, not moving, but looking at him with their black eyes.

Chapter 26

Sugamo and Osaki did *janken* rock, scissors, paper to see who would drive. Sugamo lost and took the starter fob from Osaki. Outside, rush hour traffic had started, and headlights and streetlights were coming on already.

Hiroshi got in the back and opened the tube of maps and layouts of buildings managed by Kurono. He unrolled them over his lap and turned on his cell phone light to see better. Most places were just inside the Yamanote Line, clustering around Nippori, Nishi-Nippori, and Tabata Stations. Another group clustered near Komagome Station, where the Silver Center was.

He pulled up the photos of the same area he got from Keisuke. It was hard to see how anything lined up. The Silver Center was quite large compared to the smaller rectangles, but Hiroshi had no idea what he was looking at. It was all a tangle.

Osaki twisted over the back of the seat to see what Hiroshi was looking at. "It's the oldest part of an old city. What do you expect?"

"Those areas are going to be the first to catch fire and burn down in the next earthquake," Sugamo said. "My wife refused to live around there."

"Where did you decide on?"

"Out west." Sugamo braked for a car that cut in and then pulled forward. He looked in the rearview mirror. "Tokyo's a hundred cities, connected to the others by train."

Hiroshi put aside the pages with building rules, lists of repairs on heaters, elevators, water pipes, and structural updates for earthquake retrofits. He didn't remember asking for these. The office staff must have tucked them in there. They were as much of a tangle as the streets.

Osaki turned back to the front. "Are we going to check all of the management company's buildings?"

Hiroshi rolled everything up and stuffed it back in the storage tube. "Maybe not all. Something will connect before we get to the end."

"Let's hope so." Sugamo turned east onto the Shuto Expressway going north, the same route they'd been transversing, back and forth, the last two days.

Osaki said, "I thought we were getting something to eat." He started searching on his cell phone.

Sugamo looked at him. "You didn't say anything."

"One of the best ramen places in the city is back there."

"We're already on the expressway."

Osaki growled.

Hiroshi pulled up the map on his cell phone. "Ishii and I found the video cameras quickly this morning, and the tech guys will confirm it immediately. It might not take long. Then, we'll eat."

Osaki leaned back. "No, then something else will interfere."

Hiroshi leaned back in the seat and looked at the photos of the maps, trying to decide if there was a better or worse way to tackle the task. "Let's start with the ones by Nippori Station." Hiroshi held up his cell phone map.

"You can send the address directly." Sugamo tapped the car navigation screen. "Bluetooth."

Hiroshi fiddled with his phone, found the Bluetooth, connected to the device, and sent the address.

Ayana texted him, and Hiroshi pulled up the conversation.

"When do you have time to talk?" she wrote.

Hiroshi sat up and texted back. "Finally, you answered. I've been texting—"

"We need to talk. Not in between work, but when you can listen."

"Are you OK?"

"I'm fine, yes."

"Didn't you have a doctor's appointment today?"

"I called them."

"Are you staying there or coming back? Why—"

"I'll explain when we talk. Like we used to."

Used to? Hiroshi sighed. Had he gotten so bad?

Ayana stopped texting, and Hiroshi held the phone out, staring at it with the stupid hope there was more to the conversation—more positive—than he could figure out. He was the uncommunicative one, not her. She was always there. Was a fugue state part of her hormonal changes?

Despite all the stories he'd heard, Ayana was more reasonable after getting pregnant. Yes, she had a few picky food requests, but no complaints. She laughed at him for reading books about raising children, consulting sites on how to pick a name, and fretting about the future. Then, after her mother arrived, she took off for Nagoya without a word.

"Wife?" Osaki asked.

"We're not married."

"But she's pregnant?" Sugamo asked.

"Did your wives do anything unusual when they got pregnant?" Hiroshi shoved his cell phone into his pocket.

"My wife worked until the last minute, and once we finally found childcare, she returned to work." Osaki shook his head. "Now, I just worry about my daughter alone at home, but she likes to study. I can't believe all the programs she watches online, English, art, music, Japanese history."

Sugamo surveyed a long line of cars ahead. "Sons are easier. You worry less, maybe. My son sends me photos with emojis all day. I can't figure out what they mean half the time, but it doesn't matter. He loves sumo and sends me updates and news."

Takamatsu texted. Ishii had picked him up. He didn't say where he had been.

Hiroshi told them to meet at the first building on the list. They could be there in ten minutes, Takamatsu wrote.

Hiroshi called Nakada and told him to stand ready to check the feeds. Nakada seemed to be in the tech room every time he called.

Sugamo pulled up to the first building on the list, a ten-story building with a 1960's-era front that was well-kept and neatly retro. It was on a quiet corner closer to Tabata than Komagome.

Hiroshi got out and went in. Ishii parked behind Sugamo, got out, and opened the trunk. She'd brought an LED light on a tripod from the crime scene.

Takamatsu got out and lit a cigarette.

The building manager wore a well-washed uniform too large for his thin frame, but he was helpful and opened the door to the basement. He led them down into a basement where a light, steady flow of water had helped grow a big patch of muddy green mold.

Hiroshi watched where he stepped as he headed into the dark with Ishii right behind. She shone her light along the path, checking for spiderwebs.

Takamatsu came down but stayed in the dry area by the door. He fiddled with the LED light Ishii brought until he got it working. It cast light through the basement, illuminating discarded office furniture, old filing cabinets, and half-used buckets of paint. The place smelled of damp concrete and fresh mold.

Ishii roamed her flashlight before walking forward.

Osaki came down, and Takamatsu pushed him forward.

Hiroshi moved his flashlight in a circle. The basement ran to the left. Rectangular vents and insulated pipes crisscrossed the ceiling. Their flashlights threw shadows in all directions.

"There it is." Hiroshi shone his light on a little camera and caught a glint off the glass cover.

If the tech guys confirmed one camera feed, they would have another hit. But what would that mean? He called Nakada while Ishii kept her light on the camera.

Nakada answered right away. "Hey, take the light off the camera. Shine it to the side."

Hiroshi pushed Ishii's hand down.

Nakada said, "Another hit. Will you keep going?"

"We have a dozen more buildings," Hiroshi told him.

"I'll be here."

Hiroshi walked to the end of the basement. A set of stairs led to a landing with another door. He yelled to Takamatsu, "Get the keys to this door from the guard." His voice echoed from the basement walls.

Takamatsu took the keys from the guard and waited for Osaki to get them. Osaki jingled the keys as he trundled back, careful where he stepped.

Ishii took the key ring, bumped the two men aside, and went through the keys. She tried several until she found the right one, and the door swung open.

Hiroshi and Ishii walked up the stairs to the landing and turned right. The air was even mustier than in the basement they'd just traversed.

Osaki moved the light closer. "What do we do if we find another camera?"

Hiroshi kept going forward. "We check it off the list."

"But we still won't know why," Ishii said.

"We'll find something," Hiroshi said. "It'll connect."

Hiroshi looked at the map from Keisuke's office, but looking from the top and below felt too different. It seemed the two buildings were both managed by Kurono. The door must be a connecting passage. The concrete was newer around the door. Was it added later? Not part of the original building?

Hiroshi held his flashlight up as he walked into the cavernous space of the second building's basement. He looked for something to prop the door open. Osaki came in and pushed over an old car tire with his foot.

Inside the larger, high-ceilinged space, their footsteps echoed, and their lights seemed weaker. The worn lines and arrows on the dusty floor indicated it must have been a parking lot, but there were no cars. It was as dry and dusty as the first was wet and moldy.

Hiroshi called Nakada to check the video feeds on the computer. All three started roaming their flashlight beams through the murky, giant space, in and around the support pillars, and along the dingy walls. The concrete pillars were immense, like for some ancient temple.

Hiroshi called Nakada. "What do you see, Nakada? Anything?"

"There's a glimmer, but far away," Nakada said. "Walk forward and try again, can you?"

Hiroshi waved Osaki and Ishii forward, motioning for them to spread out.

"What's this space for?" Ishii asked. "Or what *was* it for?"

Osaki pointed the light at the wall. A thin line of mud ran across the concrete. "Must have flooded. I wouldn't want to be down here when it does."

Osaki's light went out. "Damn batteries. I have another in the car."

They moved forward on two flashlights.

Hiroshi stopped and called Nakada. "Anything?"

Nakada said, "It seems to come from below."

Hiroshi ran his light along the ceiling. "There?"

"Move forward a little and keep it pointing up."

Hiroshi waved Ishii forward.

Osaki stayed where he was.

"Here?"

Nakada said, "Yes, I think we have another one."

"We're on a roll," Ishii said.

"A roll towards what?" Osaki asked.

Hiroshi told Nakada, "Put that feed on the map."

"What map?" Nakada asked.

"The map I'll bring in in a little while."

Nakada laughed. "I'll be here all night."

"Don't you ever go home?"

"Home?" Nakada asked and hung up.

Hiroshi wondered if he slept in the office like he'd been doing before he moved in with Ayana. He'd ask him next time, tell him to get a life, to find a woman like Ayana, and not work so much.

Hiroshi looked around the empty underground space one last time.

When he turned around, Ishii was talking on the phone.

Ishii hung up and looked at him. "We need to go."

She took off for the door. Hiroshi got to the door in time to see her running through the hallway, careful not to slip on the floor. At the end of the basement, she brushed past Takamatsu without a word and headed upstairs.

Chapter 27

Halfway there, Ishii put on the siren, and Sugamo did the same. Police cars and ambulance trucks filled the road below Keisuke's real estate office. Red and white lights spun in circles, illuminating the trees and buildings. The acrid smell of smoke saturated the evening air.

Near the Silver Center, a crowd had gathered in the blocked-off street. The crime scene crew had cordoned off a wide swath of the street and put up tarps to block the media. Ishii parked halfway on the curb, and Sugamo pulled up right behind. Ishii bounded upstairs to Keisuke's office. Smoke had left black marks up from the windows. Takamatsu got out, lit a cigarette, and spoke to the detective at the bottom of the stairs up to Keisuke's real estate office.

Stretching from the back of the firetrucks, high-pressure hoses crisscrossed the street outside the building. Two box-shaped ambulances spilled bright light from their rear doors. In one, a crew was working around a patient on the gurney. From an overhead rack, IVs and oxygen lines dangled at the ready.

Hiroshi looked in the ambulance truck. Was that Keisuke? He asked a crew member standing at the back doors. "Can I talk with him?"

"He's been beaten very badly. In and out of consciousness. Can't it wait?" the ambulance crew member blocked his view. She looked remarkably young.

"Is that Keisuke Sugata?"

The head of the ambulance crew came over. "We just gave him something for the pain. We need to get him to the hospital right away, or you may never have a chance to talk again."

Hiroshi snagged a mask from a tray and headed for the entrance to Keisuke's building. He felt like he was being stalked.

Every place he visited, something happened.

Firefighters carried extinguishers and a smoking trash can down the stairs. The sickening smell of burning plastic filled the room. Hiroshi started coughing even with the mask.

Black smoke marks stretched like tornados up the wall. Papers were strewn in all directions, and notebooks ripped from the shelves lay open with pages burned, soaked, or torn.

"What happened?" Hiroshi asked one of the firefighters.

The firefighter looked up. "It wasn't very professional. Is that what you're asking?"

"How does an amateur start a fire?" Hiroshi asked.

"Without accelerant."

"Was it an accident?"

They both shook their heads. "The only professional thing they did was to start it in several places. That helps it get going."

"So, they knew what they were doing?"

"Not the best fire I've seen, but efficient enough."

"Can you give me all you have on this?"

"We'll have more for you tomorrow." The firefighter went back to checking all the possible surfaces that could reignite.

Ishii started coughing. She waved her hand and went downstairs, and Hiroshi followed. They met Takamatsu and Osaki coming up and waved them back downstairs.

Downstairs by the ambulances and firetrucks, Hiroshi looked through his cell phone for the phone number of Keisuke's nephew, which he'd gotten when they'd met in the office.

He called and looked at Takamatsu, who, for once, wasn't fiddling with his lighter. He left a message for the nephew.

When he finished the message, Takamatsu said, "That old guy, Keisuke Sugata. I was wrong about him."

"You suspected him?" Ishii asked.

Takamatsu shook his head. "The skateboard kid has been following him, taking videos."

Ishii and Hiroshi frowned in unison.

"The videos are a bit shaky, but they're clear enough. He's who he said he is. My mistake." Takamatsu shrugged.

Hiroshi leaned close to Takamatsu. "You're going to screw up this whole investigation with stunts like that. How could you think bringing in teenagers was clever? Not even Sakaguchi can protect you if someone—"

"All I did was tell them where Sugata was, and the kids did the rest." Takamatsu looked more contrite than Hiroshi had ever seen.

"Why didn't they let you know?"

Takamatsu nodded. "They're just helping us. They're our eyes. They're not cops. They couldn't have stopped this."

"That doesn't make it OK." Hiroshi wanted to shout, but the scene was filled with young detectives, firefighters, and local police.

"The skateboarders cover a lot of territory, and you don't notice them. We should start a special brigade." Takamatsu didn't sound so sure.

"You can work on that when you're on probation again."

Ishii intervened. "Did they find anything?"

Takamatsu gestured like Ishii was being reasonable. "One group watched Keisuke, and another waited outside Kurono's office. That was harder because he drives—"

"Maybe Takamatsu's right. We can't keep searching basements." Ishii looked from Takamatsu to Hiroshi.

Takamatsu nodded. "These kids trail people well. No one notices them. I told them to stay at a distance and contact me about anything at all."

Hiroshi was shout-whispering, watching for any of the police higher-ups. They sometimes showed up for photos. "The skateboarders, the ones who didn't let you know about this, where are they now?"

Takamatsu checked his phone.

Hiroshi stared at Takamatsu. "Do you think any of this will be admissible as evidence?"

"What does it matter if it works?" Takamatsu fiddled with his phone.

"It matters if that's the only evidence, and it's inadmissible, and we have to let the guy go."

"So, you don't want me to show you what they just sent me?" Takamatsu took his cell phone out. "Their videos are a bit shaky."

Ishii reached out for the phone. "Let me see."

Takamatsu handed her the phone, and Hiroshi crowded over to see. Five men in masks broke the lock and went inside. In a few minutes, smoke came out of an opened window. In a few more minutes, they came back down. A tall, thin man stood to the side of the door.

Hiroshi looked at Takamatsu. "You can't see their faces."

Takamatsu shrugged. Ishii handed the phone back to him.

Hiroshi heard raised voices from the other side of the ambulance, and he walked around to see.

Setsuko stood at the back of the ambulance talking with a young detective who had her arms spread to keep her from the back door of the ambulance.

Hiroshi felt Ishii brush by him. She wrapped an arm around Setsuko.

Hiroshi looked around for Takamatsu, but he was already gone.

Ishii looked over Setsuko's head at Hiroshi while she whispered to Setsuko.

Setsuko nodded at whatever Ishii had told her and straightened herself.

Ishii turned to Hiroshi. "Setsuko has several things she needs to say."

Setsuko's face was wrinkled in a way it hadn't been under the light of the office. Hiroshi had thought her youngish for her age, but now, he could see all the worries of her life and—when she closed her eyes and took a breath—the fear.

Setsuko wiped her eyes with her palms and snuffled. "This isn't the first time."

Hiroshi leaned closer. "First time for what?"

Setsuko spoke louder. "For him to be attacked."

Hiroshi looked at Ishii.

Ishii shook her head. It was the first she'd heard about this too, it seemed.

Setsuko sighed. "He's so stubborn he can drive you crazy." Setsuko looked at the ambulance. "My husband died. I thought I was done with all that. But our feelings blossomed. That's how it works at any age, isn't it?"

Hiroshi waved over one of the young detectives. "I'll have one of the detectives accompany you, and we'll put a guard on the door. It would be best if you had someplace safe. So, the attacks?"

"Keisuke didn't tell me much. He was beaten up one time. Bruised so badly he wouldn't let me see. When I finally saw him, he was still in bad shape. He said, 'Just part of being a real estate agent.' That kind of macho stuff."

"Why was he beaten?"

"It was after he started attending city meetings."

"What meetings?" Hiroshi asked.

Setsuko shook her head. "He disrupted so many meetings that they banned him."

"What meetings?"

Setsuko shook her head. "At the city office. I thought it was just regulations, new laws about abandoned buildings, ownership, boring real estate stuff."

"But it was something more?" Hiroshi asked.

"Someone caught him alone near his office."

Ishii prodded Setsuko. "Tell him about the disturbances at the Silver Center."

Setsuko nodded. "We had one rather disturbed individual who kept showing up at many of our functions. He wasn't that old, young for the Center. He interrupted a lot of events. Keisuke helped to quiet him down."

"Quiet him?"

"But one day, there was a big argument, and the local police came, but it seemed resolved. I guess it wasn't. I didn't think it would be like this."

"The disruptive guy was angry? Threatening?"

"Very threatening. He said he was from around here, but he didn't know anyone, didn't even know the area." Setsuko's words tumbled out. "I told Keisuke to stay quiet, but he doesn't listen. He does what he wants. The more he complained at meetings, the more that guy came around. Keisuke did get the *sento* public bath designated as an important property. He tried for a higher cultural level but at least got it protected from demolition."

Hiroshi felt confused. "That sounds like a good thing."

"Some people disagreed. Protesters gathered."

"In front of the bath?" Hiroshi looked at Ishii, but she had not heard any of that story.

"They wanted to stop the restoration of the bath building. You'd think that wouldn't be controversial." Setsuko looked down. "They were not locals."

Hiroshi waited.

Setsuko looked up. "I want to be at the hospital when he wakes up."

Hiroshi nodded at Ishii, who walked her off to find a car accompanied by one of the younger detectives.

Sakaguchi arrived. He climbed out of the car in a long wool coat, making him look larger than usual. He wore an extra-large mask, which still looked small on his large, round head. He was immediately besieged by the crime scene crew, each vying for his signature on their forms. Hiroshi walked over to update him.

"How is this connected to the *hikikomori* kid and the fatal accident two days ago?" Sakaguchi passed a clipboard back to one of the crew members. He turned to Hiroshi and Takamatsu. "And why do more things keep piling on to this case?"

Hiroshi wanted an answer to that himself. "We used to hide everything from the last chief so he wouldn't screw it up. But we don't have to do that with you. The more that happens, the closer we're getting."

"You're starting to sound like Takamatsu," Sakaguchi said.

"I'm starting to feel like him too."

Chapter 28

Takuya walked from Roppongi, vaping and wondering what Imada wanted beyond what he said. Imada was Tokyo through and through, saying one thing, meaning something else, talking only to people who could help him, and calculating on multiple levels. It made him miss the countryside.

Imada's condescending attitude was like coming to Tokyo with Yasui all over again. Tokyo people took every chance to look down on anyone not born there, and people like Imada doubled that, being from Tokyo and being wealthy.

What sounded good from Imada was the income and the chance to move out of scamming. Times were catching up with scammers, and public information was spreading. Murayama and Noguchi were already looking ahead, he knew. He and Yasui needed to do the same.

It would be nice to tap into Imada's network, wealth, and real estate, where the profits were sky-high. He had had enough of running on a broken heel through back alleys. Now, he had to figure out precisely what Imada asked him to do.

He turned north on Sakurada-dori Street. Tall scaffolding lined both sides of the road, rerouting pedestrians with sand-filled plastic barriers, warning lights, and carefully placed mats. That was one thing he never got over in Tokyo—the constant construction. Instinctually, he eyed the gate to the construction site, locked for the night.

Near Toranomon, the buildings stretched up taller. Maybe the future of Tokyo was up, as Imada said.

He cut toward Shinbashi. The smaller, more affordable drinking spots, eateries, and nightlife venues were opening up for the night. Shop owners and touts were putting out street signs to drag foot traffic inside. Misaki or one of the so-called OL Office

Ladies would be doing the same outside her shop.

As he got close to Shinbashi, he saw people waiting outside the station, checking their cell phones. The Yamanote Line and all other trains north and south had stopped because of a "human incident," a euphemism for suicide. He could take a subway, but there were several transfers and two long walks to Misaki's OLzakaya.

He headed for a narrow street parallel to the train tracks and turned in a *tachinomi* standing bar filled with salarymen. They had the same idea—drink and eat until the trains got sorted out. The bar had a counter running along the walls, wide enough for a beer mug and two small dishes.

Takuya ordered *nanbanzuke* deep-fried mackerel drowned in vinegar and onions, *tamagoyaki* fried, rolled egg, and a large mug of beer. The counter staff handed them over the counter with a small potato salad dish and a teensy dish with a few edamame.

He carried them to the corner, ignoring the loud banter of the salaryman, and took a soothing slug of beer. He worried he should have told Imada yes from the beginning. He said no, but not a firm no. Imada was a businessman. He'd understand the need to think things over. Negotiations took time.

Misaki called. He took another slug of beer before answering. He wanted to tell her the good news about Imada's offer of better money and easier work.

"Takuya, come quick!" Misaki's voice sounded strangled and whispery. "It's terrible."

"That new cook didn't work out? I knew he—"

"No, it's bad, awful. Just come. Now."

Takuya set his beer down. Misaki sounded like she was about to cry.

"Where are you? I need you here now."

"All right, I'm coming."

She hung up.

Probably one of the girls slugged a customer. He choked down a slice of mackerel and finished the egg with two neat cuts of his chopsticks. He washed it down with the rest of the beer and hurried out toward the station.

He looked up at the overhead platform. A train was still stalled on the tracks. The taxi line stretched along the front of the station. An announcement said the trains would restart operations in another thirty minutes.

A taxi pulled across the street under the tracks to let out a passenger. Takuya hurried over and pushed into the back seat before the door shut. The driver started to complain until Takuya handed a five-thousand-yen note over the seat.

When they got close to Misaki's, he directed the taxi driver as close as possible. The narrow streets of small eateries and love hotels were blocked off.

"That'll be three thousand two hundred," the driver said.

"I just gave you a five-thousand-yen note," Takuya protested.

"That was to let you in before all the people waiting in line." The old driver looked at him in the rearview mirror.

Takuya handed over two thousand yen. "This'll have to do." He opened the door and hurried toward the OLzakaya.

Around the next turn, he saw the rhythmic flash of police lights. Two firetrucks angled across the street and local police directed traffic. Misaki was talking to the police. Two of the waitresses huddled under blankets. A third stood smoking to the side under a man's jacket. The smell of smoke filled the street.

He pushed forward towards Misaki. The front window of her shop was busted. Black soot spiraled along the outside wall. The far window was shattered, and though he couldn't see too far inside, he could see the interior was destroyed.

He nodded to the police and took Misaki in his arms. He pulled off his coat, draped it over her shoulders, and leaned down to her. "What happened?"

The local cop held up his pad. "Who are you?"

Misaki straightened up. "This is my boyfriend."

The cop folded his notebook shut. "We can talk in my car."

"Just a minute, OK?" Misaki pushed Takuya aside.

"Was it that new cook?" Takuya worried about the kitchen. If it had burned, he was screwed. Insurance would cover everything but the money hidden in the ceiling.

Misaki pulled him further. "These guys came in from the back. They lit a fire that made it look like the kitchen…"

"Where was the cook?"

"He must have run off."

He must have been the one to let in the guys, Takuya thought.

"After the kitchen caught fire, I got the girls out front."

"And then?"

"They came in the back door and started to break the place up. It only took a few minutes, and then they took off."

"Did they set fire in the front too?"

"I guess. I don't know. I couldn't see. And then the firetrucks and police came and pushed us away." Misaki burrowed into Takuya's chest.

Smoke was still trickling out, the smell horrible.

Takuya pulled Misaki tighter. "Tell me what they looked like."

Misaki continued. "There were five of them. The main guy stood outside."

Noguchi pulled up on his motorcycle and parked across the street. Takuya felt a wave of relief he was there.

"Did they touch you? The guys who came in."

"Just Nami."

Takuya looked at her, wrapped in a blanket, waiting patiently. Nami worked as a plus-size model and part-time at the OLzakaya. She was the only one who had actually been an OL office lady. She hated it.

"Nami started bashing them in the head with a tray."

Takuya smiled at her.

Takuya wanted to go inside to check, but the cops probably wouldn't let him in. The firefighters were still inside.

Misaki wiped her eyes. "What am I supposed to tell the police?"

"Tell them what they look like so they can find them."

A detective came over and asked Misaki to step into the car. Takuya watched the firefighters work through the mess. He vaped and glanced at Noguchi, not wanting to get him involved until the cops left.

After fifteen minutes, Misaki got out of the detective's car and walked back.

Takuya draped his coat over her shoulders. "I'll stay here and lock up. Why don't you go home?"

Misaki pulled his coat tight. "Here's a list of places that will put plywood over the windows and a locksmith. The detective gave it to me."

"Go home. Shower. Sleep. I'll call them. Noguchi will help." He looked over at Noguchi and saw that Murayama had come too. They stood talking quietly. He felt better with them there. They had work to do.

Misaki finally started to cry.

Takuya wrapped her in a hug. He didn't want to say it was OK because it wasn't, but maybe the money he'd hidden in the ceiling would be there. That was the main thing. He looked over at Nami. "Nami will walk you back."

Nami took Misaki's arm, and Misaki let herself be walked away.

A police officer came over and gave him permission to go inside.

He turned on his cell phone flashlight and walked in with his handkerchief over his mouth. The front room was in shambles, with tables and chairs knocked over, glassware smashed, liquor bottles busted, and the front counter kicked in. He picked his way to the back room.

The room divider to the closet, which served as an office, was torn off its track. Inside, invoices, bills, orders, and receipts had been stomped to mush on the wet floor.

He went to the kitchen and the storage area. The back door stood open. Inside, cases of beer had been overturned, the bottles broken. Tomato juice splashed out from a box. Cans of spices spilled over the floor.

He climbed on one of the shelves and pushed up a tile in the ceiling. He climbed up one more shelf and poked his head inside the dropdown space.

The lock boxes were still there, all three of them. He should have moved them further from the gas range. He should have moved them out long ago. He didn't even tell Misaki it was there. The ten-thousand-yen notes would be safe, but he couldn't carry it out with the police there. He'd have to figure out how to lock the place up and wait to get it later.

He returned to the front door and pulled out the list of service providers. If he could get someone to board up the windows and call in a locksmith, he could sort out the rest in the morning. He got to work calling from the front sidewalk.

The police lingered for a while, promised to stop by during the night, and left.

Once the police left, Noguchi and Murayama came over.

Noguchi spoke first. "Is this because you told Imada yes or because you told him no?"

Hearing Noguchi's question, Takuya quit denying it. Maybe the cook was part of it, but Imada had something to do with this. Or he sent Kurono. He seemed like the one Imada wanted them to replace so he could stay safe while they handled the messy work, like setting fire to places.

But if this was Kurono's work, how did he set it up so quickly? He must have had it planned long before he even talked with Imada.

Takuya looked at them. "I told Imada I'd think about it."

Noguchi peered inside at the damage. "It's good you didn't tell him no. The whole block would have burned down."

Chapter 29

Takamatsu, as always, knew the woman behind the cash register at the *kushiage* restaurant. She dropped her glasses on a strap and took Takamatsu's elbow to lead them upstairs. Her patterned skirt and lace sweater were as traditional and neat as the rest of the interior. Hiroshi, Osaki, and Ishii followed wearily behind. The rich aroma of deep-fried battered vegetables and breaded meat followed them from the first-floor kitchen.

The wood stairs creaked under everyone's weight. Ishii used the handrail, her fatigue showing. Osaki stopped halfway up the stairs to take a call, saying the restaurant's name and nothing more.

The private rooms upstairs lined the hallway across from narrow serving tables with a steamer of hot *oshibori* towels, neat rows of small beer glasses, and upside-down sake cups.

The owner chuckled at whatever Takamatsu was saying. A waitress hustled out from the prep room, wiping her hands and bowing to the orders the owner briskly delivered. Osaki scrunched in the booth, and Ishii and Hiroshi slid along the cushioned bench. Takamatsu hung his coat on a thick peg on the outside post, smoothed it out, and squeezed in next to Osaki.

Osaki moved closer to the wall. "Sakaguchi's coming in a few minutes."

Takamatsu pulled out his cigarettes and leaned in the corridor to call for an ashtray.

Ishii started studying the menu.

Takamatsu waved his unlit cigarette at the menu. "She already ordered for us."

Ishii put the menu back.

The waitress brought them steaming *oshibori* towels and handed them over one by one, deftly popping the plastic and pushing out the towels. She crumpled the plastic, rushed off, and returned with beer bottles and small glasses.

Osaki grasped the beer bottle and took charge of pouring the first round. They toasted, and everyone leaned back to down the bubbly relief, nestling their tired limbs in the *zabuton* pillows against the thick wood of the booth. Osaki poured another round, and they downed those just as quickly.

"One of the oldest *kushiage* places in Tokyo," Takamatsu said. "Couldn't let Ishii outdo me."

Hiroshi felt instantly lightheaded from the beer. He hoped another glass would bring him back, but the fatigue fell on him like a weight. He hadn't drunk any water or eaten anything all day. What was he thinking? Ayana would ask him, and he'd have to lie that, yes, he was taking good care of himself while she was gone.

He wondered if what Takamatsu often said was true, that distracting his mind made it work better. Sometimes, looking away revealed the patterns that let him finish investment scams or company embezzlement cases. But he first had to load it all into his mind. Sleeping, eating, or doing something else lets the connections emerge.

But with this case, a drink or a good night's sleep wasn't likely to do much if there was nothing to work on in his mind in the first place. He had only bits and pieces that didn't fit together. The video basement feeds were particularly confusing.

At least the food and drink made sense.

The waitress arrived with small dishes of green cucumber, white daikon, and black eggplant pickles. Another waiter, Asian but not Japanese, passed around plates, chopsticks, and a brown ceramic container for the used skewers. Takamatsu told her more people were coming, and she brought more dishes for them.

The two waitresses worked to set out flat plates with thick miso, salt, and sauce for dipping. The head waitress handed over bowls of square-cut cabbage, daikon radish, carrots, and cucumber from the second server. Their raw, fresh texture was the perfect balance for the deep-fried skewers.

Hiroshi thought he felt the first tremor of an earthquake. The floorboards of the old building creaked and rolled. But it was just Sakaguchi coming up the stairs. The second waitress, maybe from Southeast Asia, bowed and pointed him in the right direction.

Sakaguchi peeled off his overcoat and hung it up beside Takamatsu's.

After Sakaguchi wiped his hands, the waitress handed him a second hot towel. He needed two.

Osaki poured beer for Sakaguchi and then for everyone else again. They toasted silently, too tired to reach out for a touch of glasses.

"Sugamo had to hurry home to watch his kids so his wife could go care for her mother." Sakaguchi sighed and poured himself a refill.

The waitress brought a large round serving platter filled with deep-fried skewers of vegetables and meat. Each one trembled slightly beneath the crinkly golden-brown breading. Everyone reached for their favorites, dipped them in their favorite sauce, and crunched into them.

They ate silently, dipping each skewer in the miso, salt, or sauce, thinking, not thinking, and washing it down with beer before sliding the empty skewers into the container and reaching for the next.

Hiroshi tried to balance the pork and beef with yam, squash, lotus root, and bitter melon, but he felt his body was deprived of everything. He felt too tired to chew, but the taste kept his jaw moving. The waitress brought a special plate of deep-fried seafood, shrimp, scallops, and small river shrimp.

There wasn't much to talk about, and there was everything to talk about. Even Takamatsu was quiet. He finally broke the silence by ordering sake.

The head waitress set out a row of small glasses in saucers and plopped a big brown bottle on the table. Hiroshi tried to read the label, but the calligraphy was too artistic to decipher. With the younger waitress watching, the waitress hoisted the bottle in one arm, plucked off the cap, and poured sake into the five glasses without spilling a drop over the edge of the saucers. She plopped the top on and carried the bottle off like a bell.

They toasted.

Hiroshi felt the cold sake chase the deep-fried vegetables into his inner being.

Another plate of *kushiage* skewers arrived, radiating like spokes on a wheel of culinary delight. The second server brought another plateful, moving the last two uneaten skewers to the new plate.

Sakaguchi turned to Hiroshi. "So, Hiroshi, what about the basement video feeds?"

Takamatsu groaned.

Osaki and Ishii kept eating.

Hiroshi took another sip of sake. "Maybe the tech guys will find something."

Takamatsu said, "I think they're too professional to find things that way. The videos show us masks, not faces. Masks are a low-tech defense against a high-tech search. Low-tech always wins."

"Maybe the basement videos were something legit," Sakaguchi said before sinking his teeth into a breaded shrimp, slipping it off the skewer with bared teeth.

Hiroshi slid his empty skewer into the container. "Could be it was some security thing."

"From a kid?" Takamatsu finished his sake. "The guard said that the building was just sold. He was being let go at the end of the month. Those are pretty old buildings."

"Earthquake standards?" Ishii suggested. She took a skewer of lotus root. "Companies who want to develop an area push to enforce strict earthquake regulations."

"Isn't that good?" Osaki asked.

Ishii finished her lotus root, nodding. "Yes, of course. But it favors new developers with deep pockets."

Takamatsu smiled at her.

Ishii caught his smile. "It was Keisuke who told me that."

Hiroshi thought about that. "They use safety concerns as leverage to tear down instead of retrofitting. They manage the building, tear it down, build it back, and then manage that."

Takamatsu nodded. "Repurposing land is the prime skill of Tokyo developers."

Hiroshi said, "I think that guy Keisuke probably knows more than he lets on."

Takamatsu took another sip of sake. "He probably knows the whole area in detail, which buildings are going to be torn down, which sold, which owners are the most stubborn."

Osaki cleared his throat. "That's just business as usual. Not a motive for murder."

Ishii finished the last of her sake. "I think Keisuke's trying to keep the community in place. I'm more confused about the videos. It seems like a lot of effort to make, monitor, and store them."

Osaki slid another skewer into the container. "The basements don't hold vital info, do they? Even if we figure out where they all are."

Sakaguchi poked his head outside the booth, and the waitress came right over. "Another round of sake."

She brought the same sake again, with fresh glasses. Everyone pulled them carefully along the table, trying not to spill. They were way past toasts.

Sakaguchi drained his glass and set it down. "We need to see who owns what."

Hiroshi said, "I'm going to the lands and deeds office tomorrow."

Ishii said, "I'll go with you."

"I think you should stick with the Silver Center for now. The two deaths must be connected through there." Sakaguchi looked at her. "And someone's got to talk to Keisuke. If he wakes up."

Ishii and Hiroshi both nodded.

Sakaguchi nodded. "What about the delivery health girl?"

Hiroshi shook his head. "No word."

Sakaguchi said. "We need to follow up on her."

Hiroshi hoped Takamatsu wouldn't make a joke about it, but he looked tired.

Takamatsu finished his sake. "You must look for the precise moment when one detail clicks it all into place."

Hiroshi stared at his empty sake cup. "We're a long way from that point."

The waitress brought bowls filled with slivers of black *hijiki* sea vegetable and dried kelp on a bed of rice. She went back for a large teapot from which she poured thick green tea on each. The tea filled the bowls, softening the rice and unleashing the sea-salt smell of the kelp and *hijiki*.

Everyone took their spoon and dug into the warm, mushy mix, hoping it would solve something inside, if not outside.

Chapter 30

Hiroshi hadn't wanted Ishii to go with him back to headquarters. He wanted to get some work done on his own, but she insisted. When they returned to the annex building, the halls were quieter than he'd heard in a while. The construction was done for the night.

Akiko had left a stack of folders on his desk and layers of stickie notes on the back of his two monitors. He flipped through them, looking for insights, updates, or reversals, but there wasn't much more than follow-ups on old cases, details that would have helped months ago, forgotten forms, and missing info he needed to send.

At the door, Ishii looked a little peaked, mumbled, "I'll be back," and walked down the hall.

As soon as she was gone, Hiroshi took a moment to call Ayana. She picked up right away.

"Did I wake you up?"

"I was awake."

Hiroshi could tell she'd been asleep, but he let it go. It was his fault for calling late.

"It's my mother." Ayana hesitated. "I'm not sure how to—."

"Just say it." Hiroshi waited while she figured out how.

"My mother has cancer."

"What? What...what kind? Why didn't you—"

"I didn't know. It spread quickly. She only found out two weeks ago. She didn't tell me until we were here."

"I thought she came because of the baby."

"She did. But also because of this. I went with her to the hospital today."

Hiroshi flopped into his chair.

"The doctors were helpful, but they said the next step was

easing the pain. She refused medication."

"She's tough. Like you."

"Not like me." Ayana snuffled but wasn't crying. "She wanted to be with me before deciding what to do."

"Isn't there something they can do?"

"They have a new type of chemotherapy. I guess they always do. So, she'd be a test case. And she'll have to go twice a week. But it might be too late."

"Why not try it?"

Ayana was silent.

Hiroshi waited. "Let me come to Nagoya."

"There's nothing you can do here."

"I can be with you."

"No, you're busy."

"This is what we talked about. Taking more time for important things, for us."

"This isn't me or us. It's my mother. You don't even know her."

"I want to come."

"No."

Hiroshi stayed quiet. He'd never heard Ayana talk like that. "You must be upset."

"Of course I'm upset."

Hiroshi decided to stay quiet. He was irritating her. He was drunk, and it was late. He'd woken her up. "I hope she can hang on until the baby's born."

"What kind of thing is that to say?"

Hiroshi tried to think of what to say that wouldn't make it worse but couldn't, so decided to say nothing.

"She looks so old." Ayana blew her nose. It didn't sound like she was crying, but he couldn't tell. He hadn't heard her cry all that often.

"Don't we have another appointment for a check-up next week?"

"I'll change the date. I'll do everything."

"I was just going to offer to change it."

"Have your secretary Akiko change the time, you mean?"

"I don't have her do personal things. I—"

"You wanted to help. That's what you always say, but all you do is work."

Hiroshi stopped and waited, but maybe being quiet was worse. "You can bring your mother to the apartment if you want. Move her to Tokyo."

Ayana coughed. "Bring her to our apartment for hospice while I'm giving birth? Great idea, Hiroshi. Maybe we can find one home care worker to do both."

Ayana being sarcastic was something Hiroshi hadn't encountered much, either. She joked, but with the situation, never angrily. "I thought your mother had a sister?"

"They're not close, but she's going to call her. She's not close to anyone. Me included."

"You're there now. She came to get you."

Ayana sighed.

Hiroshi knew she was lying on her back. Her voice sounded different. "Let me do something," he pleaded. He had no idea what he could do.

"I didn't bring enough clothes."

"I'll bring you some."

"You'll get the wrong ones."

"I can—"

"I wish she'd told me all this before." Ayana sighed. "At least there's an extra room here. I've got to sleep. We'll talk tomorrow." Ayana hung up.

Hiroshi watched his phone revert to the photo of her he used as the main screen. Did they just have an argument? Hiroshi wanted to call her back to be sure. They never argued.

Or maybe he just never noticed. Even when they did have a misunderstanding, she was always there to make up afterward. This time, all he was left with were words.

He started checking the Shinkansen schedule to Nagoya. He could catch the first Shinkansen train there in the morning around seven.

He looked up to see Ishii standing in the doorframe.

"Everything OK?" she asked.

Hiroshi wasn't sure how long she'd been listening, but he didn't want to get into it.

Ishii looked at the stack of folders. "I'm falling asleep."

"Only two ways to go. Futon chair or espresso." Hiroshi pointed at his two emotional supports.

Ishii went to the futon chair.

"The pillow flips up. Undo the velcro."

Ishii pulled the pillow around, slipped off her shoes, unfolded the blanket, pulled it over her, and fell asleep before Hiroshi could whisper, "*Oyasumi nasai*, good night."

Hiroshi pulled out the black tubes of rolled-up maps and building diagrams. Another rolled map sat to the side. Akiko must have printed it on the main office's big printer. It was so big it fell over the side of his desk.

Most of the younger detectives used online apps that focused in and out, but the paper let your eyes roam without resizing the image. The big paper map allowed you to look until you internalized it.

Ishii started snoring.

He looked at each station along the northeast section of the Yamanote Line. The buildings were clustered around Nippori, Nishi-Nippori, and Tabata Stations. And what of the management company? On the one hand, it was just a map of one company's business.

Kurono was managing buildings spread out in different areas, some near the stations, some a fair walk away. Hiroshi shuffled the maps and tried to connect the dots. He looked at the Silver Center, Keisuke's office, the bank, and the neighborhood. He clicked on his computer and typed, "Silver Centers *shitamachi*."

Several popped up. He tried to see how they fit.

As a Go player, you sometimes didn't see the pattern until it was too late. The most skillful opponents wouldn't telegraph the pattern they were constructing. Just the opposite, they would distract you from seeing it until there was no defense and the surrounding pieces fell in place.

Ishii snorted, coughed, and dropped back into the rhythm of deep sleep.

Hiroshi looked up to see the tech guy Nakada hunched by the door. He whispered, "It's nice you still use paper. It's an amazing technology."

Nakada tiptoed in, casting an eye at Ishii sleeping. He had a laptop under his arm and looked for a place to set it down.

"How did you know I was here?"

Nakada shrugged.

Hiroshi waved Nakada to Akiko's chair. Did the guy ever sleep? He didn't look tired in the least.

"I think I might have found something." Nakada sat down and opened his laptop. "Do you know what video masking is?"

Hiroshi scooted over, shaking his head, as Nakada's computer sprang to life.

Nakada looked at his screen and around the room. "Your Wi-Fi's not so good."

"Can you fix that for me?"

"I'll send a mesh router down for you." Nakada surveyed the room.

"Video masking?"

Nakada hunched forward. "So, every photo, every video, has its own DNA. I used to work in the child pornography section. We could track how most images were sent. They were often masked."

"What does that mean?"

"One on top of another. Of course, it's not physically on top. It's all digital. Once you start unmasking, it's easy, but sometimes, even the layers are layered, with the worst at the bottom."

"Worst what?"

"For the porn, the worst image." Nakada stopped and looked away from his laptop. "Homicide is much easier to take than child porn. I'm glad I transferred." Nakada moved his laptop around. "Let me show you."

Hiroshi scooted over to see. A video of the basement started. It could have been any one of the basements they'd just wandered through.

"This is just the top layer. The *hikikomori* guy was very sophisticated. He masked them in several ways."

"I don't get the masking."

"Masking is simply putting one video on top of another. Like wrapping a present digitally. You peel off the outside layer, and underneath is another layer."

"Is that hard to do?"

"Standard masking software."

"There's software for that?"

"There's software for everything." Nakada pressed a button, and the video of the basement switched to a video of a busy lobby, with people coming in and out. Nakada pressed another button, and the lobby switched to an entryway with part of the sidewalk visible.

"These are all on top of one another?" Hiroshi leaned back.

Nakada nodded.

"So instead of two dozen cameras, we now have...how many?"

"Potentially infinite, but the ones I cracked open go three layers deep." Nakada hummed in appreciation. "He used all the cameras to cover the other cameras. So clever."

"We'll give him a posthumous prize." Now Hiroshi was being sarcastic. "So, how do you find the layers underneath?"

"Peel them off one by one. You can undo some of the layers on some software, but then you have to know which software or technique to use for the other layers. It's not that complex technically, but he did it well. Like having a password for other passwords."

"He hid the important videos underneath the basement videos?"

Nakada nodded. "Only he would know where—and how—they were hidden, though."

Hiroshi looked at the video of the lobby on Nakada's laptop and looked at Nakada. Maybe the videos had nothing significant in the bottom layer. Or perhaps they held the connection he couldn't see from the maps. "So now we have to look at all the videos again?"

"If all the layers are from one building, it might not take long. We can peel back the digital layers and then run each layer through a motion sensor separately. But what are we looking for?"

"Repeat visitors, a building inspection, a disturbance, repairs…anything."

"Broad parameters." Nakada shut his laptop quietly and stood up. "With child porn, it was always some small detail that cracked the layers of nothingness. Maybe it'll be the same here. Let me try."

Ishii turned over, gurgling, and pulled the blanket over her head.

Hiroshi looked at her enviously.

Chapter 31

Hiroshi's cheekbone throbbed as he lifted his head and squinted into the harsh light. The world was sideways. Pain rattled through his skull. The source of the light seemed to be Akiko. Hiroshi squinted and groaned as Akiko set her bag on her desk. "Back to your old habits," she said, heading to the espresso machine.

Hiroshi leaned back in his chair, watching her push the foldout futon chair against the wall, turn on the espresso machine, and press grind. His eyeballs felt like someone had dried them with a towel. He had eyedrops somewhere.

As Akiko's espresso dripped, the revitalizing morning smell reached him. He felt his body resign itself to being awake.

From somewhere in the building, the rat-a-tat of a jackhammer kicked against concrete.

They groaned in unison.

Akiko nodded at the foldout futon chair. "You slept here all night?"

"Ishii did." The blanket was neatly folded on the pillow.

A quick frown passed over Akiko's face as she handed him a double espresso.

As he sipped the espresso, he thought of Ayana smiling across the kitchen island. He still wondered about what she'd said. He couldn't tell how angry she was. He checked his cell phone, but there were no messages.

Akiko was making another espresso for herself when the room rattled. The crunch-thud of a sledgehammer gave way to a loud, heavy crumpling as something fell over in the hallway just below. The sound was closer than before.

"Are they coming up to our landing?" Hiroshi asked.

"The notice said all the hallways would be refurbished. I guess that includes the stairwells." Akiko pulled the carpet over the door and sat down to focus on her espresso.

Hiroshi tapped his keyboard. His screen, at least, woke right up. He stood to stretch. His throat felt as dry as his eyeballs. He needed water, inside and out.

The jackhammer went back to work. It was so loud Hiroshi had to wave to Akiko as he dragged the carpet aside and walked out. He headed down the underground passageway to the locker room. A few other detectives were getting dressed and washing off the night shift with a shower.

The shower felt restorative. The cold water dispenser in the drying area offered just what he needed. He looked in the mirror, which was fogged over. Just the way he felt. He had to put on the same clothes, which felt grungy. He hoped he had at least a new shirt back in his office.

He grunted hello to some of the younger detectives as he walked through the underground passageway back to his office. They gestured and winced at the noise echoing around them. Halfway back, he realized the towel was still draped over his shoulders. He was too tired to return it, so he climbed the last flight to his office and started pushing the door open.

Inside his office, Ishii and Akiko were discussing a file whose pages were spread out over her desk.

Hiroshi walked to his file cabinet to see if there was a fresh shirt. There was a clean shirt and pants but no underwear. "What's in the file? I looked at so many last night." Hiroshi tucked the dry cleaning bags with his shirt and pants under his arm and went to the men's room to change. When he came back, they were still looking at the file. "What's in there?"

"Tax breaks," Akiko said. "I thought it might connect."

He looked at them.

"Your specialty." Ishii leaned forward. "Not just any tax breaks. For buildings."

Akiko looked at Hiroshi. "Mainly for earthquake

reinforcements."

Hiroshi shuffled through the documents. Most were stamped with a row of red *hanko* stamps along the bottom. The forms had passed through a long series of meetings, offices, and officials, each with their red stamp of approval.

Hiroshi looked up. Akiko and Ishii nodded for him to keep reading. He read on.

Akiko and Ishii waited patiently.

Hiroshi looked up. "So, these are scams. It was passed through for approval without inspection. The subsidies for earthquake-proofing were paid, but the work was left undone. But it still doesn't answer who put the cameras in the basements."

"We can guess, can't we?" Ishii said.

"We can guess, but we need to know." Hiroshi closed the file. "Where did you get this?"

Akiko smiled. "Where do you think?"

Hiroshi shook his head.

"Watanabe. In the tax office." Akiko opened her eyes wide. "Inter-departmental cooperation."

It dawned on Hiroshi slower than it had Ishii. "When did you see him?"

Akiko tilted her head to the side without meeting Hiroshi's gaze.

"You've been seeing him?" Hiroshi thought Akiko had blushed ever so slightly.

He'd introduced them on a case a few months ago. They'd talked enthusiastically at that time, but he didn't think anything more about it. Akiko had asked to join him when he visited Watanabe at the tax office about another case, but he hadn't noticed anything. He felt happy she was happy enough to blush a little.

Hiroshi folded the file shut and set it on his desk. "The videos could be someone trying to find who had failed to put in structural reinforcement. Or someone was using this information to blackmail the owners for the deeds to the buildings. The cameras explain the first possibility, and the masking explains the second."

Ishii clasped her hands. "Setsuko told me once that developers regularly came through the neighborhood handing out pamphlets, talking to the owners, and making offers to buy old homes. It was hard to resist until Setsuko, with Keisuke's help, organized information sessions. It wasn't a crime, so I didn't think about it. Keisuke had some of the small building owners as clients. They mostly wanted to sell. I was focused on the women's task force."

"You mean, there were not many women owners of the bigger buildings?"

"There were a few, but they were savvy enough not to get scammed."

"About their buildings?"

"About anything. They'd mostly outlived their husbands. But they didn't want to sell their places. Out of loyalty, maybe, fear of moving, letting old habits go." Ishii looked at the wall, frowning. "We focused the task force on the scams cheating the elderly. They cut their budgets tight. A missed payment would be all it would take. Some were down to the last yen every month. It's how they lived."

Ishii continued. "At first, the women's initiative focused on crimes against young women, mostly sexual exploitation, credit card debt, loan scams, and the like. But one of the other women on the team found that the worst effects, in monetary terms, were scams against older adults, most of whom were women. We redirected our efforts to the Silver Centers."

Hiroshi unrolled one of the maps from Keisuke. "If the buildings fail to pass inspection, their resale price drops. And with tightened standards after the Tohoku earthquake, it can take a year to get inspected." But there was something else, he felt, something he'd seen last night. "I think we better pay a visit to Keisuke in the hospital. I want to know why he had that map in the first place. He knew a lot about Kurono Management. I should have asked."

"You think he's involved in this?" Ishii asked.

Hiroshi shrugged. "Maybe getting beaten up and having his office burned will encourage him to talk."

Akiko sat at her computer. "I'll dig into the buildings, the present owners, the past owners. Anything else?"

Hiroshi smiled. "Maybe talk with Watanabe again too."

Akiko blushed and busied herself at her desk.

"I meant about the case." Hiroshi raised his eyebrows at Ishii. "Could you also find exactly where the proposals for upcoming urban renewal projects are located? By stations or in *shitamachi* or where? And see if you can find whose *hanko* seals are needed for these proposals. It must be someone inside the city offices. We need to know who approved these. I want to talk with them. Set up an appointment." Hiroshi looked at Ishii. "And I think we need to talk with Setsuko again too. She knows more than she's said."

Ishii hummed. "She'll probably be at the hospital with Keisuke."

Hiroshi called Sakaguchi to tell him where he was going.

Sakaguchi was in a meeting, but took Hiroshi's call as an excuse to step out in the hallway. "Where's Takamatsu?"

"He keeps running off."

"Let's hope he's running off in the right direction."

Hiroshi, for once, felt a surge of trust in Takamatsu. He had to trust something about the case. Maybe he just wanted some sense of certainty.

Akiko took a call. She nodded and checked her email. "Hiroshi, Nakada from tech will send some video. Do you want to see it before you go?"

"I'll look in the car."

Akiko pointed at his desk. "There's the printout of the building names and addresses."

Hiroshi checked his phone—no news from Ayana.

"Don't you want to eat something? You know, breakfast?" Akiko looked at him.

Hiroshi touched his stomach. "I still feel full from the meal last night."

Akiko checked her email. "You don't want to wait for the video? It's downloading."

"Waiting is all we've been doing for two days." Hiroshi waved Ishii to follow him. She held up the car remote starter and waved at Akiko as they left the office.

He wanted to get as much done as possible so he could go to Nagoya and straighten things out with Ayana. He'd lived his whole life focusing in two directions, pulled apart by things he hadn't always chosen. He'd gotten used to it, but it was catching up with him. The baby, small and hidden as she was, weighed more heavily than he'd imagined, pulling him strongly in that direction.

Chapter 32

At the hospital where Keisuke had been sent, they found the correct ward after asking for directions several times. Ishii stopped at the nurses' station while Hiroshi headed to the room. Nurses made rounds, checked charts and supplies, and talked with patients.

The top-floor ward felt upscale. A large lounge area with vending machines and a kitchen and tables spread out just off the hallway. The private rooms were widely spaced, and the carpeting, walls, and room signs were tasteful.

Hiroshi checked the name on the door. Keisuke's name used Chinese characters meaning "auspicious good luck." He hoped that would ensure his recovery.

Setsuko was dozing in a chair.

Keisuke lay in the bed with pins screwed to the right length to hold his skull in place and a chin strap around his jaw. Oxygen tubes curved into his nostrils. The rest of him was buried under sheets.

The light was low in the room. Setsuko woke, uncurled herself, and reached for Keisuke's hand. She stood and ran her fingers over his cheek between the stabilizing rods and the jaw sling. When she noticed Hiroshi, she didn't seem surprised. "He's sleeping."

Hiroshi nodded. "We need to ask him some questions."

Ishii came in the door and went straight to Setsuko. They clutched hands and looked at Keisuke.

Setsuko shook her head. "He's been in and out."

Hiroshi stepped to the bedside. Keisuke's face was severely bruised, the skin dark blue in spots. Around the skull screws, the skin caved in under the metal.

A nurse came in and turned the dimmer switch to brighten the room.

Keisuke stirred.

The nurse checked the monitor, IV drips, and halo. She picked up her tablet and checked the boxes, pointing at each to confirm completion. She tucked the tablet under her arm and turned to Hiroshi. "Please don't talk too long. He needs to rest."

She walked out, and Hiroshi tapped the bed rail. Keisuke's eyes opened.

Setsuko turned to Hiroshi. "I know what you're going to ask. So let me answer as much as I can." Setsuko wiped her face with a handkerchief. "When he got beat up before, it was a renter in one of the buildings my husband owned. That's why he asked his nephew to start handling collections and helping out."

Hiroshi looked into Setsuko's bloodshot eyes. "So, what about his office? It seemed like whoever broke in was looking for something."

Setsuko shook her head. "He said it was a robbery. But I'm not so sure."

Setsuko continued. "Sasaki put several properties, including the Silver Center building, into a shelter, and Keisuke set it up so that it would stay as it is forever. We got approval from the city office to designate the neighborhood as a culturally important area. It hasn't reached the final stages of approval. Today is the final hearing on stopping the so-called beautification project."

Hiroshi wanted to tell her she should have told him this before, but that wouldn't do any good.

Setsuko looked at him like he was stupid. "That's just the name for it. Beautification. Not the reality."

"What's the reality?"

Setsuko looked away. "To tear everything down and rebuild. At a profit. Keisuke was classmates with one of the people on the board. But they had a falling out." She touched his hand, but his eyes remained closed, his head held tight in the brace.

"Where is the hearing?" Hiroshi pulled out his cell phone.

"At our city office."

Hiroshi exchanged glances with Ishii.

"His nephew's coming to stay with Keisuke so I can attend. I'll have to do his part. However, all our presentation materials were burned up in his office." Setsuko shook her head. "I'm not sure if I can do it justice. He had everything in order."

Could it be that simple? Was it a threat taken to extremes? Hiroshi asked, "Including video?"

"Yes, including video."

"Those were monitored by the kid who was killed in the dorm?"

Setsuko nodded. "He was a good kid but had mental health issues. We caught him filming in the women's showers. Sasaki did, actually. We didn't know what to do. If we turned him over to the police, would that have helped him?"

Hiroshi didn't say anything.

Setsuko continued. "We offered him a job instead. We wanted to know who was going into all the properties. There were inspectors for all kinds of things, and we were worried they weren't real inspectors."

"Who would they be?"

"We don't know. The video was taken when he was killed. You have it all."

Hiroshi frowned. "So, who saw the video feeds? Keisuke?"

Setsuko nodded.

"He paid the kid?"

"Sasaki paid. She said it was something she could help with." Setsuko looked up at Hiroshi. "Filming wasn't illegal, was it?"

"I'm not sure if anything's too legal in real estate." Hiroshi scrunched his face. "You set them up to monitor what? Harassment? Inspections? Improvements?"

Setsuko shrugged. "We got worried about the building managers. Some of them were getting paid off."

"Paid off for what?"

"Information. Access. A tipoff. The inspectors knew all the management agencies. It was all too cozy." Setsuko took Keisuke's hand.

Keisuke groaned, and everyone turned to him. He turned his shoulders toward them, about all he could do, and spoke in a faint, scratchy voice, nothing like his confident, pleasant manner before. "It's all my fault. Setsuko has nothing to do with any of this."

Setsuko squeezed his hand. "Kei-*chan*, we need to tell them everything. They'll help."

Keisuke looked at her and then looked at Hiroshi.

Keisuke cleared his throat and tried to sit up, but he couldn't move much. "The developers want to control everything. They build monstrous apartments, shopping malls, and business complexes. All in terrible taste. And then they charge so much no one can afford them. That kills the neighborhood and drives out those living on a pension." He fell back, exhausted by the effort to talk.

Keisuke's nephew came into the room. He set a bag of drinks and snacks on the table and turned to Setsuko. "I found what you needed in Uncle's house, but I'm not sure it's right. Anyway, I'm here. You can go." He handed her a folder from the bag.

Setsuko opened it up and flipped through the pages. "It's better than nothing." She patted Keisuke's nephew's arm.

The nephew looked around. "What's going on here? Uncle should be resting."

Hiroshi looked at him. "We needed to ask him a few questions. But we can ask you."

Keisuke's nephew stared at Hiroshi and then at Ishii.

Hiroshi took a breath. "When did you start working for your uncle?"

"After he got beat up. I was between jobs, so I helped with a few things. I've been working part-time at a friend's business. Pop-up restaurants and boutiques. Some people still pay by cash, if you can believe it. And my uncle isn't always the most discreet person." The nephew shrugged. "You meet a lot of women."

"Did you know about the videos?"

The nephew looked at Setsuko and then at his uncle. "Uncle was very worried about them. He wasn't sure the young kid could handle it, but from what I could tell, the kid was a genius. I guess it always seems that way if you don't know computers. But Uncle Keisuke was trying to put them together for everyone's protection."

"Protection from what?" Hiroshi couldn't quite get what they were worried about, but he was sure it connected to the deaths.

The nephew shook his head. "He was putting together a presentation for today's city meeting. He'd been working hard on it. I handled most of the day-to-day stuff recently."

Setsuko nodded. "I finally got him to take all this to the right government departments. He's a bit old school that way."

"Old school, what way?" Hiroshi asked.

The nephew cleared his throat. "He didn't even have contracts for some of the buildings. The people had been there so long. So, he couldn't raise the rent, either. It was all locked in old property regulations, some dating back to World War Two."

Setsuko said, "It wasn't his fault. He inherited some of the properties, and others, he just helped collect rent and do repairs. The whole city ran on trust back then, and all of a sudden, it didn't."

The nephew shook his head and looked at his uncle. "He should have formalized everything long ago."

"What about the *hikikomori* kid?"

Setsuko said, "We should never have asked him to do that."

The nephew looked at his uncle and sighed. He looked at Hiroshi.

Hiroshi didn't have anything more to ask. Or rather, he wished he knew what else to ask.

The nephew pulled out an ebook reader and flopped into the

chair. Setsuko patted his shoulder.

He patted her hand. "Good luck at the hearing. I'll help sort things out as soon as it's over."

Setsuko pulled a jacket on and gathered her things, including the folder the nephew had brought. She leaned over Keisuke and, through the hardware, kissed his cheek. She smiled finally and looked around at everyone. "Love gets better with age. You cherish your romantic walks and shared meals. You appreciate where you are and who you're with. Sex gets better, also. You no longer hurry."

Keisuke's nephew scrunched his face and looked away.

Setsuko clamped her eyes shut. Tears trickled out. She wiped them away with her sleeve and clutched the bag. "I have to go."

When she was gone, Keisuke's nephew fidgeted in the chair. "You should check into the large development companies. They're the ones who would do anything to acquire the land."

"Any other suggestions?" Hiroshi had misjudged the nephew the time before.

He exhaled in exasperation and shook his head. "My uncle talked with someone in the city office all the time, someone on his side. Maybe an old friend or a classmate, I'm not sure."

"Do you know his name?" Hiroshi asked.

"Terajima."

"And his number?"

"Is it important?"

"Yes."

"I'll ask Uncle when he wakes up. If he can't remember, I'll go to his office and look."

Chapter 33

Takuya pressed Murayama and Noguchi to help with one thing all morning—find the hospital. He kept calling them while he took care of the repair people who, smelling the income, came early to do estimates.

After she woke up, he'd let her sleep late, he set Misaki on the insurance, but she was too unsettled to accomplish much. He had only slept a few hours himself.

The police came snooping around, but they were considerate enough and said they'd keep an extra watch, even while implying the OLzakaya's staff were working on the side, perhaps in the back room. Takuya was too busy to take offense. It was partially true, but none of the police's business after all.

Takuya called Misaki. "Are you coming in?"

Misaki sounded surprised. "I thought you wanted me to get all the insurance sorted out. Which is it?"

"I've got to go out for a while. Bring someone with you. Can't you get some of the girls to come in and help clean up?"

Misaki was shuffling papers. "They don't like to do that. They'll break their nails."

"Well, too bad. Get them, or someone, in here."

"How are the repairs coming?"

"It will take four to six weeks to get this done. With no income." Takuya looked around the place. It was a total wreck. Not a centimeter of anything, including the floor and ceiling, had been left untouched. They'd have to strip it down to the studs.

Misaki sighed. "I'll be there in a few minutes."

A delivery man from a disposal company brought six large trash bins. He tossed them onto the sidewalk outside the OLzakaya and hopped off the back of the delivery truck to drag them over.

"Do we need to sort the trash? Glass, paper—" Takuya looked at the bins. Three had wheels, and three didn't.

"Just throw it all in together. Give me a call when they're full. You need more than these?" He opened the cab, waiting to climb back in.

"I'll call you when they're full."

Takuya hoped some of the employees could come in and help, but maybe they chose the job precisely because they didn't like cleaning. There were piles of pieces of everything. Nothing heavy.

He sat on the edge of the bench, vaped, and looked around. He went to the counter and pressed the imported espresso maker, but nothing happened. Misaki had been so proud of the machine when it was delivered. She giggled at the directions, trying to translate from English. She'd learned to make faces and designs in the foam. Maybe it could be fixed, but he dragged a trash bin over and tipped it in.

Takuya went back to survey the kitchen, dragging along one of the trash bins on wheels. Some canned goods might be OK, but Misaki would probably want to throw them out. The cases of booze were smashed. One box of top-shelf liquor seemed salvageable. He called Murayama to see if he knew where to sell the unbroken bottles of booze. The rest would have to go. He'd already cut his finger picking up some of the broken glass.

"Make any progress?"

Misaki's voice startled him. She had come quickly. He looked at her and looked around the kitchen. "Does this look like progress?"

"It looks like a mess," Misaki said. "Nami's coming in, and two of the other girls."

"Finally, get some work out of them."

She looked into the bin with the espresso machine and let out a sad little groan. "They won't come back, will they?"

"Not likely." Takuya wasn't so sure. He'd call Noguchi to help clean up, but mostly just be there. "I've got to go out for a while."

"For what?"

"I need to check on something."

"Can't you stay and help clean up?"

"I'll help when I get back."

Misaki looked at him.

"There's something I have to find out. I'll be back later."

Nami, the plus-size waitress, came in dressed in jogging pants and a bright pink sweatshirt with a towel tied around her head, carrying a bag of what looked like cleaning supplies. She looked cute, more so without makeup.

Takuya turned to Misaki. "Now, you have company. Noguchi said he'd be by to help. You call the police first and me second if something happens. But it won't. Nothing more to break."

Misaki didn't look scared, but she didn't look like she had the focus or energy to clean up, either. She was as messed up inside as the shop was outside.

He turned to Nami. "Thanks for helping out. There'll be a bonus, not to mention we appreciate it."

Nami smiled and nodded.

Takuya breezed out the door and pretended not to hear Misaki call his name.

He walked to the corner, vaping, and held his hand out for a taxi, checking the message from Murayama about the name of the hospital.

* * *

The hospital entry required him to sign in, and he put a name from one of his recent scams. He remembered the address and made up a phone number.

He found the elevator and rode up to the ward. The elevator had an antiseptic smell, as if it had just been cleaned, which he hoped it had.

The nurses' station was busy, so he slipped by, pushed through the swinging doors, and walked down the hall. It was not like other hospital wards. The windows were tall, and the doors closed. Most rooms had four patients, but some had only one or two.

At the end of the hall, two large rooms opened on either side. He checked the name. It was the one Maruyama had found. He should have visited the day after he was chased, but better late than never.

He was the only person in the room. He was attached to monitors and draped in white sheets. A kind of whirring noise emanated from the room, a fan vent or filter.

A nurse came by, and Takuya waved her over. "Can you tell me how he's doing?"

"Are you family?"

"His cousin. I'm his only family in Tokyo."

"You know what this room is?" The nurse checked her tablet computer and pulled up his chart. "You're supposed to have gloves and a mask on in this ward." She pointed at boxes at the side of the hallway.

Takuya pulled on a mask and gloves from a stand by the door. "I know he was scraped badly. Loss of skin is bad, I know. Anything broken?"

She was reading his chart. "I don't see anyone contacted besides his friend, and his father stopped by during the night." She looked at Takuya.

Takuya tried to think who would have visited. A couple of people stood on the sidewalk, but he'd mainly focused on the undercover cops before he took off. "How's he doing now?"

"He took a turn for the worse. Infection. I'm not sure how that happened, but he was missing a lot of skin, so infections easily occur. We're testing for other allergies, illnesses, or sources of infection."

"Is that the problem? His scraped skin let in infection?"

She cocked her head and closed her tablet. "If you're family, you must still register at the nurses' station."

"I signed in downstairs."

"Nurses' station too." She pointed down the hallway.

"I just want to talk with him."

"There's a microphone. Not long, OK?" She folded her tablet under her arm and walked down the hall. "Are you sure you're family?"

Takuya put on his best smile. She frowned. Takuya watched her go. He looked through the window into the room at the unknown sleeping someone, the one person who could tell him about Imada. Murayama had traced a police call to find the right hospital. So, he'd found the kid, but couldn't talk to him. He just wanted to ask if he knew Kurono or Imada, and if not, who had put him up to snatching the bag. Imada seemed to know everything, and he wasn't sure how.

Takuya stood there for a long time before he turned to go.

Standing at the end of the hallway was a young kid carrying a skateboard. His mask, booties, and gloves looked odd against his baggy pants and long, loose hair. He stared at Takuya.

Takuya stared back. He recognized his way of standing. Maybe all skateboarders stood the same way. No. He was there that day. He'd run past the kid, not thinking anything about it. Now, he was thinking a lot about it.

Takuya walked toward him.

The kid picked up his skateboard and cocked it over his shoulder.

"Who are you?" Takuya asked him.

"Who are *you*?" the kid asked.

"I'm a friend—"

"No, you're not. I'm his friend. Who sent you?" He held his skateboard at the ready.

"I was there the day he got hurt. On the sidewalk. I just wanted to be sure he was doing OK."

The skateboard kid squinted and looked more closely. "You're the guy who took the bag."

"He was robbing the old lady. Who paid you to steal the bag?"

"What about you?

Takuya slowed down and looked into the room. "I'm Takuya."

"I'm Sho." He readjusted the skateboard and reset his mask.

Takuya decided to be upfront enough to get his trust. He needed to know. "I run a group that sometimes does business with elderly people."

"You run a *sagi* scam ring."

"So, who was it?"

"I don't know. I didn't handle the arrangements. We met a guy along the riverfront."

"What riverfront?"

"Sumida River. We skated down until he saw us and called out."

Takuya had been told to do the same thing. It had to have been Kurono. But how did he know to send the kids at the same time as Takuya was doing the pickup? Yasui wouldn't have told him, wouldn't have let it slip. But how did Imada know so much?

The kid let his skateboard down, balancing it on his foot. "My friend said a man stopped by last night."

"What friend? What man?" Takuya saw two nurses coming down the hallway, followed by a security guard.

"My friend was watching him all night. A man visited and said he was his father."

"Whose father?"

Sho pointed into the room. "His."

"So?"

"So, he grew up in foster homes. It couldn't be his father."

Takuya could tell the kid wrapped up in the isolation room wouldn't recover. "And his condition got worse right after his 'father' visited?"

Sho nodded.

"Would your friend recognize this 'father' if I showed him a photo?"

"We already know who he is. He's the guy who hired us."

"Are you sure?"

"Yeah. I'm sure." Sho hoisted his skateboard over his shoulder and looked at his dying friend.

Chapter 34

Ishii pulled up outside Hiroshi's uncle's accounting firm. Hiroshi got out and leaned in. "I won't be long. But he's called a dozen times just this morning."

Ishii pulled out her cell phone. "I'm fine here. I have a hundred emails to answer. And more to delete."

Hiroshi hurried into the building and pressed the call button for the elevator. A large *ikebana* flower arrangement dominated the entryway. It featured a sprig from a cherry tree with blossoms set off by bright yellow flowers. The buds were opening. Did his uncle hire someone to do that? Or was it one of the office staff? He'd encourage his daughter to do *ikebana*. Maybe he'd start studying it himself. Ayana had several beautiful holders.

He turned to the brass elevator door as it opened and got in.

An office staff member bowed to him as the door opened on the fifth floor. She led him to the same conference room.

Before he could sit down, his uncle came in. He wasn't wearing a tie. Even when they met for drinks after work, his uncle kept his tie on. He loosened it but never took it off.

An office staff came in with two cups of green tea.

"Sit, sit." His uncle's voice sounded tired.

Hiroshi eased into an ergonomically designed chair.

"Watanabe told me about your case." Hiroshi's uncle eased into his chair. "You wanted to know about the developers, he said."

"Do you know them?"

"I know their books. Who are you looking at?"

"That's just it. We don't know who. We have the present buildings but not the future developers. By the time we figure that out, more people will be dead."

"Dead?" His uncle cleared his throat. "What *is* this case? Give me the names."

Hiroshi cocked his head. "Kurono, maybe, Imada, maybe. But they might be subsidiaries of larger companies."

His uncle looked at him.

"You thought I came here to discuss taking over your firm?"

"Did you think it over?"

"I...well...the baby's coming and—"

"All the more reason."

"Ayana's mother has cancer. She's in Nagoya now."

"I'm sorry to hear that. Is it serious?"

"I'll go down as soon as I can."

"So, what do you need to know?" His uncle had an odd way of focusing on what was needed while considering other issues. He'd always been that way—business first, everything else second. His father, from what he remembered, had been the same. But he moved between the two easily.

"Hold on." His uncle called one of his aides on his cell phone.

The first woman who'd walked him from the elevator immediately came in with a folder. His uncle flipped through the pages, nodding. "Kurono is connected to Imada Industries. Their holdings aren't large. They owe one of our affiliated accounting firms three years' back payment. They keep saying a big project is coming. But there's only so long you can file deferrals and carryover losses. Their office is in Roppongi."

"They don't pay their bills?"

"It's more common than you think." His uncle shrugged. "Kurono manages buildings in the northeast of Tokyo. In *shitamachi*. Usually, the development companies are the ones with big budgets. And the management companies are more like subsidiaries picking up the crumbs. But the accountant at our affiliate said something was odd in their relationship."

"Odd?"

"Maybe the management firm was calling the shots."

"Kurono is in charge, but hiding it?"

"It's a common set-up when the real decision-makers are—"

"Corrupt." Hiroshi thought that over. "Have you met them?"

"At a perfunctory business meeting. I'm sure you'll hate that kind of thing if you take over my firm."

Subtle sarcasm was the other trait Hiroshi's uncle had in common with his father. He wondered if it was genetic or skipped generations. "Sounds like you're tired of your job."

His uncle smiled. "That's why I want to get this over with."

"This?"

"The transfer of the firm to you."

Hiroshi looked at the desktop. "I am thinking about it."

"Then I can send you some of the figures."

"On Imada and Kurono?"

"I can do that because you're part of the firm. So technically, I'm not divulging any secrets."

Hiroshi felt out-maneuvered. "We have a secure site where you can upload files. My assistant Akiko will get them." Hiroshi sent the address for the secure file transfer site to his uncle. "Did you get it?"

His uncle checked his phone and nodded. "And talk to Watanabe too. The tax office knows everything and everyone."

"I'll do that. I've got to run. Thank you." Hiroshi got up.

His uncle stood up slowly. "One more thing."

Hiroshi stopped.

"I've got surgery scheduled. My bladder."

"Surgery?"

His uncle shrugged. "Bladder's off. They'll move things around, tighten things up, and put in something to keep it working."

"Why didn't you tell me?"

"What am I supposed to do, call you and tell you I can't piss?"

"When is it?"

"Next week."

His uncle looked tired. Hiroshi put a hand under his uncle's elbow as they walked to the elevator. Walking seemed to pain him.

* * *

Hiroshi knocked on the window to get Ishii's attention. She was lost in her cell phone, working it with two thumbs faster than Hiroshi could type with ten fingers on a full-size keyboard.

Ishii unlocked the door and started the car. "Where to?"

Hiroshi got in. "Office of deeds."

Hiroshi inputted the address into the car navigation and thought about the layout of the buildings and how they fit together—or didn't. He'd have to talk with Ayana about his uncle's surgery and his offer, but not until he had some idea himself.

Along the street, all the buildings lined up neatly. Each building was a small fortune, a high-turnover mint that kept churning out rent. Tearing down a four-story building to build a ten-story building, even if it took time, was worth it. So, the churning never stopped. The only direction was up. The air was the last contested space in Tokyo.

Tokyo could be considered a collocation of villages that arose organically. But recently, neighborhood-sized living was being cleared away for skyscrapers. Even when the designs paid homage to traditional Japanese layouts or recreated old-style streets, they remained under the control of a company, far from the soft pressures of the human community that shaped Tokyo for centuries. The concept remained but was easily repurposed.

Ishii pulled to a stop on a tree-lined street with buildings whose fronts looked like one of the basements they'd searched the day before. They all needed cleaning and didn't get enough sun. Hiroshi got out, threw a leg over the sidewalk railing, and stepped around a ginkgo tree whose roots had broken the pavement.

Hiroshi showed his badge to the guard at the Deed Registry. He was a heavyset man with a plump face and calm manner, one of the hordes of rehired workers spending their retirement scrambling to supplement their state pension.

Hiroshi took the visitor's pass, hung it around his neck, and waited for the elevator, which arrived with an unpleasant clunk. He got off the elevator on the tenth floor, and the secretary pointed him toward the counter for land deeds.

He stood at the long counter until a woman stopped ignoring him and reluctantly got up. The other workers in her section pretended not to notice. She was a pleasant-looking woman with long, straight hair and a grey business vest over a white blouse and grey skirt. She came to the counter but didn't say anything.

Hiroshi showed his badge and pulled out the list Akiko had printed for him. "We need to find the owners of all of these buildings. We also need all the purchase and transfer dates." Hiroshi handed over the list along with his *meishi* name card.

The woman bent to a small plastic lettercase, found the right drawer, and pulled out a form. "You'll need to fill this in."

Hiroshi frowned. He took a pen from the holder and quickly started ticking off the boxes. He signed it and pushed the paper across the counter.

She took it, checked it, and asked him to sign one more box. She took a *hanko* seal from a shelf under the counter, pressed it into an ink pad, and then onto the first square along the bottom of the page. "Do you have an official letter of request?"

Hiroshi looked at her. "No, I don't."

"Normally, we ask for a letter from the head of your department. In your case, that would be the head of—she stopped to look at his *meishi*—the homicide department." She adjusted her mask and glanced at Hiroshi.

"This is urgent."

"I understand, but—"

Hiroshi raised his voice enough to draw the attention of the other workers hunched over their desks. "I don't have time to get a letter drawn up."

She sighed. "Let me see what I can do for you." She walked to an area broken up by low dividers and leaned in to speak with someone Hiroshi couldn't see. She nodded and bowed.

She came back and, without explanation, started to tick off new boxes. She pulled out a new form from a different drawer. "You'll have to fill this one in too."

Hiroshi took the new form and filled in all the boxes the woman pointed to.

When he was done, she took the two forms, surveyed them again, pointing at each filled-in section, and said. "It will be ready next week."

Hiroshi wanted to scream. "As I said, this is an ongoing case, a murder investigation."

She straightened up and held the two forms in her two hands. "The deeds are not stored here. We have to get them brought in." She turned to look at the large clock on the wall. "Even if I sent this over now, it would take a day to retrieve them. We need to check all the information too."

"How can I expedite that?"

She looked at the clock again. "Maybe I can catch them before today's requests are sent to the storage facility. But it still won't be back here until tomorrow."

Hiroshi started to ask where the storage facility was, but gave up. "Tomorrow then. Can you text me as soon as it arrives?"

She looked at the *meishi* again and nodded.

Downstairs, Hiroshi flopped into the car. "Fucking bureaucracy," he said in English and pounded the dashboard.

"You can't do anything in Japan without the right documents. And you can't do anything with them, either." Ishii started the car. "Half of my work at the women's task force is filling in forms."

"OK, if it's bureaucracy they want, it's bureaucracy they'll get.

Let's talk with our favorite bureaucrat." Hiroshi pulled out his phone and made a lunch appointment.

Chapter 35

The streets of Yotsuya were busy with people heading to lunch. Ishii pulled onto the loading palette of a carousel parking lot that stretched up a dozen stories. Hiroshi got out and went to get the claim ticket from the attendant. She eased the car onto the rack, put the brake on, and turned off the ignition. They stood and watched their car spin away into the vast carousel of parking in the air.

People strode across the sidewalk, some carrying their lunch to enjoy under the first blossoming of cherry trees along the train tracks and canal that stretched from Yotsuya to Ichigaya. The raucous *hanami* flower-viewing parties would start soon, in the evenings, but lunch was a quieter time to enjoy the blossoms.

Ayana preferred the cherry trees in Chidorigafuchi Park. She worked in the National Archives nearby. That was where they had reconnected a couple of years before. When he got to Nagoya, he'd remind her how quickly their college love affair rekindled there. They'd take their daughter to the same spot for her first cherry blossom viewing next year. She wasn't even born and was making all the decisions.

The place to meet Watanabe was just across the street from the parking tower. As they walked on the sidewalk closer to the lunch place, some 1960s Blue Note jazz, a song Hiroshi knew but couldn't remember the name of, flowed up the stairs from a speaker at the bottom of the basement landing.

"Cool." Ishii pointed around as they descended the staircase past a neat row of framed record covers of iconic albums. The rich aroma of fresh-brewed coffee wafted out of the open door.

The jazz *kissaten* coffee shop was one of the older ones in Tokyo. Their vinyl collection filled the shelves along one wall, and a pair of massive speakers filled the front. The record player had a selection of stylus needles that customers could request to match their album request. Hiroshi tried to remember the last time he'd come here, maybe at college.

Inside, Watanabe was looking through a stack of albums near the turntable. A display stand held up Dexter Gordon's "Go." That was it. Hiroshi had that CD. It was still in a box in the basement storage in their building. He'd go down and bring them up, play music for their child from day one.

Watanabe returned the album to the display case and waved them to a table. He snapped his suspenders. His dark pink shirt stood out in the light wood interior of the corner booth. Lunch was a choice of two set meals, "Napolitan" spaghetti or Japanese-style hamburger, with salad, bread, and coffee.

"Thanks for taking the time to meet." Hiroshi wanted to say something about Akiko and his relationship but decided to wait.

"I've only got a few minutes," Watanabe replied. "Some information came in on a company we've been looking at for years. The investigators are meeting. Their taxes are in arrears, to say it politely."

Hiroshi settled onto the cushion on the bench. "We'll take as much time as you can give us."

Watanabe handed Hiroshi a thick envelope tied with eyelet strings. "What you need is in there."

Hiroshi took the envelope and unwound the strings. He started reading the tax records of the development companies. He wasn't sure what it meant, but he knew it would reveal their operations. You couldn't just acquire land and not file an income report, even if it was full of misdirection and concealment.

The manager came over, a young woman with an efficient manner. "Spaghetti or hamburger?"

Watanabe looked at her. "I'm not...oh, screw it, I can be late. Hamburger."

"Spaghetti," Ishii said.

They looked at Hiroshi, who was lost in the documents.

"He'll take hamburger," Watanabe said. "And blend coffee for all of us."

Watanabe slipped his hand into his suspenders and let them slap against his chest. His coat was hung neatly over a chair with his bright red and pink necktie tucked neatly in a pocket. The music shifted to a new album. "Here's what I requested. Horace Silver. He's so easy to listen to that he doesn't get the respect he deserves."

Hiroshi put the documents away and turned to Watanabe. "So, the big companies get the deeds to the land without paying any inheritance taxes?"

Watanabe laughed. "If they're good at what they do, they get away with it. Land taxes are trickier in Tokyo than personal or corporate taxes. It's easier to hide things in the regulations."

Hiroshi sipped his coffee. "How do they hide it?"

"If the land doesn't change hands, and if the deeds are kept in the original owner's name, it can be nearly impossible to track down who owes what taxes for what land." Watanabe shook his head. "Half the city, it seems, has deeds in the name of deceased owners. If no ownership transfer is filed, it's impossible to tell who owns it. And that's not even counting the buildings and homes that are abandoned."

"Abandoned?" Ishii shook her head. "How—"

Watanabe smiled. "The inheritance tax is more than some people can pay. So, they get squeezed between paying that or selling the land. So, the land sits empty."

"Until someone manages to snap it up." Hiroshi sipped his coffee. "I heard the government was claiming those?"

"They are. But that's when some inheritors decide to claim the land for themselves." Watanabe smiled. He turned to Ishii. "And since you're on the women's task force, you probably already know it's the older generation of women who are cheated the most often."

"It still surprises me how often." She looked at the speakers.

"Aren't all land transfers required to be registered?"

"People let them sit for generations to avoid taxes. Typical bureaucratic ambiguity. It lets you do everything or nothing. But of course, the tax office doesn't have the resources, so they do nothing." Watanabe sighed. "And can you imagine how many inspectors it would take to check all of them? The problem is worsened with the new '*Tokyo no Shareta Machinamizukuri Suishin Jorei.*'"

"The what?" Ishii laughed. "That's a mouthful. What's that?"

Watanabe chuckled. "It's what's going to ruin the rest of my career. It's an 'Ordinance for the Promotion of Stylish Cityscapes in Tokyo' or some such idiocy. They want to tear down the oldest parts of the city and hand them over to developers."

Hiroshi leaned back. "Developers?"

Watanabe sighed. "Yeah, they claim the old buildings are dangerous, infested firetraps. And then, the developers create projects to 'upgrade' everything, which means tearing it down and building new. They use the beautification policy to get tax breaks and enforcement of pushing out holdouts."

"Holdouts?" Ishii looked confused.

"Some landowners never want to sell. Don't you remember that rice farmer who held up the expansion of Narita Airport? His rice paddies blocked one of the runways. He held out until he died. Lots of the post-war generation think like that. More power to them, I say." Watanabe laughed. "At least they pay their taxes. Or some of the taxes anyway."

The lunch dishes arrived, plump, round hamburger patties covered in a demi-glace sauce with a neat mound of white rice and steamed vegetables on the side, for Hiroshi and Watanabe. She came back with the spaghetti Napolitan for Ishii. The spaghetti was neatly folded under a hefty dollop of tomato sauce and a sprinkling of grated cheese.

Hiroshi tapped the folder. "Is there a list of those developers?"

"Must be." Watanabe straightened his suspenders again. "But

it's got to be at the Office of Deeds."

"I was just there," Hiroshi groaned. "It's where office workers go to die. Are all the projects approved?"

"If you're a developer with connections with the right government officials, it's smooth sailing. All you have to do is offer an apartment in one of the new buildings, and it's done."

Ishii wiped the tomato off her lips. "Is an apartment that much of a bribe?"

Watanabe smiled. "The buildings provide in-house restaurants, gyms, libraries, viewing platforms, grocery stores, entertainment rooms, and pretty much anything the ultra-wealthy and the corrupt bureaucrat might want. You never have to leave. And when you do, you're chauffeured."

Hiroshi put down his fork. "Hidden Tokyo."

Watanabe nodded and dipped a forkful of hamburger in the demi-glace sauce. "Tokyo without the streets of Tokyo."

"And without the neighborhoods," Ishii said. "They're like *hikikomori*, hidden in enclaves dozens of stories high."

Watanabe smiled and pointed with his fork. "Money does strange things to people."

"That's what Takamatsu says." Hiroshi pulled out his cell phone to message Akiko to check what projects had been filed recently.

Watanabe turned his attention to the music and pointed at the speakers. "I love the sound in here." Horace Silver's chord progressions had tightened, every note connected, and his quintet locked in the pocket, the rhythms, harmonies, and melodies in synergetic flow.

"I didn't know you were a jazz person." Hiroshi smiled.

"I'm trying to up my profile." Watanabe sipped his coffee in an absurdly pretentious manner and laughed.

"You mean for Akiko?" Hiroshi asked.

Watanabe looked up, surprised. "Well, yes, we did go out a few times. I don't know, though..."

Hiroshi tapped the table and wiped the last of the sauce with a forkful of rice. "You can't do better than her."

"I know." Watanabe nodded. "But that's the problem. I'm busy all the time. I don't have time to read restaurant reviews or articles about where to go in Tokyo. I can't entertain her in the style—"

Hiroshi chuckled. "Let her take the lead. Whatever you do, she'll be ahead of you."

"Become a good follower?" Watanabe laughed. "I can try that."

Ishii twirled her spaghetti slowly before turning to Watanabe. "If you hurt Akiko, you will be sorry."

Watanabe choked on his rice, coughing and covering his mouth. "You'll put your task force on me?"

Ishii hummed. "I'm the least of it. It's Detective Takamatsu you'd have to worry about."

"I will keep that in mind." Watanabe snapped his suspenders and started to pull on his jacket. "I better go. I haven't read all the documents before my meeting. Not that that ever helps."

Hiroshi's cell phone buzzed. It was a message from Keisuke's nephew. He'd sent the contact number for Terajima, the city office worker whom Keisuke knew. "We have to go."

Chapter 36

While Ishii waited for the parking lot carousel to deliver the car, Hiroshi stood by the entrance and made a call.

"*Moshi-moshi*," a low voice whispered.

"Is this Terajima-san?" Hiroshi spoke in a low voice in response.

"*Hai*."

"I'd like to talk with you."

There was a pause before Terajima answered. "Who are you?" he whispered.

"I'm Hiroshi Shimizu. A friend of Keisuke Sugata. I'm a homicide detective."

"Homicide?"

"I can explain in person."

"I have a lot of work, and there's a hearing this afternoon. Can we do it later this week?"

"I'll go where you are. The city office?"

"Don't come here."

"Where then?"

Hiroshi waited.

"There's a *kissaten* coffee shop called Kojo. Near Ueno Station," Terajima whispered. "In half an hour."

"I'll find it."

Hiroshi hung up.

"All OK?" Ishii asked.

"We're heading to a *kissaten* called Kojo. Akiko found his *hanko* on all of the projects. And Keisuke's nephew had his name from his uncle."

"Both? But which side is he on? He's got to know something."

"If he read what he stamped for approval, he'll know a lot." Hiroshi found the directions and inputted them into the car navigation.

* * *

Ishii pulled onto a back street lined with an iron railing in an old flowery design. The back street was quiet, with a few ramen and yakitori places on the first floors of narrow office buildings. On the rolling shutters of several stores, faded signs gave hand-sketched maps to new addresses.

Hiroshi rechecked the GPS map. Ishii had to circle again. They'd missed the entrance.

"Let me out," Hiroshi said. "I can find it easier on foot."

"I'll park and meet you inside." Ishii pulled to the curb at the main street.

Hiroshi kept one eye on his cell phone and one on the street until he found the shop sign. Beside the door was the menu with faded photos.

The stairwell down was covered in brown marble with a wide chandelier. Hiroshi walked down and pulled open the door to the interior, squinting in the dim light. Backlit stained glass murals with ornate designs of European kings and queens, princes mounted on horses, and marble staircases covered the walls. Carved stone divided the interior into booths. It was the least Tokyo-like interior Hiroshi had ever seen, but it wasn't quite Western, either.

A thin, concave-chested man caught his eye and looked away.

Hiroshi walked over to him. "Terajima-san?"

Terajima nodded at the plush chair. "Can I see your badge?"

Hiroshi sat down and passed it over the table.

Terajima looked at it closely, folded it shut, and pushed it back across the low table. His face was as pale and gelatinous as over-boiled rice. He wore a white undershirt beneath a white button-down shirt and a plain black jacket.

Hiroshi leaned forward. "We found your *hanko* on almost every document for a case we're investigating, and we hope you might be able to offer us some insight."

"Officially, I shouldn't talk to you until you file a request form through the city office and the Ministry of Land, Infrastructure, Transport, and Tourism."

Hiroshi nodded. "That could take a long time."

"That's the point." Terajima sipped his coffee.

"Keisuke Sugata was beaten up badly. He's in the hospital."

Terajima winced. "Will he be OK?"

Hiroshi shrugged. "Hope so."

"Did you find out who did it?"

"That's why I want to talk with you." Hiroshi let that sink in. "The city beautification projects are a front for renewal projects that profit development companies. One name that keeps coming up is Kurono Building Management. The other is his associate, Imada Industries. Do you know them? They were on a lot of the forms you approved."

Terajima leaned back into his chair and rested his arms on the thick armrests. He took a breath. "Why do you need to know this?"

"We have two deaths, a near-murder, an arson attack, and the possibility of more. Your *hanko* is on all of the documents. You must have approved them."

Terajima cleared his throat. "My stamp means the document came through my office. Nothing more. It's a big office."

"You've seen all the applications."

Ishii walked up, and Hiroshi waved for her to sit. "This is my colleague, Detective Ishii."

Terajima looked at her. "A woman homicide detective. My office also has more women. Nice change. Too bad I'm retiring soon."

"So, how and why do the developers need the city's approval?"

"Which developers are we talking about?" Terajima leaned forward.

"Imada and Kurono."

"One is a developer. One a management company."

"You must know them well."

Terajima's pasty face darkened. "The ward office is a mess if you want the truth. It's not transparent. The office deals with many developers."

"Some more powerful than the others."

Terajima continued. "The successful development moguls have connections everywhere from the city offices to the ward offices to the Tokyo government. And from there, they know Diet members and ministers. They all know each other from university days. From high school even."

"And Imada and Kurono?"

"You wouldn't be asking if they didn't control more than you can imagine. You figured that out, I see. There's Japanese bureaucracy for you. They are flexible when they want to be and rigid the rest of the time. They bend over backward to please people like Imada and Kurono."

"You don't sound like a government employee."

"I should've been fired years ago. But not for my attitude. I have a tattoo. That's against the rules. I have a partner. It's not against the rules, but it could be."

"If they wanted to enforce the rule."

"Worse was I talked to a reporter about these beautification projects. That's definitely against the rules. Now, I'm talking to a homicide detective. It adds up."

"But you're retiring."

"At the end of March."

Terajima waved to the owner, a grey-haired woman in a neat apron. She brought over a shiny silver coffee pot and refilled his cup. She snapped her fingers for a waiter who hurried over with two cups. She poured for the detectives.

The owner shuffled back to the counter by the kitchen. "So, why do they need to push the locals out of the way if they already have their projects approved?"

Terajima took a careful sip of coffee. "Essentially, any landowner can refuse to move pretty much forever. You remember the farmer who wouldn't sell to Narita Airport?"

Hiroshi looked at Ishii and laughed. Watanabe had just used the same example.

Terajima frowned, confused.

Hiroshi sipped his coffee. It had a nutty, bitter taste with a lingering smoky aroma. They must roast their beans. "So, after they buy the properties, they move people out quickly."

"And quietly. That's probably more important." Terajima looked at the stained glass wall behind Hiroshi and Ishii. "But that doesn't always work. When a neighborhood unites together, resistance can go on forever. Negotiation, offers, counter-offers, demands..."

"So, to avoid all that?"

Terajima looked at Hiroshi. "Usually, they use money. The problem is that the longer they hold out, the higher the buyout price. Then, it gets serious."

"Is that happening anywhere now?"

"You mean the project in Komagome?"

Hiroshi leaned back. Terajima knew much more than he was letting on.

"Tomorrow's the deadline. It looks like the developer has enough for the project to proceed." Terajima shrugged. "The final hearing is this afternoon."

"That's where Setsuko was going." Ishii put her hands on her knees, ready to get up.

Terajima held his hand out. "The hearing's just to let them vent in public. It's good for them, and they can try to broker better deals for the last holdouts."

"You mean, it's already done?" Hiroshi sighed.

Terajima looked away at the stained glass of a castle. "It's how things are done. The developers run Tokyo. They do things their way."

Terajima looked at them like he had said more than enough. But he took a breath and continued. "Some sections of Tokyo have now been designated to remain as they are for tourism. Tourists won't come to Japan to visit another skyscraper. So, the older areas are essential to bringing in tourists. They have character. They're more Japanese. Our support staff for tourism has almost tripled in the last few years, and the budget has more than tripled."

"So, there are some in the government ensuring the old flavor of Tokyo isn't whittled down to nothing?" Ishii asked.

Terajima smiled at her. "It'll be Disney-fied in places, made cute, but some of old Tokyo will remain, at least for tourists." He shrugged. "Eventually, someone's going to find the circumvented regulations."

"Circumvented?"

Terajima fidgeted. "For example, there are a lot of abandoned homes. When their official status is registered, and due diligence to find the owners is completed, they are up for grabs."

Hiroshi closed his eyes. "Up for grabs by who?"

Terajima opened his hands wide. "Whoever knows how to find them. Developers have deep pockets and lots of resources. They pretty much do what they want."

"Isn't it all on record somewhere?" Ishii asked.

"Where? Even if some enterprising journalist found all that, the buildings are already in place. It would be too late."

Hiroshi sipped his coffee. Ishii stared at the walls as if noticing them for the first time. Lit from behind, the stained glass princes and princesses seemed to be in motion.

Terajima said, "They stay ahead by having the right information. Which comes from contacts. Which is helped by the occasional well-placed incentive."

"A bribe?"

"Call it what you want. The information they need is buried deep in the files, so someone on the inside has to find it, but there's probably other ways."

"Like what?"

"Like doing the legwork. So, I've never been sure if they have someone on the inside, or they dig around themselves on the outside, or both. Plenty of people would be happy to do that for them. They probably hire people. However they do it, they're good at it. Kurono is one of the best."

Hiroshi looked at the bright-colored castle design on the wall. "And Imada?"

Terajima looked away. "He's the connection to the elite. He married into the family of the biggest developer in Tokyo, but he hasn't made his mark yet. He keeps starting and never finishing projects. But his plans are bigger every time I hear them. All he needs is one to work, and he's set for life."

"Even better set, you mean?" Ishii said.

"His marriage will have paid off then." Terajima finished his coffee.

Chapter 37

Ishii got a call as they walked to the car. She stopped in the middle of the street with her eyes closed and breathed deeply as she listened.

Hiroshi stopped and turned back. "Ishii?"

She looked up, shook her head, and looked away, squeezing the car remote. She let out a big breath and started jogging for the car.

By the time he got to the car, she had already paid at the machine and put the light on the roof.

Hiroshi got in, and she wheeled out of the lot, popped the siren, and pulled into the oncoming lane. Drivers eased to the side of the road, and she sped down the empty center lane.

They got to the Silver Center in record time. Ishii killed the siren and turned left down the same street Hiroshi had chased the *sagi* guy down. The road was filled with police trucks and an ambulance just outside a tarp strung across the narrow lane. Another tarp. Ishii hadn't spoken, but he knew what the tarp meant.

Ishii parked, hopped out, and hurried inside.

Hiroshi got out and hesitated by the car—another crime scene. Hiroshi imagined the nauseating scene inside, worse because Ishii hadn't said a word.

Ishii walked out from under the tarp with her arm around Setsuko. Setsuko's face was buried in her hands. Hiroshi held back.

Setsuko stared in the direction of Keisuke's half-burned office. Crime scene tape still covered the entrance. She looked at Ishii, said something low, and stormed away.

Ishii followed her, but Setsuko waved her hand in a leave-me-alone gesture. Someone should be with her, but if Ishii didn't follow, there was no point in him trying. Ishii yanked aside the flap of the tarp and ducked inside.

The LED lights glowed white over the top of the tarp, lighting up the cherry blossoms on the branches over the small lane.

Sakaguchi would be inside so he could look for him. Was this going to be another dead body? On the street? Or inside one of the old wooden homes? Or some other horrible combination he couldn't picture? He wanted to go back to the safety and sanity of his office to piece together the puzzle of buildings, companies, and killings.

Takamatsu stepped out, realized he still had on his nitrile gloves, and yanked them off. Hiroshi turned away, but Takamatsu called to him and strolled over, lighting a cigarette with his hands cupped around his gold lighter.

"Your smoke is contaminating the scene," Hiroshi told him.

"No, just my lungs." Takamatsu looked up at the cherry blossoms overhead. The white LED lights over the top of the tarp lit the blossoms in sharp relief against the black night. "Only an idiot trims cherry trees," Takamatsu said, smoking and looking up.

"I thought that was plum trees?" Hiroshi looked at the blossoms.

"Both, I think. My wife says that. She takes care of the gardeners."

"You have a garden?"

"Only place I can smoke at home. I'm allowed one small ashtray." Takamatsu pointed at the tarp. "You can go on in. There's no blood. They used a pillow."

Hiroshi stayed where he was. Blood was the worst, but death in any form made him faint.

Takamatsu blew out smoke toward the blossoms overhead. "Older woman. Worked in the Silver Center. Maybe you met her the other day. I think that fits the mission of the women's task force pretty well."

Hiroshi grunted. "Anything else in there?"

Takamatsu smirked. "I wish we had this one first. Security camera down the street caught a good image of him running away. Two of the students living in the dorm found her. The house was torn apart. They left a safe. Couldn't get into it, or it was too heavy."

Hiroshi sighed. "When did it happen?"

"The students discovered it when they stopped by. I've been here an hour. Could have been in the morning."

"Morning?"

Takamatsu shrugged his 'not sure' shrug. "They tortured her."

"What?"

"Maybe just one guy."

"The same *sagi* gang, you think?"

"Probably not. They don't use violence." Takamatsu took in another lungful. "Internal bleeding is what got her, the crime scene crew surmised. She weighed no more than a child. She was skin and bones. There used to be meatier victims. Greying society, I guess." Takamatsu put out his cigarette in his portable ashtray.

A gurney wheeled out between the flaps of the tarp. Two ambulance personnel hurried over to help navigate the gurney to the ambulance. Takamatsu put his hands together and bowed to the deceased, hardly visible inside the body bag. Hiroshi bowed until he heard the doors of the ambulance close.

Takamatsu lit another cigarette. "Can you talk to those students who found her? They're upset. And they don't speak Japanese, do they?"

"They speak Japanese just fine."

"Doesn't make it any easier to talk with them."

Hiroshi looked around. "Where are they?"

"I sent them to wait in a car." Takamatsu pointed with his cigarette in the opposite direction.

Yellow crime scene tape was strung across the end of the lane, and local uniformed police blocked access, waving gawkers away. Just outside the restricted area, the two students sat inside a police car.

The two detectives assigned to watch them looked relieved to see Hiroshi. Most of the younger detectives spoke English, but these two were older. Hiroshi nodded, and they scurried off.

The two students, the Russian woman and the Indonesian woman, looked shaken. They'd been the ones asking the most questions when he talked to them in the dorm. He got in the front seat and turned to where they leaned on each other in the back.

"Do you remember us?" the Russian student asked with a smile.

"Natasha from Russia. And Annisa from Indonesia."

"You remembered." Annisa smiled.

Hiroshi nodded, of course. "I'm sure you told someone here already, but could you tell me again what happened?"

Annisa nodded. "We were coming to finish our interviews—"

"Interviews?"

"For our school project," Annisa said.

Natasha pulled out a notebook from her backpack. "As we told you, we're urban studies majors. One of our projects involves interviewing older women about their lives in Tokyo and their reactions to the changes in the city since they were young." She held out her notebook. It was filled with notes in careful rows.

Annisa pulled out her cell phone. "We've been recording everyone, so it'll take forever to transcribe it, but they have amazing stories. Some remember the firebombing of Tokyo. Others came from the countryside in the fifties."

Natasha chimed in. "They give us a qualitative record of life that's different from our urban studies classes. Our advisor likes our approach."

"The other teachers are pretty conservative, I guess?" Hiroshi asked.

They both shook their heads. Natasha said, "I was a bit shocked that such a modern, progressive city and a famous university was so…" she turned to Annisa.

Annisa shook her head. "Old-fashioned. Their idea of research is looking at maps and urban renewal projects."

Natasha shook her head. "If I never see another map or blueprint again, I'd be happy."

Hiroshi held his hand up. "Did you take many classes on the mapping of Tokyo?"

They both nodded.

"Could you look at one more map?" Hiroshi pulled up the photo he had taken of the buildings managed by Kurono and handed his cell phone to them.

The two women scrolled the map open and shut, scowling and pausing.

Natasha leaned back and looked at Hiroshi. "We can check this against some of the maps we were forced to study and ask our advisor, too. We can go to the grad students' room right now."

"Later is fine." Hiroshi wondered what they would see. "Can you tell me what you saw when you found her?" He realized he didn't know the name of the latest victim.

Annisa wiped her eyes with the back of her hand. Natasha patted her back. "We were excited for the interview with Sasaki-san."

"Sasaki-san? Who works in the Silver Center? Setsuko's friend?" Hiroshi knew Ishii would be devastated.

"She always brought us students little cakes and things. We still…" Natasha held up a plastic bag filled with *sakuru mochi* rice cakes. Seeing the undelivered treat, Natasha burst into tears. Annisa rubbed her back.

Annissa let Natasha get herself under control and talked for them both. "Sasaki-san loved these pink *mochi* rice cakes with sweet *adzuki* beans inside and pickled sakura leaves on the outside. We went to Ginza to get them for her." Annisa couldn't hold back any longer and burst out crying. Natasha dug tissues out and shared them.

Hiroshi gave them a minute. "So, when you got to her door today, what did you find?"

Natasha looked away. "We arrived at four o'clock. The door was open. We thought maybe she had left it open for us. So, we stepped inside the *genkan* and called out to her. But there was no answer. We didn't know what to do. We took off our shoes and walked inside."

Annisa patted her again and took over. "We found her on the tatami. It was obvious she was dead. The house was a mess. There was a safe. I tried CPR, but she didn't respond."

"And then you called the police?"

Natasha said, "The local police came right away."

"Did you see anything or anyone?"

Natasha and Annisa shook their heads and wiped their faces.

Natasha said, "I wish we'd come earlier. We might have interrupted—"

"Or you might have been hurt." Hiroshi made a mental note to get more police to guard the dormitory, Silver Center, and maybe the whole neighborhood.

But if the surveillance videos were as clear as Takamatsu said, maybe they wouldn't need protection for long. Perhaps they'd get the safe open right away too.

Chapter 38

Misaki put away the sponge mop she'd been using on the floor behind what was once a counter, now splintered wood and a leaking sink. She pushed her hair back under the white towel around her head.

Takuya stopped sweeping the floor and bent over to get the bigger pieces into the dustpan. He dumped it all into the least full of the trash bins. The others were filled with busted tile, broken mirrors, and bits and pieces of the tables and chairs. The larger chunks of the booth were jumbled in the corner.

"Taku, honey, come on. That's enough. Let's get a drink. And I'm starving."

Takuya watched her reflection in the cracked mirror. He heard her checking the plywood he'd nailed in place over the back door, knocking on it to be sure it was secure.

The back room hadn't been busted up as badly, but it was smoke-damaged. A few supplies were salvageable, but not much. At least no one dropped a match where the alcohol spilled. Or maybe they didn't get to it.

Takuya took out his vape pen and sucked in a blast of rum and cigar. He surveyed the barrels, bags, and broken furniture. He'd be by to pick up everything in the morning. There was not much to the place, to any business. It was a space to exchange money for food and drink and a chance to ogle girls in tight clothes.

The employees had stopped by all day, commiserating and hinting about how to get paid. Some helped for an hour or two, then flitted off, making excuses. Some had new jobs already.

Takuya pulled off his coveralls and tossed them into one of the barrels.

Misaki stood in the spot from where she had commanded the room. She could rebuild if she wanted, but he was done with it.

He'd given Misaki the seed money, proud he could support his practical, pretty girlfriend and give her what she wanted—her own shop. The place came apart quickly enough.

"Taku, that's enough for today. We need to eat. We need to sleep." Misaki gave him that pouty look. She ruled over the other women as much by her earthy good looks as by her bossiness and efficiency. The employees and customers all said Misaki was a natural *bijin* beauty, and she was. The girls studied her taste in clothing, how to make their eyes seem big, their lips full, and how to accessorize.

Was the OLzakaya any better than lightening the savings of retirees? It was lightening the pockets of losers. He'd called Yasui all day, wanting to ask him that question, but he was still in the hospital with his grandmother.

Someone knocked on the wood over the front door. Takuya stomped towards the door and pushed it open. The hinges still worked. Standing on the sidewalk was a plump man in a rumpled suit with stringy hair. His belly hung over his belt, and his suit coat couldn't button. "Closed!" Takuya shouted.

The man bowed, his oily hair falling forward over his plump face.

"Closed!" he shouted.

The man stood there stupidly.

Takuya twisted the lock open and yanked the cracked glass door aside, and stormed out, shouting, "Closed, you asshole. Closed! Can't you see?" waving at the disaster inside.

The man backed away and held his hands up.

"Takuya, stop." Misaki was pulling his arm. "That's Eto-san. He's the insurance lawyer." Misaki pulled Takuya back. "One of the regular customers."

Misaki held the door open and waved Eto inside. He clicked on the LED work light he'd had to buy that afternoon to see what they were cleaning.

Eto bowed politely, and Misaki waved him to the last

remaining section of the counter.

Eto looked around and let out a sad harrumph before opening his briefcase backpack and pulling out a plastic folder. "Misaki-san, I'm so sorry to see this happen. I found the forms and the company. I think you're all right. I need you to sign where I put the Post-it notes." Eto handed her the papers on a clipboard and kept a wary eye on Takuya.

Misaki wiped her hands on her apron, took the clipboard, and looked through it, nodding as she flipped the pages.

"Put your *hanko* seal on each page on the lower right-hand side." Eto bowed again to Takuya.

Misaki pulled out her seal, set the pages on the counter, and put her red ink seal in the small squares Eto pre-marked for her.

Takuya vaped by the door, holding it open. The outside air felt good and clean.

Eto looked around the shop. "I can file for clean-up expenses, so keep track of everything. I'm glad you decided to get insurance with me."

"So am I. Thank you!" Misaki turned her smile on, and Eto looked away, tugging on his ill-fitting jacket.

"Is the wait staff OK?"

"You're going to support them too?" Misaki laughed.

"I wish I could. They can file for unemployment insurance." Eto blushed and pushed his oily hair back. "I think that's it." He bowed, put away his papers, and walked carefully around Takuya before hurrying off.

Misaki smiled at Takuya, who was still holding the door open. "I thought it was stupid at first, but Eto came twice a week and never pushed it on me. Funny, huh? The extra insurance covers a lot. The girls will be fine with unemployment benefits." She took Takuya's arm. "Now, come on, let's get something to eat."

"Who was it who did this?" Takuya vaped deeply without moving from where he held the door open.

Misaki picked up her bag. "Look, the insurance will cover this.

We can restart someplace else."

Takuya gave her a stern look. "So who was it?"

Misaki shook her head. "It doesn't matter, does it?"

"No, it very much does matter. Who was it? You saw someone, right?"

"Takuya, no, it doesn't matter."

Takuya scowled. "Was it the same person who demanded payments last year?"

"No, it wasn't the same. Last year, they were local guys. The police ran them off. I told you all that. Old history." Misaki pulled out the new keys and nodded for him to go first.

Takuya took her hand with the keys. "But it was the same group?"

Misaki kissed him on the cheek.

Takuya pulled away.

She grabbed his arm. "That's why I didn't tell you. You act like this."

"Like what?"

"Like you're going to do something."

"So, these people were not the local *chinpira* shaking you down last year?"

"I don't know that a hundred percent for sure. But the guys yesterday were more...well...professional."

"Like how?"

"They got everyone out first and worked quickly, all four of them with a task."

"I thought you said 'five'?"

"One stood outside." Misaki pulled her hand free and clenched the keys.

"What did he look like?"

"I was trying to get the girls out of the way. He was tall and dressed in black. He left quickly after they got started destroying the place."

Takuya stared at the front door, furious.

Misaki put her arm around him. "We got the insurance money, and no one was hurt. And I'm ready to move on. I want to think about what to do next."

"The collectors last year, was that what they wanted? You to move out?"

"That's part of what they wanted. Or to own the place."

"Take it from you?"

"Yeah, I guess." Misaki nodded. "One of the girls told me. She'd seen the same guy at another club. She told me to be careful. Another girl heard that all the buildings on the next street were coming down."

"But those people last year and the people yesterday were not the same people?"

"You asked me that before." Misaki looked at him. "I'm tired and hungry. And my period just came. I want to eat something and get so drunk you have to carry me home. Can't we do that?"

"OK." Takuya took a hit from his vape pen and turned off the LED lights.

"Nothing lasts forever." Misaki pushed him out on the sidewalk and turned to lock the door. It was a new lock, and she twisted it several times to be sure it worked.

Takuya thought she loved the place. Now, she was ready to move on.

A motorcycle pulled around from the back alley. Takuya couldn't see who the rider was in the headlights. He shielded his eyes and squinted into the light.

The motorcycle roared towards them.

"Go back inside," he said to Misaki. "Back. Now!"

Misaki fumbled for the keys and got the door open. She tried to pull Takuya inside as she pulled out her cell phone.

It was two of them on the cycle. They pulled forward and braked to a hard stop. The back rider dismounted.

When the driver clicked off the headlight, Takuya shouted, "Yasui? What are you doing here? I thought you were with your grandmother in Ibaraki?"

Yasui came forward. "I had to come back when I heard about this." He looked at the OLzakaya. Yasui had helped build the interior. He was a whiz with the air ducts, ceiling panels, flooring, the bar area, and the kitchen shelving, saving them a lot of start-up expenses. Yasui looked stricken.

Noguchi pulled off his helmet. "I picked him up from Tokyo Station."

Misaki re-locked the door and went over to hug Yasui. Yasui had always been very huggable. He'd never grown up, staying plump as a baby, his hair uncombed and clothes wrinkled.

Yasui walked over to look inside the OLzakaya. He turned back and shook his head.

"Want to see the rest?" Takuya asked.

Yasui shook his head. "That was a lot of work. We did the whole interior."

Noguchi walked over carrying his helmet. "Murayama has some ideas."

Takuya looked at Misaki and turned back to Noguchi, whispering, "I'll get her home and meet you at the coffee shop."

Noguchi pulled his helmet on and went back to his motorcycle. Yasui followed him, threw his leg over the back of the bike, and balanced himself as they pulled off into the night traffic.

Misaki grabbed Takuya's arm. "Don't."

"What?"

"Just don't."

Takuya held her by the arms and looked into her eyes. "We're just talking." There wasn't much to say, only things to decide.

"You didn't eat since breakfast and barely slept last night. And now you're going to...what...do something?"

"I need to talk with Yasui. We'll get something to eat." He waved his cell phone at her. "Put the insurance forms someplace safe."

Misaki put her arms around him and tucked her head into his

chest. He held her until she leaned back and started thumping his chest with her fists, slow at first, then harder. He held her until she stopped.

Chapter 39

Setsuko knew what she needed to do. She wasn't sure she could do it without Keisuke, Sasaki, and Ueno. But she'd have to. Keisuke was a long way from dispensing advice. She hadn't even started to arrange Ueno's funeral, much less Sasaki's. Ueno was older, eighty-six, but always in good health, and Sasaki was so young, just seventy-nine.

She glanced behind her at the lights in front of Sasaki's place. Instead of turning toward home, she turned left, hurried to the corner, and waved for a taxi. The first two were full, so she pulled out her cell phone and fiddled with the taxi app until she got one. It was Sasaki who'd taught her how to use the app.

She closed her eyes to stop herself from crying and opened them to watch for the taxi. It came quickly. She got in and gave the driver the directions.

It didn't matter what happened now. Whatever happened would happen. She had to know and had to do what she could. Ueno always knew what to say, and Sasaki knew what to do. She'd always relied on them. Those days were gone. They'd never return. She was on her own. But she could do what was needed now. She could become the active one of the three at last.

Sasaki had found them an apartment when Tokyo was rebuilding from the firebombing after the war. Ueno was the one who went with her to the countryside, where Setsuko's father had the foresight to move all his deeds and documents to a safe. He died in the war, as he must have known he would. He was one of the last to be sent to the Pacific. Some safes in Tokyo homes had melted in the flames of the firebombing, the heat had been so intense.

Setsuko's country cousins had a big farm home with plenty of room and, more importantly, food. She and Ueno had stayed there for a week, filling their bellies after the shortages and black market hassles of Tokyo. When the time came to return to Tokyo, her cousins had loaded them up with dried, pickled, and salted everything. They had not even asked about the documents Setsuko took from the safe. Her father had her memorize the combination of the chest-high, arm-length-deep safe and explained what was there before he was conscripted.

After they took the train back to Tokyo and she had time to read the documents, Setsuko discovered her father had owned ten buildings, mostly in *shitamachi*, but one in the hilly area of Shibuya. Sasaki helped find a lawyer whom they could trust. She first sold the family home in Shibuya, which was falling apart.

That was partly a mistake as Shibuya became prime real estate as Tokyo developed, but they needed the money right away, and the profit was more than enough for the three of them to move into a better apartment. Setsuko wasn't sure she could manage the other buildings, but she quickly found veterans educated before the war to help.

Sasaki and Ueno married well, though not as well as they might have. Ueno's husband died from cancer. Sasaki never minded working. Her husband was lovely, but his heart condition made it hard to work, and he spent his last years in decline, though still in love.

They were done with men after that. But years after Setsuko's husband died, she met Keisuke and realized love was not done with her.

All three threw themselves into study groups, education tours to famous areas around Japan, and local charity projects. Sasaki, Ueno, and Setsuko had always told each other everything, down to the most intimate details.

With their husbands gone and no children, they made their wills to each other and kept them together in a joint safe. That way, if something happened to one of them, the others would know what to do.

After Ueno was killed by the scooter, Sasaki and Setsuko were too shocked even to begin going through her documents. After Sasaki's death, Setsuko couldn't even get to the safe where everything was kept. She felt her anger and grief grow inside her, doubled by their deaths. She had to do something, and she knew exactly who to do it to.

* * *

As she approached Roppongi, the evening revelers irritated her beyond belief. Young people laughed in groups. People fondled their cell phones, draped their arms around each other, and chatted freely. Skateboarders shot by between the cars and the sidewalk railings, oblivious to the danger they posed. Others hung out on the street, not moving at all.

The new office/shopping/entertainment complexes had changed the entire character of Roppongi. It was neat, clean, open, and untangled. The top of the skyscrapers had become some imaginary heavenly space you had to buy your way into. The companies designed every interior to turn people into consumers, eternal customers. "Predators" and "scavengers," Keisuke called them. He had stood up to them at one meeting after the next. He wasn't afraid of them, and she wasn't, either.

She got out of the taxi at the corner of the vast plaza of Tokyo Midtown and hurried toward the entrance. There wasn't anything here to dislike. It was too bland for that.

She stormed into the office building lobby and told the receptionist at the counter, "I'm just taking something up to my nephew," pulling a grandmotherly smile as she headed for the elevator.

"Um, excuse me..." the receptionist nodded to the security guard.

The guard followed her, confused, looking back at the

receptionist. Several elevators arrived, and Setsuko hopped on before the guard could catch her. The door shut, and the elevator whisked her to the top floors.

Setsuko got out on the floor for Imada Investing and Development. A young woman who got out after Setsuko pulled the security card from her neck. "Are you seeing someone here?"

Setsuko looked as cute and calm as any eighty-year-old woman could when lying. "I'm bringing something to my nephew."

That was enough for the young woman to usher her in and show her a sofa in the waiting area inside the security doors.

"I know the way," Setsuko told her with a smile. She remembered the way from the one time she, Ueno, Keisuke, Sasaki, and her lawyer had come to try to work out a compromise the year before.

She walked to the back and charged into the office. It was strikingly empty, a hollow space for hollow plans, the opposite of Keisuke's messy stacks of papers and mementos, his genial aimlessness.

Imada looked over Roppongi's bustle and twinkle, talking on the phone. That's all he did—talk on the phone. She saw her reflection—a blurred older woman—in the window and waited for him to spin around in his ergonomic chair.

Setsuko wanted to scratch his eyes out. She should have turned him in when she had the chance. Keisuke had talked her out of it. She wouldn't make the same mistake twice.

She put her hand in her purse and fondled the small canister of pepper spray Keisuke had bought her after Ishii's talk on self-protection. She wasn't sure she'd be quick enough to hit him in the eyes, but at least she'd be close enough to try. Then she'd kick him for all she was worth. She'd taken a self-defense class at the gym with Ueno and Sasaki. Her favorite technique was kickboxing.

Imada saw her in the window's reflection and turned as he

finished his conversation. Framed by the lights stretching to the horizon behind him, he seemed minute in the vastness of Tokyo.

Imada leaned back with a casual smile. "Are you finally coming to negotiate?"

She wanted to shove him out of the window and see him sail to the concrete below. She fingered the canister in her right-hand pocket. "No. I'm coming in to look you in the eye. I know it was you or one of your underlings. Try to deny it."

Imada folded his arms over his turtleneck sweater and kept his eyes on her.

"I should never have even tried to negotiate with you." Setsuko wanted to spit on his desk, on his face.

Imada smiled. "Your boyfriend's the one who can't negotiate."

"You're the kind of vile punk I had to deal with after the war. I was never scared of gangs then, and I'm not now."

Imada nodded his head quietly. "You spied on me."

"You paid off inspectors, lied about earthquake upgrades, threw out tenants, threatened owners, and coerced women with Alzheimer's. How much lower can you get? I know it was you or one of your people who killed that poor kid and beat up Keisuke and set his place on fire. You were probably behind Ueno getting killed by that scooter, and now Sasaki." The pepper spray felt cool in her hand.

Imada stood behind his enormous black desk. "And what about you? Your properties are not up to code, either."

"They're getting there. Besides, I live *in* Tokyo."

Imada laughed and rocked against his desk. "I live here too."

"No, you live *here*." She pointed at the office. "This is not Tokyo. And it never will be. You can build your little pseudo-Shibuya in *shitamachi*, but it will never take hold. People will go once or twice, then start to hate it. And you know why? You have no humanity, no sense of beauty, no soul."

"You're angry."

"Your idea of a city is a place to take, take, take. You can bribe all the local city office workers you want, all the ministers in the Ministry of Land, Infrastructure, Transport, and Tourism, but you'll never catch up with your brother-in-law. You're going to be the failure in the family, the one who didn't quite measure up."

Imada's attention flickered to something behind her.

Before she could turn around, she saw a glimmer of motion behind her and felt a sharp poke in her butt that surprised her more than hurt.

She turned to stare into the cold, black eyes of a tall, thin-faced man. She rubbed her butt and realized she had not been careful enough.

She whipped the pepper spray out of her purse and pointed it at the man's face, but before the spray shot out, he snatched her wrist in a single, quick cross and duck. The sharp, acrid smell of burning pepper spread through the room, but the stream hit the wall. He twisted her arm until she dropped the can.

Setsuko stomped on his foot with all her might.

He grunted and reeled to the side, but held her tight. He wrapped his arm around her neck, kicked the pepper spray to the side, and dropped her into a chair.

Setsuko looked up at him. "You're Kurono." She tried to stand, but her knees buckled.

She fell back into the chair, knowing what was coming. She would soon be as blurry as the distant lights, and then it would all turn to darkness.

Chapter 40

Hiroshi sent the students back to the dorm with two younger detectives. He asked the local police to help watch. He wanted the two students, Natasha and Annisa, to review the maps. Maybe they could find something he couldn't, something that would be the connection they needed. He watched them walk away. It was only a few blocks, but a lot had happened in those few blocks during the past couple of days. More still could.

Sakaguchi dropped his hard, heavy hand on Hiroshi's shoulder.

"What now?" Sakaguchi asked.

Hiroshi didn't have a good answer. He didn't have any answer at all.

Sakaguchi grunted. "Maybe the cameras will find something. There were good ones on a convenience store at the end of the block, and some old guy rigged another one to his front gate."

Osaki and Sugamo were clearing the way for a safecracker from the safe company. They helped him hoist his rolling tool case up the few steps into the house. The crime scene crew was starting to pack up and turn things over to the detectives assigned to guard the scene for the rest of the night.

Takamatsu ducked under the tarp with his cell phone held up. He ground his cigarette underfoot and put his phone against his ear. He started peeling off his gloves and booties and tossed them in one of the trash bags. When he hung up, he turned to Sakaguchi. "We need helicopters."

"Again?" Sakaguchi sighed.

Takamatsu pointed at Osaki and Sugamo. "You two take one car, and Ishii and Hiroshi can accompany me." He started towards the end of the street, then stopped and turned to Sakaguchi. "Helicopters," he shouted. "I'll let you know where."

Sakaguchi shook his head, knowing it was easier to get the helicopters arranged than to argue Takamatsu out of them.

Takamatsu hurried off with Hiroshi and Ishii right behind.

Osaki shouted to Hiroshi. "When he figures out where we're going, call and let us know?"

Hiroshi shook his head. "Will do."

Ishii got in the driver's seat, Hiroshi settled in the back, and Takamatsu lit a cigarette in front. Ishii pulled to a stop at the end of the street. "I need a direction to drive in."

Hiroshi leaned back. "Why didn't you tell Sakaguchi where to send the helicopters?"

Takamatsu pulled out his cell phone and checked his messages. "It's the skateboarders. I didn't want Sakaguchi to know about them."

"He already knows."

Takamatsu leaned over to Ishii and said, "Just head towards the Sumida River. I'll tell you more in a minute."

Hiroshi got a call from the tech guy Nakada.

Nakada had a calm voice. "Detective, I've found a lot more videos. These were not masked very well."

"What was on them?"

"Old houses."

"Houses?"

"I have all of them here if you want to stop by."

"I'll do that. What time are you there?"

"I'm always here." Nakada hung up.

Before he put his phone away, Akiko called.

"Did Nakada call you?" she asked.

"Why are you working so late?"

"It's not that late. I started looking at the houses and couldn't stop."

"And?"

"They match up with the map from Keisuke."

"They're all in that same area?"

"Close to the Silver Center, spreading in several directions. Do you want me to combine these with the other map of the bigger buildings?"

"We're going to need that. Send me whatever you finish as soon as you can."

Hiroshi was about to hang up, but Akiko said, "One more thing?"

"Yes?"

"I checked for deaths around Komagome Station and the Silver Center."

"And?"

"There were quite a few more than average for similar areas in *shitamachi*."

"You crosschecked with public records?"

"There were no autopsies."

"And no inheritors?"

Akiko hummed. "For many places, none."

Hiroshi smiled. Akiko always came through. It was why he wanted to spend more time in the office himself. "OK, can you pull all that together, and we'll cross-reference it with the maps and info from the deeds office?"

"I'm half finished."

Of course you are, Hiroshi thought. "We're going to need that soon."

He wanted to say something more, but Takamatsu turned around and said, "Tell Osaki and Sugamo to head down the east side of the Sumida River."

"I've got to go," he told Akiko. "Thank you."

Hiroshi texted the info to Osaki and Sugamo.

Takamatsu said, "A woman pushed in a wheelchair by two men."

Ishii sped up. "A woman in a wheelchair. No one will think much at this time of year—a grandson taking his senile grandmother out for her last *hanami*."

Ishii picked up her phone.

"Let me do that. You drive." Hiroshi reached for her phone.

Ishii handed it to him after putting in the passcode. "It's under 'Setsuko.'"

Hiroshi tried but got no answer.

"Try the Silver Center." Ishii looked back at him in the rearview mirror.

Takamatsu tossed his cigarette out the window and held up his cell phone to Ishii. "Here. Where the Kanda River flows into the Sumida. Yanagi Bridge."

Ishii looked at the map and then looked at Hiroshi in the rearview mirror. "Try the nurses' station at the hospital. She's probably there with Keisuke."

Hiroshi found the number and called.

Ishii turned to Takamatsu. "Siren?"

"No. We go in quiet." Takamatsu turned to Hiroshi. "Tell Osaki and—"

"Let me finish this call, can you?" Hiroshi held his hand up. "You have their number."

Takamatsu growled in reply.

Hiroshi finished his phone call. "The nurses knew who Setsuko was but said she wasn't there."

Ishii fidgeted and sped up.

Takamatsu called Osaki and Sugamo and told them to pull down to the next bridge south of Yanagi and walk north. Ishii made a sharp left turn that rocked Hiroshi to the side of the back seat.

Hiroshi's cell phone rang. It was Ayana. The worst time to talk was the time she always called. He leaned back and answered.

"How are you doing?"

"I'm fine. My mother's not so good. She fades at night."

"I'm sorry about that. Listen, I'll call you back in an hour. If you're asleep, don't pick up, OK?"

"OK," Ayana said and hung up.

He had to go to Nagoya as soon as possible.

Ishii pulled to the right and found the street parallel to the Sumida River. They couldn't see the river on the other side of the bank, but the humid, musky air told them it was close.

Takamatsu held up his tracking app. Hiroshi leaned forward and watched a blip move north up the Sumida River.

"What's in the river?" Hiroshi asked.

Takamatsu smiled. "Our water taxi driver."

"The guy we talked to on the canal?"

"The very same. He got a call for a pickup. And called me." He turned around, pleased with himself. "It must have been the cigarettes I gave him."

Hiroshi coughed. "So, he's leaving from Kachidoki Marina?"

"I don't know if he picked someone up yet, though. He might be alone." He switched the app's focus to see further west from the river. Another blip, then two, moved through the streets near Kanda Station. Then, the blip turned east, heading toward the river.

"What are the other two blips?" Hiroshi asked.

Takamatsu smiled. "The skateboarders. They posted themselves outside Kurono's and Imada's. There are a hundred exits. They—we—got lucky."

Ishii headed to the end of the street, where it dead-ended at the park that ran along the river. She parked halfway up on the sidewalk.

Hiroshi hopped out. The revelers in the park were noisy, and people strolled along with coolers, bags of food, and tarps to sit under the cherry trees. *Hanami* cherry blossom parties were underway.

Takamatsu got out. "We should head down the riverside walkway. I guess he'll tie the water taxi up there."

"Let's hope we catch them before he gets to it this time," Ishii said.

Takamatsu jogged up the steps of the embankment leading to

the riverside park. "I'll call the local cops. Tell them to join us." When he finished, he called to tell Sakaguchi where to send the helicopter.

In the park, long strings of *hanami* lights lit up groups of people on pegged-out tarps. Paper plates filled with food, delivery plates of sushi, plastic containers of homemade nibbles, and beer, wine, sake, and *shochu* bottles tilted and tottered inside the circles of people enjoying the night together.

Ishii and Hiroshi spread out across the walkway. Takamatsu stayed close to the barrier fence nearest the water, his eyes on his cell phone, looking up to see if anyone was coming.

Takamatsu stopped and looked over the river. "There's nowhere they can go. I'll tell Osaki and Sugamo to come towards us. What's that bridge called?"

"Kototoi Bridge," Ishii said.

Hiroshi called to tell Sugamo and Osaki to come up and squeeze them for the capture.

Takamatsu called Sakaguchi to check on the helicopters.

Hiroshi looked over the river, still moving forward.

Ishii checked her friction-lock baton.

Takamatsu tapped his ash into the dark water and checked his tracking app.

Ishii looked at everyone passing by, looking far down the river walkway.

Hiroshi got a message from Sugamo. They'd parked farther south and were walking upriver. They'd hopefully pinch them in between.

Hiroshi texted back their location.

The lights were on in most of the buildings on the other side, and the voices of partiers formed an exuberant echo from the closer buildings.

The click-clatter of skateboards turned his head, and two skateboarders shot past. He stepped towards them, but they were going too fast to chase.

Was that Takamatsu's guys? They went by, leaving nothing more than a blurry glimpse.

Another skateboarder zipped past them just as fast.

He could only watch them disappear into crowds ahead. Ishii had taken a few steps after them but gave up.

Both the park and the walkway were dense with *hanami*-goers. A gentle rumble of human laughter and talk mixed with the slosh of the river.

Hiroshi walked faster toward the skateboarders, glancing for a signal from Takamatsu, who checked his cell phone for messages.

When he looked back, from the middle of the crowd, came a man pushing a woman who flopped over in her wheelchair.

A tall man in black followed close behind him.

Behind them, farther down the walkway, the skateboarders had stopped. They kept a foot on their boards, talking to each other, looking at the trio.

Chapter 41

In the glass block room of the coffee shop, Takuya explained what happened to Misaki's shop. Yasui, Noguchi, and Murayama listened carefully and leaned back in their chairs to think.

The coffee shop manager brought them a second round of beers and took the empties away. He returned with small plate-sized pizzas for each of them and a bowl of cut vegetable sticks to share and told Takuya he was leaving.

Takuya stood up, shook his keys, and followed him to the door. Before he walked away, Takuya asked him, "Do you want this place back?"

The manager, who'd been addicted to gambling, stared at him sullenly. Takuya rescued him from his gambling debts. In return, he'd tapped the revenue stream and used the books to hide money. He knew this would be the last time the group needed a meeting place because it would be the last time they worked together.

The manager looked at Takuya. "I'll see what I can do." He turned to go but then turned around. "Thank you."

Takuya wasn't sure if he was still going to Gambler's Anonymous, but he seemed less beaten down than he used to be.

Takuya locked the door and walked back inside.

Murayama was interrogating Yasui. "How did you meet Kurono in the first place?"

Yasui shrugged. "He found me. He said I'd taken money from a woman whose home he wanted to buy. I don't know how he found me, but he did. He didn't care about the money but wanted my help with the house next door. And a ten-story building next to that."

Murayama pressed him. "And did you help him?"

"No, I found out about my grandmother and forgot about it."

"So, it was recent?"

"Yes. I would have talked about it with you, but I didn't get the chance." Yasui never got ruffled, but he rubbed his eyes.

Noguchi took a pull on his beer and lit up a cigarette. "Imada's the same as us. Difference of scale, though."

Yasui took another daikon stick. "That ten-story building had a fire."

"Where was this?" Takuya asked.

"Up by Tabata Station, not far from Komagome." Yasui tilted his head back and finished his beer in two big swallows.

"That's his game?" Murayama started typing on his computer.

"What did you tell Kurono exactly?" Takuya asked Yasui.

Yasui crunched his daikon and looked at Takuya. "Not much."

"How not much?" Takuya asked.

Yasui shrugged. "I don't know how he could've found the time and place. I really don't."

"Was anyone following you?" Noguchi asked.

"What? Of course not." Yasui leaned back and shook his head.

Takuya looked at the glass blocks, black in the night, and thought of when they barely had money, how they took girls out for meals and drinks and screwed them right in the karaoke room. That was long before he met Misaki and long before they'd met Noguchi and Murayama and switched to the *sagi* scams. But someone had slipped up, and Yasui was the most likely candidate.

Noguchi drank his beer. "Yasui, think closely, how many times did you meet him?"

Yasui thought about that. "A couple."

"You told me one time," Takuya said. "Did you talk to him on the phone, too?"

"I wasn't thinking exact numbers," Yasui said. "Yeah, I did."

"He asked you about our operation?" Murayama asked.

Yasui sat forward. "What is this? I'm to blame for this? He said something about different work that could be more profitable, and that was it."

"He already knew?" Takuya asked.

"He did," Yasui said.

Takuya drank his beer. "Imada knew a lot when I talked to him, too."

Murayama turned to Takuya. "So, you're sure it was Kurono who broke up Misaki's place?"

"I can't figure out why he'd do that if he wanted to work with us, though." Takuya finished the last bite of pizza.

"To push you his way. You'd be in need and easier to control." Murayama tapped his keyboard.

Takuya didn't like being manipulated, but that was how Imada did things. He was a street-level punk in a high-rise office.

Murayama tapped his laptop. "Are you sure Kurono hired the scooter kid?"

Takuya looked at the highway signs on the wall. "Yasui must have left something slip and—"

"I didn't let anything slip." Yasui slammed his beer down. "I'm as careful as any of you. Maybe more so."

They all looked at him and then worked on finishing the last scraps of food and final swigs of beer in quiet.

Noguchi said, "It's pointless to blame each other. Let's decide what to do now."

Murayama sighed. "You're right. Let's figure out how we handle them."

Takuya drank the last of his beer, thinking he shouldn't give the shop back to the gambling-addicted manager but buy the place outright. It would be a clean investment, with much less anxiety and less trouble.

Noguchi stabbed out his cigarette in the large glass ashtray. "So, Imada and Kurono know exactly who we are. They probably thought you got away with the documents, that it wasn't all just paper."

"That's why they broke up Misaki's place?" Takuya wondered how much they knew, and how much they didn't.

Murayama looked up from his screen. "Was anything there in the OLzakaya?"

Takuya shook his head. "Nothing they'd want." Except for the money he hid in the ceiling, but they couldn't have known about that. Not even Misaki knew.

Yasui took his beer and drained the last of it.

"As we talked about, let's lie low for a while," Noguchi said. "But before then, let's push back hard."

Murayama started typing on his laptop. "We hit Imada and Kurono, and we take a break."

Takuya set his vape pen down and leaned forward. He had nothing to prove to anyone except himself. None of them were fighters. They'd only gotten rough when they had to, usually to get away. But it was doable if it was four against two, or they could catch one alone.

Murayama looked up from his screen. "Let's tie them to the scams we pulled. We're moving on, so we might as well blame them. Redirect the police to Imada and Kurono."

"How do we do that?" Noguchi asked.

"We list all the names, dates, banks, and convenience stores we used and tie them to it. Not so hard. And maybe we can even tie them to the fire Yasui mentioned too." Murayama was making a list.

Everyone nodded.

Takuya tapped his vape pen on the table. "For a direct hit, probably the parking garage is best."

Yasui frowned. "They don't seem like people who let their guard down. Couldn't we hire someone more in that line of work?"

"Then there's a trail," Murayama said. "We're trying to refocus attention on them, not on us."

Noguchi swigged his beer. "Hitting them in the parking lot or at their office will only work once."

"Agreed." Takuya felt one time would be enough. They'd have

to be sure it worked.

Yasui stopped them. "Wait, where do we send the documents?"

None of them wanted to say "to the police." It felt like breaking a code. But then again, it was the only way.

Noguchi looked at Murayama's computer. "Are you sure you can cut any traces to us?"

Takuya looked at Murayama. "You can send the info anonymously, right?"

Murayama stopped typing and looked at them. "We're not connected to any bank transfers or cash deliveries. That's all in other names, other company names, not ours. I can send all the info on a Tor browser. That'll keep it anonymous, and safer than the post office."

Takuya hummed. "OK, and as for hitting Imada and Kurono, let's do it tonight. We can head off after that." Takuya felt ready. Imada and Kurono must pay for messing up their *sagi* ring, ruining Misaki's place, and putting them all in danger. He couldn't believe he considered working for the guy.

"Tonight?" Noguchi looked up.

Takuya said, "We hit him in the parking lot. We can ask the scooter kid. In the hospital, he told me they've been watching them and know their movements."

"Do you trust him?" Noguchi asked. He was the toughest one from his biker gang days and knew how to fight on the street. Takuya had survived the reformatory, which taught him all he needed to know—hit first and hit hard.

Takuya sighed. No, he didn't trust that kid.

Yasui got a call. He listened. Nodded. Held up his phone. "That was the hospital. My grandma died."

"You better go," Noguchi said in a calm voice. "We'll get this done tonight and come up tomorrow. You coming with us, Murayama?"

"Wouldn't miss it." Murayama smiled. Takuya remembered

him kicking a security guard when they lifted a case of caviar back in the day. Noguchi had to pull him away, or he would have killed the guy. Were they going that far again?

"You go back to Ibaraki." Takuya put a hand on his shoulder.

"I've got my bike outside." Yasui looked like he was in a daze.

Noguchi said, "Take the Shuto to the Joban Expressway."

"I'll be there in two hours." Yasui stood up. Takuya followed him to the door. When they stepped out, they found Misaki coming up the brick steps, jingling the extra set of keys to the coffee shop he'd given her.

Takuya caught her eye. "Yasui's grandmother died."

Misaki wrapped him in a hug. "I'm so sorry, Yasui."

Takuya kept speaking for him. "He's heading to Ibaraki now."

Misaki looked at him and gave him another hug. "We'll be there to help."

Yasui mumbled thanks and headed off.

"Was he drinking?" Misaki asked.

"Just a beer. What are you doing here?" Takuya stared at Misaki.

"I should ask you the same thing." Misaki pushed up the stairs and shoved Takuya back inside.

"I told you to rest." Takuya tried to speak in a commanding tone.

"*Told* me?" She stared at him. "I went out anyway. I came here to get you."

"We'll talk about this later." Takuya took her arm and started moving her toward the door.

"No, we're not going to talk about this later because there's nothing to talk about." She pulled free and brushed past him.

Takuya followed her.

When Misaki looked into the glass block room, Noguchi bowed, and Murayama shut his laptop, pulled his bag over, and slid the computer inside.

Misaki stared at him.

Murayama bowed to her, put on his coat, and was about to say something, but left without another word.

Misaki turned her gaze to Noguchi.

Takuya heard the bell on the door jingle as Murayama left.

Noguchi looked at Misaki. "Maybe we should get Yasui's grandmother's funeral over first. We can sort out the other later."

Misaki looked at him. "There's no other. Whatever you're planning."

Takuya said, "Misaki, this doesn't concern you."

Misaki looked at him. "Who does it concern? The insurance company? The arsonist? The police?" She shifted her bag and set her shoulders. She'd hit a customer once and gut-punched Takuya one time when they argued about his flirting with one of the staff. Everyone could flirt except him.

Misaki folded her arms. "Let all this go. I can guess what you've been doing. We have a chance to change things. Change jobs. Change our lives. And that's what we're going to do." She stared at Noguchi, waiting for him to agree.

Noguchi put his cigarettes away, picked up his keys and cell phone, and took his helmet in hand. He nodded once and left.

The front doorbell jingled again, and after a moment, Noguchi's motorcycle started up outside.

Takuya looked into Misaki's eyes.

"Let's go to Ibaraki until this blows over," Misaki said. "Yasui's grandmother's funeral will take a few days. Don't we need a break? I can handle the insurance and repairs by phone."

"A break would be good, yes." Revenge would be sweet, but getting away would be sweeter. The only thing he didn't need a break from was Misaki.

Chapter 42

Takamatsu flicked his cigarette into the water and put his cell phone away. Ishii's friction lock baton snapped open. Hiroshi took a readying breath and searched the crowd for Sugamo and Osaki. These two must be Imada and Kurono.

Imada and Kurono kept coming forward, Imada pushing the wheelchair and Kurono watching the river. Imada checked his cell phone, looked over the water, and back at Kurono.

Farther down the river walk, the skateboarders stepped off their boards and tipped them into their hands. Their loose clothing and long hair stood out among the passersby on the walkway.

Then suddenly, the skateboarders nodded to each other, dropped their boards for a running start, hopped on, and pushed to speed. Weaving around pedestrians, they headed straight for Imada and Kurono.

Takamatsu ran towards them, but the skateboarders squatted low, push-kicked for speed, and closed the distance.

The last of the three pulled his bag tight around his wrist and held it to the side, loose and heavy, an improvised flail.

The first two skateboarders cut in front of Imada. He yelled at them.

The third skater swung his bag and caught Imada square in the back of the head. Hiroshi could hear the clonk when the heavy-looking bag walloped Imada's skull.

Imada let go of the wheelchair and staggered aside, clutching his head.

Kurono started running but couldn't get close.

The woman in the chair fell to the side. Her hat fell off, and before Imada could retrieve it, Hiroshi saw Setsuko, her eyes closed.

Yelling at Kurono and still clutching his head, Imada looked down at the river. The water taxi pulled up to the stairway.

Kurono went for Setsuko, plopped her hat back on, and wheeled her to the stairs.

Hiroshi took off with Ishii right behind him.

Imada shouted and waved at the water taxi. He looked around for the skateboarders and back at Kurono.

Before they could get closer, the skateboarders wove around Ishii on the far side and sped toward Imada.

This time, something flashed in the hand of the third skateboarder. He'd slung the bag over his back and was holding a knife.

Imada didn't see them coming, and neither did Kurono, as the first two skateboarders shot past. Imada swung at them, but they dodged and kept going.

Imada hustled over to take Setsuko from Kurono and started down the stairs with her. Kurono peered after the two skateboarders and readied himself.

The third skateboarder came in from behind, squatting low, pumping hard, zipping forward. Kurono turned, but too late. The skateboarder plunged his knife into Kurono's thigh.

Kurono yelped and clutched his leg with both hands.

Hiroshi stopped, unsure which way to go.

Kurono stood unsteadily, searching the crowd for the skateboarders, but they were already out of reach.

They'd pulled up a hundred meters down the walkway, boards in hand. One of them slung the knife into the river, and without further hesitation, they dropped their boards, pushed hard, and skated out of sight.

Ishii got to Kurono first and swung her baton, but even after being stabbed, Kurono was strong and skillful. He grabbed the baton and sent Ishii tumbling across the tile. His leg was bleeding, but he could still kick. He landed his foot on Ishii hard and fast but almost fell over from the pain.

Hiroshi headed for Imada, clambering down the stairs to the water taxi with Setsuko over his shoulder. Hiroshi spun around the wall and ran down the stairs. He got a hold of Imada's belt from behind. There was no rail along the stairs, and he worried Imada would toss Setsuko into the river, so he snagged part of Setsuko's sweater.

Imada continued down, shouting, "I'll throw her in." He struggled toward the taxi tied up at the bottom of the stairs.

Hiroshi tugged on his belt, held Setsuko's sweater for several steps, and then let Imada go. They could track him down later, but Setsuko seemed drugged. She wouldn't survive a dunking. He got another hand on her arm and pulled back, losing his balance. His shoes were slippery on the wet stairs.

Terada, the water taxi driver they'd talked with, stared at the scene. Seeing Hiroshi, he frowned. Then, he reached over the stern, slipped the hitch knot holding the taxi to the cleat, and twisted the wheel. He put it in reverse, and the boat arced away from the landing.

Imada yelled. But he was stranded.

Terada dropped it into neutral, and the taxi rocked gently on the current.

Imada twisted to drop Setsuko at the bottom of the stairs, half in the water. He turned to face Hiroshi.

Hiroshi kicked at his head, but Imada dodged and came up a step, throwing a punch at Hiroshi's balls.

Hiroshi twisted aside and stayed close to the wall, hoping someone else would come. Where was Takamatsu? And Osaki and Sugamo? Was Ishii still fighting with Kurono?

Imada came up another step.

Hiroshi swung a round kick at his head, but Imada blocked again.

Hiroshi lost his footing. He waved his arms to stay on the stairs.

Imada gave him a shove and jumped up the steps.

Hiroshi felt for a foothold, caught his balance, and grabbed Imada's ankle.

Imada twisted and kicked until he could slip away and sprint for the top.

Setsuko was in a heap on the landing, river water washing over. Hiroshi took a step toward her, saw she wouldn't fall in, and took the stairs up two at a time.

At the top, Ishii was bent over double, trying to catch her breath. She pointed down the walkway.

Takamatsu stood in Imada's way. Imada dodged one way, then the other, and almost made it free. Osaki and Sugamo arrived. Osaki dove at Imada, dropped him to the pavement, and knelt on him with all his weight.

Passersby screamed and backed away.

Sugamo dropped a thick leg onto Imada's back and snapped on the cuffs.

Ishii was still trying to catch her breath, but she moaned, coughed, and pointed toward the *hanami* parties under the cherry trees.

"Setsuko's on the stairs," Hiroshi shouted to her and took off.

Hiroshi raced forward, searching the crowd under the trees. From the direction of an over-loud karaoke machine, a dark figure moved too fast to be partying. Hiroshi hopped up on the wall and started through the dense nests of partiers. Kurono was moving along the upper grassy area by the fence. He was limping, but swift.

Hiroshi picked his way through the circles of people, but there wasn't much room to step. He dodged through the party goods, and people spread out like a massive, messy checkerboard. Hiroshi didn't see a drunk heading for the toilets and smashed into him. They tumbled over in a heap. Everyone scrambled aside. Apologizing, Hiroshi got to his feet. The drunk wobbled in place, his face wet and red from drinking, and laughed.

Kurono's loping figure moved through the open space behind

the temporary trash collection area. There was no way to get to him without cutting across the middle of the packed-in groups.

If he could keep him in sight, he could catch him at the next set of stairs that led to the street, but no matter what he did, Kurono managed to stay ahead.

Ishii came running along the walkway to the left, her baton in hand. She'd make better time, and he could stay behind Kurono through the partiers on the upper edge of the park.

Hiroshi kept moving, but cups, paper plates, plastic containers of yakitori and fried rice, bags of chips, and *senbei* rice crackers sat at the edge of the tarps, slowing him down. He had to look every time he put his foot down. He kneed a man leaning back, apologized, but kept going, trying to speed up, dodging back and forth.

At the fence, Kurono cut toward the river.

Ishii scurried around the last circle of partiers and headed directly at him.

Kurono saw her coming, so he pulled up and braced himself.

Ishii swung her baton sideways and caught him in his ribs. Before he could answer, she swung again on his thigh.

Kurono screamed and bent over in pain. Blood spilled down his pants.

The circles of revelers had scampered aside as best they could, staring at the fight. He could hear their shouts as he dove at Kurono and tackled him low. The two of them pitched into the middle of the next circle of people and rolled forward. He could feel bottles and plastic containers crunch beneath him.

Hiroshi caught Kurono's wrist and bent until he rolled over. He tried to grab the other arm, but Kurono had plenty of fight. Hiroshi felt his leg hit someone's midsection, but there was no time for apology. Kurono swung a punch and twisted out of the wrist hold.

Hiroshi dodged as Kurono swung for him again. Hiroshi bent low and dove onto him. They collapsed into the middle of another party's space, scattering bottles, plates, and bags. Kurono whipped an elbow into Hiroshi's chest, then another to his face that sent Hiroshi reeling.

Ishii caught up, looking for an opening, and landed a baton blow on Kurono's shoulder. Hiroshi lost his grip, and Kurono rolled over, got to his feet, and punched Ishii.

Hiroshi grabbed Kurono from behind and wrestled him to his knees.

Kurono fell forward into what had just been a party, and Hiroshi got a knee in the middle of his back. Kurono swung an elbow at Hiroshi's head but missed.

Ishii dropped her knee onto Kurono's arm, got his hand, and twisted for all she was worth. He shouted and shook with the pain. Ishii twisted until he gave up and let his body slacken.

Ishii dropped a knee in his back, and Hiroshi felt a heavy weight drop beside him. He saw two thick arms. Osaki. Finally.

Osaki stuffed Kurono's head into the tarp as Ishii slipped on the first cuff. Kurono gasped for breath but then stopped squirming. Osaki kept hold. Ishii slipped the other cuff on and snapped it shut. Osaki held Kurono until Ishii got plastic cuffs around his ankles.

Ishii put her handkerchief over Kurono's wound, applying as much pressure as she could to staunch the blood. Osaki yanked him to a sitting position, but she kept her hand over his wound. Osaki called for backup and an ambulance.

Hiroshi clambered to his knees to catch his breath. He felt like kicking Kurono in the head, but he noticed the people whose *hanami* party he'd demolished staring at him. Around them, a larger ring of people had circled to stare.

He got to his feet and looked down to find his clothes covered in food and soaked with sake and red wine. Around him, a wide swath of parties had been demolished within the surrounding circle of cherry trees. Plates, trays, bags, and bottles were scattered every which way.

The helicopters arrived. One hovered right overhead, lighting up the scene and blowing the trash further in all directions. People squinted and shielded their eyes from the brightness of the spotlights.

Ishii didn't look disheveled in the least, but she rubbed her jaw where Kurono had punched her, her other hand still pressing on Kurono's bleeding.

She asked Osaki to push the handkerchief on the wound. "I better check on Setsuko," she said and ran off.

One of the women from the closest ruined party walked over and handed Hiroshi a roll of paper towels. He took them from her and looked at his messy front.

Before he could wipe himself, someone took a photo, and everyone else, coming out of shock, remembered their cell phones and started taking pictures of Hiroshi and the fight scene from all angles.

Chapter 43

Back in his office, Hiroshi dropped his wine, sake, and food-soaked clothes into a plastic bag. He managed a shower, some water, and a short snooze on the fold-out futon chair in his office. The office still smelled like a party, so he dropped the bag with his clothes into another bag and tied it tight.

Kurono and Imada were being run through processing, but Kurono had to be seen by a doctor for the knife wound in his thigh, and Imada had demanded a lawyer before he would say a word. He might not get one, but either way, that added a delay. There wasn't much to do until they could get them into an interrogation room.

He sent a message to Ayana to tell her he'd be coming to Nagoya that afternoon. He made a double espresso, drank it, and made himself another. With all the espresso, he felt some inner energy had been tapped. Maybe it was an illusion, but he'd worked with less.

When the construction work started rattling the walls at eight-thirty exactly, Hiroshi stood up and headed out of his office as quickly as his fatigue allowed.

Outside the interrogation rooms, the hallway was empty. There were no lights on over the rooms. Hiroshi looked around, a bit confused. He knew Imada and Kurono had been processed, but there must have been some further delay.

Sakaguchi came out of the elevator with Takamatsu. Sakaguchi stopped by the first room and peered inside. Someone was in there, but no one had turned on the notice light.

Sakaguchi looked at Takamatsu. "Can you not smack this guy?"

"Is that Imada in there?" Hiroshi asked.

Sakaguchi put a finger in Takamatsu's face. "This guy has good lawyers. Outstanding lawyers. They're already here."

"Where?" Takamatsu looked around jokingly.

"Upstairs." Sakaguchi pointed, serious. "I don't know how they found out, but they did. We have enough trouble as it is. *You* have enough trouble as it is. The skateboarders, for a start."

Takamatsu hummed. "They got it done."

Sakaguchi turned to Hiroshi. "You go in with him. Don't screw this up. He'll walk out of here. And it's not just the lawyers. The up-and-ups found out about this case, too. There's going to be a hearing. Probably a week of hearings."

"They should never have rehired the old chief as an advisor." Takamatsu flipped his lighter.

"Yeah, but they did," Hiroshi said.

Osaki came out of the elevator, holding a folder. He must have been working straight through, but he didn't look tired or not as tired as Hiroshi felt.

"We searched Imada's office and then Kurono's office." Osaki handed over the folder to Sakaguchi. "Want to see the photos? There are hundreds of them. The most boring two offices in Tokyo. Except for a can of pepper spray."

"Is that right?" Takamatsu smiled. "Any bets on whose prints are on it?"

Hiroshi looked at the folder. "My money's on Setsuko. She must have gone there after Sasaki was killed."

Sakaguchi said, "The lab will let us know soon enough."

"The guard at Tokyo Midtown already confirmed it," Osaki tapped the folder. "He identified Setsuko. Remembered her because she didn't stop."

Takamatsu put his lighter away. "The water taxi driver said Kurono wanted to go out to the bay. He saved the fax. Plenty of planning involved there. Can't get better evidence than a fax. Too old school to deny."

Sakaguchi pulled another piece of paper out of the folder. "The drug in Setsuko's system was Rohypnol."

"Same as the *hikikomori* kid," Osaki said.

"Same dosage twice. Same place." Sakaguchi nodded. "Good enough for me."

"What was in the safe at Sasaki's?" Hiroshi asked.

"Deeds and documents about properties in the area," Sakaguchi explained. "The videos were shaky, so I sent Sugamo back with a tech guy for something more."

Osaki turned to go but stopped and turned back. "One more thing. The hospital video got a clear shot of Kurono visiting the skateboard kid's room."

"And going in?" Hiroshi asked.

"Unfortunately not, but on the same floor. Right before the kid took a turn for the worse. We'll look through more, though." Osaki nodded.

Still looking through the folder, Sakaguchi nodded.

Hiroshi ran all the evidence through in his head. "With everything Yumi sent us, especially the payments for her services that came straight from Kurono, we have him tied to a larger conspiracy."

Sakaguchi and Takamatsu looked at Hiroshi, waiting.

"The properties line up on the map," Hiroshi said.

"What properties?" Sakaguchi asked.

"The ones Imada and Kurono bought. All around Komagome, they have been snapping up properties for years. And, not coincidentally, the beautification project needed those same properties to move forward." Hiroshi pointed in the air with his finger, dotting some invisible *Go* board.

"You're sure about that?" Takamatsu asked.

Hiroshi nodded his head. He was sure.

"Let's see if Kurono will flip on his boss." Takamatsu smiled.

"Let's connect a few dots for Kurono and see if that moves him." Hiroshi opened the door.

Kurono was sitting upright, his hands cuffed to the table. He wore a prison uniform with one leg cut off above the bandages wrapped around his thigh. Takamatsu walked over and peered down at the bandage.

Hiroshi waved for the video camera to be turned on. He wanted to get this over.

Kurono kept his eyes on the wall.

Takamatsu pulled out his cigarettes and offered one to Kurono.

Kurono twisted his head a few degrees to stare at Takamatsu, dead-eyed, before returning his gaze to the back wall.

Takamatsu blew the smoke into Kurono's face as he pulled out a chair and sat down. "Stabbed by a skateboarder." Takamatsu chuckled. "You've got to learn to be more careful."

Hiroshi leaned forward. "We have you for drugging and kidnapping a victim. That's serious enough right there. Taking her out to drop in the bay. What's that?" Hiroshi turned to Takamatsu.

"That's attempted murder. Depending." Takamatsu nodded.

Kurono scoffed and reset his leg, eyes on the wall.

Hiroshi tapped the table. "We'll also add extortion and coercion. All those properties you and Imada managed to acquire around Komagome have a connection to crimes. And we haven't even begun to look at all the other ones you've bought over the years. After we charge you, we'll have plenty of warrants to search everything."

Takamatsu jumped in. "And falsifying documents. That adds prison time. One of the kids you hired died in the hospital this morning. We had a pretty good image of you on the video cameras. Hospitals always have good equipment. And good lighting."

Hiroshi looked at him to be sure he wasn't going to throw a punch.

Takamatsu put his arm on the back of his chair. "You might get off on one or two of these, but not all. And we'll keep re-arresting you for suspected crimes until we get you on every one of them."

Kurono resettled himself in the chair, careful of his leg. "Go ahead then. See what you can do. None of that will stick."

Takamatsu smiled. "It must have been your associate, Imada, then."

Kurono shook his head. "Imada had nothing to do with this."

Hiroshi laughed. "You were both there pushing a drugged woman to a water taxi heading out into the bay."

Kurono fidgeted, trying to take the pressure off his leg. "They were old friends."

"Setsuko and Imada?" Takamatsu laughed. "They were going on a little boat ride to take in the night panorama of Tokyo?"

Hiroshi leaned forward. "We have you on video when a crime was committed."

"They were old friends." Kurono leaned back and looked at his leg.

"And you're just a building management company chief." Takamatsu stood up.

Hiroshi didn't want him doing anything, even off-camera. "Imada's going to let you take the blame."

Takamatsu put his cigarette out on the table right next to Kurono's hand.

Kurono didn't flinch.

Takamatsu leaned back.

Hiroshi braced for Takamatsu's attack, but Takamatsu said, "We also have phone calls from your number to a young woman who left us a stack of information. And guess what?" Takamatsu swung his arms wide and laughed. "She disappeared. That doesn't look too good. She tells us all about you, and then she's gone?"

Hiroshi wanted to punch Kurono too, but he opened his cell phone instead. "Do you know any of these places?" He showed him the videos Nakada had sent him.

"Basements, it looks like. Even a cop should know that." Kurono leaned back.

Hiroshi got a message on his phone. He pulled his phone back.

Sugamo sent a message they found nothing in Kurono's office. That would have helped, but they had plenty on him. Imada would take more time.

Hiroshi swiped his photo album for photos of payments, bank transfers, and account numbers. It was an extensive list that Akiko had helped compile. He set the phone down in front of Kurono. "Any of these look familiar?"

Kurono leaned forward. "I hire someone to do all that for me." He leaned back.

Hiroshi sighed at the thought of connecting everything Kurono had just denied. Akiko and he could pull the rest together after he returned from Nagoya. They could hold Imada and Kurono for twenty days and re-arrest them again if they needed more time. Probably, they wouldn't.

Takamatsu waved for the camera to be turned off.

The video recording light went dark.

Kurono pulled his wrists tight against the handcuffs chained to the table. The chain didn't stretch far enough to get an elbow up to defend himself.

Hiroshi put a hand up in front of Takamatsu, but a buzz of commotion interrupted any impulse Takamatsu might have had. Raised voices were coming down the hallway, arguing back and forth just outside the interrogation rooms.

Osaki pushed his head inside and waved for Hiroshi and Takamatsu.

In the hallway, two men in business suits stood beside Imada. The head of the police department and two upper-floor police bureaucrats stood to the side.

Sakaguchi spoke in a loud voice, telling them to leave. The two men spoke back in loud but lawyerly, formal Japanese. Sakaguchi took a step forward, and the lawyers took a step back, but Imada stayed where he was.

"What is this?" Hiroshi demanded.

Osaki whispered. "They're letting Imada go."

Hiroshi stepped forward right up to the lawyers. "Did you see the charges?"

The lawyers stared back. Imada moved behind them, watching silently.

The police chief, department head, and defense lawyers looked back and forth.

Takamatsu solved the impasse by diving between the lawyers and popping Imada in the face.

Imada crumpled as Osaki grabbed Takamatsu and pulled him back.

Takamatsu struggled free and landed several quick punches to Imada's face before Osaki could drag him away. Hiroshi put his arm out and helped pull him down the hall. Takamatsu straightened his jacket and walked it off, shaking his hand.

This wouldn't be some second-hand, toned-down report with a short suspension. The police chiefs were standing there, witnessing Takamatsu strike an elite developer. It would also be recorded on the hallway cameras. Every space in headquarters had video cameras.

Hiroshi looked at Takamatsu, rubbing his knuckles at the end of the hallway. This could be permanent.

One lawyer reached down to help Imada to his feet. Imada's nose looked broken.

The other lawyer turned to the chief. "We'll add assault to unjustified arrest, false detention, and harassment."

"With what evidence?" Sakaguchi asked in a deep, angry voice.

The lawyers pointed at the hallway cameras.

Sakaguchi cleared his throat. "Those don't work. Budget cuts."

Hiroshi wondered if Nakada could get to the stored files quickly enough to erase those few minutes.

The lawyers patted Imada's back and turned him toward the elevator.

The police chief and other admin cops looked back and forth, shaking their heads.

Chapter 44

When Hiroshi explained where they were going, Sugamo and Osaki whispered to Hiroshi that Takamatsu could not be left anywhere near the interrogation rooms, so they dragged him along for the ride.

In the car, Takamatsu said, "If Ishii wants backup, she gets it."

Sugamo parked in front of the city offices, and Takamatsu hopped out to ask the guard, an older man with a red, wrinkled face and a crisp blue uniform, to watch the car.

The guard saluted.

Hiroshi asked the receptionist on the first floor where the hearing was taking place. They hurried to the elevator. The upper-floor hallway outside the conference room was packed. Inside, it was so crowded people lined the walls and shared chairs.

Sugamo and Osaki stayed by the door, and Takamatsu skirted around to the side door.

In the middle of the aisle toward the front was a wheelchair with a woman talking at the microphone. No, it couldn't be. It was. Setsuko.

Hiroshi looked around for Ishii but didn't see her anywhere.

At the front of the room was a U-shaped line of desks covered in microphones, behind which sat city officers. Smartly dressed men sat along the left side of the U. The developers leaned over sleek, thin computers, as impatient as the city officers were bored. In the back of the U sat a couple of up-and-ups from the Ministry of Land, Infrastructure, Transport, and Tourism, Hiroshi assumed, confident in their bureaucratic disinterest.

Silence fell over the room as the chairperson adjusted the microphone, checked the U again, and cleared his throat. "This concludes the evaluation of the proposed project. The project is rejected."

Hiroshi wasn't sure what that meant, but a cheer went up from the crowd. Two women by Setsuko leaned down to hug her. Everyone in the audience talked at the same time.

Hiroshi saw Annisa and Natasha. He made his way toward them.

"Did you hear the whole thing?" Hiroshi asked Natasha and Annisa. Their faces were beaming.

Natasha smiled. "You gave us all that information, the maps, and everything."

Hiroshi nodded.

Natasha twisted her shoulders proudly. "So, we compiled it all and connected it to the people cheated out of money. It all lined up. Then we checked the houses in the area and figured out who were the landowners. It turns out that the buildings set for demolition were all in the way of the beautification project. All of them were bought up by someone named Imada. Do you know him?"

Hiroshi opened his mouth to explain, but Annisa took over. "But none of that mattered."

They both laughed.

Hiroshi was having a hard time understanding.

Natasha said, "What mattered was what we found beside the buildings."

More cheers went up from the crowd, and Hiroshi recognized a couple of the people from the Silver Center.

Natasha laughed. "Annisa remembered from her studies that courts always side with the landowners in land ownership claims. That goes back to World War II when soldiers refused to go to battle if their wives and families were not allowed to stay in their homes."

Natasha took a breath and kept going. "We're going to change our research topic to this, by the way. We found a new advisor who's very enthusiastic. We can access old ownership papers and make a short history of the area's development."

Hiroshi smiled. "That sounds like a great direction for your research. But what does that mean?"

Annisa continued. "You know about the redevelopment plan for Meiji Jingu Gaien Park. Many people organized to fight putting skyscrapers inside the park. And they won! So, we thought that would work for us."

Natasha interrupted. "The key point was tearing down the trees, destroying green space, and blocking one of the biggest green areas in Tokyo."

Annisa giggled. "Then, we got lucky. We found that the cherry trees in the area—"

Hiroshi held up his hand. "You mean around the Silver Center?"

Annisa nodded, excited. "Komagome used to be called Yoshino, named after the famous Somei-Yoshino variety of cherry trees that originated there. It became the most common type of cherry tree from Edo times to now."

Hiroshi couldn't quite follow. He hoped their graduate papers were written more logically.

Natasha smiled. "So, we woke everyone in the dorm to send texts, posts, and messages about these cherry trees. Musicians, artists, and writers who spoke up about Meiji Jingu stay up late. After several famous people reposted, we went viral."

Hiroshi frowned.

Annisa wiggled her phone. "With a little help from some late-night researchers, it turns out that Emperor Taisho planted the cherry trees along the road by the Silver Center. He took clippings from trees from his grandfather."

Someone wheeled Setsuko over. "I never even liked those blossoms. They're too showy. I like the subtler *shidare-zakura* weeping cherry trees. These two students wrote what I read out in the hearing today."

Hiroshi looked back and forth.

Setsuko laughed. "We told the bureaucrats about species diversity, inbound tourism, transpiration, and the imperial lineage of the trees. Those scientific words in English threw them off."

"Her English is excellent," Natasha said.

Setsuko waved her hand to disavow any English skills. "The specialists on Tokyo's cherry trees we invited reported that our trees dated back to the early Edo period. They said they should be labeled a protected species. But it was really that no urban planning board in Japan would allow trees planted by the Emperor to be cut down!"

Hiroshi had to smile.

"One of the famous musicians, I forgot his name, came to this hearing this morning with his lawyer. Even the bureaucrats at the front were impressed." Annisa looked around for him. "He left already. He had bodyguards."

Sugamo pushed his thick head in the side door and waved for Hiroshi to come.

Hiroshi smiled. "Congratulations!" Sugamo still waved at him, so he hurried to the side door.

In the hallway, Hiroshi found Ishii lecturing the developers. Osaki blocked their way down the hall. The city managers were nowhere to be seen. They must have slunk off already.

Ishii poked her finger in the face of the developers and raised her voice. "You used illegal means to line your pockets."

Sugamo held her back.

Hiroshi stepped between Ishii and the developers. "You're from Imada Enterprises?" Hiroshi looked at each of them before he spoke. "You might have gotten Imada out of jail, but someone will pay for those murders."

The head of the developers frowned. "We decided to go with another firm, not Imada's. We were under pressure to use him as we tried to coordinate beautification projects across firms, but apparently, we outsourced to the wrong person. We won't work with him again."

Hiroshi took a step forward. "You can cut him loose, but if we find you were aware of his methods, we'll hold you and everyone else accountable."

The head of the team was young. He'd be pushing another generation of so-called beautification projects, sitting in meetings and hearings in designer clothes with their thin, little laptops. It would never end. But maybe it wouldn't always end with murder.

The team head smiled. "You'll excuse us. We have a long afternoon of meetings."

The detectives watched them retreat. Ishii walked down the hall to calm down.

Hiroshi got a text message from Terajima, the city office worker they talked to the day before. "Are there protections for whistleblowers?" Terajima asked.

Hiroshi texted the city office worker right away. "We can work out whatever you want."

Terajima wrote back. "I'm using my vacation days next week. Can we meet?"

"Anytime." Hiroshi had a hundred questions for him. Terajima must know the whole scheme.

The detectives headed back to the elevators. The crowd had thinned out. In the corner of the lobby, Takamatsu stood talking with Sho, the skateboard kid. He dressed the same, in baggy pants, oversized T-shirts, and floppy shoes.

Hiroshi joined them.

Takamatsu turned to Hiroshi. "Sho tells me he doesn't know where his friend is who knifed Kurono. He's hiding somewhere." Takamatsu turned to the kid. "You know who will take the blame for that, don't you?" He pointed at himself.

Sho said, "I didn't know he would do that. I don't believe in revenge. Or in knives."

Takamatsu sighed. "Well, it's lucky his aim was bad. He could have hit Kurono's femoral artery."

"What's that?" Sho asked.

"You hit that, and the person bleeds out too quickly to save."

"I don't even know his real name. He goes by 'Board.'" Sho shrugged.

"It'll catch up with him." Takamatsu reached inside his leather jacket and pulled out a thick envelope. He handed it to Sho.

"I couldn't take this." Sho pushed it back. "My fuck-up," he said in English.

Takamatsu pushed it on him. "You're going to need it over there."

"Over where?" Hiroshi asked.

Sho took the money with both hands and bowed before tucking it away in the interior of his loose layers of shirts. "Over in California. I was born there and went to school there for a couple of years until my parents split up. I got a job offer to work in a skateboard shop there."

"You lived there before?" Hiroshi asked.

"When I was a kid. I want to try it again now that I'm older."

Takamatsu laughed. "Yeah, you're so old now."

Sho smiled. "I'm old enough to appreciate the cool vibe, great chicks, and good weed. Everything's a hassle here in Tokyo. A friend there needs someone who speaks Japanese and English and knows boards."

"You still have a US passport?"

The kid patted his chest. "And now I got the cash."

"Where in California?"

"L.A. The main shop is in Little Tokyo, but he has outlets near Venice Beach, Stoner Skate Plaza, and El Sereno. I do shoe and board designs too."

"Young entrepreneur." Hiroshi smiled.

Takamatsu said, "Keep in touch. In case you need work when you come back to Tokyo."

He patted the money inside his shirt before putting his

skateboard over his shoulder and heading for the door to the stairway.

"He's not taking the elevator?" Hiroshi asked Takamatsu.

When he was out of sight in the stairwell, they heard the grind of wheels and a clack clunk that echoed down the stairwell.

Was he skateboarding down the stairs? They looked at each other and listened to the fading sound, which soon disappeared altogether.

Takamatsu pulled his head back and laughed.

Chapter 45

Outside the city office, Hiroshi texted Ayana and told her he would get the next *Shinkansen* to Nagoya.

"Don't come today," Ayana texted back. "My mother had tests all day and is worn out. I'll text you later."

"I'll come this evening, then?"

Hiroshi stood on the sidewalk and waited for an answer. He waved as Sugamo and Osaki left with Takamatsu.

Ishii waited, sending her messages. "I'll take you to the *Shinkansen* if you want?"

Hiroshi sent Ayana three question marks but still got no answer. He sighed. "I guess I'll go tomorrow, wrap this case up today."

Ishii squinted at him. "More work?"

"Lots of files I want to finish before I head to Nagoya." Hiroshi tried to look confident, but maybe the argument with Ayana the other day really was an argument. Anyway, he could pull everything together on Kurono and Imada and leave without that hanging over his head.

"I'll catch a taxi," Hiroshi said.

"I'll take you." Ishii turned to the parking lot.

Hiroshi checked his messages and followed her to the car.

* * *

Akiko was working away in the office but didn't hear Hiroshi come in because of the construction noise and she had her earbuds in. Hiroshi waved at her, and Akiko reared back in her chair, startled. The remodeling noise had moved down to the lower hall but still echoed up the stairwell. He shoved the carpet over the door.

She pulled out her earbuds. "I thought you were going to Nagoya."

"Tomorrow." Hiroshi eyed the espresso machine and decided against it. He didn't want his fatigue battling the caffeine.

Akiko put her earbuds back in and settled into work.

Hiroshi pulled up the maps and layered them on top of one another. Then, he went through the deeds, noting where they were, who had bought them, when and how, and he knew the why. The scale of the extortion and buyouts was immense.

Akiko came over with a document. "I think this one is important." She had to shout over the noise.

"Ah, nice. His letter of acquisition of those properties is right there, isn't it?" Hiroshi looked at it and smiled. "That's from Terajima?"

Akiko wiggled her eyebrows. "That's just the tip of the iceberg from him."

Hiroshi hummed. "He wants witness protection. Can you check into that?"

"He won't need much if Kurono's in prison. I heard about Imada, but we'll get him too." Akiko tapped the document.

They worked on compiling past ownership and purchase dates for the rest of the afternoon. From there, they moved on to mapping out and cross-referencing the purchased land with the beautification project proposals.

The construction noise ceased at five, and Hiroshi looked heavenward in thanks. Akiko took out her earbuds and kept typing.

At seven, Akiko stood up and stretched. "Do you want me to stay?"

"No. Go home."

"You should go home yourself. When's the last time you were home?"

"I don't know, but I'll finish here soon."

Akiko yawned at the door. "I'll come in early if you want?"

"Regular time is fine."

"What's regular?" She yawned again and laughed at herself.

"We got two days' work done this afternoon. Sleep in." Hiroshi looked at her. "Call Watanabe."

"We're going to an *onsen* hot springs next weekend, so I'll leave early on Friday."

Hiroshi smiled. "*Onsen* sounds great. Where?"

"Up in Gunma. I can't remember the last time I went to an *onsen*. Maybe before I went to America." Akiko took a big breath, brushed back her hair, and left.

The *Shinkansen* trains to Nagoya started again at six the following day. He wrote Ayana that he'd catch one of the early ones. "Are you angry at me?"

"Angry? What are you talking about?"

"You're not?"

"Not yet. Don't come early tomorrow. We have doctors' appointments, both of us."

"You're going to a baby doctor there now?"

"Just for an ultrasound. No big deal."

"I wanted to go."

"You can next time. Come after lunch. We might have to wait at both. Maybe evening is better."

Hiroshi wrote back, "Fine."

Ayana didn't write back anything more.

Hiroshi wandered down to the tech room to find Nakada.

Nakada was sitting on a stool in the middle of five large screens, each split into smaller screens.

"What did you find?" Hiroshi asked him.

Nakada hadn't heard him come in but wasn't surprised to see him. He stood up and pointed at the screens. "I got some new motion detection software from a friend working for Japan Railways security—they pay much better than the police. This software works great. It halved the time. More than halved."

"Shouldn't we have the best software at the police agency?"

"As I said, private companies pay better."

"I hope you're not going to leave?"

"Not yet." Nakada pulled his monitor around.

Hiroshi wasn't sure if he was being ironic or not. Maybe he should start thinking that way too. Money and ease. His uncle's firm. All he had to do was say yes. He'd be home with Ayana every evening instead of running around the city or going to crime scenes. For shitty pay. "What's the software do again?"

Nakada wiggled his eyebrows at the chance to explain. "It lets you look for a specific shape, size, face, or physical feature. Once we had Kurono's photos in the station, I turned them around from every angle, dug out the unique points, and input those to let the software work its magic."

"And you got hits?"

Nakada nodded. "He was all over the place."

"What about Imada?"

"I also ran him through. He's not at as many places, but enough. I'll pull those together and cut out the dull parts."

"That'd be great. And the software worked through all the video masking?" Hiroshi still didn't quite understand what that was.

"The video masking didn't get in the way. It adds to search time, but this new software works faster, so it hardly matters. It's an amazing application of multiple advances in visual digitalization—"

Hiroshi held his hands up. "I'll come down for a motion detector software lesson next week. For now, what do you have?"

Nakada looked disappointed as he stared at the screen. He pulled at his loose black sweatshirt and then smiled. "Well, if I had to summarize it, we have him in many basements, lobbies, and building fronts."

"You have Kurono at all the sites? Even the small places?"

Nakada pointed at all the screens and nodded in satisfaction. "I love it when it all comes together on one screen."

"And you have the times and dates for all of those?"

"It's on the video, right there." He pointed at the screen. "What was he doing at all those sites?"

Hiroshi had to laugh. "I'm still not completely sure. He was faking inspections or gathering data, it seems. And the *hikikomori* kid was keeping an eye on him for the Silver Center people. It's a bit hard to keep track."

"Having cameras everywhere can make you paranoid. It makes you want to put more cameras there." Nakada stared at the screens.

Hiroshi scoffed. "That's how it seems. But if we have Kurono and Imada near to the scenes of crimes, the videos will have done their work."

Flipping through videos was making him nauseated, so Hiroshi looked away. He leaned back. "Can you pull all of that into a single file for me? I have to present it at the meeting."

"No problem. I used to do that in the child porn section all the time. You need it like a timeline."

"If you can." Hiroshi leaned back and felt the fatigue in his legs. "Can you pluck off all the times and dates and a still shot of Kurono at each one?"

"Easy. When do you need it?"

"Tomorrow morning?"

Nakada nodded. "Don't you want video clips?"

"I don't know if they can play that at the meeting. It takes too long to watch the videos. But we need them as evidence."

"I'll make two versions, one with video and one with still shots."

"Perfect."

"And what about—"

"Imada?" Nakada shook his head. "We had his official arrest photos." He clicked on the closest keyboard. "But we only have him a few places. I'll keep looking for more. There might be another few layers in there."

Hiroshi's fatigue was clouding his brain. "Give me everything on Kurono now, and then see if you can find Imada on others. Look at the other cameras again too. Not just the basement and entryway cameras from that *hikikomori* kid."

"Can you give me another day for Imada's search?"

"Sure." Hiroshi turned to go.

Hiroshi started back toward his office. The construction noise had finished, and he didn't want to be there when it began again, though it looked like he might be.

He emailed Ayana, and she texted back that there were more tests, so it was better not to come before evening. Was she putting him off? Again? He couldn't tell.

But maybe that was the problem. He should be able to tell. If he wasn't going, then at least he could finish the case and catch up on his sleep before the eight-thirty a.m. crash of construction started. If he got up early enough, he could avoid that and return home to change before heading off to meet Ayana.

Chapter 46

Hiroshi awoke on the fold-out futon chair when the construction started at eight-thirty precisely. He'd meant to get up earlier but felt heavy and listless. He wandered to the shower. The pants felt too big, and he had to cinch his belt tighter. Other than being desperately hungry, he felt better.

Akiko was in the office when he returned. She'd brought a bag full of croissants, pastry, juice, milk, and fruit. "I ordered a refrigerator, by the way. I hope you don't mind?"

Had she read his mind the other day? "We need one."

"I thought it might be delivered already. That's why I bought all this."

Hiroshi picked through the pastry and made a double espresso for Akiko and another for himself. It was nice to have a little milk with it. He stood by his desk, wolfing things down.

"I brought you an extra pair of earbuds I had at home that I never used."

"Thank you." Hiroshi swallowed his last mouthful. "Not sure I can take another day of the noise."

Takamatsu knocked on the doorjamb and walked in. "Breakfast time?"

Akiko smiled. "Espresso?"

Takamatsu bowed.

Akiko made a double in their nicest espresso cup and handed it to Takamatsu.

Takamatsu sipped his espresso with his little finger up and turned to Hiroshi. "What about a short trip up to Ibaraki?"

Hiroshi looked at him. "Sure, why not? I have nothing to do here." He put as much sarcasm into his words as they would hold. "Anyway, I can't. I'm going to Nagoya."

Takamatsu opened his arms wide. "We can drop you off at the

train station on the way back."

"Ibaraki's in the opposite direction from Nagoya."

"Ishii's driving. It'll be faster than you think."

"What's in Ibaraki?"

Takamatsu shot his cuffs and straightened his smooth leather jacket. "It would have been much easier if you'd run faster that first day and caught him."

"I didn't notice you running at all the past few days. How did you find him?"

"I also came into possession of important documents relevant to this case."

"What documents?"

Takamatsu pulled up an email on his phone. "This was sent anonymously through a Tor browser last night. It connects Imada and Kurono to all the *sagi* scams in the area. Lots on Kurono. And on Imada."

"I don't think so. They were working at another level."

"Evidence is evidence. If we can add on the scams, why wouldn't we?"

"We don't want to find the real perpetrators?"

"That's why I want you to come with Ishii and me up to Ibaraki. Akiko will have this new information organized by the time you return."

"Sure." Akiko looked at Takamatsu's phone. "Won't take me long."

"How would you survive without her?" Takamatsu asked Hiroshi.

Takamatsu was right about that.

* * *

Ishii headed them to the expressway. Hiroshi kicked off his shoes, rolled his coat into a pillow, stretched out in the backseat, and fell fast asleep.

He didn't wake up until Ishii slowed for the exit from the expressway off-ramp.

He sat up and yawned. Then it dawned on him. He leaned forward to Takamatsu. "You're trying to avoid the disciplinary hearing about the fight in the station, right?"

Takamatsu pulled an innocent face.

Ishii looked over at him.

"Wasn't that today?" Hiroshi yawned. "Takamatsu, you should—"

Takamatsu turned around and held up his hand. "Suspend me or don't suspend me, but I refuse to be scolded, especially by incompetent assholes. Sakaguchi can handle it. And I'll handle whatever they decide."

"And did they find out about those skateboarders too? That will make it worse."

Takamatsu cracked the window and lit a cigarette. "I know I should never have hired those kids, but they got it done, didn't they?"

Ishii spoke seriously. "What are you going to do if you're suspended?"

"*When* you're suspended," Hiroshi said.

Takamatsu hummed and smoked. "I'll do some part-time snooping for my old friend Shibutani. As always, he has more divorce cases than he can handle. COVID divorces on top of the usual ones."

They rode quietly through the wide streets of Mito City. Ibaraki was more spacious, with a higher sky and wider streets than any place in Tokyo. There were no tall buildings.

Ishii pulled to the entrance of an old shopping Ginza that curved away from Mito Station. The nearby *Koban* police box had plaster walls needing a coat of paint. Ishii parked on the gravel in front.

Takamatsu hopped out and went inside. One of the local cops came out with him, hung up a "Back soon" sign, and wheeled out his bicycle to lead them.

The shopping street was a portrait of faded glory. The *torii* over the entryway was painted red, but the light boxes were faded and chipped. Half the shops were shuttered, and walkway tiles were loose underfoot.

But a little further on, a British pub had a sign outside for lunch and an early happy hour. Past there, an Indian restaurant had a line in front. Next to it, a *rakugo* theater showed the week's performance schedule on hand-painted slats.

The cop stopped at the first side street and pointed at a fruit and vegetable stand on the corner. Three young people, their heads wrapped in white towels, were cleaning up. Flat baskets of root vegetables, well-wrapped strawberries, and round melons were laid out with handwritten prices on thin-cut wood slices taped in place.

Hiroshi and Ishii spread out on either side of the corner shop. The cop parked his bicycle and stood ready.

Takamatsu walked up to the store. "Are you Misaki Kono?" Takamatsu asked the woman. "The manager of *OLzakaya* in Nippori?"

Misaki put down her broom. "Did you find who broke up my place?"

Takamatsu cleared his throat. "I want to ask you about your boyfriend, Takuya."

Misaki gestured with her thumb. "Why don't you ask him directly?"

Takuya wore a thick apron and rubber gloves.

The other man straightening the vegetable display baskets

was plump and baby-faced.

Takamatsu looked at Takuya. "Can you tell me where you've been the past week or so?"

Takuya pointed at the baby-faced man. "His grandmother just died. She was like a mother to me too. We're here taking care of her things. And her funeral."

"We have video footage of someone who looks like you near several crime scenes in Tokyo." Takamatsu looked at him hard. The local cop reset his leather belt.

Takuya shrugged. "I look like a lot of people."

Misaki spoke up. "I had to run the OLzakaya myself for the past several weeks while he went back and forth."

"And whose shop is this?" Hiroshi gestured at the place.

Yasui set his broom to the side. "It's my grandmother's. She ran it for fifty years."

Takamatsu turned to the local cop. "It's easier in Tokyo to rip off old people. And here in Ibaraki, you rip off your relative's property."

"I inherited this. It's been in my family for years." Yasui knew how to act unruffled. "We'll sell fresh vegetables here and online. Farmers around here need a little help with the logistics."

"Logistics?" Hiroshi scoffed. "I'd say your gang was good with that. What's the scam here?"

Takuya took off his gloves and dropped them on a tray. "We'll sell fresh local produce here and online," he repeated. "Cut out the middlemen and sell directly." He nodded at a stack of empty mailing boxes in the corner. "A friend is creating a site for us."

"Food scam?" Takamatsu started flipping his lighter.

Takuya ignored Takamatsu's accusations. "We're going to open an *izakaya* over there." He pointed across the shopping street. "Farm to table."

Misaki put on her prettiest, most dimpled smile. "You should go after the *chinpira* punks who destroyed my place. We've had enough of Tokyo. Better quality of life here. No extortion."

Hiroshi pulled out copies of the info Takamatsu had received anonymously. Akiko had sent it while they were driving. "Any of this look familiar?"

Takuya wiped his hands on his apron and came over to take a look. He shrugged. "Some kind of bank transfer thing?"

"Evidence of *sagi* scams." Hiroshi looked at him closely.

Yasui shrugged.

"You don't know anything about this?" Hiroshi asked.

Takuya wiped his hands on his apron.

Misaki smiled her big smile. "Like I said, we're done with Tokyo."

"Tokyo might not be done with you." Hiroshi looked from Yasui to Takuya to Misaki. All three of them looked calm and innocent, Hiroshi thought. The local cop took their cell phone numbers and address. Hiroshi took a photo of it.

Takamatsu looked at them, laughed, and lit a cigarette. "You know, Takuya, it's just lucky you wore a mask. Otherwise, we would have had your face on numerous surveillance cameras."

Takuya wrinkled his face and shook his head in feigned innocence. "Would you like something to take back to Tokyo?" Takuya shook open a bag and pointed at the long onions and mountain potatoes.

"Next time," Takamatsu said. He blew out a big lungful of smoke, and Hiroshi knew he would let them go.

The local cop got his bicycle, and they all walked back down the shopping street to the car parked outside the *koban*. Takamatsu chatted with the cop while Hiroshi and Ishii got in the car. Hiroshi was looking forward to napping on the way back.

When he got in, Takamatsu said, "I think it was those two who were behind the scams, but at least we have Kurono and Imada. Just my hunch."

"Hunches don't count in court." Hiroshi slipped off his shoes and put his feet on the back seat.

"Those kids didn't commit murder, anyway. Ishii, you can

bring them in under your task force."

Ishii pulled out, the tires crunching on the gravel. "They've just set up a dedicated unit for *sagi* scams, so I'll send it to them. I know one of the women put in charge there. She'll track the details down."

Hiroshi folded his jacket under his head and drifted off.

* * *

When he woke up, they were pulling up in front of Tokyo Station. Trains left every quarter hour. He'd be there in an hour and a half. Ayana hadn't written back, but he was going anyway.

Hiroshi and Takamatsu got out. Hiroshi leaned over the window by Ishii. "Where are you off to today?"

"Back to the women's task force. High school girls." Ishii shook her head and rubbed her bruised chin where Kurono had punched her.

"Let me know if their accounts are too complicated."

"They probably are." Ishii waved and pulled off.

Hiroshi headed toward the station, checking the *Shinkansen* schedule on his phone. Takamatsu walked beside him.

The station was crowded with the pre-rush hour throngs of people trying to get home before the full-on rush hour.

Takamatsu stopped at the stairs to the Yamanote Line.

Hiroshi paused.

"I might not see you for a while." Takamatsu patted Hiroshi on the shoulder.

"You've come back from suspension before."

"It'll be a longer one this time." Takamatsu looked serious for once. "Fortunately, I've got a new hobby."

"I thought you were working divorce cases?"

"I am. But a hobby seems like a good thing. I'm getting older."

"What is it?"

"Hot yoga." Takamatsu's face broke out in a wide grin.

Hiroshi groaned. "How did you find her?"

Takamatsu smiled. "Same way I found the Ibaraki crew. Detective work. I'm just glad she's not at the bottom of Tokyo Bay."

"You can still mess up the case by socializing with witnesses."

"It's healthy, hot yoga. I want to sweat out all this tobacco. Maybe I'll stop smoking."

"That'll take a lot of sweating."

"That's what I was thinking." Takamatsu gave a half-salute and headed up the stairs to the Yamanote Line platform.

Chapter 47

Hiroshi got his *Shinkansen* ticket at the counter inside. He only had a few minutes to spare and hurried to buy a bento box lunch and a beer. He made it to the platform as the doors slid open. The passengers filed in, the door shut, and he found his seat.

The train was nearly empty, and he stretched out. He opened the beer, and the soft fizz-clink of the can resounded in his ears. A beer wasn't always just a beer. Some were better.

He wrote Ayana when he would arrive. He realized he didn't know the Nagoya address and asked her to send it.

She sent it without further comment.

She was upset about her mother, probably angry with him, and feeling the weight of the pregnancy. Whatever it was, it was better for her to be angry in person than in an endless series of messages. A full-on, in-person argument was better than a dribble of half-meanings.

Yes, he was overworking again and not attending to the upcoming birth, but he'd been to every appointment with the OB-GYN, except the last ultrasound, which was more than most Japanese men did. He'd have to figure out what to do when the baby arrived. And his uncle would hound him until he made a decision about taking over his firm or not.

He pulled the top off his bento and opened his chopsticks. Egg, chicken balls, vegetables, and seaweed toppings he should know the name of but didn't. He sipped his beer and watched Tokyo slip away. The tall buildings faded to lower buildings on the other side of the fields, and finally to just fields and the first sight of mountains. Tokyo and its heights were left behind. Tokyo's buildings provoked his inner fear of heights, even when he was on the ground.

As he finished his bento, he got a message from his cousin. Like his aunt, she was perfect in dress, conversation, and manners.

They remembered to send presents and cards on time. His mother and father were sullen and quiet, but his aunt and cousin were lively and friendly, always fussing over him. Even his uncle, so reserved at work, turned energetic in their company.

Their family was full of love, talk, and activity. His own had been full of silence. Hiroshi knew which kind of family he wanted to make with Ayana. He wasn't sure how to do it. He would have to shuck off the last of his parents and move on.

His cousin Nana called, so he picked up. Even her voice was a delight. "My dad's in the hospital. I wondered if you could stop by?"

"I just got on the *Shinkansen* to Nagoya. He said his surgery was quick and easy."

"That's the kind of thing he says. But he had another pain he probably didn't mention. They'll know more tomorrow."

"Can you call me when you find out?"

"Of course. What's in Nagoya?"

"Ayana's mother has cancer. Ayana's there with her."

Nana let out a sympathetic sigh. "Can I do anything? If I'd known you were alone, I would have sent you food or something."

"I've hardly been home working on this case."

"Did my father talk to you about taking over his firm?"

"He did."

"Are you thinking about it?"

"Tell him I'm thinking about it. But right now, I've got to help Ayana and her mother. Not that I can do much."

"You can be there."

"Can I talk to him?"

"He's right here."

Hiroshi could hear her handing him the phone and explaining who it was.

His uncle's voice sounded strong. "Hiroshi, I'm fine. Once they open you up, they want to look at everything. Like accounting."

Hiroshi shook his empty beer can and looked out the window, wondering how to be in two places at once, or how to lead two lives.

"I'm heading to Nagoya, but I'll stop by as soon as I return to Tokyo."

His uncle paused, and Hiroshi wasn't sure why. "I do want you to take over. I can half-manage it until you're ready."

"Give me some time to think it through."

His uncle paused again. Maybe they had him on some painkilling medicine.

Hiroshi took a breath. "We're going to have a baby, and Ayana's mother is seriously ill. It's all such...all so unknown."

"That's why I love accounting. The unknowns get known."

But not all got known. You had to accept that. The unknowns lingered. "I'll go see you as soon as I get back."

His cousin got back on the line and talked about her daughter until a doctor came in and she had to hang up.

Hiroshi stared out the window. Was this what it was going to be? One illness, surgery, death, and loss after the next? Was that what getting old meant?

A child felt like locking him in place for many years. He felt ready, and he liked the idea of being locked in with Ayana. He wasn't sure he'd make a decent father. He was willing to change what needed to be changed to try. He felt sure Ayana would be a great mother. That was enough.

He took a taxi from Nagoya Station to his mother-in-law's place. The taxi driver went in the wrong direction twice, and Hiroshi didn't know how to guide him, but at last, they pulled up in front of a prim house on a row of new homes.

Some of the trees, saplings really, were still supported with staked posts and wrapped in burlap. The whole place seemed recently built. But it formed a real neighborhood, open and light, with room to play and a park at the end of the street. It would be a treat for kids. He'd started evaluating everything from a child's perspective after seeing the first ultrasound scan with Ayana.

Hiroshi paid the taxi driver and walked to the door. He didn't know whether to go in or knock. So, he knocked.

After a minute, the door opened, and there was Ayana. At last.

She looked different.

"Well, come in." She frowned and let go of the door, so he had to catch it.

The *genkan* was neat and narrow. She leaned down to hug him, and he kissed her neck. He held her as he moved to kiss her lips. At last.

"Where's your mother?"

"Shopping."

"Is she OK to go shopping?"

Ayana sighed. "She said she was. She'll be back in a few minutes."

He stepped up with his hands open. "I didn't bring anything."

"We have everything."

Ayana never looked more beautiful. That was another thing he kept saying to himself since the ultrasound. But it was true. He just wanted to stare at her.

He took off his shoes and stepped up on the floor. He put one arm around her and one on her stomach. "I want us to get married."

"That's the first time I've heard that word out of your mouth."

"Do I need to say it?"

Ayana wiggled closer and put her arms around him. "Married, huh?"

"I wanted to buy you a ring but didn't have time."

"A wedding ring?" Ayana laughed.

"Engagement? Wedding? How does that work? Are there two?"

"I don't need a ring. We don't need them."

Hiroshi pulled her closer. "Well, I'll get one for you anyway. In case you change your mind."

"I won't change my mind, and we could use the money for something else."

"We already have everything you just said."

They stood quietly in the hallway of the strange house. It

smelled different from theirs, some incense, maybe for her father, and some boiled something. He wasn't sure what. And underneath all that, a clean smell. Unlike all those basements.

"Why did you run off?" he asked.

Ayana looked at him like he was crazy. "Run off?" She laughed the laugh that said he was being ridiculous.

Hiroshi pulled her closer. He could feel the belly bump as he pulled her tight. "I know I'm always busy. I know. But I'm taking time off when the baby comes. I've decided."

"We'll be fine."

"It'll make your mother happy if we get married, won't it?"

"Is that why you're proposing?"

"No, for my own reasons."

"Like what?"

"Like this." He pulled her against him for a deep kiss, pressing against her in every spot he could press against. He didn't want to let her go. He kept kissing her, short and long, dry and wet, hard and soft. She didn't resist.

Finally, he leaned back for a breath. "I want your mother to see how good we are together."

"I told her already."

"I want her to see it."

"Why does that matter?" Ayana pushed back, testing to see if he'd hang on.

He did. He kept his hands firmly on the curve of her waist.

"My mother is afraid of new things. She wonders why I'm not. She hasn't recovered from the disaster of my first marriage. Or from hers."

"What about you?"

In answer, Ayana ran her hand up to his neck and kissed him hard. "I was over my first marriage the day you and I walked under the cherry blossoms."

"Can we take our daughter there for her first *hanami*?" Hiroshi asked.

"I've been planning on it."

"My uncle wants me to take over his accounting firm. He's having surgery."

"Surgery? Take over the firm? Are you going to?"

"I want to get married first." Hiroshi kissed her again on the mouth.

The door opened. "Oh!" Ayana's mother said.

Hiroshi pushed back, but Ayana held him close and, ignoring her mother, kissed him again. Ayana let him go so he could bow and say hello.

Ayana's mother was just as pretty, an older pretty, as Ayana.

"I figured he'd turn up sooner or later." She kicked off her shoes and hoisted two full shopping bags as she came inside. "I've kept the fridge full."

Hiroshi reached for the bags. "Let me help with those. I didn't bring anything. I'm the worst Japanese person."

"All those years abroad." Ayana's mother handed him the bags and turned to Ayana. "He's nicer than your first husband." She started down the hall.

Ayana gave Hiroshi an apologetic smile.

"We're getting married," Hiroshi said. The words seemed to echo in the hallway.

Her mother stopped. "I know it'll be better than the first one." She turned at the end of the hallway. "I ordered beer for you the other day. They're nice and chilled. Want one? I need one. There's wine too. No alcohol for the pregnant girl, though."

Hiroshi thought he saw the flicker of a smile on her face—a tighter version of Ayana's smile—but the hall was a little dark, and she walked on before he could be sure.

Ayana took Hiroshi's hand and led him into the kitchen.

THE END

About the author

Michael Pronko is the author of the award-winning Detective Hiroshi series and the Tokyo Moment series. He has written about Japanese culture, art, jazz, and politics for Newsweek Japan, The Japan Times, Artscape Japan, and other publications for over twenty years. He has appeared on NHK Public TV, Tokyo MXTV, and Nippon Television. He also runs a website, Jazz in Japan, about the vibrant jazz scene in Japan.

Michael is a professor of American Literature and Culture at Meiji Gakuin University in Tokyo. He teaches courses in contemporary American novels, film adaptations, and American art and music. When not teaching, writing, or listening to jazz, he wanders Tokyo contemplating its intensity and figuring out the stories to come.

***

For more on the Hiroshi series: www.michaelpronko.com
Follow Michael on X (Twitter): @pronkomichael
Michael's Facebook page: www.facebook.com/pronkoauthor
For more about jazz in Japan: www.jazzinjapan.com.

Thanks to everyone who helped.

Allen Appel
Anne Brewer
Matt Kineen
Nancy LaFever
Marco Mancini
Richard Sheehan
BeauteBook

And thanks also to friends, family and students.
And always, to my miso and my mayonnaise, my wife.

If you enjoyed this book, please consider taking a minute to write a review on your favorite book-related site. Reviews really help indie writers like myself.

And if you're interested in future releases and news and insights from Tokyo, sign up for my newsletter here:

www.michaelpronko.com/newsletter

About the author

Michael Pronko is the author of three mystery novels and three collections of writings about Tokyo. He has written about Japanese culture, art, jazz, and politics for Newsweek Japan, The Japan Times, Artscape Japan, and other publications for over twenty years. He has appeared on NHK Public TV, Tokyo MXTV and Nippon Television. He also runs a website, Jazz in Japan, about the vibrant jazz scene in Japan.

Michael is a professor of American Literature and Culture at Meiji Gakuin University in Tokyo. He teaches courses in contemporary American novels, film adaptations, and American art and music. When not teaching, writing or listening to jazz, he wanders Tokyo contemplating its intensity and figuring out the stories to come.

His award-winning collections of essays about life in Tokyo are available at online retailers and from his website, as are the Japanese language versions. The novels in the Detective Hiroshi series have won numerous awards.

***

For more on the Hiroshi series: www.michaelpronko.com
Follow Michael on X (Twitter): @pronkomichael
Follow Michael on Instagram: @michaelpronko
Michael's Facebook page: www.facebook.com/pronkoauthor
For more about jazz in Japan: www.jazzinjapan.com.

Printed in the USA
CPSIA information can be obtained
at www.ICGtesting.com
LVHW021701290224
773137LV00001B/60